Where Madness Lies

A Novel

Where Madness Lies

A Novel

Sylvia True

TOP HAT BOOKS

Winchester, UK
Washington, USA

JOHN HUNT PUBLISHING

First published by Top Hat Books, 2020
Top Hat Books is an imprint of John Hunt Publishing Ltd., No. 3 East St., Alresford,
Hampshire SO24 9EE, UK
office@jhpbooks.com
www.johnhuntpublishing.com
www.tophat-books.com

For distributor details and how to order please visit the 'Ordering' section on our website.

ISBN: 978 1 78904 460 7
978 1 78904 461 4 (ebook)
Library of Congress Control Number: 2019951304

A CIP catalogue record for this book is available from the British Library.

Design: Stuart Davies

UK: Printed and bound by CPI Group (UK) Ltd, Croydon, CR0 4YY
US: Printed and bound by Thomson-Shore, 7300 West Joy Road, Dexter, MI 48130

For Oona and Finn

Author Note

Both of my parents fled from Frankfurt before the start of World War II. My mother's side of the family moved to Switzerland. Their reasons for leaving Germany were multi-layered. It wasn't only because they were Jewish. There was another factor, something that in 1935 might have been even worse than Judaism. There was mental illness, kept secret for many years.

My mother's mother, we called her Omama, was the family matriarch. She cared deeply about her grandchildren and desperately wanted us to master the art of refinement so that we could be accepted into the highest circles of society. When she left Germany, she lost her money, her position, and her status; but she still played the role of aristocrat, though there were moments when her guard came down and loneliness poked through.

This is her story, and mine as well. The names have been changed, and some of the details are how I imagined them, not exactly as they might have been. But the bones of the story are true.

Prologue

Partial Testimony of Dr. Paul Viktor Bohm—Medical Director of Sonnenstein Psychiatric Hospital and Deputy Director of Action T4.

Q: When mentally ill patients were selected and sent by transport to euthanasia stations, such as the one you were director for, by what methods were the mercy deaths given?

A: They were led to a gas chamber and were disinfected by the doctors with carbon monoxide gas.

Q: In other words murdered.

A: Yes, I suppose so.

Q: And you agreed to this because of orders from Bouhler?

A: I agreed to it because we were releasing patients from lives of misery.

Q: And these patients, some children, were placed in this chamber in groups, I suppose, and then the carbon monoxide was turned into the chambers?

A: The basic requirement was that the disinfection should not only be painless, but also imperceptible. We photographed patients, for scientific reasons, before they entered the gas chambers, thus providing a diversion. Then they were led into the chamber which they were told was a shower room. They were in groups of perhaps twenty. They were gassed by the doctor in charge.

Q: And these patients thought that they were going in to take a shower?

A: If any of them had any power of reasoning, they had no doubt thought that.

Q: What diagnoses would lead a doctor to believe a patient should be euthanized?

A: Feeblemindedness, Schizophrenia, the congenitally crippled, to name a few.

Q: After Sonnenstein had constructed their gas chamber, you were asked by the Reich Committee for Research on Hereditary Diseases to visit Buchenwald Concentration Camp. Can you tell us the purpose for the visit?

A: To provide assistance and advice in the construction of similar chambers.

Q: In order to euthanize mental patients?

A: I believed that was the case, yes.

Q: You believed Buchenwald to be a mental hospital?

A: No, of course not, but I believed they had some mental patients there and that the doctors would employ a similar protocol to the one we used.

Q: Did you survey any of patients?

A: I did not.

Q: Dr. Bohm, from what you have told the court, are we to understand that you are in part responsible for the prototype for the gas chambers used to kill millions of Jews?

A: A number of psychiatrists were consulted.

Q: But you would agree that the gas chambers used in the concentration camps were fashioned after the chambers you and other doctors constructed in mental institutions?

A: It could be viewed in that way, yes.

Chapter One

McLean Hospital

Belmont, Massachusetts
1984

Sabine knew there was no molecule that made fear, yet fear was what she breathed on that cold, damp November night, as she stood in front of the steel door with a wire-mesh window.

She wanted Tanner to step up and press the bell, to show her that he was with her on this. Instead, he played Eskimo noses with their three-month-old baby, as if they were at home about to eat spaghetti, not standing at the entrance of a mental hospital.

When Sabine finally pushed the red button, a man, wearing a tan sweater and faded jeans, who looked about twenty-six, her age, stepped into the hallway.

"Visiting hours were over at eight," he said, nodding toward the stairs.

Sabine didn't think she could speak without her voice cracking. She glanced at her husband, who looked away.

"I saw Dr. Lincoln an hour ago," she managed. "He told me I should come here. To get admitted."

The man gave a tired sigh and led them down the hallway. Her head lowered, Sabine took furtive peeks. If not for the glassed-in nurses' station at the end of the corridor, North Belknap Two might have passed for a college dorm, with its wooden doors decorated with posters of Bon Jovi, Van Halen, and kittens dangling from trees with the words, *hang in there*, in bold.

The man pointed to a dining area where a few scattered people sat alone at tables of varying shapes and sizes.

"You can sit in there," he said.

"Let's go to the back," Sabine whispered to Tanner, wanting

to get a sense of the place, to make sure there weren't any people like in the movies—zombies wearing stained gowns and spewing nonsense.

Tanner unzipped Mia's purple snowsuit. The moment she was out, she kicked her legs and smiled, her dark eyes glistening with the joy of being free. Sabine kissed her baby's forehead and felt like the luckiest most miserable person alive.

A heavy man with a mop of blond hair shuffled in from a swinging side door with a bowl of cereal filled to the brim, milk lapping over the edges. His expression was hollow, and Sabine's heart raced.

"Maybe we should go," she said.

Tanner jumped up, his round eyes shaded with fear. "Yeah, you don't belong here."

The scar that ran through his right eyebrow looked more prominent.

But she couldn't go back to the bed where she couldn't sleep, to the kitchen she couldn't clean, to the back steps where last night she'd smoked a cigarette for the first time in over a year, hoping it would calm her. Instead, the smoke stung her lungs and made her dizzy. When she looked at the burning tip, orange with specks of black and gray, she couldn't resist. Sabine brought it close to her wrist and felt the heat. The ember point singed her skin, and a tendril of smoke curled upwards. This kind of pain was much easier to bear. After the fourth burn she put the cigarette out, carried the butt to the back of the yard and flicked it into the woods behind the fence.

"Let's wait," she told Tanner now.

A tall, thin, elderly man approached with loping steps. Maybe he was the doctor. Maybe he would help. But as he came closer, Sabine noticed his slippers and yellowed fingernails.

"There's cyanide in the coffee," he grumbled. With that he turned and walked away, leaving behind a vague scent of mold.

"Come on, Sabine," Tanner pleaded. "I'll stay home from

work tomorrow. We'll figure this out. This place isn't right."

If a doctor hadn't walked into the room at that moment and introduced himself, she would have left. He looked how Sabine imagined a psychiatrist should: salt and pepper beard, dark hair graying at the temples, wire rim glasses. The only deviation was that one of his pant legs appeared to be haphazardly trapped in his black sock.

"Sabine Connolly?" he asked.

"Yes," she answered, feeling excited, as if by knowing her name he'd confirmed that this was all going to be fine.

Dr. Baron brought them to a small, windowless room beside the nursing station. It was a stark and institutional. Sabine sat and reached for a tissue, but the box was empty. For a moment she wondered if it meant something. Was it some sort of sign she shouldn't ignore? But the thought vanished as she watched Tanner bounce Mia on his lap.

She sat across from Dr. Baron, making sure the sleeve of her baggy green sweater covered her burns that had blistered into the shape of a four-leafed clover. With her back straight and her ankles crossed, she smiled, determined to show that she wasn't a lost cause—even if her hair was a frizzed-out mess and her eyes were red and swollen.

Dr. Baron glanced down at his clipboard. "So, you saw Dr. Lincoln?"

Sabine nodded.

"Major depression. Suicidal ideation," he mumbled.

"I might be a little depressed," she said, embarrassed at how glaring he'd made her condition sound. "I mean, I just met Dr. Lincoln today for the first time. Maybe I'm fine."

A part of her hoped this new psychiatrist would agree. If he believed she was fine, maybe she'd believe it, and that might stop the panic, the feeling that she was walking on a tightrope and about to fall off.

He asked a series of standard questions. Age. Physical health.

Occupation.

"Mother," she answered, and felt a swell of shame. Sleeplessness and agoraphobia had forced her to drop out of grad school in biochemistry. She was too anxious to hold down a full-time job. The last part-time job she'd had was at an animal shelter, but she stopped that near the end of her pregnancy. Lately she'd felt incapable of being a good mother. Her hands trembled at the wheel of a car. The aisles in the grocery store made her claustrophobic. She couldn't cook or do laundry without feeling overwhelmed.

"Do you ever feel euphoric?" Dr. Baron asked.

"I was happy when Mia was born," she replied, knowing that she wasn't actually answering his question.

"Hallucinations?"

"None."

"Any mental illness in the family?"

"Absolutely not." She was the weak link in an illustrious chain.

He jotted a few notes.

"Will they be able to help me here?" she asked, hoping her desperation didn't show.

"We will certainly try," he said, giving her a piece of paper. "If you could just sign where the X is, we can get you checked in and show you to your room."

She noticed the word "voluntary" written in bold, which comforted her. She signed the form and passed it back as Mia began fussing. Tanner handed the baby to Sabine, who put Mia on her breast. As she suckled, Sabine forgot where she was for a few moments. The only thing that mattered was making sure Mia's needs were met.

"There's a nurse waiting for you," Dr. Baron explained. "She'll show you to your room."

When he stood and walked to the door, he seemed shorter than when she'd first met him.

"Wait," she said, surprised by the sharpness in her voice. "How many days do you think it will take for me to get better?"

If he had an answer, he didn't share it. "I'm afraid babies are not allowed to spend the night."

But it was a hospital. Surely they didn't separate mothers and babies.

"I nurse her." Sabine snapped her bra closed, pulled down her sweater, and wrapped her arms around Mia. A few fibers brushed against her burn. She took a deep breath and stopped herself from wincing.

"I'm sure she'll do fine on formula," Dr. Baron said. He looked down at his feet and straightened his pant leg.

Get out. The voice was clear, as if it were spoken into Sabine's ear. But she knew better. She didn't turn—would never give away that she'd heard something the others hadn't.

"I won't leave my baby," Sabine said. She glanced at Tanner, who had shifted forward on his chair, his eyes darting around nervously, as if he might be the next one to get trapped. "You can't just stop breastfeeding like that," she told Dr. Baron.

"I am sure this is very hard."

"I can't stay." The words came out hushed and terrified.

Tanner stood. Sabine looked up at him. She'd leave with him. They couldn't stop her. Tomorrow she would find a better plan.

"The form you signed states that you have to stay for at least three days," Dr. Baron explained. "Three business days. Weekends don't count."

Tanner reached for the baby.

"It was voluntary." She held onto Mia as she glanced around the room, looking for something, anything that might help. The dingy, white walls felt too close, and yet when she looked at Tanner, he seemed farther away. Her eyes were playing tricks.

"Good luck," Dr. Baron said, and walked out.

Sabine stared at the door.

Tanner tugged Mia away and put her back in the purple

snowsuit. Sabine's hands clapped to her chest. She wanted to protect herself, and Mia. And to stop the small shoots of splintering pain. It hurt to breathe.

Tanner zipped the snowsuit. "We should have left before."

"I'm walking out with you," Sabine said. "They can't stop me."

The door opened and a woman, who introduced herself as Nurse Nancy walked in.

"I'm leaving with my husband and baby," Sabine told her.

"If you try to leave we will have to restrain you," Nurse Nancy said too perkily, before locking her eyes on Sabine's. "You don't want to be in a straitjacket."

Sabine glared at Tanner, who looked at the door, ready to bolt. It was her fault she was stuck here. She'd found Dr. Lincoln's name in the Yellow Pages that morning. She'd asked Tanner to take her, she'd pressed the red buzzer—and signed the form. But that was before she knew they would take Mia.

"I'll accompany you to the door where you can say goodbye," Nancy said.

Sabine walked alongside Tanner, clutching Mia's mittened hand.

The man who had let them in opened the steel door and stood in front of Sabine. A dull static pulsed through her. How many years had she feared a place like this? How many nightmares had she had about it? How many warnings?

She remembered the orange tabby she had killed. It had attacked her in her college dorm room, flying through the air with its claws aimed at her chest. It gripped her T-shirt and hissed. Just as it was about to sink its fangs into her face, she ripped it off by the scruff of its neck and slammed its body against the wall. When the tabby whimpered, she felt a pang of remorse and loosened her grip. The cat lunged. She slammed it harder. There was a high-pitched wail and then a moan of defeat. Its limp body, a large clump of fur, was stained red.

The tabby had befriended her, slipping in at night, and nuzzling on her pillow. She never really understood how he got in, and she didn't think about it much, because when he curled up next to her, the feeling that she wanted to tear off her skin subsided.

The night she killed him, as she stood paralyzed in the middle of the room, holding his bloody body at arm's length, someone knocked.

"Come in," she called.

It was the RA, Cindy, a passionate rule-follower. "You were screaming."

Sabine held up the cat. Only there wasn't a cat. And Sabine could see the confusion on Cindy's face.

"Just a bad dream." Sabine turned to face the window. Of course, there had never been a cat.

Her slips into delusion happened infrequently, after bouts of sleeplessness and panic. They only happened at night. When she was alone. A blessing. A relief not to have to explain. Not to get thrown in some institution that would lock her up.

Yet here she was. Inevitably.

Now she stood in a locked ward, feeling paralyzed once again as she watched her daughter's purple hood descend through the wire-mesh window.

* * *

Arlesheim, Switzerland
1984

Inga pressed her fingers on the envelope, enjoying its plumpness. Yes, there would be parts of this long letter from her daughter that rambled, but that didn't matter much. She would read Lisbet's letter at least three times. It would take half the morning, which would make the rest of the day breeze by. The drab, vague emptiness would be lifted today.

She used her silver letter opener and began reading, skimming the weather report that filled the first two pages. Next came stories about Lisbet's skating students, then something interesting about Inga's grandson, about how the bank he was working for insisted on paying him a higher salary. Page six had a sweet account of a bunny in the garden, and then suddenly, Inga read a sentence that didn't belong. She took off her glasses, rubbed her eyes, and tried again. But the words didn't change.

She put the letter down and held onto the edge of the desk. The room seemed to darken, and the fir outside the window appeared almost black rather than green. She remembered herself as a young woman, kneeling next to a hospital bed. Vials of medicine littered the floor. A metal bowl with traces of yellow stomach fluid sat next to her.

After a minute or two, she felt more settled. She wiped her brow with a handkerchief, made tea, and checked all of the clocks in the house, even though she'd already set them all hours earlier. Each clock had a certain tone, a bell, a cuckoo, or a chime, and she liked them all to ring at exactly the same time. It was fastidious, but it was also a task that kept her busy. Distractions, she had learned decades ago, helped one move forward, kept time plotting at a bearable pace.

By the time she returned to her desk, the tree was once again its handsome forest green, and she was once again herself. She reached for the miniature painting that sat on the top shelf. In it, her sister Rigmor wore a red gown that showed off her slender shoulders and porcelain skin. But it was her stance, deferential and poised, that revealed her soul.

Forty-nine years ago, when Inga and her mother left Germany (she did not like the word fled), the large portrait of Rigmor that hung in the main drawing room had stayed behind. She had taken the miniature, the test-sample that the artist had painted.

Rigmor had been Inga's better half. Yes, the phrase was used for spouses, but it was better suited, in Inga's case, for a sister.

Interesting, how in the past few days, even before the letter had arrived, she had been drawn to the portrait.

She straightened her spine and picked up the letter once more. In the ten pages Lisbet had written, there was only that one line, a deathblow of a sentence, nested in trivialities.

Sabine has been admitted to an asylum with the name of McLean.

Inga went to the kitchen, where she put three jars of her homemade jam in a basket. Then she slipped on her tweed coat, put the letter in her handbag, and set out to visit Arnold.

A year ago, she had not been entirely pleased when he reentered her life, but she had come to look forward to visiting him, to reading him the correspondences from her daughter. Their conversations brought comfort to her, perhaps because he'd known her in her prime. He'd seen her at her best...and her worst.

Her right hip nagged with arthritis as she climbed the hill that led to the nursing home, called, of all things, The Sonnen Heim. The Sun Home. It was absurd that institutions used the word sun in their name, as if they were trying to mask the darkness inside their walls.

At the door, Inga composed herself and pressed the bell.

"Frau Sommer," the matron exclaimed. "I don't believe we were expecting you this morning." Inga noted a slight disapproval.

"I have come for an informal visit and was hoping Arnold would be available."

"Of course." The matron gave a small, almost imperceptible bow. "Will you wait in the green room?"

Inga placed her basket on a chair in the foyer. Invited or not, she never arrived empty-handed.

The green room, a small lounge that looked onto the gardens, was furnished with a beige couch and two burgundy colored armchairs. Inga sat on the smaller chair and perched her handbag on her lap, gripping the thin leather strap. The room had the advantage of good light, and the disadvantage of harboring one of the worst paintings of the Matterhorn that Inga had ever seen.

A nurse wheeled Arnold in. As he met Inga's gaze, he did not hide his concern. His brow furrowed, and the right side of his mouth, the working side, curved downward.

The moment the nurse was gone, he asked, "What has happened?"

"Are they feeding you well?" she replied.

"My dear Inga. That is not why you are here."

She pulled a handkerchief from the breast pocket of her starched blouse and kneaded it. He waited. His eyes misty from cataracts, looked a bit like marbles covered with thin white tissue.

She undid the clasp on her handbag, took out the letter, and handed him the relevant page.

"The third sentence in the second paragraph," she said. "It is underlined."

As she watched Arnold read, she thought of the day, almost a year ago, that he knocked on the door of her chalet, wearing a three-piece suit and holding a cane. She'd recognized him immediately, though it had been forty-eight years since she'd last seen him. He still had all of his hair; it had turned completely white. She had no idea what to say. They had promised each other there would be absolutely no contact. No letters, telegrams, or phone calls. He had honored the agreement until that point.

He said he had come to see her one last time, for a final truce. Truce seemed the wrong word—they had never battled, after all. She agreed to meet him for dinner later in Basel, but only with the promise that he would not speak of their time together before the war.

The evening had been more pleasant than she expected. She enjoyed his stories about his work in the States, and was pleased that he'd found love. A month later he telephoned from a hospital. He'd had a stroke after their dinner, and his left side was paralyzed.

He had no one left. Inga found a nursing home in her village, and took meticulous care of the logistics in getting him placed there. She even helped with some of the expenses. She knew she owed him nothing, but it saddened her to imagine him alone.

"Well?" Inga asked now.

"Tell me again, how old is Sabine?"

"Twenty-six," she replied.

"And there were no signs?"

"Some melancholy as a child perhaps." Inga thought of how Sabine had sometimes been withdrawn. "Certainly nothing recent that I was told of." But Lisbet had often kept Inga on the outside, viewing her as meddling and even controlling, regardless of Inga's good intentions.

"She just had a baby, did she not?" Arnold asked.

Inga nodded. "Three months ago."

"Post-partum depression, perhaps?"

From where Inga sat, she could see the words: *Sabine has been admitted.* Inga thought of Lisbet, of how she would not be able to manage this, how she would put her head in the sand. Inga loved her daughter, though she did not always understand her.

"I doubt you really believe that," she said and snatched the letter from Arnold's lap. Tears stung her eyes. The thought of Sabine in some institution, forlorn and in distress, pained Inga. She fought to regain her composure as she stared down at the Oriental carpet.

"Inga," Arnold said gently. "You must not jump to conclusions. There is not enough information, yet, to assume something terrible."

The air felt close, the room hot. She folded the letter and fanned herself with it. "Then I suppose it will be up to me to get the information. I will go there myself."

"Surely Lisbet will go; she can tell you what you need to know." He took a breath. The stroke made it difficult for him to talk sometimes. "I think it's unwise to rush."

"I am not rushing, and Lisbet will not go." Lisbet was likely fretting and rubbing an eyebrow. Such a handsome, kind woman, but with the disposition of a nervous mouse. "Sabine, could be on a ward with truly mad people, or be given the wrong diagnosis."

"Things are different now. Very different. Medicine has come a long way. There are some excellent drugs." He put a hand on the arm of her chair. "You mustn't worry."

She felt as if she had a piece of coal inside of her chest, black carbon that had been inert for many years, and had just now begun to smolder again. "Yes, of course I know times are different." She pressed a hand on her heart. "But I cannot just sit in Arlesheim and wait for a letter that may or may not come and may or may not have any useful information. I cannot do nothing."

"You could make some phone calls," he said.

She shook her head. "It is always best to have conversations face-to-face, especially when there is difficulty, and the chance of misunderstandings."

"Your hip is bad. You are not young. I worry this will be difficult for you."

She held up her chin. "My granddaughter is ill, and she will need me."

"Inga." He sighed. "I fear a journey like this could put you in a precarious situation."

"Nonsense," she told him.

They sat in silence. She gazed at the dappled window pane and thought that this felt familiar, the two of them together in disagreement.

"The weather is miserable," she said.

He gave his lopsided smile. "Is that what you'd like to talk about?"

"My decision is firm." She opened her handbag and placed

the letter inside.

"May I ask something?" he began.

She nodded.

"What do you think Sabine might in fact need?"

Inga felt as if there was a large, invisible hand on her back, pushing her forward. Saving, she thought. Although that sounded lofty and pretentious. She only said, "Sabine will need someone."

Arnold tugged at the faded collar of his shirt. "You are strong. But..." He hesitated. "But on the inside, we are all vulnerable."

Of course she was vulnerable. More now than when she'd first told him of the letter. Exactly the opposite of what she'd hoped for. It might have been nice for him to have shown some faith in her.

"I will not be talked out of going," she said, gripping the strap of her handbag.

He bent his head, relenting. "I know of the hospital mentioned in the letter. An old colleague of mine has a top position there. It's not a lot, but it's all I can offer."

"Very kind of you," she said, sounding colder than she intended.

"You may very well help Sabine. But please, you must also look after yourself. Don't only stay at the hospital. Go for a walk or out to a nice dinner." He paused. "And if it gets to be too much, and you can't manage, call me."

Although the surface of his eyes had been altered by age, the essence of them, the kindness, hadn't changed from the first time she'd met him in her family home in Frankfurt. He had come to them recommended, eager and naïve, perhaps too ordinary a man to take on what lay ahead.

The walk home was more difficult than Inga had expected. The damp weather had seeped into her hip, which ached sharply. And though nothing Arnold said would deter her, the apprehension she'd been feeling earlier was now doubled.

But she simply had to go. She owed it to Sabine, to Lisbet, and to Rigmor.

Chapter Two

A Parasite

Frankfurt am Main, Germany
1934

At twenty-seven, Inga was young enough to believe her actions could change the course of fate, and mature enough to set about doing so, starting with the household. The grandfather clock had not yet struck eight, and Inga had already instructed the cook to boil the eggs for three minutes and fifteen seconds, not three minutes. She had written thank-you notes to two acquaintances, and had given them to the butler to be delivered. Now, as she sat in the great room, she looked at the portrait of Rigmor, admiring her sister's wide-set eyes, and how the morning light wove threads of gold through her dark hair. Rigmor's episodes might have worsened since the painting was completed a few years ago, but Rigmor was as beautiful then as she was now.

The day promised to be bright, and the room was certainly not cold, yet Inga felt a chill. A cardigan was called for. At the landing of the staircase she watched her mother descend with heavy footfalls, and a stone-like expression. In her black dress, Frieda seemed more like a recent widow than a divorcee of fifteen years.

She was a study in contradiction—a stoic matriarch who held firm political views, and yet also believed women, other women (not herself), should always carry an air of subservience.

"What is it?" Inga asked. It would be just like Frieda to walk past, without acknowledgement.

Frieda stopped and looked at the paring knife in her hand, its tip red. "She has hurt herself."

Inga raced up the stairs and burst into Rigmor's room.

The heavy ivory drapes were closed, something Inga had advised against. The room smelled of camphor, another of Frieda's prescriptions. And there were no open windows to let in fresh air.

Rigmor was sitting on the bed, in her white nightdress, with her arms wrapped around her knees as she rocked back and forth. Her hair, which naturally formed perfect ringlets, looked as if a flock of birds had flown through it. Likely she'd spent much of the night tugging at it.

"Trouble with sleep," Inga began, and walked toward the bed. She sat next to her sister so she could look into her eyes.

"Mother took away my knife," Rigmor whispered. "Will you get me another?"

"Are you preparing an apple tart?" Inga asked.

Rigmor smiled, and Inga felt relieved that her sister was lucid enough to understand the small joke.

"So tell me," Inga said. "Why does a woman need a paring knife in her bedroom?"

Rigmor lifted her head. Her gray eyes seemed confused. "It's the botfly larvae," she answered.

"But it is much too cold for them to survive in the winter. They live in South America," Inga replied, playing along.

The botfly larvae crawled under people's skin and grew into a boil until it was ready to escape and pupate. It was a deliciously squeamish topic that the sisters had laughed about as children.

Rigmor extended one of her thin arms, revealing a small wound next to her wrist.

"Can you tell me why you did this?" Inga asked, gently.

"Last night I put hot compresses on the larvae, thinking that would kill it. But it only moved from the heat. I needed to cut it out."

"And so you went to the kitchen to get a knife?"

Inga had mentioned to Frieda that it might be good to have a nurse sit outside Rigmor's room during the night. But Frieda resisted, insisting that Rigmor did not need a child minder. Had Inga and Frieda agreed just a bit more about Rigmor, Inga might have suggested she and her husband move to another home. But she needed to keep an eye on her sister. And there was also the recent appearance of Fred. To move away with her husband would make things more difficult with her lover.

Inga took Rigmor's hand and studied the cut, a square laceration about two centimeters in length and width. Most often when Rigmor's imagination took such dark turns, it happened in the middle of the night, when she was unable to sleep.

"Perhaps you do have some sort of insect bite," Inga said. "Maybe a mite, or a bedbug. Sometimes when we have those, they feel as if they are moving from one place to another."

"No, it's a maggot." Rigmor shuddered. "I can feel it."

"Come," Inga said. "We will wash your arm, and it will go away. We'll drown it."

Rigmor walked with her sister to the sink, and Inga lathered the soap and cleaned the wound, grateful that it was quite small. It could have been much worse.

After the cut was dried and bandaged, Rigmor changed into a long-sleeved cotton dress, and Inga buttoned the back.

"Tea?" Inga asked as Rigmor sat next to the window.

Just then, Frieda appeared with a cup of hot bullion. "Cook prepared this. It will be good for your nerves."

Rigmor smiled obediently. For a woman of twenty-three, well-read and talented in music and art, she sometimes behaved like a young girl in front of their mother. That Frieda elicited this docile response, purposefully or not, irritated Inga. If she stayed, it would only be a matter of seconds until she bickered with Frieda about the windows or the light. Or Rigmor needing to go out more and get some exercise. And so Inga kissed her sister's forehead and took her leave.

Soon after, as Inga walked to the library at the University of Frankfurt, she imagined Frieda sitting next to Rigmor, coaxing her to have one more spoonful of bullion. Frieda had always doted, sullenly. The rare times she looked happy were when she listened to Rigmor play the piano. Then Frieda's face would take on an air of giddy intoxication, as she would talk about the suppleness of Rigmor's fingers and the grace of her body. Inga admired her sister, but she could not tolerate Frieda's fawning. Some might say Inga was jealous, but she would disagree. Her mother's attention was not something she sought.

Inga climbed the steps to the library. She was a regular on the second floor, where they housed the books and journals on psychology. Helmut, the young librarian, with bright blue eyes and white blond hair, kept a stack of readings he thought Inga would find interesting. He smiled brightly at her and seemed to find the need to walk past her numerous times as she read. Inga would glance up at him, tilt her head, and shift in her chair so that her legs were visible. Never ashamed to flirt, Inga knew she was attractive, with high cheekbones, a slim figure, and fine features. More than once she had been compared to Katharine Hepburn.

Today she scanned through an article about the recent developments of the Health Courts; Hamburg and Berlin had already assembled a number of them. Professor Rudin was leading the cause. Very soon, those courts would make determinations on who was to be sterilized.

Had Inga come from a middle-class family, she might have gone to medical school herself. But she was bred to be an aristocrat, a hostess, and a good wife; all things she could do, though none interested her.

She took a small notebook from her handbag and turned to the second-to-last page, where she kept a list of illnesses. Inga crossed out schizophrenia, feeblemindedness, and mania, things she was sure Rigmor did not have.

It still wasn't clear what Rigmor had; most doctors categorized her as a hysteric, and although Inga found that word vague, she also found it reassuring. A touch of hysteria could be treated at home; it would not get Rigmor institutionalized or sterilized.

When she was finished, Inga gathered her things and walked to Helmut's desk.

"I know it's strictly forbidden to take home these journals," she began, tucking back a few strands of her wavy hair. "But I would like so much to show this article to someone."

Helmut looked down at the article, then glanced at Inga, who had set her elbows on the desk and was leaning in. His face turned bright red.

"It is against our policies," he said. Then, without another word, he produced a pair of scissors and cut out the article. Inga folded the paper and patted Helmut's hand.

She waited until nine that night, when Frieda took her two whiskeys in the drawing room. Inga sat across from her mother and explained her idea of finding a doctor, someone who could keep an educated, watchful eye on Rigmor.

"No more doctors," Frieda said, slamming her glass on the end table. "We have seen five in the last six months. It has done nothing." She looked like a bull ready to charge. "And you have a husband to take care of. I will look after Rigmor."

Klaus was likely reading in bed, immune to the turbulence.

"My husband is perfectly fine," Inga said. She paused. "The man we would hire for Rigmor would not be acting as a doctor. He would be a friend. Someone we could trust, who could take her to a museum or café, watch her for a longer period of time, make a more accurate diagnosis. A correct diagnosis is the clearest path to successful treatment." Inga unfolded the paper in her hand. "I can phone Dr. Rudin." She handed the article to her mother. "You have met him. He came to a dinner party here once."

Frieda waved the paper. "I have no idea who he is."

"He is one of the most famous psychiatrists in the world. He can make a recommendation. I'm sure it will be excellent. What could it hurt?"

Frieda paused, appearing to consider Inga's suggestion. "If we do find someone, I will conduct the interview," Frieda said. A small concession, Inga thought, pleased she had won.

Chapter Three

Confessions

Belmont, Massachusetts
1984

Strips of morning light streaming through the locked window played on the floor. Sabine lay in bed watching the shadows and felt relief that she had managed a few hours' sleep.

She pulled aside the thin cotton blanket. As her feet hit the floor, the door opened. She didn't bother looking up. She knew it was only the checks person.

"Room change," a man said.

Now she looked. The man was Paul, the aide who had let her in the night she arrived.

"Why?" Sabine asked.

She was just getting used to this room. It had its advantages. It was next to the lounge with the piano and orange shag carpet, where people gathered and smoked. It was bigger than most rooms, and the ceiling cracks were in the shape of a dolphin. Its main disadvantage was that it was on the five-minute check hall, which meant that every five minutes, the door opened, and a staff member peered in. Although at night Sabine felt oddly comforted by the intrusions.

Paul had zero interest in the patients he served. "Just doing what I'm told," he said.

"Is it only me who's moving?" Sabine asked.

"Nope. You and Cecelia. Ten minute check hallway." He looked at his watch.

"Can we just wait a little, until she wakes up?"

Sabine needed to call Tanner. Now. Before she had coffee, before she went to the bathroom, before she gathered any of her things, she needed to know that she would see her baby today.

"I'm up," Cece grunted.

She'd had another difficult night. At around two in the morning, she'd screamed that there was a man wearing a red bandanna around his neck, trying to kill her. Staff came when they heard her yell, and made her stand up and count backwards from one hundred. After she calmed down, she returned to bed and cried quietly as Sabine whispered that she was so sorry.

Cece gathered her black hair into a ponytail, rubbed her eyes, and stuck a cassette into her boom box. Prince belted *Purple Rain*.

In their new, smaller room, Sabine once again took the bed near the window. The bad spirits, Cece said, came through windows at night. After Sabine finished moving her clothes and toiletries, she walked to the phone booth and called Tanner collect.

"Can you and Mia visit today?" She bit her lip. She should have started differently. Asked him how he was. How Mia slept.

"Uh...." He yawned. "Haven't had my coffee yet."

Her throat tightened. "Can you?" she whispered, as she read some of the graffiti etched in the wooden walls of the phone booth. *You're OK. They're fucked.*

He yawned again. "Listen, Sabine. I'm exhausted. Mia got me up twice during the night."

"Please." She traced a finger along the word HELL. "Today will be the fifth day."

"The thing is, my mom said she would pick her up from daycare later so I could stay in the city. You know, maybe meet a friend. It's been a while since I've had the chance to do anything for myself."

Somewhere under the shame that she was weak and needy, there was a spark of anger, of wanting to tell him he was a selfish bastard. Yes, he'd had to set up the daycare, and work, and help his father fix the roof, and yes, on the second day he'd brought Sabine all of her things in a garbage bag. But five nights had gone by.

"Sabine," her husband said. "Are you there?"

The spark drowned. "Tomorrow?" She tried not to cry and reminded herself that it was difficult for him to have a wife like her.

"Yeah, tomorrow is good."

"Thank you." She wiped her tears with the back of her hand.

As she dressed, she thought again about signing a three-day, which considering it was almost the weekend would mean she would be out by next week. But then she remembered everything she'd tried pre-McLean: relaxation tapes, advice from the La Leche League, walks around the neighborhood, phone calls to her mother, herbal teas from her best friend, and in one of her lowest moments, an evangelical television program, which flashed a phone number across the screen. For only $9.99, she could be prayed for.

In the dining room with the large wooden-framed windows that rattled on windy days, Sabine sat and stared at the snow-covered lawn.

Helen approached. "May I?" she asked. "You look like you could use some company."

Sabine nodded. Helen was poised and articulate, the kind of woman, Omama, Sabine's Swiss grandmother, would approve of—upper class with shiny dark hair, understated makeup, defined cheekbones, and impeccable manners.

"Coffee?" Helen asked.

"Sure."

Something about Helen, about her surety of convictions, about the way she observed everyone and everything, comforted Sabine, at least a little. Helen would help. She would have answers.

As Helen poured coffee from the urn, Sabine glanced at the slab of plywood covering an old fireplace.

Helen set a yellow cup in front of Sabine.

"What's wrong?" She reached across the table, but stopped just short of touching Sabine. No physical contact, PC, was allowed. But Sabine didn't believe it was the rule that stopped Helen. It was that she was too professional, even if she was a patient.

"Tanner can't bring Mia," she said. The coffee had a strange gasoline aftertaste.

"Sorry," Helen said.

Tears welled. "I need to figure out how to get better fast."

Helen picked up her cup the correct way, at least correct according to Omama, without her pinky sticking out.

"Let me know if you figure it out." Her large brown eyes shined with a mixture of laughter and cynicism. This was her thirteenth hospitalization.

"What's helped you?" Sabine asked, as the general din, the whooshing of the swinging door to the kitchen, patients asking staff for matches, and an argument about protocol for signing out, surrounded her.

Helen paused long enough to make clear she wasn't going to answer that question. "What are the three things you would never tell your therapist?"

Sabine considered the question, understanding both its merit and difficulty. "Have you done that?"

Helen chuckled. "God, no."

Frank barreled in, pulled a chair right up to Sabine, and crossed his long, spindly legs. He put an elbow on the table and stared at Helen.

"Frank," she said. "We're busy."

"She wants to operate on your brain," he told Sabine, who rubbed his arm gently, ignoring the PC rule.

"No, she doesn't. I swear I'm OK. She's a friend." It was strange how quickly Sabine felt comfortable around most of her fellow patients. It was easier than making friends on the outside. Once you reached the bottom of the social strata, there was no point in pretending.

Paul walked toward the table. "Frank, time for a shower," he said.

Frank dashed out of the room. Showers, he believed, could kill you.

"So why wouldn't you tell your therapist the three things?" Sabine asked. "I mean, if it would help?"

Helen tucked her hair behind her ears. "I'm not here to get help."

She'd told this to Sabine before, but it was hard to fathom. Everything about Helen was hard to fathom. The first time they met, Helen had asked Sabine if she voted for Reagan. When Sabine said no, Helen smiled and asked Sabine to sit.

A cool veil glided down Helen's face now, and Sabine knew she was crossing the line. No more questions about Helen.

"So, three things," Sabine began, taking a deep breath. "There was this period of time when I was growing up"—she ran her finger along the cup—"when I took plates from the cupboard." She pictured herself quietly opening the glass cabinet. "They were expensive plates. From Europe. I took one each day, and I'd walk to the end of our street and then drop it."

"How old were you?"

"Nine. I wasn't a destructive kid. I didn't break things or steal. It was weird." She shrugged. "I don't know what I was thinking."

"And no one saw?"

"My next door neighbor did. Mrs. Zandichek. She made me come to her yard one day. I remember how perfectly green her lawn was. She told me that she had seen me break the plates. I lied and said it wasn't me. Then she told me that if I was lying my tongue would turn black, and if I didn't show her my tongue, it was proof that I was guilty. I knew tongues didn't work that way, so I showed her mine."

Helen laughed. "So she lied to try to catch you lying. And

27

your mother? Didn't she miss her plates?"

"I don't think so." Sabine looked at her hands, feeling the shame now that she hadn't felt then.

"You needed some attention," Helen said. "Maybe from your parents. But it sounds as if they weren't able to give it."

"My mother was busy," she said, and bounced her knee. "There were three of us, and she was also teaching skating."

Sabine remembered something her mother had said a couple of years after the plates disappeared. She told Sabine about a child in her village—*a strange child, who had stolen his mother's gold bracelet and stomped on it at the bottom of the street where everyone could see. The neighbors thought the boy was mad, but the mother of the boy was wise. She pretended it didn't happen, and because she did that, the boy had to pretend as well, and he pretended so hard for so long that he ended up being perfectly fine.*

"Want to move on to the next thing?" Helen asked.

Sabine took a sip of the coffee—now cold. "I had a psychotic episode," she whispered.

"Just one?"

Sabine shrugged, not wanting to answer that. "I lied when Dr. Baron asked me when I was being admitted."

"Everyone lies at those screenings. We have to."

Sabine felt relieved, although she wasn't sure why it was that people had to lie.

"I was at home, cooking spaghetti," she said. "Mia was in a bassinet sleeping in the living room. When I dumped the spaghetti into the colander, and looked at it, it was this huge bowl of squirming maggots."

Helen let out a gasp. "What did you do?"

"I screamed. Thankfully no one was home. I reached for a broom." Sabine forced a laugh. "I don't know what I thought a broom would do."

Helen covered her mouth. Her face blanched. "You could have run."

"I guess," Sabine said. "But I remembered something I had read about maggots cleaning wounds, so I decided they weren't really that bad; all I had to do was put them in the trash. I stuck my hand in the bowl, and as soon as I did, it was spaghetti again. So maybe it wasn't really a psychotic episode."

"You stuck your hand in a bowl you thought was full of maggots?" Helen's eyes were wide and watery.

"I guess. But not really, because there weren't actually any maggots in there."

Helen shivered. "I would rather die than put my hand in a bowl of maggots."

"Oh." Cold air streamed through the window. Maybe she shouldn't have been talking about psychosis. Maybe that was the line between a little crazy and really crazy.

Helen pulled at a few of her eyelashes. Her shoulders rounded as she seemed to withdraw. "Once," she said, her gaze fixed on the wall behind Sabine. "A maggot crawled on my face. It curled up and rested in the crook of my eye."

"You didn't move it away?" Sabine asked.

"I was tied to a chair," Helen answered flatly.

This was the first crack Sabine had seen in Helen, the first inkling that something had gone terribly wrong.

"Why?" Sabine asked, softly.

"I was in Texas."

Sabine nodded as if that made some sort of sense. "Is that where you're from?"

"No. I hate Texas." Helen had a small spot on the side of her nose where she had no melanin. It brightened like a white star when she got emotional.

"Right," Sabine said.

Helen waved a hand. "We're not talking about me. My stories are not interesting." The star dimmed.

"What is the third thing?" Helen asked.

"I'm in love with Dr. Lincoln," Sabine blurted, which was by

29

far the most embarrassing of the three confessions.

"Oh," Helen replied. "That's just transference. It means therapy is working."

"No, I really feel like I'm in love with him," Sabine said.

"Of course you do. You transfer your feelings of the love you might have felt for your parents onto him, hoping that this time someone might actually listen and understand."

"My parents listened." Although as soon as she said that, she thought about her father, how he would stomp around the house yelling that he needed his peace and quiet even when Sabine and her brothers were playing silently in the basement.

Helen raised her impeccably shaped eyebrows.

"Really," Sabine declared. "My mother was perfect."

Helen picked up her cup. "The perfect is the enemy of the good," she said to Sabine, before leaving her alone at the table.

The room had filled. Patients ate their toast and Cornflakes. Hot breakfast was served in the large cafeteria in another building. You had to have privileges to go there.

Sabine thought of her mother—her tall, beautiful, made-of-honey mother, who had been a champion skater, who people gathered around at the pond in wintertime when she did a sit spin on the ice, whose accent made everyone ask her where she was from. Who said *vonderful* and *vhat* instead of *wonderful* and *what*. Who was too terrified to speak to Sabine the night she was admitted. Who still hadn't called, after five days. Who had once whispered to Sabine that being mentally ill was the most terrible thing that could befall a person, and God forbid if it was schizophrenia.

Chapter Four

An Invitation

Frankfurt am Main, Germany
1934

Arnold glanced at his diary; three patients in the morning, and research in the afternoon. He carried his breakfast dishes to the sink and heard a knock on the front door. Odd. He had neighbors, but none he was close to. His stomach lurched. What if it was the Gestapo coming for him because he owned some of Freud's books? The raids were happening more lately, especially to intellectuals and left-leaning socialists but, thankfully, no one he knew personally.

He opened the door. A man in a chauffer's uniform handed Arnold a wax-sealed envelope, gave a bow, and turned away.

There was no family crest Arnold would recognize. He was not a man of high society. That he had worked his way up to a solid academic life was a tremendous accomplishment, considering that he'd come from a small farming family in Holdstadt.

On the front of the envelope, his name, Herr Doctor Arnold Richter, was scripted beautifully.

It seemed a shame to break the seal, but he could hardly just stand there admiring it. He opened the letter and discovered it was an invitation to a dinner party hosted by the Blumenthals, a well-known Jewish family. Arnold had heard the name from a colleague who had received a visit from one of the daughters. His colleague had reported that this woman was interested in psychiatry, but that after about thirty minutes, she left in a huff, dismissing his ideas as old-fashioned. Arnold found the story amusing. What sort of woman waltzes into a doctor's office and criticizes his ideas?

He held the cardboard invitation and wondered if this Blumenthal woman wanted to speak with him about psychiatry. But why invite him to a dinner party? Why not just make an appointment? Puzzled and intrigued, he left the card on the front table in the foyer and headed to his office.

The brisk April air was particularly good walking weather. He decided to take the route along Bockenheimer Landstrasse, and identify which home belonged to the Blumenthals.

His thoughts drifted back to when he and his mother would take the train to Berlin once a year. She wasn't interested in shopping or architecture, or theater. She only wanted to see the big houses. Together they strolled the tree-lined streets, as she would invent all sorts of stories about the goings-on of the wealthy. The servants, she imagined, were always relegated to horrible rooms in the attic. One afternoon, two women emerged from one of the homes, and Arnold's mother stopped and gaped. One of the women, who wore a hat with a blue feather, looked at him and seemed perplexed. Young farm boys in lederhosen didn't walk those fancy streets. He tugged at his mother's hand, anxious to hurry away. Shame snaked around his heart, tightening the muscle. But his mother, who felt only joy at being in such close proximity to the women, turned to Arnold and proclaimed that one day he would marry such a lady.

Her dreams for her only child were of immense proportion. She was sure he would become a doctor, which he had, although disappointingly not a surgeon. She came from more educated stock than Arnold's father, who was a hulking farmer with dirt permanently etched around his fingernails. After Arnold was born, his mother, once a nurse, stayed home to raise her son, milk the cows, and slaughter the pigs. Never one to shy from hard work, she did whatever was needed to save her pennies so that Arnold could go to boarding school.

Her husband had little interest in their boy. He never understood Arnold's attraction to books, and he claimed to be too busy on the farm the day Arnold graduated from Wurzburg Medical University. Arnold had been relieved not to have to introduce his father to his classmates.

Now, as he strolled along the wealthiest street in Frankfurt am Main, Arnold thought of his mother's prophecy regarding his marriage. She believed in the mystic arts, and sometimes read palms for the villagers. He adored his mother, but he was a man of science, and had no faith in her divinities.

Arnold stopped in front of the Blumenthal home, set back from the road but still visible through the budding trees. Smoke curled from the chimney. Here lived people with old money and social currency, whose connections might prove useful. He imagined himself standing behind a podium in a large lecture hall filled with doctors and professors, everyone dazzled by his latest discovery.

On the evening of April 13th, Arnold dressed in his new black tuxedo. He had researched the latest operas, and given himself a hurried course in modern art. He already possessed solid knowledge of literature, and could quote Goethe. Boarding school had not been for nothing.

He tried to make a fair assessment of how he would be viewed. His features were plain, but he had a sturdy physique and a full head of brown hair. He had a large forehead, which a colleague, an expert in morphology, had once commented was a sign of intelligence.

The butler took Arnold's overcoat and led him from the enormous foyer to the drawing room, where cocktails were served on golden platters. Arnold sipped champagne as he scanned the room, recognizing no one. His gaze stopped on a painting of a woman above the mantel. Unlike most portraits, in which the subject stared out directly, this woman looked downward. She was pretty, although not classically beautiful. Her dark hair, swept up off her neck, was arranged elegantly. She wore a red gown that showed off her pale shoulders. But what struck him most was the innate gentleness he sensed. That a painter could capture something so internal and private impressed Arnold.

"You must be Dr. Richter." In front of him stood a true beauty. Her wavy hair, cut in a modern angle, framed a perfectly symmetrical face with a strong chin and striking green eyes.

"I am," Arnold said, and shook her hand.

"I am Inga Sommer, daughter of Frieda Blumenthal." She glowed.

"Your home is magnificent." He glanced at the walls, covered with oil paintings in gilded frames.

"Technically, it is my mother's home," Inga said. "Although my husband and I reside in the east wing." She smiled. "I'm glad you decided to join us."

"It's a pleasure to be here."

"You must meet my husband, Klaus. He is also at the University. A chemist." She turned and tugged at a man's sleeve.

Klaus, who by any standards was extraordinarily handsome, gave Arnold's hand a firm shake. "Good of you to come," he said, as he puffed his pipe.

"I will leave you two to get acquainted," Inga said and dashed off.

Klaus carried a certain bemusement in his eyes, as if this was all an entertaining game.

"Is the painting above the mantel of Frau Blumenthal?" Arnold asked.

Klaus's deep laugh complemented his tall stature and wide shoulders. "I shouldn't think anyone would want to be in a room in which her portrait hovered."

Arnold smiled, the acceptable response, but wondered what undercurrents lay beneath this family. "This Frau Blumenthal, your mother-in-law, is she quite a character then?"

"She is steel," Klaus said, not seeming to care if anyone overheard them. "A mixture of an iron will with the darkness of carbon."

"Spoken like a true chemist," Arnold said.

"Alloys are my specialty." He smoked. "The painting," he said, gazing up at it, "is of the favored child, Rigmor." He tipped his head to the corner. "She is over there, more than likely attempting to fade into the background." Taken at face value, the words could have sounded caustic. Yet Klaus's tone was considerate, almost warm.

Arnold saw a woman who held her glass close to her chest. Her hair was in a bun, and her ivory dress was simple and understated. She watched rather than mingled.

"Are they alike, your wife and your sister?" Arnold asked, although he had already guessed they were not.

"How they came from the same parents is a mystery. But one can never be sure of paternity, can one?"

The question was stated so objectively that Arnold wasn't sure if Klaus was asking earnestly or making a joke.

"One of my interests is the genetics of personality," Arnold answered, mirroring Klaus's impartiality.

"Well, the two sisters would certainly make a good case study."

"And their mother? Which daughter is more like her?"

Klaus gave Arnold a hearty pat on the back. "Answering that question could mean the end of my marriage." He winked. "Enjoy your evening."

The dining room was something out of a picture book. Each place setting had multiple silver utensils and the chandeliers were lit with real candles. Arnold found his name card. He was seated next to an elderly woman who wore too much perfume and kept asking him if he really was a psychiatrist. "I simply don't understand why you would get a medical degree to become a mind reader."

Dinner consisted of five courses, and everyone, aside from himself and the woman next to him, was absorbed in conversation.

After dinner the party moved back to the drawing room.

Klaus sat in one of the larger armchairs smoking his pipe. Arnold had thus far met no artists, writers or doctors. Klaus was the only person he felt any connection to. Just as he headed over, someone tapped his arm. He turned and saw a woman, in her mid-forties, wearing a plain black dress.

"I am Frau Blumenthal," she said.

All evening he had tried to guess which lady was the matron of this home. He couldn't even remember seeing the woman who now stood in front of him.

"A pleasure." Arnold held out a hand.

She glanced at his hand as if he should put it away. "Would you be so kind as to have a word?" she asked.

"Yes, of course." Finally, the purpose of his invitation was to be revealed. "What can I do for you?"

"Not here," she murmured.

He followed her to a small sitting room where the paintings were light in color and theme, mostly of flowers and fruit—a ladies' parlor, he guessed.

Frau Blumenthal's hair, wrapped around her head, looked like a turban, the kind he'd seen in pictures from India. He declined her offer of a drink.

"Please sit," she said, pointing to the sofa.

She sat across from him, holding herself unnaturally straight. Arnold liked to think of himself as an expert in body expression. Her stiffness, he surmised, was due to nerves. He had absolutely no idea what she wanted with him, but her posture told him it was something of great concern.

She took a deep breath. "Inga found your name."

"Oh?"

"A man by the name of Ernst Rudin gave it to her. Have you heard of him?"

"Of course I have heard of him," Arnold answered. "I think any reasonable psychiatrist in the country—in the world—

knows who he is." He crossed his legs. "I have attended a few of his lectures. I am a great admirer of his work."

He restrained a smile, wanting to put on the façade that it was nothing out of the ordinary that he was known by someone like Rudin. In fact, it was a shock of the most pleasant nature.

"Inga feels he is something special as well," Frau Blumenthal said. She folded her hands on her lap with her index fingers pointing upward like a steeple, an unusual gesture, as if part of her wanted to pray.

"I must say I am very curious how I play into all of this," Arnold said.

"I have two daughters. Inga, who you have met, and Rigmor, who you might not have had a chance to speak with yet."

"I have not had the pleasure."

"She suffers from fits." Frau Blumenthal held herself completely still. Arnold nodded.

"She has some sort of nervous disorder." She paused. "I hope this will stay between us."

"Of course."

"I am no expert on these types of illnesses. Inga, on the other hand, seems to throw herself into learning everything that she can. I believe she and Rudin are on friendly terms."

"And he knew of me?" His voice squeaked, betraying his lack of ease. He re-situated himself.

Frau Blumenthal shrugged. "How else would he have known to recommend you?"

"I did publish a paper last year on manic depressives. Perhaps he read that?"

"I am not familiar with his reading habits," she said.

He smiled. "So you are worried about your daughter."

"I am her mother."

"Are you looking for my professional opinion?"

"In a way, yes. What we are looking for is a bit out of the ordinary. She has seen many doctors. We have had many opinions." She took a labored breath. "None have been particularly useful."

"Even Rudin's?"

"I am not interested in his opinion. He seems to focus only on a particular type of mental illness that Rigmor does not have."

Arnold doubted that Rudin would be so narrow-minded. But he understood. Rudin's work was primarily on the genetics of schizophrenia, and that was a diagnosis that no one wanted.

"The doctors you have seen, what have they said?" he asked.

"She has a combination of hysteria and depression."

"Do you think their assessments are correct?" He believed that parents, if they were willing to be completely honest with themselves, were the most reliable source of information about their children's illnesses.

"Their words mean nothing to me. What I see is a young woman who gets herself worked up over nothing. Sometimes she cries for days, pulling at her hair, and saying that she just can't carry on anymore."

"I have no doubt you are telling me the truth, but the few times I glanced at her this evening, I saw a woman who seemed very self-contained."

"But of course. She would hardly be joining the party if she was in the middle of an episode. If I gave the impression that she suffers from these all of the time, please excuse me."

"No, you have been very clear. May I ask what she means when she says she *can't carry on anymore*?" Arnold asked.

"Well that is the thing, is it not? There is nothing for her to do. She can relax all day, and yet still she has a lack of control of her nerves."

"Has she always had these fits?"

Frau Blumenthal exhaled. Her posture softened. "She was a sweet child, shy and kind. I remember how readily she felt shame. It saddened me to see her suffer." She hesitated, her eyes distant for a moment. "But the fits didn't begin until she was fifteen."

"It's not uncommon that women begin to suffer from illnesses around the time their bodies develop. Has anyone else in your family suffered this way?"

She relaxed her hands from their rigid formation and sliced one through the air. "There is no mental illness, no deformities of any type, on either side of the family. I do not want to make it sound as if we are superior. I am horrified at the recent talk of a superior race. But genetically speaking, we are above the norm."

Arnold nodded. "So how can I be of assistance?"

"I believe she needs a compassionate friend."

"She doesn't have any friends?"

Frau Blumenthal shifted and sighed. "I am speaking of a compassionate friend, who is also a psychiatrist, and is not terribly far from her in age."

"And you thought I might be a good candidate?"

"I have watched you all evening. I think you have a kind nature."

"That is generous of you to say."

"I am not here to give false flattery. I am here to offer an arrangement. I want you to become her friend. She will confide in you, and feel as if she has someone to talk to about her problems. It will not be a secret that you are a psychiatrist, and you can offer casual advice. In this way she can stay clear of other doctor's offices, where people look at her as if she is a subhuman specimen."

He didn't like to think that any of his colleagues would view a patient that way. "And if she doesn't want to become my friend?"

"You are an intelligent man. You will figure it out."

How absurd. It wasn't as if he could just snap his fingers and become friends with a strange woman.

"I appreciate your faith in me, but I am not sure I'm a suitable candidate."

"Don't think we haven't done our research. You are the right age. You have the correct background." She paused. "May I assume you are not a Nazi?"

He laughed. "Most certainly not." He thought it best not to inform her that doctors, especially psychiatrists, were leading the way in joining the Party.

"Then I will invite you to a smaller dinner party next week and you will be able to spend time with Rigmor. After that, you can go on walks, or play cards, whatever suits you. I will come to the University to talk to you every so often and find out how things are going."

"I could not share anything that was said in confidence." If she wanted a pawn, she would need to look elsewhere.

"You will not technically be her doctor, so you needn't worry about that. If there is someone with whom she can relax, be honest with, not be afraid of some horrible treatments they may prescribe, then perhaps we can get to the bottom of why she has these fits in the first place."

"Would she be aware that you would come to talk to me?"

"I think that would be counterproductive. I don't want her to feel as if she is being spied on."

"Yet in essence that is what you would be doing."

Her face soured. "I am trying to help my daughter. I don't see anything wrong with that." She gripped the arms of the chair.

"I am not faulting your intentions. I am only saying I might not be the right person."

"You would be well paid."

"I would never take money for something like this."

"You would be a regular guest at our home. Your friend, Rudin, comes sometimes, as does the mayor of Frankfurt."

Arnold was not interested in politics. "I'm sorry," he said, getting ready to stand. The thought of meeting Rudin was tempting, but his ethics must come before anything else.

Frau Blumenthal touched his arm. "Just come to dinner next

week. Don't make a decision now. At least meet her."

Under the hard exterior, he saw the desperation in her eyes and remembered his mother with a similar expression when she learned her husband had congenital heart disease. She had begged Arnold to find a cure, which naturally was impossible. Arnold looked at Frau Blumenthal and gathered she had become a master at hiding her anguish.

"Very well," he told her, finding it simply too difficult to say no.

When she smiled for the first time, he noted that she was an attractive woman.

"I will send my chauffer over with a date and a time."

He bowed his head. Frau Blumenthal stood abruptly, extending an arm, now agreeable to a handshake.

How different she seemed from Rigmor, a woman who moved like a gentle breeze and seemed content to remain in the shadows.

* * *

The party was over, and Inga was anxious to find out how things had gone with Arnold. She found Frieda in the drawing room, taking her two glasses of whiskey.

If Inga was perfectly honest with herself, she would have appreciated a sliver of gratitude, some kind of recognition that her plan to enlist Arnold had potential. But Frieda showed no signs of softness, no smile, nothing that might intimate that she was pleased in any way with her daughter.

"How did it go with Arnold?" Inga sat straight, formally. If her mother was going to be aloof, then Inga would play along.

"He has a weak chin."

Inga laughed, although she knew Frieda did not mean to be funny. "I thought him quite good-looking. But if the dimensions of his chin are what interest you, perhaps we should start a different sort of search."

"He was not as agreeable as you indicated he might be."

"I had never met him."

"Since you enjoy going to the library so much, perhaps you could have done a bit more research." Frieda's jaw tightened.

"I found out what I could," Inga said. "But I do wonder if it would have made a difference if I had explained the situation to him." She wanted to keep her tone light, as if she was doing nothing more than being curious.

"Are you suggesting that I am incompetent? You may view me as your old mother, but I do know how to manage people." Frieda finished her whiskey.

"Sometimes it isn't about managing. Sometimes it simply takes a bit more finesse." Inga glanced at Rigmor's portrait.

Frieda stared at her daughter. "You talk about finesse, about discretion and delicacy? There have been rumors. A number of them. You are seeing that little man, Frederick Silbermann. I would suggest a bit more tact." Her face reddened.

Inga remained still. "He is a friend. Nothing more."

"You go to nightclubs with him," Frieda said. "He has been seen with a hand on your backside."

"You have spies in nightclubs?" Inga pretended she thought the topic entertaining, although that was far from the truth. She had been strict with Fred, telling him not to touch her in public. But sometimes it was impossible, not to reach out and brush a hand against the person you were so in love with.

"You have married a good man," Frieda said. "Why not be content with him?"

"I have no intention of ending my marriage." She crossed her legs. Divorce was not something she or Fred wanted. He was also married, and they both agreed that upsetting their family order was not wise. "What I do in my spare time is my business. Now please tell me what Arnold had to say."

"Your husband is a good-looking man. He is well educated. I

have never heard him raise his voice. He does not seem interested in other women. So why?"

Inga would never talk about the root problems in her marriage with her mother, and she understood that her mother's harshness was born of fear. Fear that Inga's husband might leave Inga for another woman, fear of loss, fear of gossip—of shame.

"Please tell me about Arnold," Inga said.

"I simply don't understand," Frieda persisted. "Fred is not attractive. He is married with children. It is selfish not to see how you might be hurting his wife."

Of course that would be Frieda's perspective. *The poor wife.* "I am here to talk about Arnold."

"He is not eager to do our bidding," Frieda began. "And not interested in money."

"I told you he would not take money."

Frieda stood. "He will come to dinner again. We shall see. In the meantime, I don't think it's wise that you sneak into Rigmor's room in the evening. She needs her rest."

"She enjoys my company."

"You have a husband to keep." Frieda walked to the door, stopped and turned.

With her hair wrapped around her head, her dark clothing, and her lack of willingness to even wear lipstick, she made her position clear. She did not want to draw people close to her. She could not withstand the hurt that might follow.

"More attention to your own affairs is in order," Frieda said.

Left alone, Inga slumped, relieved to be out of Frieda's line of fire. All she wanted from her mother, all she had ever wanted, was respect. When Inga was four, her nanny had helped her to embroider a handkerchief with small blue flowers. Frieda had patted Inga's head and said, "Good work, my girl." Inga still had that handkerchief.

Frieda's first misfortune was discovering her husband's indiscretions. She might have eventually moved on from that, but then Rigmor became ill, and Frieda, a much more sensitive soul than she let on, kept people at bay. Except Inga, who took the brunt of her mother's anger, and who understood that Frieda needed to lash out at someone who was completely loyal and also had the strength to remain standing.

Inga thought back to when Rigmor was born, how all of the attention naturally went to her. She was a captivating baby. Everyone felt that. Most of all Inga.

She remembered the very first day she saw Rigmor. It was the nursemaid who introduced them, handing Inga the baby wrapped in a yellow blanket trimmed with ivory silk. Rigmor's mouth made sweet sucking motions as she glanced upward. In that moment, Inga felt transformed, as if some sort of light warmed her heart. Perhaps it was merely what all older sisters felt, or perhaps it was because Rigmor was truly extraordinary. Either way, Inga spent as much time as she was allowed with her baby sister. When Rigmor first toddled in her white shoes, Inga was there to clap and cheer. It was Inga who taught Rigmor how to read, how to make daisy chains, and which trees in the garden were best to hide behind. Inga held Rigmor's hand when she was shy, told her not be afraid of adults or horses, and taught her that sometimes splashing paint on a canvas, making a mess, and rolling down hills were just as important as good manners.

* * *

When Arnold came for the second, more intimate dinner party, he sat next to Rigmor, and they spoke about painters and musicians. Conversation flowed smoothly, and by the end of the night, after they had talked about Agatha Christie's latest murder mystery, they were laughing and devising plots of their own. Had he known nothing about Rigmor from Frau Blumenthal, Arnold would have thought her perfectly normal. The few notations he made were that she did have a tendency to lower her head quite often, and her cheeks turned pink readily. But she was very intelligent, curious, well-read, and engaging. He doubted she needed much help at all, and he wondered if her mother's need for her to be looked after came from a need to control. After all, Frau Blumenthal was not married. Arnold assumed she was a war widow, and from his experience widows often clung to their youngest child.

At the end of the evening, Frau Blumenthal cornered Arnold.

"It seems to have gone well," she said.

He glanced at Rigmor who was talking to Inga. "I enjoyed myself. Thank you for having me."

Rigmor approached to say good night.

"Tea next Thursday?" Frau Blumenthal asked Arnold, as her younger daughter slipped quietly behind her.

"Yes," he replied, without hesitation.

The following day, as Arnold listened to a patient carry on about her dog that died recently, and how she wished it was she who had died instead, his thoughts kept wandering to Rigmor.

When Thursday arrived, Arnold was surprised to discover that at this event, he and Rigmor were the only two participants. They sat together in the smaller, lighter drawing room.

"Your mother and sister couldn't join us?" he asked.

"My mother has business with the bank, and Inga, well, she is always here, there and everywhere." As Rigmor smiled, she held a hand in front of her mouth.

"May I be so bold as to ask what happened to your father?"

Color sprang to her face. "My mother and father are divorced."

He nodded, wanting to know more, but not wanting to cause embarrassment. "I see." He kept his posture open, showing a willingness to listen without judgment.

"He had an affair, and my mother couldn't tolerate it."

"That must have been difficult." He bit into the moist lemon cake.

"I don't recall much. I was eight at the time, and it seemed that everyone around me spoke in whispers. Except Inga. She was twelve, and said my mother had no right to tell my father to move out."

"Do you see him often?"

"Never. My mother said that if he remarried, she would not allow him to see us." She brushed a hand along her skirt. "She even said it was illegal. I remember him sitting stiffly in the drawing room in his military uniform with the thick cuffs, an iron cross pinned to his lapel, and large silver buttons on the cape. I wanted to touch those buttons." She smiled. "He had a long mustache that twisted at the ends. I can't really remember what he was like, but I remember those buttons."

Arnold pried gently. He learned that Rigmor was a family name, that her governess had been strict, something Rigmor adapted to, being submissive by nature. Inga, on the other hand, was constantly scolded. He learned that Inga, although the more boisterous sister, was fiercely protective of Rigmor.

Near the end of the afternoon, he asked her if there was one thing she could change in her life what would it be.

"I have seen a number of psychiatrists and no one has ever asked me that question."

"I am not here as your psychiatrist," he reminded her.

"No, of course not." She gave a half smile.

"Would you change anything?" he asked.

"I would like to go to bed at night and know that I will be able to sleep."

He had not expected that answer. He thought maybe she would want to study at the University, or leave home, or travel, but to wish for sleep? She had no discoloring under her eyes, or any other signs of sleep deprivation. Aside from the fact that she was perhaps a bit too thin, she looked in the prime of health.

"Do you always have trouble falling asleep?" he asked.

"And what would you wish for?" she replied.

He chuckled. She was very good at deflecting. "Many things,

I suppose."

She poked his arm. "This isn't a fair game if you don't tell me." Her gray eyes reminded him of light sparkling off the ocean.

"No, that wouldn't be fair." He had never told anyone of his real dreams. "I know it's very unlikely, and it would take an enormous amount of work, but I would like to make a name for myself one day. Perhaps even write a book."

Her eyes shone as she clapped. "Of course you will do it."

Over the next two weeks, he saw her four times. Twice they walked through the Palmengarten, and twice he visited her for tea. She wore clean cut dresses with conservative necklines. Everything about her—the way she walked, spoke, and carried her handbag—had a modest, unpretentious air.

She was interested in Darwin, animals (especially insects), mystery novels, the piano, and art. She was not fond of poetry, politics, or fashion. She hated anything loud, such as night clubs, and felt anxious walking down a crowded street. She loved to talk about Inga, who had an extraordinarily busy social schedule and seemed to know everyone on the planet. Inga's descriptions of people, which often included comparing them to some sort of animal, (her mother was naturally a mule) made Rigmor laugh.

But for every piece of information she gave, she extracted something from him. A description of his childhood farm, the nature of his mother, and the reason he chose psychiatry. He paused and smiled when she asked him this, even though on the inside, he was hardly feeling lighthearted. He told Rigmor he had gone into the field because he was interested in the dynamics of the human mind. In part that was true. But the larger part, the part he didn't say, was that he had hoped to find a way to cure his sexual perversions, perversions that the Nazis found particularly abhorrent. Not that he agreed with their beliefs, but one could hardly escape their views of late.

Chapter Five

Reunions

Belmont, Massachusetts
1984

Inga booked a ticket and packed her suitcase. If there was one thing she had learned from traveling the globe with Fred, it was how to avoid bringing unnecessary items. She lifted her bag, pleased that it was quite light. She would not be one of those elderly people who needed assistance with luggage.

Once in Boston, she took a taxi to the Holiday Inn. The lobby smelled of cleaning fluid. The flowers were silk imitations, and the browns and oranges of the walls were drab. But it was the closest hotel to the hospital, and as long as the mattress was firm, which they had promised would be the case, all would be satisfactory.

Under the constant distractions of wall colors and smells, Inga felt a dull and permanent ache. There was the missing of Fred, the worry about Lisbet, the anxiety concerning Sabine. But she could only do what she could do. And carry on, she must.

The view from her third-floor room, of a parking lot, was tolerable, but the lack of space was unbearable. There were two beds covered with spreads that felt synthetic and itchy, and a particle-board armoire that had a television inside of it.

Inga marched down the hallway and took the elevator back to the lobby.

"I'm afraid I need a different room," she told the man behind the desk, who appeared to be half asleep.

He studied his ledger for what seemed a long time. "What's the problem?"

"There is no space to move." She placed a hand on the counter.

"Perhaps you have a larger room."

"That's our standard size."

"I noticed a door to the adjoining room. Would it be possible for me to have both rooms?"

He glanced at his ledger again. "If you want, but you have to pay for it."

"Of course. But I will need someone to help me rearrange the furniture." She opened her handbag, took out an envelope of cash, and handed him two twenty dollar bills. "If you could send up a couple of young men to help, I would greatly appreciate it."

His eyes became alert. "Yes, Ma'am. We'll move the TV to the storage room. We can get you extra blankets or pillows, if you'd like."

Three men came to help, and a fourth, the manager, supervised. Inga explained that she was from Switzerland, and that she was impressed with how Americans were always so willing to help. The men moved out one bed and the television from the room she would sleep in. In the adjoining room, they took out another bed, and were able to make some space so that it resembled, to a small degree, a sitting room. Inga gave them all handsome tips and thanked the manager profusely.

In her sitting room, she placed the photograph of Fred on the desk. The picture, taken from behind, showed him in his waders standing in a stream on a sunny day. But what gave the photo its sublime intimacy was the moment her memory filled in: his blissful expression when he turned to her just after she set her camera aside.

* * *

The following morning, Inga woke early and did her exercises — toe-touches, neck-stretches, and half-sit-ups. She dressed in a straight-lined navy skirt, her white starched blouse and a light-blue cardigan. She applied a minimal amount of blush and lipstick, then went downstairs for a breakfast of weak coffee and a stale roll.

A man and a woman, neither of whom wore wedding rings, sat a few tables away. The woman laughed as she brushed a crumb from the man's face. Inga remembered being in Paris with Fred, eating croissants in bed under the white eiderdown that smelled freshly laundered. She had watched him read the paper that morning, had wanted to paint a portrait of him, wanted to capture his look of concern—the deep intelligence in his brow. He had understood sooner than most the hideousness of the Nazis.

An hour later, she peered out the window of her taxi at the old stone walls and brick buildings that made up McLean. She imagined this was once the estate of a very wealthy family.

After climbing to the second floor of North Belknap, she pressed the red button, and suddenly felt dizzy. She clutched the strap of her handbag and thought that maybe Arnold had been right, perhaps this would be more difficult than she had imagined.

The door opened, and in front of Inga stood a young man with disheveled brown hair and dull eyes. He wore a tatty red sweater. She assumed he was a patient, perhaps feebleminded, who had earned his way to a quasi-butler status. It pleased her that he was given a task, for it demonstrated that those in charge cared that the patients felt a sense of purpose. Inga told him she was here to see Sabine Connolly, her granddaughter. He gestured for her to wait inside, where the air smelled of stale cigarette smoke and dirty laundry. The lighting was poor, but on a positive note, there was no wailing or screaming and a normal-looking man with a dark beard sat a few meters away strumming a guitar. Inga took a deep breath and continued to focus on her surroundings rather than her fears.

The last time she had seen Sabine was at her wedding, held in a quaint New England inn a year and a half ago. Her hair had been twisted and plaited into an exquisite updo, and although Inga would have advised against so many beads on the wedding dress, Sabine seemed happy. But even as a child, Sabine kept herself at arm's length from Inga, who never understood why. Inga went out of her way to buy her granddaughter nice clothes, and to teach her manners and good posture.

The man returned. "She'll come in a second," he said. "I'll need to check your bag for sharps."

"Are you a resident here?" Inga asked.

"I work here. I don't live here."

"I see." She smiled. "But you wear no uniform?"

"We don't like to differentiate ourselves that way."

"Ah."

She handed him her bag. She understood the theory of patients and staff being on equal ground, but as he walked away, she heard the jingling of keys and noticed the metal hook that hung from his belt loop. Keys dangling so obviously might give an impression of power, but Inga was not here to comment on how best to run a ward. Her focus would be on her granddaughter—on any other topic, she would keep her opinions and advice to herself.

Then she saw Sabine. She was heavier, which was understandable as the baby was still young. But her hair, worn loose looked expansive. Something Inga would bring up gently another day. At the moment, she didn't want to say anything that might make Sabine uncomfortable.

"Omama," Sabine said, a note of surprise in her voice. "Why are you here?" She stopped just far enough away so that Inga could not shake her hand, as was the custom in Switzerland.

"I am here to help you," Inga said, stepping forward and reaching for her granddaughter's shoulder. It was meant to be a reassuring gesture, but Sabine moved back, and Inga glanced away, picking a piece of lint from the arm of her own coat.

"But I'm fine," Sabine said.

"My dear girl," Inga said. "You are in an asylum."

Sabine cringed and looked down at her boots. "We don't call it an asylum."

"Sometimes my English is not perfect," Inga said, although what she called it seemed of little consequence. "Can we go somewhere to talk? Perhaps where it's a bit quieter?"

Sabine gestured to a dining area at the end of the hallway. The most immediate and important thing was that the room had a good number of windows and the light was pleasant. The walls could have used a fresh coat of paint. The veneer tables were occupied with people Inga assumed were patients, but now that she knew the staff dressed in similar clothing she couldn't be sure.

The women sat at a table near the back, next to a window. Inga felt a draft and pulled up the collar of her tweed coat.

The man who had come to the door returned Inga's handbag. She thanked him and took out her small spiral notebook with its attached pencil. Inga found a clean page and considered the fact that Sabine had not smiled yet, nor had she given any indication that she was grateful her grandmother had come to help.

"You must tell me everything. How you got here? Who brought you? Why they decided on this place?" She smiled at Sabine, hopeful.

"Do you want something to drink?" Sabine said. "They have coffee here."

"Thank you. That would be very nice." Inga understood the need to be a good host and that conventional practices were often soothing.

The coffee was bitter and cold, and served in a yellow plastic cup that looked as if it belonged to a child. As Inga made a note that the ward could use some nicer cups, she reminded herself that she wasn't going to interfere.

A youngish woman, with a dark ponytail, bounced toward the table and sat next to Sabine.

"This is Cece," Sabine said, finally smiling. "She's my roommate."

Inga jotted the information. She also noted, but did not write, that Sabine seemed very comfortable with this woman. Inga remembered Sabine, at seven years old, running off to the home for feebleminded children near the chalet. Sabine had wanted to stay and play, but Inga dragged her away.

"Nice to meet you, Cece," Inga said. "I am Sabine's grandmother, Omama."

"Omama! I love that name."

"It is merely the German translation for grandmother," Inga explained.

But Cece wasn't paying attention. Her gaze had shifted upward. "There is a woman standing behind you."

Inga turned, but there was no one. Cece likely suffered from delusions.

"No," Cece said, and smiled. "She's passed. She's on the other side. She's kind of young. Maybe in her late twenties. She's on your right side, so she's probably related to you or your family, not your husband's."

Inga lifted her eyebrows, unsure of how to respond. "Very interesting," she said.

Cece laughed as she kept her gaze fixed on whatever it was she saw behind Inga. "She has a brush in her hand, like she wants to brush your hair."

"Would you mind terribly," Inga said to Cece. "I have only just arrived, and it's been some time since I've seen Sabine. We can talk later if you like. But at the moment, I would like to speak to my granddaughter alone."

Sabine cringed again as Cece's chair scraped along the floor. She walked away with the same happy skip in her step that she'd come in with.

"She's a cheerful sort," Inga said. "You seem concerned, but I'm quite sure she took no offence."

"I guess," Sabine mumbled.

Rigmor would have behaved so differently in this situation, Inga thought. Her gray eyes, even in her worst states, would have shined with a glimmer of gratitude. But comparisons were rarely helpful. Nor was it wise to think of Rigmor.

"Did Mutti ask you to come?" Sabine asked.

Inga paused, taking care with her answer. She wasn't sure what had transpired between Sabine and Lisbet, and to say that she thought Lisbet was wrong for not visiting might upset Sabine.

"Your mother did not advise me, but it's good to have family in these sorts of circumstances."

Sabine looked confused. Inga would explore the topic of Lisbet at a later time.

"Can you tell me why your doctor decided this was the place you should come?"

Sabine tapped her fingers on the table. "I had trouble sleeping. I was having panic attacks, and I guess I couldn't really cope."

"You guess you couldn't? Or you really couldn't?" Inga asked, as a cloud of cigarette smoke drifted to their table.

"I'm sorry, but I have to go," Sabine said. "I have therapy in a few minutes."

"I see," Inga said, sitting even straighter, trying to hide that she felt unwanted. "I would be happy to accompany you. If you'd like I can meet your doctor. Is he a man?"

"Yes—and you can't," Sabine said. "I mean, I have to talk to him and ask him if it's all right."

"Perhaps tomorrow then?"

"Sure."

Inga gave Sabine her phone number at the Holiday Inn, neatly printed on a page torn from her notebook. She would have liked a few more minutes with her granddaughter, to get a better sense of her illness, and perhaps even to see a modicum of warmth or joy that Inga had travelled all the way from Switzerland. Was it age that caused the distance in their relationship? Cultural differences? Lisbet had a similar aloofness, although hers seemed to stem more from fear than anything else. It would take time and persistence for Inga to make headway with Sabine, but she would find a way in.

* * *

Dr. Lincoln gave his introductory nod, which meant, simultaneously, how are you, hello, and what have you been thinking about? There wasn't a flicker of levity about him, except that he had a paperclip on the cuff of his shirt in place of a missing button.

Sometimes, as Sabine sat on the armchair in his small office on the third floor, she tried to wait him out, see how long it would take for him to actually say something. But today there was no time.

"My grandmother showed up. Totally unexpected." She poked her finger in a small hole on the arm of the chair and felt the coarse stuffing.

Dr. Lincoln nodded.

"The one from Switzerland. The one who thinks I'm wretched."

"I remember," he said.

"She can't be here."

Sabine scuffed the heel of her boot along the carpet and looked out the small window near the ceiling. The sky was a sharp blue. The office was over-heated, yet she could feel the chill of the winter day. She was uncomfortable in her own skin and she knew it wasn't Dr. Lincoln's office, or his serious expression, or the heat in the room, or the cold outside; it was her anxiety and fear and guilt, now all made worse by the fact that her grandmother was here.

Dr. Lincoln nodded again. He was over six feet tall with

black hair and black eyebrows, and an uncanny ability to show enormous compassion with the slightest change in expression.

"You have to tell her that she can't stay," Sabine said.

"I think that's something you will have to do." His baritone voice would have been comforting in any other situation.

"She won't listen to me. I can tell, she's on some sort of mission. Once she wanted to buy me the right raincoat. We had to go to eight stores. It took a whole day, and I didn't even need a raincoat."

"So what's her mission now?" Dr. Lincoln asked.

"I have no idea." Sabine's hands shot up as she spoke. "But she will tell me my hair looks terrible, and my clothes aren't right. She'll tell me I shouldn't talk with my hands. She'll tell the nurses what to do." She stopped for a second. "You could tell her it's best for me medically to be without family."

He shook his head.

"Doctors tell other people their family members can't visit," Sabine said. "Helen's brother isn't allowed to come."

"Perhaps this is an opportunity for you to understand why you have given your grandmother so much power." He sounded ponderous, missing or ignoring the urgency of the situation.

"Because," she began and stopped.

"Because?"

"Because she'll try to tell everyone what's wrong with me, and she doesn't have any idea. Because she'll meddle and judge me, and I already feel judged all of the time without someone actually judging me."

"Can you talk about why you feel so judged? Where you think that comes from?"

"It comes from her," Sabine said, and poked her finger back into the hole. "She has opinions on everything."

"Did other people in your family have opinions?"

"Of course," she said, irritated. "But it wasn't the same."

"So she is the wicked witch?"

"I think my grandmother will try to take Mia away from me," Sabine said. "She'll make sure I get stuck here for good, and then she'll use her money to bribe Tanner, and Mia will be gone. I know it sounds ridiculous. And I know you probably don't believe me. But." She hesitated. "And this will sound crazy too. But I had a dream that she did that. Took my baby. Only it wasn't exactly me."

"Who do you think it was?"

"I don't know." Sabine's face flushed. "It's stupid."

Her father had told her once that analyzing dreams was for people who didn't have real problems to solve. She needed to focus on the concrete issue in front of her—getting Omama back to Switzerland.

"It doesn't matter," Sabine told Dr. Lincoln. "It just matters that she leaves. She's never liked me. I don't think she really liked my mother much either. She likes men. My brothers can do no wrong. She'll probably think you're perfect too. I'll bring her tomorrow and you'll see."

"Do you want to bring her?"

"No. But." An idea struck. "I could ask her to call Tanner. He'll bring Mia for her."

Both of Dr. Lincoln's eyebrows went up, his way of saying, *please explain.*

"Tanner and Omama like to admire each other."

"Tanner still hasn't brought the baby?" he asked.

Sabine teetered at the opening of a dark crevice, a place where she could have plunged into sadness, but she pulled herself back.

"Is it difficult to watch them get along?" Dr. Lincoln asked.

"Not really." The sooner she called, the better the chance of success.

"Do you ever want to be admired?" he asked.

"No, of course not." It was a ridiculous question.

"It seems that Tanner likes to be admired. Your mother as well. Perhaps there are similarities."

"No." But then she thought about the way her father shouted, and how her mother always said that no other woman would put up with him but her. "Maybe," Sabine said. "I don't know about admired exactly. But my mother wanted us to know that she was the only one who could tolerate my father's screaming."

"Interesting." His brow creased. "She was the only one?"

Sabine felt confused. "He was never married to anyone but her."

"But other people had to tolerate his yelling."

"No."

"There were three children in the house."

"That's different," she said.

"How?"

"Because we were children."

"Would you think it was OK if someone yelled at Mia the way your father yelled?"

She shook her head. "Obviously not. I would never let that happen."

"But your mother let it happen."

She banged her heel on the carpet. "I don't want to talk about this. I need to go back and call my grandmother."

"We still have some time."

"I need to see Mia."

"Can you talk about how it feels not to see your daughter?"

She slapped her hand on the arm of the chair. "Really," she began. "You want to know what it feels like to have a baby — to feel like you can't breathe if she's not around? To nurse her, and then suddenly, some doctor you barely know, tells you that you need to be locked up?" She was aware that she was mischaracterizing what had happened, but she rushed on. "He doesn't tell you that you won't see your baby for five days or that you'll cry yourself to sleep because it hurts so much. Like you're missing the most important part of yourself."

Dr. Lincoln's eyes looked a little proud, as if he'd been waiting for her outburst.

"I have to go," Sabine said. And with that she jumped up and walked to the door.

Chapter Six

Yellow Roses

Frankfurt am Main, Germany
1934

Inga waited until Frieda was in bed before making hot cocoa. She added a dollop of cream and two extra teaspoons of sugar to Rigmor's cup. When she slipped into her sister's room, Rigmor lay on the bed, staring at the ceiling.

"Would you like company?" Inga asked.

Rigmor sat up, her smile strained, as Inga handed over the cup and then climbed on the bed. Rigmor's dark curls fell around her delicate shoulders.

"Tell me," Inga said.

Rigmor shook her head and sipped the drink. "It's nothing."

"You don't have to hide from me," Inga told her.

"I will feel better tomorrow."

"Can you tell me what you are feeling now?" Inga had read about anxiety, agitation, depression, hysteria. She would keep reading, keep going to lectures, keep learning until she understood exactly what ailed her sister.

Rigmor caressed the silk eiderdown. "I cannot bear being in my own skin. I know I am not trapped, and yet I feel as if I'm in a cage." She paused. "Most of all, I hate that I have so much and am so miserable."

Inga lifted Rigmor's chin and looked into her eyes. "I also hate that you feel miserable. But I promise you that we will find a way to help."

"Can we talk about you?" Rigmor asked.

It seemed to relax her, hearing the details of Inga's life, and if that helped, then that's what she would do.

"I spend far too much time planning and scheming when I will see Fred again." She grinned. "I think he has me under a spell."

Rigmor chuckled. "That is hard to believe. That anyone would have that much power over you."

"He is witty and intelligent," Inga said. "When I'm with him, I am not always thinking of the next thing that must be done. I live entirely with him. In the moment."

She thought about the night she first met him, at the Rothchild's dinner party. She felt her heart jump after talking to him for only a few moments. He owned a leather business, had a bald head, a wife and children, and an impishness in his eyes that made her smile. She had wanted him to thrust her against the wall and kiss her. It was strange to feel such immediate, intense desire. But the attraction was not only sexual. They also shared a love of art and painting. He did oil and she did watercolor, which was a perfect match. If they both had used the same medium there might have been an unhealthy competition.

"Is it fun?" Rigmor whispered. "To be with a man?"

"To have sex?" Inga said. "You mustn't be afraid to talk about it. It's a wonderful thing." She smiled. "One day you will know for yourself."

"No," Rigmor said.

"But you are lovely, and warm, and charming. Of course you will find a man. And he will be good to you." She touched Rigmor's cheek. "If he isn't, he will have to answer to me."

Rigmor shook her head and put her cup on the nightstand. "I would be a burden."

"You must never say that," Inga said. "I have read that when you think negative things, you make a sort of track in your brain. The more you use that track, the more difficult it is to veer to a new one."

"You must stop reading about all of these horrific things and live your life," Rigmor said. She rested her head on Inga's lap.

"When will you see Fred next?"

Inga ran her fingers through her sister's hair. "In a week's time. I take a train to Hamburg. He has a business meeting there."

Inga coiled a strand of Rigmor's hair around her finger, and a thought occurred to her. Until Fred, she had not fully understood what it meant to be in love, to feel as if one is dancing in the clouds. A man, the right one, could be just the thing for her sister.

"Has mother found out about Fred yet?" Rigmor asked.

"Of course. She has spies everywhere. This just gives her more reason to dislike me."

Rigmor sat up. "You know she doesn't dislike you. She only worries and has an unfortunate way of expressing that with you."

Inga sipped her cocoa. She did not want to discuss Frieda. "Let's do something happy tomorrow. We can go into town, sit at the café you like near the Cathedral."

"The city makes me feel so closed in," Rigmor said. "Another time."

Inga felt a slight rush of air. She turned, and there, only a few meters from the door, was Frieda, looking furious.

"You are not meant to be in here," her mother said.

"I am allowed to spend time with my sister. And I don't think you even knocked."

"The door was open."

"Not true," Inga said. "I closed it."

"It was open."

"Mother," Rigmor began. "We were only talking. She brought cocoa."

"The doctor said no sugar before bed. It will keep you awake."

Rigmor pulled her legs in and wrapped her thin arms around her knees. Inga knew how her sister hated disagreements, how she could hear a different intonation in order to believe no one was ever wrong. The suppleness of Rigmor's mind, that she could find another perspective to explain obstinacy, snobbery, or ignorance, was something Inga found utterly charming. To be able to always find the good in others was both a gift and a burden. Only in her fits did Rigmor show aggressive emotions— mostly directed toward herself.

Inga stood. The bickering would only cause stress. She leaned over and kissed the top of Rigmor's head.

When she passed Frieda, Inga whispered, "You make things worse."

"Don't poison her with your ideas about men," Frieda whispered back.

In her own room, Inga climbed into bed next to Klaus, who snored pleasantly.

On the surface, everything about her husband was pleasant— his demeanor, his good humor, his intellect, his blue eyes, his ability to get along with everyone, even Frieda. But the thing that Inga did not account for, did not even think to account for, was the way she felt about him in the bedroom.

She had been a virgin on their wedding night. They'd reserved a room in a luxurious hotel and, being a romantic, she was anticipating a blissful night of lovemaking. But Klaus had grabbed her, partially undressed, and carried her to the four-poster bed, where he laid her on her stomach and slapped her behind as if she were a misbehaved child. She glanced up at him in shock, about to tell him to never hit her again, however lightly. But he was already turning her, climbing on top of her, pushing himself inside.

Inga had expected sex to be fun and exciting, instead with Klaus she dreaded it. He had even asked her once to smack his bottom with a rolled up newspaper. Every night as they got into bed, she wondered what strange, uncomfortable act he'd want to perform. She went to the library and read whatever factual material she could find about sex. She discovered an article on sadomasochism, but wasn't sure that's what she'd call Klaus's fetish. Finally she spoke honestly to him and told him she never wanted to hit or be hit, even if it was for pleasure. Klaus said he understood, and that it would have been wise if they had had sex before they married. He spoke with compassion, but also said that what people wanted in the bedroom was so primal, so deeply buried in personality, that it would be essentially impossible to change. Six months after their wedding day, they agreed to find their sexual pleasure outside of the marriage. They also agreed to remain friendly and continue to sleep in the same bed. She felt their compromise was modern and forward-thinking.

Shortly after her agreement with Klaus, Inga found Fred. Dear Fred, who ran his fingers along the underside of her arm and kissed the nape of her neck, who loved the two moles on her back, the shape of her fingernails, and the way her ankles tapered. A day apart from Fred felt like a lifetime.

She thought of Rigmor, how unfair it was that she didn't know what this sort of love felt like. Inga clasped her hands together and said a silent prayer to a god she only half believed in. For him to make Rigmor better, Inga would sacrifice anything, even Fred.

* * *

On a Friday afternoon in May, Arnold sat on the tapestry desk chair, the one cherished item he had inherited from his mother. He looked at, Johann, the sixteen-year-old patient across from him. His parents were worried he had homosexual tendencies.

"It's stupid for me to be here," Johann said, sticking out his lower lip.

He was of average intelligence and average looks. His father had found him masturbating one day while looking at a picture of Errol Flynn.

"Since you are here, perhaps we can find something you'd

like to talk about. Is there anything you're learning at school that interests you?"

Johann smirked. "Girls with large breasts."

Perhaps a denial about his own preferences. Arnold had done something similar as an adolescent. "Are you saying that because you think that's what you should say?"

"I hate you."

Arnold nodded. This was progress. Johann was finally expressing his feelings.

"Can you tell me what it is you hate about me?" Arnold asked, only to be interrupted by a knock at the door. He opened it a few centimeters, wanting to protect his patient's privacy.

"Frau Blumenthal," he said, pointing to the sign on his door that said *please do not disturb*. "I am busy at the moment."

"Then I will wait."

"There is a dining hall on the first floor. If you'd like, I will meet you there in about half an hour."

"Who was that?" Johann asked as Arnold sat again.

"Someone who does not have an appointment."

"Why is your face red?"

"Is it?" Arnold touched his cheek.

"Is she your lover?"

"No. Let's get back to where we left off. You were saying that you hated me." Arnold resented that Frau Blumenthal had intruded at such a crucial moment.

"She's your lover, isn't she? And she's married."

Arnold shook his head, but he never got the reins of the session back. Relieved when it was over, he combed his hair, and then went to find Frau Blumenthal.

Before her on the table was a cup of coffee and a strawberry tart. A handsome cane was hooked on the back of her chair. Her brown hair was braided and twisted into a bun. She wore her standard black dress that reminded him of what his mother had worn when she mourned his father.

There were no apologies for interrupting his session. The moment he sat she asked, "How do you find Rigmor?"

"I'm not sure there is anything wrong with her," he said.

"So you are unable to get her to talk?"

"We have had many lengthy conversations. I am only saying I don't find her to be unwell." He flicked a crumb off of the white tablecloth.

"Has she told you about her dreams?" Her deep-set eyes studied his face.

"No."

"In other words," she began, "you really haven't gotten a good sense of what is wrong?"

"She is intelligent and seems connected to the people around her. She has talked about difficulty with sleep, but I can't say that I see much else."

"I sometimes hear her at night." Her knuckles rapped the table. "She cries out, begging for the attacks to stop."

"Attacks?"

"Fits of fear," Frau Blumenthal clarified. "I was hoping you would uncover the cause of them."

"She hasn't told me anything about night terrors."

"She knows you are a psychiatrist." Her lips puckered. "Perhaps you behaved too much like you do with a patient. She would sense that. You were meant to be more of a friend."

He slipped a finger under his collar, feeling the need for extra air. "I think we have struck up a nice friendship."

"But you seem to be getting no results," she said, continuing to stare directly at him.

"Frau Blumenthal, it takes longer than a few weeks, in any circumstance, regardless if she was a patient or a friend. To build trust doesn't happen overnight."

She stood and grabbed her walking stick. "I thank you for your willingness to try, but I don't believe we will need your services any longer."

He jumped up. "But…" He faltered. "Rigmor and I have plans to take a walk in the park tomorrow."

"I will tell her that you won't be able to make it."

"That seems…." Again, he hesitated. "What I mean to say is that I would like to tell her myself that I won't be seeing her any more. I would hate for her to think it's because I don't find her interesting." He followed Frau Blumenthal a few steps, nearly tripping on the leg of a chair.

She turned and stared at him. "And what would you tell her?" Arnold was more than a head taller, yet she made him feel small.

"That I initiated the arrangement?"

"I think she already has a good idea of that," he answered.

"It's best you stay out of it." Frau Blumenthal tapped her stick twice on the floor and walked away.

That evening, as Arnold strolled along the Rhine, he stopped and kicked a stone wall that ran along the river, angry that he had been dismissed so summarily. Then as he continued to walk, his shoulders slumped and his pace dragged. Here he was, living in a city where he had no real confidantes, no one he could really be himself with. He thought of Schumann, who flung himself into the Rhine because of psychotic melancholia. Arnold did not consider himself a melancholic, nor was he depressed or psychotic. But he was lonely, and tonight he felt it more sharply after having lost the first real friend he had made in Frankfurt.

* * *

Inga sat in the drawing room with a cup of tea and a long letter from Dr. Benedek, a psychiatrist she had become friendly with. As she was reading the letter for the second time, the butler knocked and informed her that Frieda would like to see her in the garden.

Inga brought the letter upstairs, tucked it in her chest of drawers, and wondered what sort of lecture her mother intended on giving today. Would it be about Fred and rumors? Or perhaps Inga had walked out of a room before her mother, or violated some other inane, archaic custom. Whatever the message Frieda planned on delivering, Inga would not allow it to affect her mood.

The day was warm, yet Frieda sat at the white table under the cherry tree in a long-sleeved black dress that nearly came to her ankles. She looked like a schoolmarm.

When Inga joined her, Frieda folded her hands and rested them on the table. She was a pretty woman, but the way she dressed and sat, and the angle at which she held her chin, gave an impression of severity.

"I went to visit Arnold yesterday."

Inga sat taller. "And?"

"I have asked that he discontinue the visits with Rigmor."

"But why?"

"Rigmor is not improving. I see no benefit to their relationship."

Inga picked up an unripe cherry that had fallen to the ground. She pulled off the stem. "He wasn't meant to cure her in a matter of weeks. He is a friend, one she happens to like. Why would you take that away from her?"

Her eyes narrowed. "I am not taking anything away. I have given it much thought."

"Have you told Rigmor?" Inga asked, dropping the cherry.

"Yes. She is perfectly fine with it."

"I doubt that is really the case." Inga's good mood vanished. She knew that Rigmor liked Arnold and looked forward to his visits.

"I see what you have done to the garden," her mother said. "It looks ridiculous."

Inga ignored the remark. "We thought long and hard about Arnold," she said. "I just cannot understand."

"The more we invest in him, the harder it will be to break off relations." Frieda glanced away.

"Rigmor talks to him about how she's feeling. She can be herself around him. We need more time to assess what he could do for her." This was not an argument Inga would lose.

"I should have listened to my own counsel, not yours. Having a man around can lead to things we do not want."

So this was the crux of it: Frieda was afraid Rigmor might fall in love. "You need to let Rigmor decide," Inga said. "She is an adult."

Frieda shifted her chair, turning away from Inga. "It is decided."

Inga gripped the table. "Do you really have Rigmor's best interests in mind, or is this some selfish scheme of yours?"

Frieda did not reply.

Inga waited another thirty seconds, but then could not bear it any longer. Hot, hateful tears welled in her eyes.

The following day, Inga found Rigmor sitting at the same white table that Frieda had occupied the day before. The weather was pleasant, a bit warm for May, which brought an early spring. Rigmor wore a light floral dress with a row of buttons in the front. She lifted her pencil and paused her sketching of the rosebush to smile at her sister.

"Would you like anything to eat? Tea, biscuits?" Inga asked.

"Why does everyone always want to feed me?"

Inga glanced at Rigmor's arms and refrained from saying the obvious. That she was on the thin side. They talked about the weather, the Palmengarten, Inga's new shoes, and a servant Frieda had recently hired. Eventually, Inga broached the topic of Arnold.

"You know," she said. "Just because Mother doesn't think he should visit anymore, doesn't mean you have to agree."

Rigmor folded a loose curl behind her ear. "He's busy with his work. I completely understand."

"Is that what Mother told you—that he was too busy?" Inga's

voice strained.

"He has more important things to do," Rigmor said.

"No, he doesn't," Inga said more sharply than she had wanted. "If that's what Mother made you think, then she is even more of a shrew..."

"It doesn't matter. It's not as if I didn't realize this was all arranged by you and Mother in the first place."

Inga should have known that her sister would not be deceived. "I thought it was a good idea," she said. "I still do."

"I don't want a nanny."

"Oh, Rigmor," Inga said. "That's not what he was at all. He's a doctor. A good psychiatrist, and now a friend. He might come up with some wise suggestions. He cares about you."

Rigmor ran her finger along the ironwork on the table. "It would be awkward if Mother doesn't want it."

"But what about what you want?" Inga asked. All her life, Rigmor had struggled with asking for things she wanted—an extra biscuit, or a piece of chocolate, or to pick a flower. She could have those things, yet she didn't ask. The only thing that Inga could recall Rigmor asking for was potato leek soup.

"What I want is to sit in the garden and sketch those beautiful yellow roses," Rigmor said.

Yellow had always been her favorite, which is why Inga took such care with them.

"They are lovely," Inga said. She paused. "What if I call Arnold, and we meet him at the University? Or at a restaurant? Mother wouldn't have to know."

"She would find out. She is Mother."

"Then we won't hide it. I'll invite him over for myself."

"Inga, can we please not talk about this? I don't want any more arguments." She sighed. "It is really astonishing how that rose bush is blooming. It's early to have so many."

"I'm glad they bring you pleasure."

Two evenings ago, Inga had come to the garden with a basket

of silk yellow roses and a needle and thread. She sewed the stems of the false flowers to the stems of the real ones, taking care not to overdo it, to make sure the silk roses were placed naturally.

"I will get the shears and pick a few for your bedroom," Rigmor said.

"No." Inga held up a hand. "I don't like cut flowers. It always seems like such a shame to take them from their natural environment. Don't you think?"

Rigmor laughed. "You do have some odd ideas about things."

"Yes," Inga said, thinking that just because her idea about Arnold might have been unconventional, that didn't mean it wasn't good. Tomorrow she would call him and invite him to their garden party.

* * *

It had been two weeks since Arnold had seen Rigmor, and although he couldn't deny he was excited about meeting Rudin, the director of the German Institute for Psychiatric Research, who had recently been named president of the International Federation of Eugenics, he was more excited about the chance to talk to Rigmor.

Champagne was served in the garden. The azaleas were in full bloom, and a slight breeze carried the sweet scent of wisteria that hung from trellises. Arnold glanced around. Inga wore a blue dress, the same bright, iridescent color of the famous Blue Morpho butterfly of the Amazon. Her shoes were covered in sequins.

"Arnold," she said, approaching. "We are so very glad you could come."

He wondered who the "we" was, and again looked around for Rigmor. "Is your sister here?" he asked.

Inga moved closer. "She can't join us this afternoon."

"Not because I am here?" he whispered back.

"Why would you say such a thing?"

Arnold didn't want to admit what he was thinking, that perhaps it was Rigmor who wanted to end the relationship, and Frau Blumenthal was only the messenger. "Is she well?"

Inga shook her head. "The last few days have not been so good."

"Is she home?"

"Yes."

"May I see her?"

"My mother is a centurion," Inga said. "I doubt you will get past her. Another day would probably be better. I can phone you when my mother is out." She tugged his sleeve. "Come meet my friend, Ernst."

That she spoke of Rudin on a first-name basis felt extraordinary. They were introduced, and as Arnold shook the famous man's hand, he felt like an infatuated adolescent.

"Arnold is an ardent admirer," Inga said.

Rudin had a mane of white hair and thick, caterpillar-like eyebrows. Yet his most distinctive feature was the deep crease between his eyes.

"Yes, very ardent," Arnold said, and felt his cheeks burn. "I have been to a few of your talks."

"I see." Rudin furrowed his brow. The crease between his eyes deepened.

"You spoke about the two-recessive gene theory of schizophrenia. I am interested to learn of your new techniques. I was actually wondering how you determined..."

As Rudin placed his large hand on Arnold's arm, he anticipated a deep intellectual conversation.

"My dear man," Rudin said. "I don't think it is a wise topic for a garden party."

Arnold looked at the grass. "My apologies."

"Do tell me how you know Inga and her family?"

Arnold composed himself. "I work at the University here in

Frankfurt," he said. "It was actually you who made my meeting with the Blumenthals possible. You suggested Inga contact me."

"Did I?" he asked, as he ate light orange caviar. One of the eggs fell into his beard. "Yes, I do recall it now. I placed a call, and Dr. Hegel thought you might be the right fit. The Blumenthals are good friends to have."

Arnold stared at the tiny orange egg nestled in the white hair. "Yes." His head was a cement block. No words came.

Rudin glanced into his empty glass. "It was a pleasure to meet you," he said.

Arnold was left alone with his half-filled flute of champagne, feeling as if he had missed the opportunity of a lifetime.

Accompanied by a short, bald man, Inga practically waltzed to Arnold. She introduced him to her friend, Fred, who proceeded to interrogate Arnold about the infiltration of Nazi doctrines at the University.

Arnold, unable to answer most of the questions, kept glancing toward Klaus who smoked his pipe and spoke with Rudin. The conversation with Fred fizzled, and Arnold decided it would be best to go home. He walked through the house, stopping in the drawing room, where he stared at the painting of Rigmor and hoped she wasn't suffering too terribly.

Finishing his champagne, he placed the empty glass on the mantel. He admired how the artist was able to make the fabric in the painting look so real. He touched the dress, half expecting it to feel like silk.

"Dr. Richter?"

He spun around to see Frau Blumenthal at the threshold of the door.

"I was just leaving," he said.

"She has asked for you."

"Has she?" He tipped his head.

"Perhaps you can go up now, if you have a spare minute."

"But…"

"I was wrong," said Frau Blumenthal, wringing her hands. "I should not have dismissed you so soon."

He didn't like Frau Blumenthal, there was no secret in that, but one lesson of his practice was that it was a rare thing for a person to say *I was wrong*. Three simple words, a liberating phrase that required a certain amount of courage. Or possibly desperation.

With the drapes closed, Rigmor's room smelled like methanol and rosemary. Likely a camphor concoction that was rubbed on her chest to help with nerves. Arnold understood the need to try various potions, but they rarely did anything aside from filling the room with cloying scents.

He approached the canopy bed, and for a moment thought it couldn't be. The woman he saw looked old, her skin translucent. Plum-colored circles surrounded her eyes.

"Rigmor?"

"Oh, Arnold," she said. "What is happening to me?"

"Nothing terrible," he answered calmly.

"I feel as if there is a herd of galloping horses racing through me."

He sat on the chair next to the bed. "When did this start?"

"A few days ago. Out of the blue. I was painting in my studio, and suddenly I felt faint. But the moment I went to lie down, my heart began to pound, and I could feel it all happening again."

"The beginning of an episode?"

She nodded. Her hair looked as if it had been in a windstorm.

"These things come in cycles," he said. "This one will also pass."

"It's never been this bad. The shadows at night taunt me, their arms reach to grab my throat."

He had heard of people seeing shadows. Sometimes it was nothing but an extension of a dream, but he had also read that shadows could be a precursor to psychosis.

"You have to remind yourself that they aren't real. That they can't hurt you."

"I know. Yet I see them. That my mind can manifest such grotesque images makes me think I am mad."

"If you were truly mad, you would not have the slightest idea that they were manifestations."

He patted the blanket.

"I am not going to tell you to rest, as that will likely do little good, but if there is something you can do to distract yourself, that might be the best medicine."

She gave him her hand. "Talk to me. Tell me about you, or your work, or your colleagues."

He held her hand and talked until his voice felt hoarse. He talked about how distant his father had been, how his mother lost so much blood after he was born that she wasn't able to have more children. He talked about case studies he'd read, miraculous ones. He talked about how medicine was improving every day and how more doctors were choosing psychiatry.

He wasn't sure exactly when she drifted off to sleep. She appeared at peace, her lips slightly parted, her forehead smooth. He tucked her hand under the covers just as Frau Blumenthal came in.

"She is asleep," he whispered.

Frau Blumenthal clasped her hands as if she was about to fall to her knees and pray.

"So she will be fine?"

He wished he could promise that she would be free from future episodes, but he knew better, and he sensed Frau Blumenthal did as well.

"This will pass," was all he allowed himself.

Chapter Seven

The Baby

Belmont, Massachusetts
1984

Inga felt reenergized after Sabine phoned and asked for help, although it was somewhat disconcerting that Tanner would answer an old woman's call and not his wife's.

In the afternoon, Inga hired a taxi and drove around Belmont to get a feel for the area and where the shops were.

At six-fifteen, she sat in the hotel lobby. She kept her feet firmly planted on the floor, a practiced stillness she had developed over the years. But inside, a battle of emotions waged, curiosity at seeing the baby, fear that Tanner would want to leave Sabine for a more stable woman, sadness that Lisbet would not come to visit her daughter, and anger at Gerald, Lisbet's husband — which on some level was a constant.

The moment Tanner entered the lobby, carrying the baby seat as if it were a picnic basket, Inga smiled. He was like she had remembered him, handsome and broad-shouldered, with an easy nature.

"How good of you to fetch me." Inga stood, as he kissed her cheeks. Well done, she thought.

"I would have picked you up at the airport if I'd known you were coming." He put the baby seat on a chair to give Inga a closer look at Mia.

Her cheeks, round and pink, radiated health. She had wide eyes and well-defined lips. It was too soon to know about the nose and hair. But the baby looked wholesome, well-fed and content, despite the ordeals of her mother.

"She is lovely." Inga brushed a finger along Mia's cheek.

"Hold on a sec," Tanner said, undoing the straps that held Mia.

He swept up the baby and handed her to Inga before she had a moment to prepare herself. It had been many years since she held a baby, and in truth, it was not something she had ever been particularly comfortable with. Mia squirmed, and because of her bulky snowsuit, Inga's grip slipped. She held Mia closer and breathed in the fresh scent of baby shampoo.

Tanner grinned, his chest expanding, the picture of the proud father. "People say she looks like me."

But Inga hardly listened; she was too taken by Mia's dark eyes. "Mein Engel," she whispered, and felt her heart stir.

On the short drive to the hospital, Tanner asked the right questions. How was Inga's room? Had she slept well? Did she have jetlag? And then he told her how kind it was of her to visit, which made Inga feel as if she had just finished a cup of warm tea.

Sabine was waiting near the door when they arrived. She appeared to be a different person. Her hair was pulled back into a neat bun. She wore a nice gray sweater over a white blouse. She stood tall and smiled widely the moment she saw her daughter. If she had been diagnosed with a serious mental illness, it was not obvious. She unbuckled Mia from her seat, lifted her, kissed her, and then unzipped the purple snowsuit, revealing legs and arms with soft, plump folds.

What an unexpected joy, to see mother and daughter reunited.

They sat in the dining area. Sabine kissed Mia's cheeks again, then looked at Tanner and Inga. "Thanks for bringing her."

Inga smiled, pleased to have helped.

"No problem," Tanner said, shedding his gray overcoat. "Any chance we could get some food here? I didn't have time to eat dinner."

A well-dressed woman with dark, smooth hair approached.

"Helen," Sabine said. "Look who's here." She held up the

baby.

Inga sensed immediately that this woman, Helen, would not sit unless she was invited.

"Sit with us," she offered, gesturing to an empty chair.

"I don't want to interrupt family time," Helen said.

"It's no interruption," Sabine told her.

Inga watched Helen perch on the edge of a chair. Her posture was excellent, her eyebrows nicely plucked, and her lipstick a sophisticated burnt red color.

"Any way we could get something to eat?" Tanner asked again.

"The food here isn't for visitors," Sabine said.

Cece and an elderly man, whose limbs moved like those of a marionette, joined the group. Unlike Helen, they did not hesitate to sit.

Inga watched Tanner. He rubbed his stomach, and peered over his shoulder at a man eating. Her tummy rumbled, but she could wait. On the other hand, she had had enough experience with men to know that it wasn't so easy for them when they were hungry. He had been nice enough to fetch her and bring the baby to Sabine; he deserved some sort of recompense.

"I am also hungry," she whispered to Tanner.

"I could have stopped on the way, but I wanted to make sure you and Sabine got more time with Mia," he said. He had round eyes that reminded her of large English pennies, both in shape and in their copper-brown color.

"Is there a restaurant nearby?" Inga asked loudly.

"There's a Greek place," Helen answered. "If you go out of the grounds, and take a left, you'll see it on the right-hand side."

"Have you eaten there?" Inga asked.

"No." Helen chuckled. "I can't walk beyond the nursing station."

"Is that true?" Inga asked, shocked.

"Yes." Helen didn't elaborate.

"Well then," Inga began, resting a hand on Tanner's shoulder. "Shall we go out for a bite?"

He scratched his chin. "We have to take the baby."

"No." Sabine held Mia close. "I'm sure it's all right if you go for an hour. I'll watch her."

"But they said..." Tanner began.

"I have more privileges now. It's fine. Really. You two should go and have a nice dinner."

As they walked away, Inga threaded her arm through Tanner's. Perhaps Sabine didn't recognize this man's value at the moment. Or perhaps she was simply too overcome by the baby. Whatever the reason, Inga would make him understand how important he was to the family.

* * *

Freedom. That's what it felt like, to have Tanner and Omama gone, to be left with Mia, Helen, Frank and Cece.

"My mother told me I was a super happy baby," Cece said, above the noise of plates being cleared.

"I believe that," Sabine replied, and glanced at a teenage boy standing near the window. He was new to the ward, and had two staff members close by. Suicide watch, Sabine guessed. He had a beautiful face, thick auburn hair and a deferential way of standing. Sabine caught him smiling at Mia and waved him over to the table. He took a few steps toward them.

"Come sit with us," Sabine said.

He joined, keeping his eyes lowered.

Frank shot out a long arm and shook hands. "I'm Uncle Frankie," he said, proudly, glancing at Mia.

"Keith. Nice to meet you."

Helen, Cece and Sabine introduced themselves. No one mentioned what had brought them to this place.

"Uh oh." Helen raised a hand to shield her face.

Sabine turned and saw Brenda walking to the table. Brenda had brassy blond hair, dark eyeliner, a permanent scowl, and the need to create drama, especially if she wasn't getting attention.

"What's up?" Sabine asked Brenda.

Brenda clamped one hand on her waist and curled her lip. "Kind of loud right here. You having a party?" She took out a cigarette, and looked for a staff member to light it.

"You can't smoke with a baby around," Cece told her.

"Oh, I think I can." She strutted to one of the men who watched Keith. "Light?" she asked.

He lit her cigarette. It was all a show, since Sabine had seen Brenda pull out a lighter from her bra a number of times. Lighters, like duct tape and knitting needles, were prohibited.

"At least move away from the table," Helen said.

"I don't know if any of you noticed," Brenda said. "But this is not a fucking daycare."

Frank bolted up and stood in front of Brenda with his arms extended as if he could make a wall out of himself. Instead he resembled a tall, skinny scarecrow.

"Get out of my face," Brenda said. She took a long drag and blew the smoke upward. A small cloud hovered above the table.

"It's not a big deal," Sabine said. "Let's just move to the hallway." But there was no need; Brenda marched away, puffing on her cigarette.

Frank grinned. "Good riddance to bad rubbish," he said, which made Keith laugh.

The conversation continued in a disconnected way, jumping from one topic to another. But that didn't matter. What mattered was that Sabine was feeling something close to happy. Maybe the medicine had started to work. More likely it was holding Mia.

When Nurse John approached the table, Sabine thought he was coming to see the baby. Nurse John, with the saggy eyes, was everyone's favorite. His glasses were taped together; his brow permanently creased. He seemed intimately familiar with pain.

"Sabine," he said. "Is there a family member here?"

"They'll be right back," she replied. "They just went to get something to eat."

He sighed deeply. "I'm sorry," he said. "The baby can't be here without a family member."

Sabine gripped Mia. "They'll be back any minute."

John's smile was warm and conciliatory. "I know, and the rules might be adjusted in the future, but as of today, I'm afraid..."

"I can't." Sabine shifted Mia so that she wasn't facing John.

Keith's hands balled; his knuckles turned white.

"You will get her back as soon as your family returns," John said.

But Sabine couldn't let her daughter go. "Why can't you just sit with us?"

"I'd really like to, but I have other things I have to do, and I'm afraid we have to follow the rules."

"Except when you make exceptions," Helen said. "You told me last week that you make adjustments depending on the patient."

"I understand." He glanced over his shoulder at Brenda. "But people might feel that some patients are given preferential treatment."

"You're worried what Brenda thinks?" Sabine heard the uptick in her voice and told herself to stay calm.

"It would be good to show us you're willing to work with us," John replied. "It will help you earn privileges."

"What if I sit in front of the nursing station where you can see me the whole time?" Sabine asked.

Now Nurse Nancy joined the conversation. "Give John the baby or you will go to the quiet room."

Sabine stood. "Fine. I'll wait in there with Mia."

"The baby stays with us." Nurse Nancy stood in front of Sabine and placed her hands on Mia, who squirmed as if she understood what was happening.

Sabine stepped back. "You don't ever get to touch her."

"Reinforcements," Nancy shouted.

A few staff members ran in. Surrounded, Sabine sat back down. Nurse John knelt, and with great care took the baby from Sabine's arms.

* * *

Inga sat across from Tanner. Behind him, a mural with poorly depicted turquoise waves of the Aegean Sea covered the wall. Tanner was a pleasant dinner companion and over the course of their meal, as he finished his steak and drank two glasses of scotch, she managed to learn that he was a financial planner, something apparently different from a banker. He helped people with monetary goals, which sounded promising. But as she pushed further, he admitted that he worked on a commission basis, and was still in the ramping up stage. Money was tight, especially now that Mia was in daycare.

Inga remembered when they met, and she learned that he was the first in his family to attend university. She had been more dubious than she let on. Good families were educated for at least three generations—on the male side. But being a forward thinker, she withheld judgment. Upward mobility was not easy, but those who were capable of achieving it had a tenacity that Inga found inspiring.

One day Tanner would do well in his field of work. He was a natural salesman, confident, but not too loud. He listened attentively, nodded at the right moments, and didn't seem to have any nervous habits or tics. In fact, there was something almost a bit too polished and Inga wondered what was under his veneer. As the waiter cleared the dinner plates, Tanner leaned back a bit and allowed his arms and legs to take up proportionately more space than what his chair called for.

Inga ordered tea. Tanner asked for a coffee. She was pleased he did not have a third scotch.

Inga dropped one sugar cube into her cup and stirred. It was time find some answers to more difficult questions.

"It must be trying for you at the moment, with Sabine not well."

Tanner gave a weary nod. "I don't get to sleep as much as I want. Mia wakes up once or twice in the night. By the time I pick her up from daycare, it feels like the rest of the night is feeding her, feeding me, and then getting ready for bed."

"That is a lot," said Inga, although she hadn't meant the question quite as he interpreted. "Are you worried about Sabine?"

"She's had this kind of thing before, and she gets through it."

So, as Inga had feared, this was not a simple postpartum depression. There was indeed a history, one that had been kept from her. "When you say she's had this type of thing before, what do you mean?"

"When she was in grad school. She dropped out because she couldn't leave the apartment," Tanner said. "Sometimes she wouldn't sleep at all, or sometimes she'd sleep too much. Sometimes she'd have nightmares. It was like she couldn't get regulated."

Inga recalled getting a letter from Lisbet telling her that Sabine had decided to change her field of interest. At the time Inga thought it a good thing. Sabine might find herself isolated as a woman scientist.

"I never really understood, what the problem was," Tanner went on. "I mean, there wasn't anything actually wrong with her. Like once, she had this thing in her throat." He touched his Adam's apple. "She said it was a lump that wouldn't go away, and she made me take her to the emergency room. The doctor called it Global Hysteria. Sabine thought she was dying of throat cancer."

"I have heard of that," Inga said, thinking she could have helped years ago had she known.

"I told her that she should start jogging, get fresh air," he said. "Maybe eat grapefruit."

Inga nodded. "Grapefruit is good for digestion. And fresh air is vital."

She smiled at him but wondered how much he really grasped. Fruit and walks could certainly help, but they weren't cures.

"You care very much about Sabine," Inga said.

"She's my wife. I love her."

His words sounded more reportorial than passionate. Still it was nice to hear him say them. "That is good to know," she said.

"Sabine's a good person. She'd pretty much give anyone the shirt off her back." He paused. "She's not really into material things."

"And you?" Inga raised her eyebrows.

He laughed. "I can't deny that I have some pretty substantial desires."

"Such as?"

He drank his coffee. "I love boats and skiing. Bicycling. I've always wanted to ride through the countryside in France. Champagne tastes on a beer budget." He laughed again, this time with a bit of defeat.

But he had a zest for life, an attractive quality.

"May I be blunt?" Inga asked.

"Sure."

"Let us, just hypothetically speaking, say Sabine doesn't recover fully, that she won't be able to ski, or bicycle through France. What if she will need help? Around the house, with the baby. Would you find that terribly distressing?"

"I'll manage." He smiled. "She's never really been much of a cook anyway. Spaghetti is about the only thing she can make."

"So you will stay with her, through all of this?" Inga asked, mentally jotting that it might be helpful to look into cooking lessons for Sabine.

"Why wouldn't I?" he asked with a shrug.

For many reasons Inga thought. He was naïve and rather simple. Not in the way of a simpleton, but rather in a lack of life experience. He had had no great losses.

"You are young still. And happy, which I am glad for. But I worry that this problem with Sabine could be more difficult than you realize."

He leaned forward, looking more pensive. "Like how?"

Inga folded her serviette, and considered how to word what she wanted to say. "For instance if Sabine doesn't show you the affection you need. It sometimes happens to people when they are not well."

His eyes grew wider. "Affection?"

She pursed her lips for a moment "Her drive. It might come and go. It is sometimes hard on the spouse."

"Right," he said with a slightly mischievous smile.

Inga sipped her tea, taking a moment before broaching the next topic. "And money," she said. "If Sabine can't work. If you need to hire someone to help with her and the baby?"

"Not work," he replied, his mouth going a little slack, as he rubbed his chin. "Don't know if we can afford that."

"But if she can't work," Inga repeated, her voice dropping a note. She needed to get a clear sense of what his terms would be in order to stay with Sabine.

"Not sure," he said as his brow creased.

This was the most concerned he had looked, and Inga knew that money was his Achilles' heel. Not such a bad thing, she reasoned. There was no knowing how Sabine's illness would progress, or what other obstacles would present themselves. But barring another world war or stock market crash, she could help.

"I would very much like to pay for the child care."

"That would be great. Really great." His eyes brightened.

"And if in the future, if you might need a bit more, you can write to me."

"You know, I told Sabine the first time I met you that I thought you were a great lady. I..." he stopped.

Inga guessed he was about to say something to the effect of Sabine having a different opinion. It was wise for all of their sakes that he not continue.

Back at McLean, they found Sabine squatting on the floor next to the door of the nurses' station. The pretty woman, the one who looked nothing like a patient, sat next to her.

"Where is the baby?" Inga asked.

Sabine sprung up like a cat and wiped her mascara-smudged eyes. "The nurses took her. They said that a family member has to be here when she's here."

Tanner cleared his throat. Inga guessed he was about to admonish Sabine, say something to the effect of—*I told you that was the case.* Inga held a finger to her lips, advising him to stay quiet. Then she stepped toward Sabine.

"Be patient," she said quietly. "Stay in control. Do not give them the power to hurt you."

Sabine ignored the advice, banging on the door to the nursing station. How Inga would manage to bend the rules to Sabine's favor was unclear at the moment, but she would most certainly find a way.

A nurse handed Mia to Sabine, and they returned to the dining area. As Sabine talked and played with the baby, her transformation was staggering. Her eyes were more alert, her posture straighter, and it was clear that above all else, she needed to be with her child.

Ten minutes later, Tanner said that he needed to get going. He had to work, and it was Mia's bedtime. All understandable, and yet watching Sabine's mouth quiver at having to say goodbye made Inga wish they could stay a bit longer.

Chapter Eight

A Treatment Plan

Frankfurt am Main, Germany
1934

Arnold's third-floor office had once been used as a storage closet. Even so, it had a good view of the Frankfurt Cathedral, and easily accommodated two chairs, a desk, and shelves holding books on medicine, genetics and psychiatry. Books were the true window into a person's soul, Arnold believed. Although recently, he'd wrapped Freud's books in his mother's linens and hidden them in the attic.

He pushed his chair back, reclined, and swung his feet onto the desk, something he did when no one was watching. He flipped through The New England Journal of Medicine, a periodical he never missed.

'The burden on society resulting from this increase in feeble-mindedness is tremendous. For one thing, persons with subnormal intelligence are always potential criminals... The financial loss to the country is appalling. Including both the direct cost of supporting these sufferers from mental disease, and the loss of productive capacity due to their incompetence... the annual total cost of mental disease for the United States is around three-quarters of a billion dollars. We should recognize this danger that threatens to replace our population with a race of feeble-minded; we must study its causes and the sources from which it springs. If we wait too long, this viper that we have nourished may prove our undoing.'

Most German clinicians held similar views and although Arnold didn't like to think of the ill being a financial burden, he understood the reality. As he turned the page, a knock on the door startled him.

He hurried to the door, and there was Inga—confident, smiling, wearing a conservative blue skirt and a gray blouse, not her usual chic attire.

"I wasn't expecting anyone. I would have tidied."

"No need." She glanced around. "It shows you are involved in your work. That is a positive thing."

"Well then." Arnold smiled. "Would you like to sit?" He moved the chairs, offering Inga the one that had once been his mother's.

She sat upright. Arnold thought of something Rigmor had told him. Inga didn't like photographs of herself that made her look too attractive. She liked people to be surprised by her appearance, for them to say, *you are so much prettier than in the picture I saw.*

"A cup of tea?" Arnold could run down to the dining hall.

"I'd prefer something stronger." She dipped her head. "If you have it."

He kept a bottle of scotch and one glass in the bottom drawer of his desk. Turning his back, he leaned over the drawer, pulled a handkerchief from his pocket, and buffed the glass. He poured a small amount. He didn't want to seem stingy, but he also didn't want to offend her by serving too much.

Inga noticed the journal.

"And what do our American friends have to say?"

Arnold wasn't sure she really wanted to know. "Their views parallel ours in many respects."

"And they are?" she asked, sipping her scotch.

The fact that she wanted a drink, and the almost brusque tone of her questions, made him think she was nervous about something.

"It's all rather technical," he said about the journal. "Is everything all right?"

"I also read that publication," she said. "I am quite familiar with what is going on in this field."

"Of course," he said. They talked about the article—about feeblemindedness, about the Law for the Prevention of the Genetically Diseased Offspring. Inga told him that, had she gone to university, she would have studied genetics, and had that been the case, she would have made a fair and compassionate impartial judge on the newly formed Health Courts. Arnold was not entirely convinced.

Inga asked for a refill. Partway through her second scotch, she announced she had come to talk about Rigmor, and took out a small spiral notebook and a pencil. She flipped through a few pages, and then looked at him.

"Rigmor complains of difficulty swallowing sometimes, as if she has a fishbone stuck in her throat. Have you ever heard of something like that?"

It seemed far too easy of a question. "Yes, it's a common symptom caused by anxiety, due to tightening of the esophagus."

"I thought so." She turned to another page, then picked up her glass from the floor.

Arnold's job was to put people at ease when they had to broach difficult subjects. He smiled, showing her that she was free to tell him what was on her mind.

"I have done quite a bit of research on my own," she said.

He nodded. "I had gathered as much. You seem to really persevere. Your desire to learn is impressive." He left unsaid that even the most knowledgeable lay person could easily misunderstand some of the more complicated gradations of the field.

"I have selfish reasons." She glanced out the window before turning to him with her chin lifted. "I would do anything to help Rigmor."

"I admire your loyalty and dedication," he told her. She bowed her head as if uncomfortable with the compliment.

"I have met with another doctor," Inga said, "a psychoanalyst from the Berlin Institute."

Arnold felt his stomach sink. He was being replaced. Somehow, he knew the time would come, that he would not be good enough for the Blumenthals.

"Her name is Therese Benedek. Have you heard of her?"

"I have not," he said. "But that doesn't mean anything."

"She was born in Hungary, and also trained there." Inga paused. "Political reasons. That's why she moved here. And now, well." She brushed a hand along her skirt. "I suppose that isn't important for our purposes. But it does feel so unfair. That she had to leave Hungary because she was Jewish, and here she is, once again surrounded by people in government who hate her." Inga shook her head. "But there is nothing we can do about that at the moment. Therese is a small thing, a sprite really, and full of energy. When I met her, I found her physical appearance somewhat unappealing. I suppose that is not a nice thing to say, but with her hair a mess, and her big black glasses, I couldn't help but think it. But then as we talked, I found there was something charming about her, something so intuitive, my feelings on her appearance completely changed. Interesting how that happens."

"Yes," Arnold said. "What we consider to be so objective is often much more subjective than we might think." He thought of the first time he saw Rigmor and Inga, how he judged Inga the more beautiful sister. And now it was completely reversed.

"I have become quite fond of Therese," Inga continued. "She and I have talked about so much, and there is one thing in particular I think you might be of help with." "Please."

"She researches women's hormonal and sexual cycles and correlates those to psychological behavior." Inga entwined her fingers. "She looks at the mind-body connection."

"Oh," Arnold said, feeling his neck grow hot. He had read things, of course, and would without hesitation or embarrassment discuss women's hormones with a colleague. But Inga was not a colleague.

"Her studies on women are mostly about the differences between the pre and post ovulation states. But with me, she talks about sexual relations, and orgasm, and how that can affect psychological wellbeing."

Arnold focused on the lines in his knuckles and hoped his face wasn't too red. Inga crossed her legs and sat back in the chair.

"I began this study purely by accident. I had been reading a lot about hysteria, since that has been a common label doctors have placed on Rigmor. In my readings I came across an older practice, used fifty years ago, in which doctors would stimulate the vagina so the woman could have a paroxysm."

"I know of this." His eyelid twitched. If she was going to suggest vaginal massages for Rigmor, Arnold would be clear that he didn't agree with the practice.

"I found it interesting, as does Therese, that the doctors didn't think these paroxysms were orgasms. What do you think?"

"I'm afraid I haven't given much thought to the matter."

"Perhaps I wouldn't have either, but I think there is a connection between orgasm and a feeling of calm. I think that's what those doctors stumbled on, even if they called it something else."

Arnold cleared his throat. "It could be."

She sipped her drink. "I can only speak from my own experience. But I do find a certain peace after I have had relations in the bedroom. Have other patients talked of this?"

"I can't speak about what patients tell me." Again, he felt much too warm.

Inga nodded. "No, of course not. I didn't mean to pry," she said. "I am used to speaking about it with Therese quite openly, so I apologize if I have been too forward and made you uncomfortable."

"It's fine."

"You know my sister—you know that under no circumstances would she feel comfortable going to a doctor's office and getting any kind of vaginal treatment."

"I don't believe it's prescribed any longer," he muttered.

"The point is, I think it would be very helpful for Rigmor to have relations with a man. I realize that might sound crass, but I have thought about it long and hard, and I believe it might really help her. She's had suitors in the past, but she has a natural shyness that has kept her from developing a more intimate relationship."

"Has she always had this shyness?"

"I'm not here to speak of myself, but I do remember liking boys from a young age, and asking Rigmor who she liked. She never really knew. When I was a girl, I thought she was hiding it from me, but then I realized, she is made of a different type of cloth, and she just doesn't have the same drive that I have." Inga laughed. "Sometimes, believe it or not, my behavior even catches me off guard."

"It sounds as if you were a lively child," Arnold told her.

"I was." She smiled, her face relaxed and young for a moment. "But that's hardly the point. I have talked to Rigmor about men, and how having sex can be calming. I can see by the color of your face that I have astonished you. Please," she lowered her voice. "Remember that I have always been Rigmor's elder sister and she is quite used to listening to my ideas and thoughts. She is much more modern in her way of thinking than you might know."

It was true, Arnold had never seen this modern side. "Is there someone she is interested in?" he asked.

"That brings me to my next point." She looked directly at him, her eyes wider.

Now he understood. "No." He pushed back his chair, bumping it against the desk.

"You don't have to rush to a decision," she said.

"I couldn't. It wouldn't be ethical."

"She is not a patient. My mother was wise about that. And I think Rigmor has real feelings for you." She scuffed her foot along the carpet. "The question is, and I do realize this is delicate of me to ask, do you have feelings for her?"

"I care about her." He glanced at the window, as a few clouds drifted past. "Very much," he added, turning back to Inga.

"Do you care about her in the way. . ." She paused. "In the way a man cares about a woman?"

"What you are asking is quite ridiculous."

She tucked her head down, and for a moment seemed to realize the blatant outrageousness of her request. "It first seemed crazy to me as well."

"It is crazy," he said, hoping to end this conversation.

"It is unconventional. I will give you that. But it is well thought through and researched. And if you would like to call Dr. Benedek and have this conversation with her, I would urge you to do so."

But Arnold held firm—in appearance, at least. "I understand the theory, and I'm sure Benedek is a good doctor but I don't think that this is appropriate."

"You know by now how much I love my sister. I am only looking for ways to help her." She placed her handbag on her lap. He expected her next words to be stinging.

Instead she smiled. "I thought this would be your reaction. I'm neither disappointed nor dissuaded. You would not be the man I thought you were if you said yes. But I am planting the seed. That is all. I ask only that you and Rigmor consider it. And of course it will take time, should you both decide affirmatively." She stood, walked to the door, and then turned to him. "It would be best not to discuss this particular plan with Mother."

With that she was gone.

* * *

Inga continued to bring Rigmor cups of hot cocoa and made sure to always check that the door was properly closed.

"He makes me feel exquisitely alive," Inga said one evening, when she talked about her latest adventure with Fred. "Perhaps it's something you want to try."

Rigmor laughed. "You do have a way of saying whatever is on your mind."

Inga picked up a silver brush from the bedside table and brushed Rigmor's hair, transforming the curls into soft waves. "I am not so blunt with everyone."

"It is your bluntness that makes you such an interesting person," Rigmor said.

Inga grinned. "Perhaps you should inform Mother of your opinion."

"You are too much alike, strong-headed. That is the problem."

Inga did not like the comparison to her mother, although Rigmor was hardly the first to point it out.

"My opinions," Inga began, as she kept brushing, "come from factual information, not from some old tales passed on generations ago." The brushstrokes lengthened and slowed. "I know a woman, Therese. She is exceedingly bright. She studies women's ovulation cycles and how they relate to mental illness."

"Light reading again?" Rigmor asked.

Inga laughed. "Hormones influence mood, and I think they play a part in your ups and downs. Just as menstrual cycles affect us, so does sex. I would never have thought that until I met Fred. But I can tell you that I feel such pure tranquility after we have been together. It is as if I have taken some very potent, wondrous medicine." She stopped brushing mid-stroke.

Rigmor shook her head. "No."

"Would it hurt to try?" Inga resumed brushing.

"I couldn't," Rigmor said. "Besides, I have no one."

"What about Arnold?" Inga spoke with caution. "You both care for one another."

Rigmor pushed Inga's hand away and turned. "I would never."

"Because it frightens you? Or because you think it is morally wrong?" Inga picked up a strand of Rigmor's hair, and gently caressed it.

"I'm not morally against it," she said. "I think women have a right to do these things."

"I would help you." Inga let go of her sister's hair, and reached for a hand. "On my wedding night with Klaus, I had no idea what to expect. I was frightened. I would not leave you in that kind of predicament."

Rigmor pulled away her hand. "And Arnold? What if this wasn't something he wanted?"

Inga took this as a positive sign. "I am sure it is."

"You haven't?" Rigmor asked.

"I have talked to him about my conversations with Therese, and how she believes that I might be onto something."

Rigmor covered her mouth as if to hide the shock. "He doesn't think I proposed this idea?"

"Of course not."

"Please. Let's forget this whole conversation took place."

"But my dear, things are not getting better. There are bluish circles under your eyes. You are not sleeping. You imagine worms under your skin. Why not try something that might actually help?"

Rigmor ran a finger under her eye. "I'm sorry," she whispered.

"No," Inga said. "I don't want you to be sorry. I didn't mean to sound so forceful. I only want to make things better."

"I know." Rigmor paused. "Mother told me about the roses."

Inga felt her face heat as she shook her head. "It was meant..."

"I know how it was meant. And I love you for all of your crazy, preposterous ideas. But we are both grown women. Soon you will have a family, and move away, and I will have to look after myself."

"I am not having children." She was cautious with Fred, making sure he always used a condom.

Inga climbed down from the bed. "I won't bring up my idea with Arnold again."

"Thank you," Rigmor said.

"But just because I won't talk about it, doesn't mean you shouldn't think about it."

"You're impossible." Rigmor grinned and slid under the eiderdown.

* * *

On a midafternoon in late August, Arnold and Rigmor strolled in the Palmengarten. She wore a powder blue dress with a light cardigan and beige pumps that were good for walking.

They took the path around the lake. A few men wearing brown shirts and Nazi armbands passed them. Arnold reminded himself that it was a movement of fanatics and ultimately unsustainable.

Rigmor and Arnold sat on a bench that faced the water. The day was hot, and Arnold took off his suit coat.

"Are you too warm?" he asked Rigmor.

She tugged on the sleeve of her cardigan. "No," she replied as more men in Nazi uniforms walked by.

"I tell myself we are, above all, a sensible, analytic race," he said. "This will pass. People are not by nature bad."

"It cannot last," Rigmor agreed.

They gazed at the water, flat as paper. He closed his eyes for a few seconds, waited and then asked how she was faring.

"I feel a millimeter away from completely losing my mind," Rigmor said. "I don't know what to do anymore. I have tried sketching my fears, as you suggested, but they are still there in the middle of the night. I desperately want to feel normal. I would like to go into town, to shop for a new dress, to eat at a nice restaurant without worrying that I will faint, or feel my heart pounding so hard it will leap out of my chest."

"Have you tried the breathing exercises?"

"I have. I lie in my bed and tell myself to only pay attention to my breaths. But I've failed. I can't push away my thoughts."

"It's impossible to erase all thoughts. The main thing is to be gentle with yourself." He took a few breaths to demonstrate.

They sat, watching families with children, women in fashionable dresses, gentlemen walking with canes, and servants carrying packages. It was a colorful cast. People who appeared solid and hard working—of good quality. These were the Germans he knew.

"My sister doesn't care what anyone else thinks once she's set her mind on something," Rigmor said.

Arnold nodded. "I believe that is true."

"She's always been like that," Rigmor continued. "I remember when we were girls and we were skiing. She was told to stay with our instructor. But she didn't, and I don't know how, but she got herself to the top of the mountain. She flew down, better than any other skier. She was a sensation that day. People congratulated her, told her she was a natural. Mother was furious."

"I can imagine," Arnold said.

Rigmor pushed up the sleeves of her cardigan. At first he thought the marks on her arm were a rash, possibly from the heat, but when he looked at them more closely, he noticed scabs, small red dots, four of them.

"What are these from?" he asked her. "Were you bitten?"

She pulled her sleeves down. "Nothing."

He waited, guessing she had wanted, perhaps not completely consciously, for him to see the marks.

"Sometimes," she began. "I feel as if I have botfly larvae crawling under my skin. I know it can't be. But when I'm so tired and haven't slept, I think they're there, and I have to get them out."

"And how do you get them out?"

"I've tried to poke them with a needle. Sometimes a knife." She lowered her head. "In the light of day, I realize I have none of these worms under my skin. But at three in the morning, the world is so different."

He sighed, wishing she didn't have to suffer so. "Next time you feel them, is there a possibility that you could tell Inga, or phone me? So you wouldn't have to hurt yourself?"

"I will try."

"Things have been difficult," he said, and put his hand next to hers. "But overall you have been managing. I think it's important to focus on what's working."

"I hang by a thread." She gazed at the lake. "Inga talks to me. She doesn't hide anything, and I'm glad for it. I don't want to be some sort of breakable doll."

"No, of course not."

She poked the toe of her shoe in the grass. "Inga can sometimes have unusual ideas." She moved away, just enough for him to know what lay ahead. He could have stopped it right there. He should have stood up, said something about the sun being too hot, or the hour getting late. But he didn't.

"She cares deeply about you," he said.

"I know that." Her shoulders rounded. "And she talked to me about what she proposed to you."

This time it was he who moved away, just slightly. "She is admirable. I looked up the doctor she has been discussing this with, Therese Benedek. A very respectable woman."

"I have to ask," Rigmor said, gripping the seat of the bench. "Do you think it would help?"

"I do not."

"I see." She tucked her chin to her neck. "I shouldn't have said anything."

"Of course you should have. And it has nothing to do with you. I mean, nothing to do with how lovely you are." He wiped his brow. "It's that we're such good friends."

"I know. I would never have brought it up, but I'm feeling so desperate."

"We'll keep trying new treatments," he said.

A child threw a pebble in the water and the ripples, the movement, came as a great relief to Arnold.

"Do you have a woman in your life?" She jumped up and then added, "Oh dear, please forgive me." She covered her face and sat down again. "It is not my business."

"I have no one in my life," he said, smiling. "I wouldn't have the time. But I want you to know something." He held her hand and looked into her gray eyes. "I understand why Inga suggested what she did, but I would never take advantage of you. You must know that."

"I was the one who brought it up. You would not be taking advantage of me."

Yet he would have been, or at least he felt that way, because he did have selfish motives of his own. "Yes, but you are a woman, and I am a doctor, and people would think the worst."

"You always tell me not to worry so much what other people think." Her voice lilted.

She was right—he did say that, too often. "We will not give up." He put an arm around her, needing to protect her. As she rested her head on his shoulder, Arnold felt a change. He had not said, *you can't give up.* He had said, we, as if they were a couple. He felt lighter, hopeful, not just for her, but for himself as well.

* * *

Arnold always looked forward to his visits with Rigmor. Even when her mood was bleak, her empathy for others remained remarkable. She did not judge in regards to money, class, education or beauty. She made the assumption that humans behaved from a place of best intentions, which Arnold believed left her vulnerable. There were times she insisted she was fine, but he saw through that, saw the pensive stares, heard how her voice shrunk to a whisper, noticed the slight tremor in her hands that she tried to hide.

Twice more the topic of Dr. Benedek arose. Rigmor spoke of Inga's theory in halting sentences, and Arnold found himself opening to the idea. He had never been attracted to a woman the way a normal man might be, but perhaps it was because he hadn't given it a chance. And if there was ever a woman he felt love for, it was Rigmor. He even caught himself daydreaming about having a family with her. She would make an extraordinarily kind mother. But life was not a fairy tale: there were the complications of her illness that might very well worsen, there was the disparity in their social status, and there was the talk of new laws that would make it impossible for an Aryan to marry a Jew.

Nevertheless, they continued to talk about "Inga's idea" as they had come to call it. They discussed whether or not there might be chemical shifts in the body after sex, and finally they decided to try. They chose a date in December.

The plan was that he would pick her up for the symphony at the Festhalle but they would go to his home instead. As the date neared, Arnold occasionally fell into panic, fearing failure, recognizing it wasn't just Rigmor's mental health at stake but his very manhood too. At other moments he felt exhilarated at the prospect of a future with a woman he cared so deeply for.

The evening of the concert, he dressed in his tuxedo and took a taxi to the Blumenthals. He and Rigmor had promised each other that if either one felt any unease, they would stop immediately. They also swore that they would never tell anyone. Not even Inga.

The butler led Arnold to the large drawing room. A fire crackled behind Frau Blumenthal, who stood in the center of the room wearing one of her typical dresses. Her face, though, looked anything but usual. Her skin glowed, and Arnold might have even gone so far as to say she looked happy.

"This is one of Rigmor's favorites," Frau Blumenthal said. "Beethoven's Seventh. I'm so pleased she wanted to go. When she was only six, she already had an advanced understanding of classical music."

When the potbellied grandfather clock began to strike, Rigmor walked in. She wore a sleeveless black silk gown with matching gloves. Her only jewelry was a pair of earrings made of pearls that hung from a short string of diamonds. Her dark hair was twisted along the sides and rolled at the back.

"Thank you for coming," she said to Arnold as he passed her a bouquet of flowers.

Frau Blumenthal reached for the bell. "Shall we all have a drink?"

"I think we should go," Rigmor said. "Arnold has hired a taxi."

"No," Frieda protested. "You must take our car. It is much more comfortable. Safer too."

"That is kind," Arnold began. "But I'm afraid the taxi is waiting, and it would be unfair for the driver not to be paid."

"I will take care of it." Frieda rang the bell. The butler came in. Arrangements were made, as Rigmor looked at Arnold and shrugged. He smiled, to show her that it would be fine. A small obstacle would not thwart their plans.

In the car, Arnold instructed the driver to let them off at his home, and to pick them up at eleven. He gave the man some money and asked him to be discreet.

"My home is nothing compared to yours," Arnold said, as he unlocked his front door. Inside, he took her fur shawl and led her to the sitting room.

She looked at a painting he'd bought when he first moved to the city two years ago. Two horses stopped at a stream. An upper-class man, of the seventeen hundreds, sat on one of the horses.

"This is well done," Rigmor said.

"The dark tones obscure," Arnold answered, "to some degree, the vitality of the horses."

"I noticed that right away. It's as if the artist is pulling you inward, forcing you to look more closely, to not be fooled by the first glance."

"Yes," Arnold agreed. "I have actually looked at this painting for hours with a magnifying glass. That the man is missing a button on his shirt, and that his pocket is a little askew, is brilliant."

"Did it come from your parents?"

Arnold grinned thinking of the few paintings in his childhood home. They were of the German countryside—nice, but with no variation in tone.

"No, I found it on one of my very first walks around the city. It was in a small shop, in a little alleyway. I have been back there a few times. The owner is proud of every piece he has."

"Perhaps you can take me there one day."

"I would like that." He paused. "May I get you a drink?"

"Please." She pulled off her gloves.

In the kitchen, he poured them each a glass of red wine, and finally, after sitting and drinking, his nerves settled.

"It is a smallish sitting room," he said. "But I've grown quite comfortable with it. I sometimes imagine a dog at my side."

"Yes," she exclaimed. "I can imagine you with a Spaniel."

Rigmor appeared perfectly poised and, if she felt anxious about the evening's agenda, she hid it remarkably well.

"I'd prefer a smaller home without servants. Mother and Inga seem to feel the servants are invisible, but I don't have the ability to pretend they aren't there."

They chatted about their childhoods, how she wanted to do everything Inga did, climb trees, ride bicycles, run from their nanny, but Rigmor was too timid, even with Inga's cajoling. He spoke about how ordinary his boyhood was. How he worked hard to get where he was today, how he envied his colleagues who seemed to pass exams with such ease.

They both watched the fire, and after some time, she slipped off her shoes and curled into the corner of the couch. "May I ask you something?"

"Of course."

"Do many of your patients have such a dislike for themselves?"

"It's an interesting question." He faced her. "Generally speaking, the people who should feel shame or dislike, feel nothing of the sort. And vice versa."

"I asked Inga once if she ever disliked herself, and she was surprised. She said she had never really considered it." Rigmor tucked her head. "I probably seemed self-indulgent to her."

"You're an enigma." He watched the reflection of the flames dance in her eyes.

They drank and luxuriated in the warmth of the room. The notion of having sex had floated to the back of his thoughts. They talked about how the wrong things, money and status, were often the measures of success, how kindness and generosity were the most overlooked qualities. He moved closer to her as she explained that living with her mother and sister often made her feel inadequate. She didn't have their willpower or determination.

"But you have so much more," he said. "You are the one who is pleasurable to be with, who makes others feel good about themselves."

She smiled, and Arnold thought that they really were good for each other.

"Would you like more wine?" he asked.

"No thank you. Two is my limit."

"Would you like to see the rest of the house?"

As she stood, she swayed a bit. He jumped up and held her

arm.

"Even two glasses is a bit much." She giggled. It was a happy, pleasant sound, like a robin calling his mate on a spring morning.

"Shall we sit again?" Arnold asked.

"No, I think...." She blushed and moved closer, leaning a little on him. "I would like to see the rest of the house."

"The tour will take a total of two minutes." Taking her hand, he showed her the dining room, the kitchen, and his office. Finally, he led her to his bedroom. She stood in the doorway. "It is just as I had imagined."

"Which was?" he asked.

"Neat and tidy, and like a room a doctor would have."

She looked at the one print he had on the wall, *Four Doctors*, by John Singer Sargent. He had bought it soon after medical school. At the time, he was working in a hospital in Kiel and renting an apartment above a bakery.

He glanced at her lips, her unblemished skin, and wondered how a normal man would feel. Would he be anxious? Would he be dreading what lay ahead? Afraid of failure?

She turned her back to him. "Can you unzip me, please?" She was so much the braver soul.

His hands shook as he found the zipper. In an hour, maybe even in twenty minutes, this ordeal would be over, and if it was successful, he could say good night to his fears. Although as he unzipped her gown, he realized that thinking of this as an *ordeal* might be a sign that something was intrinsically wrong.

Rigmor stepped out of her gown. She wore stockings with a garter and a black-lace brassiere. Arnold glanced at his crotch, willing his penis to do something. To come to life with the joy of a perfect woman in front of him. But nothing.

She faced him. Her gray eyes showed a tint of blue.

Here she was, the most vulnerable, tender being, wanting to make love to him, and he wanted to race out of his home and find their empty seats at the symphony.

"Perhaps I should turn the light off," he said.

"If you like," she replied. "Shall I get under the covers?"

"That might be a good idea." He wished he could think of something witty or romantic to say. He switched off the light, but left the door open, so it wasn't pitch black. He disrobed quickly, leaving his clothes in a heap next to her dress.

Her breath smelled like honey, and as he brushed a finger along her cheek, his heart stirred. The problem was that his lower regions remained inert.

Eventually he ran a hand down her neck, as she waited, silently.

When he touched her breasts, she drew in her breath, and he wanted nothing more than to please her. But still his body was not reacting the way it should. He told her he would just be a moment, that he needed to use the bathroom.

In the mirror, he saw the weakness in his brown eyes. It might be best to stop things now, but he couldn't give up, for her sake, and his. Not yet.

He turned from the mirror and caressed himself, managing to get a small result. But it was not enough. He kept working at it, and allowed himself to think of a faceless man. A man who would push Arnold onto the bed and take him until they both shuddered with joy.

Soon he was ready.

"Are you all right?" she asked when he got under the covers again.

"Yes, very good."

"Is there something I should do?" she asked.

His erection began to shrink. He needed to act quickly if there was any chance of this working. He got under the covers and lay on top of her. She opened her legs, but by the time he got himself arranged, he was soft again.

She held her breath.

He moved off of her. "I'm so sorry."

"What is it?" Her voice was tender and concerned, but he also heard the fraying underneath, the crumbling of hope.

"I seem to be having trouble." He rested the back of his hand on his forehead. "Perhaps we are too good of friends."

"I should never have suggested this," she whispered. "I have put you in an untenable position."

"No. It was a good idea." He wanted to get dressed, and at the same time, he desperately wanted to try. "I'm a doctor. I mean, of course you know that. What I meant to say is that I have read about all of this, and if you want, we could try another position. Sometimes that can make a difference."

"Yes," she said. "I would like to try."

He got out of bed and closed the door. They needed complete darkness. He needed it. "I have read that it actually is more pleasurable for the woman if she gets on her hands and knees."

She moved under the covers, and he saw the outline of her body.

He pulled at himself, thinking of his friend Otto from boarding school. They would sneak into bed together, and rub each other's penises until one of them had an orgasm.

The thought of Otto allowed Arnold to push inside Rigmor. He gripped one arm around Rigmor's tiny waist as he imagined Otto's firm buttocks and broad shoulders. He closed his eyes and allowed himself to feel an intense pleasure he had never known. To be so intimate with another human, to be melded as one, to feel the edges of his own ego dissolve, was something he had never imagined. He was about to pull out so that he could put on a condom, but the explosion came suddenly—and so blissfully. He managed to extract himself just in time.

"Oh dear God!" he exclaimed, and felt a combination of relief, exhilaration, and immense gratitude.

"Is something the matter?" Rigmor asked, her voice oddly distant.

"No, no. Nothing is the matter. Quite the opposite." He fell onto the bed. "No, it was wonderful." He touched her hairline. "Wonderful," he said again.

She pulled the blanket up. "You had an—" She didn't finish.

"I did." He breathed heavily. "You?"

"I don't think so," she whispered.

"I can put my fingers inside of you. Perhaps we can make it work that way."

"No. I think it's enough for tonight."

He turned to her and caressed her hair. "I would like to make you happy," he said.

She met his fingers with hers. "You are a good man. It could be that more happened than I realized. I mean, the calm that Inga talks of, maybe it will just take a bit longer for me to feel that."

"Perhaps," he said, hoping she was correct. Their fingers entwined, and although he'd never been a smoker, he felt as if he understood now why people had a cigarette after sex. It would be such a perfect, languid way to top off such a perfect, exhilarating act. He had to admit that Inga had been right. There was a calm that came after intercourse.

He sighed deeply. "I could lay here forever."

She shifted so that her head rested on his shoulder. "Can you imagine what my mother would do if I didn't come home?"

He laughed. "She might call the Gestapo."

"Perhaps, except that no one hates the Nazis more than she."

"Possibly. Although they are not a particularly popular bunch."

"Inga has said that Fred fears they might sway more people into their camp."

He turned and kissed her forehead. "Germans are good people. In the end, they won't tolerate a culture of hatred." He sighed again. "Shall we go to dinner? There is a good restaurant around the corner."

He felt her head nod on his shoulder and reached for the

lamp on the nightstand, but hesitated. He didn't want her to feel awkward in the light. In truth he also felt a bit strange being naked, and wondered how others handled these moments. After a few more sighs, he suggested that he grab his clothes and give her privacy.

At dinner as they both ate the seafood stew, he noticed men glancing at Rigmor with seemingly lustful intentions. He didn't feel jealously, at least not the kind that sometimes overcame him when a colleague published in a prestigious journal. It was more of a pleasant sensation—of pride that she was with him.

They talked of small matters and when she placed down her spoon and smiled, he noticed a slight quiver in her mouth. As if she was trying to smile, but couldn't quite get there. He reached his hand across the table and held hers. Perhaps it was the two men with swastikas on their armbands that made her uncomfortable. Or perhaps it was the fact that she had to return home to her domineering mother. He wanted to protect her, and for a second he even thought he should just ask her to marry him.

"Do you like the stew?" he asked instead.

When the car pulled to the front of her home, he debated whether to kiss her. And if he did, should he kiss her on the lips or the cheek? He leaned toward her, placed his hand on hers, and decided the cheek was the wiser choice. But she had already opened the door. Was she trying to get away from him? On the drive back to his home, he convinced himself that all was fine. She was shy and reserved, and he was overly sensitive.

That night, Arnold woke at three in the morning with an erection, and a fuzzy dream of Otto. He replayed the night's events, and realized that although he had been able to make his penis work inside of a woman, he would still have to battle his perversions. He reminded himself that the night of lovemaking had been for Rigmor, not him. Hopefully she was sleeping peacefully, and would wake with a tranquil mind.

Chapter Nine

Trying to Help

Belmont, Massachusetts
1984

Inga sat on a hard Windsor chair in Dr. Lincoln's office. She was here to get information, perhaps to impart information, if that would help. Most important, she wanted to learn about Sabine, and what needed to be done to ensure she was well taken care of, not just here at McLean but afterwards as well. From her handbag, she retrieved her notebook.

Dr. Lincoln, an extraordinarily tall man with earnest brown eyes, sat perfectly still and remained quiet.

Sabine fidgeted. "So . . ."

Lincoln nodded in slow motion. Inga waited. After a few more moments of silence, she decided to speak. "What do you believe Sabine's diagnosis is?"

He turned to Sabine. No words were spoken.

Inga understood the theory of a doctor behaving like a blank wall so as not to sway the patient. But Lincoln seemed to take it to an extreme.

Sabine glanced at the carpet. "Depression," she said.

"I see," Inga began. "What about delusions or psychosis?"

"Why would you ask that?" Sabine bit back.

Inga placed a hand on her chest. "I meant nothing hurtful. I was only trying to get a sense of what you are suffering from." She turned to Lincoln. "And do you agree with the diagnosis— that it is simply depression?"

"These are never simple things," he said.

She would have much preferred a confident yes. She needed to find out if he believed Sabine's case was actually more complicated.

"How sure are you about the diagnosis?" she asked.

"I'm afraid that is confidential. If Sabine wants to speak about it, she certainly can."

"There isn't anything else to say about it," Sabine replied.

More silence.

Inga pursed her lips, unsure of how to proceed. At the moment, Sabine looked young, more like an adolescent, the way she wrapped her arms around her stomach. Inga wished she could do something to make it easier.

"We can use this time as an opportunity for Sabine," Lincoln said. "Is there anything you'd like to talk about with your grandmother?"

Sabine scuffed her boot on the carpet. "I guess I want to know why you thought I was wretched."

Inga tapped her pencil slowly and considered the question. She wanted to be accurate and honest in her answer.

"I thought that there were times you seemed very unhappy. As a child you wanted to stay to yourself, and you didn't smile much at all. I can picture you gazing out of my sitting room window. I wondered if you had a touch of melancholy."

"But you said wretched. As in vile. Worthless."

"Ah," Inga said. "I did say, to your mother as well, that you seemed, unglucklich. I thought the translation for that was unhappy or wretched. In fact, I remember consulting the dictionary."

"I don't know what the translation is," Sabine said. "But I remember the way you said it, and it felt like wretched."

Fred used to remark that Inga had a directness in her speech that some people might interpret as aloof or haughty, even if her intentions were not in any way derogatory.

"Can you remember when I called you this?" Inga asked.

"When I was seven. After you said the disabled children should be killed."

Inga felt her mouth open. For a moment she was speechless. "I am sure I never said killed." That was not a simple translation issue. "I am surprised you think I said such a thing."

"You called the children idiots."

They seemed to be going in circles. "That is the word. In German. That is what we say for feebleminded. Could it be that I just don't know the correct word?"

"You said they should be put out of their misery."

It seemed very strange that the conversation was headed in this direction. Yet if this was what Sabine wanted answered, Inga would do her best.

"I might have implied that I did not want the worst of them to suffer." She paused and looked at Lincoln. "It is a dilemma of all time, is it not? When to allow humans freedom from their misery. At what point do we allow release? I am sure that is all I meant." She felt her cheeks get warm. To sit in this office and be accused of wanting to murder children was the last thing she expected.

Lincoln nodded and then glanced at Sabine, who didn't respond.

Inga decided it might be best to change the topic. After all, they were not here to talk about euthanasia, but to help Sabine. "Sabine's husband," Inga began, "told me last night that she has suffered from these fits before."

"They're not fits," Sabine snapped.

"Again, I fear it is my English."

"Well, now people aren't kept in chains if they have fits," Sabine said.

"But my dear girl," Inga began. "People were not kept in chains. There were fine institutions, better than this. With very good treatments. In my younger days, I knew quite a lot about these things."

"Like what?" Sabine asked.

The question was forceful, as if Inga were being interrogated.

She held herself very straight. "I knew people."

"Who?" Sabine asked.

Inga brushed a hand along her skirt. If she wasn't already on such precarious ground, she might have told Sabine that her tone was impertinent. "For one," Inga said, "I knew Rudin quite well." She looked at Lincoln. "He was well known for his two gene theory of schizophrenia."

"I have not heard of that," Lincoln said.

"But you have heard of Rudin?" Inga asked.

"I'm afraid not." He appeared ready to stand. The session had only just begun, and Inga wondered if Sabine was being shortchanged. "If Sabine needs more time, I am happy to pay for it."

"The sessions are fifty minutes," Lincoln replied. "At least half the time needs to be devoted to just Sabine. It was nice to meet you, Miss Sommer."

"I do know quite a bit about mania and melancholy," she added quickly. She needed more information—more time. A better sense of what her granddaughter had and how she could help. She couldn't leave yet.

"I don't have those things," Sabine said.

Lincoln stood. "Thank you for coming, Miss Sommer."

"Frau Sommer," Inga corrected, and closed her notebook that had one word from the meeting. Wretched.

At the door, she turned to Lincoln. "May I set up a private session with you?"

"I'm afraid that wouldn't be ethical," he replied. "Sabine is my client."

She smiled. "I only want to ensure she has what she needs for now and the future."

"I'm afraid that would be impossible." He lowered his head. "Thank you again for coming," he said, closing the door.

Inga felt wholly misunderstood and booted out like a stray cat.

The last time she was in a psychiatrist's office it had been Bohm's, a man she wished she could completely erase from her memory. But there he was, suddenly so clear in her thoughts, with his bald head, erratic gestures and sickly plants. She shivered. Perhaps this Lincoln fellow wasn't the best psychiatrist in the world but his focus on helping Sabine felt genuine, and he seemed to be grounded by his own beliefs, not those of some despicable government party.

Inga returned to the hotel and decided that it would be best to put the issue of the diagnosis on hold.

* * *

Arlesheim, Switzerland
1965

In the summer of 1965, the children came to stay at the chalet — a great relief for Inga as she would not have to travel to the States and visit the yellow box of a house, and see Lisbet's husband. The boys were nine and eight. Sabine was seven. It would be nice to have a girl around, to put her in pretty dresses, brush and plait her hair, and teach her how to make jam and lay the table correctly.

They flew alone, with a stewardess watching them. Inga and Fred fetched them at the Basel airport. The moment the boys saw Inga, they ran to her with open arms. Sabine stood in the background, her hair a mess of curls.

In the mornings, the boys tumbled out of bed and raced to the veranda for breakfast. They ate rolls slathered in butter and honey, and stuck their tongues out at each other. Inga told them to behave, but more often than not, she found herself smiling at their impishness.

On the third day of their visit, Sabine came to the breakfast table in a white dress with brightly printed beach balls. It was a bad cut, with puffy sleeves, and too small. Inga retrieved a simple blue frock that she had bought for Sabine, and asked her to change.

Sabine stared at the dress. "No."

"Come now, be a good girl and put it on." Inga stood behind Sabine and tried to pull off the dress she was wearing. Sabine wriggled away and slinked under the table. Inga was patient. She cleared the plates, and washed the dishes as the boys played in the garden. Still Sabine didn't come out.

"You can't stay there forever," Inga told Sabine. "There is a nice toy shop in the village."

But Sabine stayed where she was and sulked, and Inga believed the best thing to do was to let her be, give her the space and time she needed. Eventually, she would come around.

Inga took the boys to the village where they met Fred, who was staying at the Hotel Eremitage, an arrangement he and Inga made, deciding it would be best if the children saw him as a benevolent uncle, and not confuse him and think he was the man of the house.

The boys played in a stone fountain. Eventually they splashed Inga, who shrieked and took a step back. But with another splash, and another, she felt like her younger, freer self, and smacked her hand across the water, dousing Robert, whose laugh was infectious.

Inga tried, day after day, to entice Sabine to join them, but Sabine refused.

"Do you miss your mother?" Inga asked.

Sabine shook her head.

"Is it because people here speak a different language?"

She shook her head again.

"Is it the clothes I bought for you? Your brothers? Can you tell me?"

Nothing.

One day when Inga and the boys returned, Sabine was nowhere to be found. She was probably daydreaming in some nook and would come out when she was ready. But after about twenty minutes, Inga began to worry. She looked across the street, behind and between all of the bushes, in the garden, the cellar, and the attic. She asked the boys to check under the beds and in every closet.

"I'll look in the trees," Robert said.

Inga patted his head.

"Maybe she dug a big hole somewhere," Henri said.

"My sweet boy," Inga told him.

Inga ran down the hill calling Sabine's name. She stopped at the fence where Dolligner's cows grazed and looked out at the pasture.

"Sabine," she called as she walked faster, heading toward the village.

Inga raced in and out of shops. By the time she checked the kiosk at the tram station, filled with sweets and cheap toys, she wondered if the boys had found her, and decided to head back to the chalet. She took the shortcut and passed the home for idiot children, a well-looked-after yellow stucco building with the most beautiful fuchsias hanging on the front porch.

Inga glanced at a group of children in the garden, holding hands and singing as they ran in a circle. It couldn't be. Yet that mop of hair was unmistakable.

Inga opened the gate.

"Sabine," she yelled, out of breath and tremendously relieved.

Sabine glanced at Inga and kept playing. A young woman approached.

"May I help you?" she asked.

Inga felt her temper rise. "That is my granddaughter," she said, pointing at Sabine.

"Oh," the woman answered. "What a lovely child she is. She comes down from the hill almost every day. You didn't know?"

"I certainly did not know," Inga said. "And she is not allowed to come here again. If she does, please tell her to return to my house."

"Of course," the woman replied. She walked over to Sabine and crouched to speak to her.

Inga watched Sabine nod and then throw her arms around the woman's neck. The tug of jealousy at Inga's heart was as immediate as it was surprising.

Inga thanked the woman and clenched Sabine's hand.

"I want to stay," Sabine said, trying to wrangle free.

"You are not allowed to be here," Inga scolded.

On their walk up the hill, Sabine yanked her hand away. "They are my friends," she said.

"You cannot just go off wherever you like. I had no idea where you were." Inga nodded for Sabine to move to the hedge, away from the middle of the road.

"I like them."

Inga squatted so that she was eyelevel with Sabine. "You must listen to me. You are old enough to understand. These children suffer and it would be better to play with other children. Children who are healthy." What Inga didn't say was that although befriending those less fortunate was very kind, it almost always led to pain and a child of only seven needn't go down that path.

Sabine looked at the pavement.

"You mustn't go there again, do you understand?" Inga asked, more sternly than she had intended.

Sabine nodded.

Inga sighed and patted Sabine's hand. "You are lucky you were not born with such deformities," she said. "It is a pity how some of the children suffer." Then, under her breath: "One wonders if it wouldn't be kinder to release them from their misery."

Sabine glanced up. "What is a deformity?"

She had a sweet, curious voice, and Inga felt herself soften. "When someone is not as they should be."

"Am I not as I should be?" Sabine whispered.

"My dear girl, I suppose we are never completely as we should be, but you are perfectly fine." Inga smiled. "Though perhaps a bit wretched at times. Especially when you run off where you shouldn't and give me such terrible fright."

* * *

Belmont, Massachusetts
1984

At teatime Inga took a taxi back to Sabine's ward and sat with her granddaughter in the dining room.

"Perhaps there is somewhere a little more private where we can talk?" Inga suggested.

Sabine shrugged. "We can go to my room. Cece isn't there right now."

"Yes, I think that would be good. What about a cup of tea first?"

"There's no tea here, just coffee," Sabine replied.

Inga stood. "That can't be."

There had to be a kettle or at the very least a pot to boil water in. In her purse, wrapped in a paper serviette, sat two teabags from her hotel. Sometimes a nice cup of tea could heal more than any western medicine.

Inga entered the narrow kitchen and searched the cabinets. An abundance of cereal, bread, and crackers lined the shelves. She could not find a pot or a kettle. In the fridge, she saw labeled containers and a can of baby formula with a note taped to it, *not for adult consumption.* She sniffed the milk to make sure it was fresh.

"Omama," Sabine called. "The kitchen is for patients."

She turned to her granddaughter. Her hair was a mess, and her eyes looked tired. "Are you getting enough sleep?"

"Can we talk in my room?" Sabine pointed to the door.

Inga found a cup and walked to the sink. Cold water would have to do for the moment. But a list was taking shape—teacups, kettle, tablecloths.

In Sabine's room, the large window, despite the metal clamp in the middle of it, let in a fair amount of light. The floor space was more than adequate, and the ceilings high. Sabine gestured to the bed.

"We have to sit on my bed," she said, attempting to neaten her thin white blanket.

Inga sat, put her water on the floor, took out her notebook, and added *eiderdown* to her list.

Sabine put a pillow between herself and Inga.

"Will Tanner come tonight?" Inga asked.

"I hope so. I need to see Mia."

Inga knew she had to choose her words carefully. She did not want to be misunderstood. "I can see how very important your baby is to you, and I am pleased about that. It's clear to me that when you are with her, you feel better. My sense is that you should not be separated from her."

Sabine appeared receptive. Her arms were at her sides, not crossed in front of her, and when she looked at Inga there was an openness in her expression.

"I know I am speaking as an old woman and you might find some of my views a bit outdated, but I do understand a thing or two about human nature." She paused. "And men."

Sabine's gaze shifted to the ceiling.

"I think it's very important that you show Tanner you are interested in him. Not only in the baby."

Sabine sighed heavily. "And if I'm not?"

"I understand that he is not foremost on your mind, but I'm telling you this because I want you to see your baby. If you can show him more interest, even if it's not completely genuine, he might bring Mia more readily."

Sabine crossed her arms in front of her.

"I know it might be difficult, but he doesn't seem a bad sort. He's willing to work for his family. He cares about you." She took a breath. "I think it would be unwise to let him get away."

"He isn't a fish," Sabine said.

Inga chuckled. "I imagine fish are not so difficult to understand. I suppose in that way they aren't terribly dissimilar to men. Yes?"

Sabine actually smiled and Inga felt as if she was making progress.

"People need to feel as if they matter. Husbands need to feel that." Inga put a hand on the pillow that sat between them. "Compared to your child, he might be secondary, but perhaps you could not make that quite so obvious. I am not saying this as a criticism, but to help you."

"I can't pretend," Sabine said.

Inga sipped her water. "I have also never been good at that." She smiled. "But you could try. Just a bit perhaps?" When she moved to touch Sabine's arm, to show her that she really meant well, Sabine looked as if a snake was creeping towards her. "And you must remember—now that you have a child, it might not be so easy to find another man."

"Maybe I don't want another man," Sabine said.

Inga rested her notebook on her lap. "You are certainly intelligent enough to know that life is not always easy. But a man can make it easier, and better. And it also gives you a certain place in society, to be married."

"But you got divorced."

"My circumstances were very different, and technically, I only separated." She had also been fortunate not to be afflicted with mental illness. But there was no need to say that aloud.

"Because of Uncle Fred?"

"That was one thing. But we are not here to talk about me."

"What about women who are gay?" Sabine asked. "You can't think they need a man?" There was defiance in the way she spoke.

"Gay?" Inga asked, not following Sabine's point.

"As in lesbian," Sabine said.

Inga wrote the word gay in her notebook. "I did not know that was the meaning of the word. I thought it meant happy." She paused. "Are you gay?"

"No."

"I suppose that is good. Not that I have ever had a problem with homosexuals, but I imagine they have more obstacles in life to overcome." Inga tapped her pencil. "So, tell me, how are things with Tanner, in the bedroom?"

Sabine launched herself off the bed and walked to her wardrobe. She took out a blouse and then put it back. "I can't..."

Her granddaughter was behaving a bit hyperactively at the moment. Had Lincoln considered mania? "You can't do what?" Inga asked.

"Have this conversation."

"It's interesting. Your mother also won't discuss this topic. You know, when I was young, people didn't mind talking about such things. We thought ourselves very open and modern. I would have thought that in in the nineteen eighties, after the sexual revolution, which in my mind was not so very big, young people would be more at ease. But it seems that is not the case."

"Maybe it's just hard to talk about with family," Sabine said.

"I suppose."

"And anyway, I just had a baby."

"Yes, and a beautiful one. A miracle." Inga took a sip of water. "But that was three months ago, and many women resume relationships after an even shorter period."

Sabine held up a hand. "Stop. I can't. OK. I'm sorry. I can't worry about what other women do or don't do."

"Of course not," Inga said. "It doesn't matter what anyone else does. I only meant..."

There was a knock at the door, and then a man with a long

beard poked his head in and told Sabine she had a phone call. Sabine hurried away, down the hall. Inga followed, limping a bit. Her hip had been stiff since the morning.

Sabine sat in the phone booth behind a thick door of plastic. Inga watched Sabine's head droop like a fading rose. By the time she was finished, her neck was blotchy and her eyes red.

"What is it?" Inga asked.

Sabine didn't answer. Back in her room, she sat on the floor, while Inga returned to her seat on the bed.

"Tanner won't bring Mia," Sabine said.

"That is a shame," Inga replied. "Would you like me to call him?"

"No."

"Did you compliment him? Tell him that you also wanted to see him?"

"Stop," Sabine shouted. "That won't help. And I need to be alone. I'm sorry. I know you're here to help me, but I think I have to figure this out on my own. I'm sure Mutti would be happy if you visited her."

For a moment Inga couldn't move. She thought of the foehn, the hot winds back home in the mountains that left a purple hue in the sky, and were blamed for headaches, bad moods, and even suicides. Was that how Sabine thought of Inga, as something like a foehn—an oppressive, burdensome presence?

Inga gathered her strength and stood. At the door, she took one last look at Sabine, who stayed on the floor with her arms wrapped around her knees. She would have liked to have gone to her, to brush her hair, to comfort her. To promise it would all be fine.

"Well my girl," she said. "It was lovely to see you and to meet the baby. I wish you all the best. Tomorrow I will book a flight back to Switzerland."

"I'm sorry," Sabine muttered, without raising her head.

Chapter Ten

Another Plan

Frankfurt am Main, Germany
1934

Arnold found Rigmor's gloves on his sofa the next morning. He wanted to return them, but could not get himself to walk to the Blumenthals. Although he preferred to think of anything but his encounter with Rigmor, his brain replayed the scene over and over, and shame became a constant.

He waited three days to phone her, and when he did, the butler informed him that she was unavailable, a clear message that she wanted nothing to do with Arnold. Or so he assumed.

Still, he could not give up and telephoned two days later. Again she wouldn't speak to him.

On December twentieth, he sat in his chilly office. A blanket covered his shoulders. He wished for hot tea and a warm fire. But he refused to give in to his physical desires and scribbled notes for a paper he'd been working on for months.

A knock jolted him. The blanket slid to the ground as he stood. He moved toward the door, but before he opened it, Inga strode in wearing a long fur coat, a stylish hat and black leather gloves.

Arnold froze. There was something about Inga that always pushed him left of center. Most people had good and bad thoughts, kind and unkind, but they chose to reveal more of the good. Not Inga. All thoughts and judgments seemed to be delivered with equal frankness.

She stared at him expectantly. "May I take your coat?" he finally asked.

"Rigmor is in a terrible way," Inga replied, showing no sign of removing her coat. "You have not come to see her."

Arnold stepped backed, knocking into his desk. "I have telephoned, but she won't take my calls. I thought it might be best to wait until after Christmas." He glanced out of the window. A slate of fog obscured the Cathedral.

"Christmas is just another day. Why would that make a difference?" Inga asked.

He wished she would keep her voice down. It had a piercing quality that made him wince.

"It has nothing to do with Christmas, per se," he began. "It is only that some people get more anxious around a holiday. Of any sort of religion."

Her fingers brushed the air. "I'm not interested in religion. I am only interested in helping my sister."

He glanced down, needing to shield himself from her glare. "Can you tell me a bit more about her symptoms?"

"The same. Not sleeping, not eating. She feels as if she can't go on. She imagines things that aren't there—shadows at night, insects under her skin. There seems to be no relief. I just can't understand. She seemed hopeful before this episode, and then it was as if she fell off a cliff. You must have some idea of why. You are her doctor."

"I am not her doctor." He held up his hand. "I didn't mean to sound so gruff. But it's important that you know that I can't be her doctor, as our relationship is not a doctor-patient one." He bumbled on. "It could be the lack of light. I have a number of patients who find the winter months more difficult, and there are papers that have been written on the effect of reduced sunlight. Would you like me to find those for you?"

"No." She walked to the window, touched a finger to the glass, and stared into the mist. "I don't think it's about darkness or light. Therese thinks that perhaps Rigmor's post ovulation cycle is somehow out of kilter. Did you notice anything different the night of the symphony? Were there any warning signs?"

"Nothing at all." He felt disfigured by shame and guilt. He could only imagine this downturn was his fault.

"I suppose there is no simple answer," Inga said. "Not that I thought there was." She sighed, seeming softer, more resigned.

Arnold moved his desk chair to the center of the room so that Inga could sit. She peeled off her gloves.

"Has she been able to do anything?" he asked.

"Sometimes she sits in bed with her sketchpad. But the drawings are disturbing. They are of cages and frightful faces." Inga shook her head.

"She feels trapped, perhaps," Arnold said.

"My mother hovers and paces and brings soup that Rigmor doesn't want. And yes, I do think she feels confined by the home, but she won't leave her room, so how can she not feel imprisoned there?"

"I have been wondering if it wouldn't help her to go somewhere."

"Where?" Inga asked.

"I was thinking of an institution, a place called Sonnenstein. She would have space to find her way. They have warm salt baths, music rooms, and beautiful gardens."

Inga looked horrified. "An insane asylum?"

"God, no. It does offer shelter to some who are sick, but it is more of a spa, where she can rest, where she might not feel so closed in. There are people there who are not insane, who have mild disorders, some nervousness, nothing different from Rigmor. And I happen to know the director there. He is at the top of our field."

"What is his name?" Inga asked, taking out her notepad.

"Paul Bohm." Arnold hoped she wouldn't interrogate him further. He had met the famous psychiatrist once, at a conference. It was highly doubtful Bohm would remember Arnold.

"Aside from a needed rest, might this Bohm have other treatments?"

"Yes, of course. And she would naturally have a private room. The setting is lovely. On the Elbe."

Inga jotted for a moment, then put away her notepad and stood. "Come at seven tonight. My mother will not be home." Once again, she walked out without saying goodbye.

Arnold wrapped his blanket around his shoulders. He did believe it would be best for Rigmor to try an institution. Yet something nagged at him, a sense that he was sending her away because of his own failings, as a doctor and a man. He imagined what other doctors might say, and each time he reached the same conclusion—that she needed a retreat, away from the city, away from her mother and sister, away from him.

By the time Arnold arrived at the Blumenthals', his ears were numb. Inga greeted him at the door and explained that Rigmor had been in a frantic state a few hours ago, but had calmed down since. When they reached the bedroom, Arnold sat and looked at Rigmor, who lay perfectly still, staring at the ceiling. Inga helped her sister up.

"Arnold is here." She ran her fingers through Rigmor's hair, beginning to plait it.

"We talked about Sonnenstein," Inga told Arnold.

"I want to go," Rigmor said, glancing at him. Her face was gaunt, and her voice weak. "I want to be with other people who are like me."

"There is no rush," Arnold said. "It's something we can think about."

"I don't want to wait," Rigmor said.

Inga stopped plaiting and reached for something under the bed. "I told Arnold about your sketches."

"No," Rigmor said, her voice strong for an instant.

Inga dropped the pad at the foot of the bed.

"Do you think it would be all right if I had a moment to speak to Rigmor alone?" Arnold asked, looking first at Inga, then Rigmor.

Both women nodded.

"I was so sorry to hear you weren't feeling well," he began after Inga closed the door.

Rigmor put a hand on her chest. "I feel as if an entire ocean sits on me. It's hard to breathe."

With great effort, she pushed herself up so that she was sitting straighter. He wanted to help, but he didn't want his touch to feel intrusive. "I really want to go away. I can't tolerate any more energy and time wasted on me."

Arnold cleared his throat. "Do you think that this episode had anything to do with us—with what happened at my home?"

He still had his coat on. His hands dove into his pockets and balled into fists. Yes, a part of him wished she would say it had nothing to do with him, but the larger part of him wanted the truth, wanted her to talk about her feelings of anger, or resentment, or whatever else she might be harboring.

Rigmor's eyes focused on something behind him. "Will you please talk with my mother? Tell her it would help me to go away."

"I can try," he said. "But that night…"

"I just want to go away," she interrupted.

"I'm so sorry for everything."

Her face tightened. "Don't be. That will make things worse. Then I will worry about you as well."

He loosened his fingers and put his hands on the eiderdown. The only word that came to him was sorry. He was about to speak when the door flew open.

Frau Blumenthal marched in, wearing a babushka and a fur coat. Inga followed.

"What is going on in here?" Frau Blumenthal stood close to the foot of the bed.

Inga sidled next to Arnold. "I asked him to come."

"Has there been any improvement since we have had this man in our lives?" she asked Inga, her anger verging on tears.

"It comes in waves. We know that. This isn't his fault." Inga's shoulders arched back, her stance defensive—a different woman, he thought, to the one who had braided her sister's hair minutes earlier.

Frau Blumenthal picked up the sketchpad. She flipped through the pages and fear crossed her face. As she handed the pad to Inga, Arnold peered over her shoulder. The sketch was of a woman who looked like Rigmor with chains around her ankles and a gag on her mouth. Behind her, a man carried a scythe; he had wolfish teeth and Hitler's face.

"If the wrong hands see that," Frau Blumenthal said. "We could all be carted off." She took the pad from Inga and threw it in the fireplace.

"You are making catastrophes where there are none," Inga answered.

"Please stop," Rigmor begged.

"I'm sorry, my darling," Frau Blumenthal told her.

Inga turned to her mother. "We thought that it might be good for Rigmor to go somewhere. Somewhere she could get the right treatment."

"She is not going anywhere," Frau Blumenthal answered, and then looked at Rigmor. "I don't want you at some place where you will have no one."

"Arnold will be there," Inga blurted.

Was she serious? He would not be there. Why say something like that to Rigmor? It was not just a lie but a cruel one.

"I spoke to the director today," Inga continued. "He is one of the best doctors in the world. He is against any sort of punitive treatment. Rigmor would have a beautiful room overlooking the Elbe River."

"Have you already chosen the wallpaper as well?" Frau Blumenthal asked.

"Mother, please—I want to go," Rigmor said, and then shuddered so violently that Arnold was sure she was having a seizure.

He held her shoulders to comfort her. The convulsion lasted only a few seconds, but left Rigmor paler than before.

"She really should rest," he said.

"Yes," said Frau Blumenthal, glaring at Inga. "She shouldn't be involved in these arguments." She kissed Rigmor's cheek.

Arnold glanced at Rigmor, hoping he could convey everything that he was feeling—that he was sorry for any pain he might have caused, that he understood how difficult it was for Rigmor to be tugged between her mother and her sister, and that he did believe a sanatorium might be just the thing she needed.

* * *

In the drawing room, Inga tried to find words that wouldn't anger her mother, but all she could think about was Rigmor's horrible sketch.

"Frau Blumenthal," Arnold began. "I understand the thought of an institution is frightening."

Inga nodded. He seemed to know how to approach the subject. She would keep quiet for the moment.

"Sonnenstein is modern," he continued, "not only in their beliefs, but their techniques. Dresden is nearby, and is known to have a good cultural center. Some say it rivals what we have in Frankfurt."

Inga watched her mother uncross her feet and plant them on the floor. She looked like a bulldog. "And in a year's time there will be another place espousing to be the most modern. It means nothing. Rigmor is going nowhere. I will not have her in some decrepit institution left alone to rot."

"She will not be alone," Inga said. "Arnold will be there."

"But," Arnold began.

Inga held up a hand for him to stop. "Not now," she said, and turned back to her mother. "Rigmor needs a fresh start, and a facility where there are many good doctors. Let her try at least. If she hates it, or we hate it, she can leave whenever she wants."

"You would keep a close watch?" Frieda asked Arnold, her voice dropping.

"I must be honest. I don't, at the moment, have any intention of leaving my post at the University. I am unsure why Inga thinks otherwise."

Inga met his gaze. "Because I have spoken with Bohm, and he is offering you the position of assistant director."

She noticed his eyebrows rise, even as he glanced sideways, trying to hide that he was pleased by the news. Had there been more time, had Rigmor not been in such a bad way, Inga would have managed this differently.

Frieda glared at Arnold. "If Inga believes it is best that you be there to help Rigmor, then that is what you will do." For a moment, Inga felt proud. It was rare, unheard of actually, that Frieda acknowledged Inga had such influence.

Frieda continued to watch Arnold, her mouth forming a perfectly straight line. Inga didn't know what her mother was about to say, but it was not going to be pleasant.

"Incidentally," Frieda continued. "I know you did not take Rigmor to the symphony, as you said. You could not really have thought my driver wouldn't have told me what occurred."

Arnold instantly turned red. "She doesn't like crowds," he said.

It took Inga a moment to unravel the events. Rigmor and Arnold had had sex. For some reason it did not go well, and consequently Rigmor was suffering. And of course it was in large part Inga's fault. But what could have gone so wrong?

"If Rigmor really wants to go to this place you speak of," Frieda began. "Then she will go. The two of you will work out the details." She walked to the door. "I will take my whiskey in the small drawing room," she told a servant.

As soon as the door was closed, Arnold jumped out of his

chair. "I cannot leave my post at the University."

"What happened between you and Rigmor?" Inga asked.

"Nothing." He fiddled with the cuff of his shirt. "I don't believe we can have a productive discussion when emotions are so high. I will come and see Rigmor tomorrow if that's what she wants." Inga rushed to block his path to the door.

"Rigmor was white as a ghost the morning after you were with her," she said. "I will never forget it. I asked her at least fifty times what was wrong, and she didn't speak. Not a word."

"It is between us," he whispered.

"So you did have sex?"

His head dropped. "It didn't work."

"But why?" she asked.

"Faulty machinery." He glanced at the window.

"But you are young."

"It's not about age."

"Has it worked with other women?" she asked.

"I won't answer that," he said.

"You need to tell me. If it hasn't worked, and it is clearly you, she needs to know that. It could help her tremendously. Imagine if she is sitting in a pool of self-doubt because she thinks she might be unattractive to men."

"It has nothing to do with her," he said. "She is completely aware of that."

Inga paced from the door to the fireplace. "I should have never suggested it."

"It is not your fault. I should have known better."

"But why didn't she talk to me? I could have helped."

"We decided it was best to tell no one."

The realization that she was on the outside, that they didn't want to include her, wounded Inga more than anything she could remember. She walked to the door and held it open for Arnold.

When he was gone, she sunk onto one of the couches.

Klaus came in about ten minutes later. Inga watched him, the way he lit his pipe, the way he sat as if his place in the world would never slip. Whomever he was sleeping with, Klaus did not suffer from faulty machinery.

"Arnold seemed in a state," he said.

"He and Rigmor." Inga stopped, feeling awkward with her own husband, not sure how to put it. "They. Well, they tried but it didn't work."

Klaus puffed, and then chuckled. "My dear wife," he said. "Our friend Arnold does not have a taste for women."

"But..." she began and stopped.

"You did not see it?" Klaus asked.

"No."

Klaus smoked contemplatively. "We are on tremulous ground. I suppose it would be unwise for people these days to show deviant sexuality."

"It's hardly deviant," Inga said, thinking of Klaus's appetite for bottom-smacking.

"You have a more evolved intellect. I'm afraid that is not the case with the masses."

She should have recognized it ages ago. After all, Arnold had never once, not even for a second, tried to flirt with her. She had wondered why that was the case, and decided it was his way of protecting Rigmor, of showing affection for only her. It was one of the reasons Inga had thought Arnold and Rigmor would be a good match. What a fool she was.

Klaus went to bed, and Inga stayed in the drawing room, feeling hurt that Rigmor had not trusted her. Her dear sister, her truest companion and friend had chosen another confidante.

* * *

Arnold went to a pub. People drank and sang folk songs and danced as if the world was a good and happy place. He had six beers and then, on his stumble home, he sang, and shouted, heil dummkopf.

The next morning, he sat in his office with a pounding headache. He looked at the phone, half expecting it to ring—to be Inga scolding him, or Frieda telling him she had reported him to the head of the University, or Bohm calling to talk about the position.

And what if Bohm did call? Arnold couldn't just leave his job. He had ties in Frankfurt, and the University was not some second-rate institution. In fact, it had produced a number of Nobel Prize winners.

He thought of Rigmor, how pale and thin she'd looked. But she had seemed to have her wits about her, and was clear about what she wanted.

When a call finally came, at ten minutes to four, Arnold grabbed the receiver on the first ring. He announced himself and then held his breath. It was Bohm. The conversation lasted for a solid twenty minutes. By the time it ended, Arnold felt exhausted but also deeply interested.

The truth—he hadn't published in over a year, and his patient roster had declined, which he attributed to the wave of nationalism. People pumped themselves up with extremism, a false remedy.

Two days later, when the official offer arrived from Sonnenstein, Arnold signed the document.

Chapter Eleven

Holgart

Belmont, Massachusetts
1984

When Inga woke, her nose was a bit congested, probably from the dry heat in the hotel. But her throat did not hurt and her mind felt alert, so no need to worry about catching a cold.

An idea, fully formed, sat in her brain. She knew exactly what had to be done, and it did not involve booking a ticket back to Switzerland. Instead she had the front desk place an overseas call to Arlesheim.

Arnold answered on the fourth ring. She announced herself quite loudly, even though Arnold sounded a few meters away, not an ocean's distance from her.

He asked about her journey and her health, and if the hotel was suitable. All well-meaning questions that she did not have time for at the moment.

"You said you knew someone at McLean," she said. "A man with a good position?"

"It's been a number of years since we spoke, but I'm sure he'll remember me," Arnold replied.

"Could you arrange a meeting for me with your friend? Preferably sooner than later. I am free this morning."

"I will call now. And how do you find Sabine?" he asked.

"Once I complete the task I have in mind, I think she will improve more quickly. She has had these types of episodes before, so it is not simply post-partum as we had hoped. I will let you go so that you can make that call."

It wasn't long before her own phone rang. Dr. Holgart said he could meet with her in an hour.

When Inga stepped into his office, she felt instantly at ease. Here was a room that befitted a man in charge. A beautiful Oriental carpet softened the space. On one end of the room was a long mahogany desk; on the other, a tasteful sitting area with a sofa and three armchairs. Although she lived in a smallish chalet in a Swiss village, Inga's aristocratic roots remained. She still found comfort with the elite—a fact that she did not advertise, but recognized was not easily changed.

Holgart shook Inga's hand. "I am so pleased to meet a friend of Arnold's," he said.

His skin was tight and plastic, as if he belonged in Madame Tussaud's. He wore a handsome gray suit with a polka-dot bowtie. He had small blue eyes and such thin eyebrows Inga wondered if he did something unnatural to them. She thanked him for seeing her on such short notice. After they sat, he spoke to her in his mediocre French, telling her of the places he'd visited in Europe.

She nodded politely and spoke French with a near perfect accent.

He told her that the paintings on the wall, all of distinguished directors of the hospital, inspired him, and that he hoped that his painting would someday hang on the walls of this hallowed institution. But he would have never made it this far without Arnold, he added. Inga felt warmed hearing this about her friend.

Holgart crossed his legs. "I was such a nervous, shy man when I was young." He closed his eyes for a moment as if he was travelling back in time. "It was difficult for me to get my words out."

"It is good you found your voice," she said.

"Thanks to Arnold. He knew straight away that I was gay." He looked at Inga. "I hope that doesn't shock you."

"Not at all," she replied, glad she had learned the meaning of the word only yesterday.

"I had researched conversion therapies. I didn't want to be who I was. But Arnold." He stopped for a moment of reverence. "He was such a genius, you know. He taught me not to be ashamed."

"Arnold has a good understanding of humans," Inga said, hoping they could talk soon about the reason for her visit.

"The Nazis had us killed," Holgart said.

Inga bristled. "I didn't know you were German."

"Oh, I'm not German. No, I was talking about how they killed the gays. I don't know how people survived during those times. How people like you and Arnold came through it so wonderfully and well-adjusted."

She squeezed the strap of her handbag, took a deep breath, and stared directly at Holgart. "I have a granddaughter in McLean, and I very much want to help her."

"Yes, Arnold told me that was the case."

"My granddaughter has a baby and a family member must be with the baby at all times, which is proving difficult. Sabine needs to see her child and I thought that I could hire a nurse who could fetch the baby from its child-minding center, and then I would accompany them to visit Sabine."

He fiddled with his bowtie. "An outside nurse?"

"Yes, I don't think a nurse from your institution could be hired to watch a baby."

He tapped his foot. "No, it must be someone from the outside. Would it be a female nurse?"

"Would that make a difference?"

"No, I suppose not. I do tend to think aloud." He grinned. "And when do you see this nurse starting?"

"As soon as possible. It would relieve Sabine's husband of driving so much."

"I'll have to speak to the doctor in charge of her unit." He flicked a few fingers. "But that shouldn't be a problem." He smiled at Inga. "I will have my secretary get you the names of some agencies."

"Thank you," Inga said with a tip of the head.

"Now," said Holgart, rubbing his hands together. "I have a great favor to ask you."

"Anything." She owed him a debt and would be happy to pay it.

"I have started to write a book about how mental illness affects siblings. The sick child often becomes the favorite. I would like to interview you and find out how your sister's illness might have changed your life."

The words raced out of this man without a thought, or so it seemed, for his listener.

"I would love to hear your perspective," Holgart continued. "Arnold said he was close to Rigmor."

Inga put a hand on her chest. She had not heard her sister's name spoken aloud in many years. Her breathing became shallow. She needed to hold onto the arm of the sofa, afraid she might faint.

"Oh dear," Holgart said. "I have upset you."

Upset was too mild a word. She opened her mouth, but only a soft groan escaped.

Holgart stood. "May I get you a glass of water?"

She shook her head, and he sat next to her. "No," she whispered. She had meant, no don't sit so close, but he didn't understand. He placed a hand on her shoulder.

"What can I do?" he asked.

She pushed his hand away. "It was not Arnold's family." She took a breath. "He should not have spoken about it."

"I am so sorry. When he revealed the account to me, it seemed that it was his story as well."

"It was not," she said, folding her hands and closing the topic. If she hadn't needed something from this man, she would not have stayed. "I would like to get a few things for Sabine's ward. It needs a bit of sprucing up. I think it helps people to have a nicer environment."

"How generous of you," Holgart said. "But Arnold didn't say it was a secret."

Inga clasped her handbag and stood. "I cannot speak for Arnold." She walked to the door. The room felt claustrophobic. "I will be in touch if I need anything more," she said, walking out.

"Yes, keep me posted. And come visit me anytime," Holgart called, as she was already some distance away.

Chapter Twelve

The Asylum

Prina, Germany
1935

On his last day at the University, a few of Arnold's colleagues bought him a farewell drink, patted him on the back, and wished him well. In nearly three years at Frankfurt, he had published only two papers, and as far as he could tell, made a less-than-average impression. Perhaps this fortuitous opportunity was just what he needed.

Arnold took the train to Dresden, his elbow perched on the windowsill of his compartment. He looked out at the landscape, the churches rising from small villages, the farmland, the grazing cows, the forests. As the train neared Dresden, Arnold noticed his heartbeat accelerating. It was not every day that one becomes the assistant to Paul Bohm.

A hired car met him at the station. Arnold introduced himself as Dr. Richter, then paused and added, "Assistant Director."

The car pulled into an area where there were three separate buildings. The biggest by far, a castle, a schloss, with twin towers on either side, rose above the others. Next to the fountain at the center of the courtyard was a statue of children at play.

An orderly greeted Arnold in the main entrance hall, a stunning room—the size of it, the chandelier, the deep red carpeting, the antique furnishings, all tasteful and expensive.

Arnold was led to his quarters, which consisted of a bedroom with a view of the Elbe, a study, and a sitting room. Initially, he'd felt a bit bullied by Inga into taking this position, but as he sat in his new study, looking out the floor-to-ceiling window, watching boats glide past, he felt gratitude.

He washed up, ready to take a look around the grounds, but he was not sure what Bohm had scheduled. In the end, Arnold waited in his room for further instructions. He gazed at an oak tree, a few meters from his window. The oak was native to this part of Germany, considered one of the greenest places in the world. He looked at the small buds that dotted the branches. Renewal surrounded him.

About an hour later, Arnold heard a knock. He stood and combed his fingers through his hair, expecting his visitor to be Bohm. Instead, a servant held out a tray with lunch.

He ate the sausage, potatoes, salad and peas, all excellent, but he also began to feel a rising apprehension at the fact that no one had formally welcomed him. He placated himself by rationalizing that things were done differently here, that people valued a slower, healthier, unrushed pace.

Finally, at five in the evening, a young man in a gray suit announced that he would escort Arnold to Bohm's office.

"And how do you find our humble establishment?" Bohm asked, as soon as Arnold sat in one of the leather armchairs at the desk. There was a vague scent of fresh cologne. The room was large, conservatively decorated, with filing cabinets lining one wall and bookcases along another.

"It is very impressive. It has a feel of an ancient castle with the most modern amenities."

Bohm laughed. "You sound as if you could be a good salesman."

Arnold gave a nervous smile.

Bohm's bald head appeared as if it had been shined. He had a deep voice and too many teeth in his mouth.

"I am looking forward to my work here," Arnold said.

Bohm opened a folder.

"Very good. We are proud of our institution. We believe in a therapeutic environment for all of our patients."

Arnold nodded. "I have read about your beliefs, but to hear

them from the director himself is refreshing."

Bohm picked up a pen. "What can you tell me about Rigmor Blumenthal?"

Arnold would have preferred to talk about his responsibilities. But he wasn't about to contradict the wishes of his new superior at their first meeting.

"She is from Frankfurt am Main," he said. "Her family is well off and are known in the city's upper circles. But I'm sure you know this."

Bohm's lips moved as he wrote. "Does not hurt to repeat. We are thorough here, as you will soon see. I have in my notes that I have spoken to Inga Sommer, the sister, on four occasions. Would you say she is the family member in charge?"

Arnold crossed his legs and gave the question a moment's thought. "I suppose, yes, although the mother, Frau Blumenthal, is a determined woman."

"And the father?"

"He left years ago. I believe he was seeing another woman, and Frau Blumenthal couldn't tolerate it."

"Because of nerves?" Bohm asked.

"I do not think so. I don't find her to be a nervous woman. I believe she didn't want to live with him."

Bohm touched the pen to his cheek. "Interesting. It may have been quite difficult for her. Have you gotten that sense?"

"I suppose it might have been." Arnold realized that he never felt much of anything for Frau Blumenthal. She seemed to make life difficult for others, not the other way around. But, yes, it must have been stressful—to have one daughter who wasn't well, to run the household on her own, and to have another daughter who was the most strong-willed person Arnold had ever met.

"And the mother's behavior toward Rigmor? Is she ashamed? Angry? How would you characterize that?" Bohm opened a drawer, took out two cigars, and handed one to Arnold.

"I prefer not to smoke," Arnold said. "It doesn't agree with me."

Bohm raised his eyebrows. "Interesting. I don't know of any man who doesn't enjoy a fine cigar." He lit a match and puffed until the tip of the cigar glowed, then blew out a mouthful of smoke. "So, the mother?"

"I would say she is very protective. Perhaps overprotective, although I like to stay away from making judgments." Arnold suppressed a cough.

"But we are in this field to judge human personality, are we not?" Bohm asked.

It was a rhetorical question, or so Arnold thought, as he glanced at the bookshelves behind Bohm, and noted volumes of Goethe's work.

Bohm pressed. "You do not think we should judge character?"

"I like to think we examine character," Arnold said.

"So Rigmor has no father and an overprotective mother." He smoked.

"Would you mind if I inquired about my responsibilities here?" Arnold asked. "Will I be seeing patients on a regular basis?"

Bohm smiled, showing his yellowed teeth. "What else would you be doing?" He laughed. "Although we do have the best nursing program in the country here." He winked. "I did see that you are not married. The Party wishes that all healthy German men be married by the age of twenty-six. And you are how old?"

"Twenty-nine," Arnold lied. He was actually thirty-two. "I would like to pursue my career."

"You can do both," Bohm answered. "We should be grateful that this present government supports so many of the things we believe in. We can't ignore that, even if we disagree with other views."

"True," Arnold said, reflecting that he would be imprisoned if the Nazis knew his preference for men.

Bohm walked to the windowsill, where there were a few

potted plants, all meager and droopy, none with flowers or interesting leaves. They hardly seemed worth caring for, and yet Bohm, while keeping his cigar in his mouth, dribbled some water into the pots from a small brass watering can. "There, there," he mumbled to the plants. Then he marched back to his desk, once again the bold, authoritarian doctor. But he did not sit.

"Will I be getting a list of who I am to see?" Arnold said.

"Do you think Rigmor's mother is jealous of her daughter?" Bohm asked.

"I have never gotten that sense," Arnold replied, masking his impatience.

"Tell me then, what is your sense of why Rigmor should be in this institution?"

"She is fragile." He paused. "She has trouble with her nerves. I think also depression. I believe that her condition has worsened with her mother's and sister's worrying. It is a vicious cycle. I believe she needs a good rest to escape her downward spiral. I believe—"

Bohm held up a hand for Arnold to stop, and extinguished his cigar. "You do not need to begin every sentence with I believe." He grinned. "If you are the speaker, we can assume you are expressing your opinions."

Arnold's face heated. "Of course."

"You were saying?" Bohm asked.

He had forgotten his point. Something about the vicious cycle of nerves. "I," he began, and stopped himself. "Rigmor is too keen to please others. That, I believe, is part of the problem."

"Symptoms?" Bohm sat, but then almost immediately sprung up and made a circular path around the room.

Arnold twisted his neck right and left to keep his gaze on Bohm. "There have been a number over the years. Insomnia, dizzy spells, and the like."

"Hysteria?" Bohm, sitting at his desk again, picked up a pen and tapped it on his chin.

"Perhaps some would call her a hysteric," said Arnold. "But I find that diagnosis overused in women."

"Interesting," Bohm said. "Is she pretty?"

"I suppose so," Arnold answered, not sure of the relevance.

Bohm continued with this line of questioning, asking about Rigmor's features, her nose, her hair, her figure. Arnold answered as objectively as he could.

"I sensed during my phone calls with Inga that Inga is quite sexualized," Bohm said. "Do you find that true?"

"I cannot judge that."

"But you must. It is an essential part of our job, is it not?" He glanced at his plants and looked as if he was about to tend to them again, but stopped himself.

"Then I would have to answer in the affirmative."

"Would you say the same of Rigmor?" Bohm asked. He seemed to have his questions lined up, ready to shoot, like a stream of bullets.

"No. They are completely different."

Bohm stood and picked up the extinguished cigar. "Could she be repressing her desires?" He paced. "Or is it that she is frightened she will end up with a man like her father?"

"I suppose both are possibilities," Arnold answered. "But I still think it will be good for her to get away from her mother and sister, to get some room to breathe."

"Any delusions?" He put the cigar in his mouth and chewed on it.

"I would describe them as night terrors," Arnold said. "Not actual delusions."

"But there is some break with reality?"

"Some."

"Do you see her as a good candidate for sterilization?" He made a sucking noise.

Arnold's heart lurched. "She is certainly not promiscuous. I don't imagine she will be married soon, if ever, so I don't know if it would be necessary."

Bohm looked at his watch. "It's nearly dinnertime. We have excellent food here. We believe that our patients should get the required amount of protein every day. I am very fond of fresh fish."

"I as well," Arnold said, expecting to finally hear about his position.

Bohm walked to his desk, sat, and closed the folder. "It was a pleasure to meet you."

Arnold remained seated, holding the arms of the chair. "My duties. I am not sure what is expected of me. Aside of course from being Rigmor's doctor."

"Oh, but you cannot be her doctor. You are clearly much too close to her to see her objectively. I have watched your skin redden as we talked about her. You have avoided my gaze numerous times, and when I asked about her figure, you crossed your arms." He modeled the gesture.

Arnold felt humiliated.

"This is what we do, is it not?" Bohm asked. "We study behavior. It is my job to notice."

Arnold saw the wisdom, and he would now be more aware of his own techniques. He was already learning a great deal from this unconventional man.

Bohm stood and gestured to the door. "You will like the food here."

Arnold cleared his throat. "I was wondering about my role?"

"At the moment, I don't have those details. I wanted to meet you first." Again, he gestured to the door.

"But you must have some idea of what you expect from your assistant director?"

"Ah," Bohm said. "I think I am beginning to understand now. We have many assistant directors here. The title gives families more confidence."

"Oh."

"And perhaps — and I do hate to bring up this awkward topic — but perhaps you were not aware of the money the Blumenthals have so generously donated."

"I was not." But of course they would have.

"I will honor all terms of their agreement," Bohm said.

"Agreement?"

"Oh dear," said Bohm, and sat once more. "I didn't realize they had told you nothing." He rested his chin on his fist. "I hate to leave a good man like you in the dark. They asked that you have a position here."

"You did not hire me based on my reputation?" Arnold said.

"I am afraid I had never heard of you. I did speak with a colleague of yours in Frankfurt and you seem to know your right from your left. So to speak." He picked up the folder and gave it a small wave.

"So will I have any work to do?"

"My good man, of course you will. You needn't look so despondent. This is a fine institution. You can work on the east ward. The doctors there are always complaining about lack of staff." He walked to where Arnold was sitting and clapped his shoulder. "You will be well paid for work that is not that hard. You can go for long walks, take time to read." He smiled. "I envy your position."

Arnold had signed a contract that said he would stay for a year. Of course he could get himself disqualified, but that would jeopardize future prospects. Then there was the promise he had made to Rigmor — that he would be here for her. But he felt as if he'd been deceived.

"And when will we meet again?" Arnold asked.

Bohm waved his hand, ushering Arnold out of the office. "I will talk with you after I do an initial assessment of Rigmor. In the meantime, try to enjoy all that we have to offer here." He grinned. "And perhaps a nurse or two."

Arnold managed a light, appropriate chuckle, although he

hardly felt light or frivolous. When he reached to shake hands, Bohm seemed not to notice. He was too busy for a man like Arnold, who was only here because a wealthy family had paid him to be not much more than a nursemaid.

* * *

Inga sat between Frieda and Rigmor as the black Mercedes sped them toward Sonnenstein.

"Are you carsick?" Inga asked Rigmor, who looked pale and withdrawn.

"A bit," Rigmor replied.

The past two weeks had been dreadful, with Rigmor vomiting morning and night. Her skin seemed loose on her bones, her eyes were red-rimmed, and her hair, which she now always kept in a bun, had turned brittle. A devastating decline. Whenever Rigmor seemed a little stronger, Inga tried to get a sense of how her sister was feeling about going to Sonnenstein, and being around Arnold. Her answers, although spoken with little passion, were consistently favorable.

As soon as they pulled up to the main entrance, Arnold trotted down the steps and opened the back door for Rigmor. He held her hand as she exited the car. She smiled and pretended nothing was wrong, but her movements were stiff, as if she was in her seventies, not her twenties.

"Would you like me to show you around the grounds?" Arnold asked Rigmor.

"The journey was tiring," Frieda said. "Please show us to her quarters."

Inga believed a short walk might have helped Rigmor's appetite, but this was not the time to bicker.

The air had a countryside freshness; trees were budding, and Inga imagined visiting Rigmor in the spring, taking walks along the river or into the hills, and doing watercolors of the landscape.

The lobby of the building was small and clean, decorated with a few armchairs and nice paintings. The first staircase they climbed was wide, had good light, nice carpeting, and freshly painted walls. A second staircase led to the tower room. It felt like something out of an old castle, with damp walls and a mildew smell. Frieda turned and glared at Inga.

Arnold nodded, seeming to note their discomfort. "The climb is well worth it," he said.

When they reached the top floor, Arnold led them to Rigmor's room. The lighting was excellent, something Inga believed was crucial. Other things could be changed—the furniture, the artwork—but not the light. Rigmor walked to one of the windows overlooking the Elbe. Inga joined her.

"What do you think?" she asked.

Rigmor's thin hand rested on the windowsill. "It's nicer than I expected."

A robin sang in the tree just outside of the window. "Look," Inga said. "Someone has come to greet you."

Rigmor touched the windowpane and smiled.

"It feels damp in here," Frieda said, as she walked the perimeter of the room.

"I think that was only the stairway," Inga replied. "The air in here feels dry."

"To me it feels damp."

Inga turned to her mother. "The light is good. And the bed is well positioned. The space is comfortable."

Frieda walked to the bed and pressed hard on the mattress. Then she turned on the bedside lamp. "There is not enough light from this. If Rigmor wants to read at night, it might hurt her eyes."

"I can look into getting another one," Arnold said.

Rigmor crossed the room and peered out of another window facing the hills, dotted with sheep. "It's so beautifully green," she said.

Frieda tapped her cane on the sofa and claimed the springs inside of it were old. The paintings were bland, and the armchair too soft for good posture.

"Mother," Rigmor said, approaching her. "I like it."

Frieda's gaze darted. Perhaps she was trying to find enough flaws to justify taking Rigmor back home.

"The room seems very satisfactory," Inga said. "I think what we should be concerned about is the treatments. Arnold, when will we be meeting with your director?"

His face flushed. "I don't believe he has a meeting scheduled with you today."

"But that can't be correct," Inga said. "He knew we were coming, didn't he?"

"I believe he does. But I'm afraid I don't know his daily comings and goings."

"But are you not his assistant?" Inga asked.

"I am." He shoved his hands into his pockets.

"Well then, I will go and see him now, and ask when he can meet with us." She walked to the door, and turned. "Arnold, you can point me in the direction of Bohm's office, and then perhaps get some tea and biscuits for my mother and Rigmor."

Outside, Inga said, "My mother and I expected that we would have a meeting. I'm surprised you didn't see to this."

He glanced downward. "Bohm is a busy man."

"Did you inquire about an appointment?" Inga asked.

He shook his head, looking rather small for such a tall, well-built man.

She patted his arm. "Well not to worry. I will go and see him now."

Arnold walked with Inga to the main building, then told her to take her first right; she would find Bohm's office at the end of a long corridor.

Inga stopped, opened her handbag, took out her compact and applied a fresh coat of lipstick.

Along the walls of the corridor were paintings of doctors—previous directors, she assumed. She approached an antechamber where a young man sat on a stool behind a high desk. His white-blond hair was cut close to his head.

"Is this the Director's office?" she asked, ready to knock on the door.

The young man hopped off his stool and guarded the door. "You must have an appointment to see the Director."

"Very well then—can you make one for me?"

He headed back to his desk and thumbed through a leather-bound book. "He has some time in two weeks. Would that suit you?"

"Absolutely not." Inga walked to the door and knocked.

"You cannot."

"He will see me," Inga said confidently. And if he didn't, she thought, then she would think twice about leaving Rigmor.

When the door opened, the young man said, "I told her you were busy. I told her she would have to wait two weeks."

Bohm waved a hand for his secretary to go back to his desk, and then took his time looking at Inga.

"I am Inga Sommer," she began. "Rigmor Blumenthal is my sister, and we have just arrived."

"So good of you to come and see me," he said, extending a hand.

His small eyes were alert and intelligent. "I did not mean to barge in," Inga said. "I thought Arnold would have set up a meeting for us. But it must have slipped his mind."

His eyes registered a vague acknowledgement. "Yes, of course. Dr. Richter sent you. And you are the sister of the patient. It is now all coming together for me." He held the door open for her to come in.

His office was spacious, but she didn't like that the curtains were half closed, or that the room smelled of cigar smoke.

"I would like to discuss Rigmor's treatment plan," Inga said.

Bohm gestured to the leather sofa. "First you must tell me all about your journey."

"My journey was thoroughly uneventful."

He laughed. "I suppose that is what we want from a journey."

"It depends on the type," she said. She had recently taken a train journey to Moscow with Fred. Their cabin was small and with every movement they seemed to bump each other, which led to constant lovemaking. Far from dull.

Bohm glanced up at the ceiling as if he was following the path of a fly. "You have chosen the best institution in the world for your sister."

"Her room is nice. But she is not here for the views."

He laughed again. A nervous habit, she decided.

"You are so amusing." He studied her. "And quite a beauty."

It was a common remark, one she had learned to ignore with decorum. "My mother is here, and of course she will also want to meet you. But you needn't go into too much detail with her about treatment plans, as she is not as well read as I am."

"Yes, I see," he said, and smiled again. "But I have not yet had the chance to meet your sister, so I'm afraid it would be impossible to give you any details."

"You do know of her case. Arnold, Dr. Richter, has surely spoken to you about her. And we have also spoken on occasion."

He slapped a hand on his knee. "I remember every word of our conversations. Naturally. I so look forward to meeting your sister and making sure she gets the best care."

"You must have some ideas from what you have heard."

"I do," he said. "But sharing my ideas at this point would be a terrible mistake. Without the whole picture, and doing a full interview, I would not want to give you the wrong impression. Imagine if I was an art critic and I saw only the first rough sketch of what would later become the Mona Lisa. Imagine if I told Da Vinci he was hopeless?" He circled his hand and laughed.

He had a point.

"How long do you think it will take for you to give us your opinion?"

"Excellent question," he said. "I like to have at least eight sessions, and also do some Rorschach tests. Have you heard of those?"

"Of course. I find the location aspects of the tests the most intriguing."

"I see," Bohm said. "You are very well read then? I think we will get along famously. Would you like a drink?"

"Not now. I will fetch my mother. Rigmor is too weak to come at the moment." She glanced at her watch. "I will return in about fifteen minutes. Does that suit you?"

"Yes," he replied.

She stood. "A word of caution. My mother can come off a bit hard sometimes, but you must understand that this is a very difficult day for her. To leave her daughter here."

"I understand." He hurried to the door and held it open.

Twenty minutes later, Inga was back in Bohm's office, this time with her mother and Arnold.

Bohm asked his secretary to get them a bottle of champagne and four glasses. Then he directed Inga, Frieda and Arnold to the small sitting area.

"This meeting calls for a toast, does it not?" He grinned.

"I do not find this is a joyous occasion," Frieda answered.

"Oh no. That's not what I meant at all. I only meant that we are so grateful to have you here."

Frieda held onto her cane as if it was a staff, and Inga thought Bohm overly solicitous.

"I have been told by my daughter, and Arnold, that you are an excellent clinician," Frieda said.

He placed a hand on his heart. "How kind of them."

Frieda shook her head. "We are not here for kindness or niceties. We have not come for tea or champagne. I am worried about my daughter and I would like to know what you can do here that we cannot do at home?"

Bohm nodded quickly, and Arnold shifted in his chair.

"I will myself be seeing her and providing you with a diagnosis and treatment protocol."

"You believe she will be cured then?" Frieda asked.

"I'm afraid I cannot say that with certainty at the moment. I think sometimes people misunderstand psychiatrists to be some sort of seers. But we are merely scientists. Wouldn't you agree, Arnold?"

Arnold sat straighter, like a student surprised the teacher had noticed him. "Yes, we are scientists."

"We follow the scientific method," Bohm continued. "Any deviation from that would be a mistake."

"What is Arnold's role in all of this?" Frieda asked.

Bohm turned to Arnold and studied him for a moment. "I believe him to be a good doctor." It sounded a bit like a question.

"That is not an answer," Frieda replied.

Inga cut in. "Will Arnold be keeping an eye on Rigmor? Making sure she eats well and goes on walks, and paints?"

"I see. Yes, that is exactly what he will be doing," Bohm told Frieda.

The secretary brought in a bottle of champagne and four glasses.

Bohm popped the cork. Glasses were filled. Frieda refused hers, yet Bohm proceeded with a toast anyway. "To good health," he said, clinking his glass with Inga's.

Frieda coughed.

Inga understood what her mother wanted. "We do have a matter we would like to bring up," she said. "I have read about your views on sterilization and although I do agree with them in theory, we are against Rigmor undergoing any unnecessary medical procedures. She is not physically strong."

Bohm waved a hand. "Yes, yes, I know exactly what you mean. It's when the practice affects someone we love. Then suddenly the whole thing appears in a different light."

"Exactly." Inga sipped her champagne, which was not very good.

"Can you promise that Rigmor will not undergo this process?" Frieda asked.

Bohm walked to his desk but he remained standing. "Unfortunately, I only have limited power," he said. "The Health Courts decide who will undergo the procedure. I can assure you they are very objective. And if, well if, it should come to that. Then, we will see."

"So there are ways to circumvent," Inga said.

"I certainly have some sway, but it will depend on Rigmor's diagnosis. Do you know that some studies have found that women have decreased symptoms of hysteria after the procedure? I am not suggesting that Rigmor has hysteria, but please do keep that in mind. It's not a terrible operation. In fact, biologically speaking, it is very simple, and not very intrusive." He looked at Inga, who smiled.

"I am firm on this point," Frieda said.

"I see," Bohm said. "And she is not promiscuous?"

"How dare you!"

"I did not mean to offend. But if I am going to defend her against the hereditary health courts and argue that she does not need to be sterilized, I must be completely prepared. Patients who appeal the court's decision are asked invasive questions."

Frieda leaned on her cane and stood. "I'm afraid this won't be an acceptable place for Rigmor. I thank you for meeting with us."

Bohm's mouth opened. But for once he was speechless.

"Mother," Inga said. "We thought long and hard about placing her here. Why not at least allow Director Bohm the chance to give us his professional opinion?"

"Under no circumstance do I want Rigmor to undergo any sort of operation."

"I really don't think we need to worry about that," Inga said. "We have Arnold watching over her, and Doctor Bohm might provide us with insights that we haven't yet heard."

"Frau Blumenthal, I do understand that this is difficult, and that coming to this decision was not easy, but I promise, we will provide her with excellent care," Bohm said. "Your daughter has been suffering now for how long?"

Frieda sat again. "For many years."

"Exactly. And I am sure you have tried everything you could think of. So I ask you, why not try this?"

Frieda sunk her head.

"You have fought so hard for so long," Bohm said. Inga watched him, pleased that he seemed to feel real compassion. "Let *us* try now. We have the skills, the medicine, and the facilities."

Frieda looked at Arnold, then Inga. "All right," she sighed. "But if anything happens, I will hold the two of you responsible."

Inga nodded, relieved that Rigmor would be given a chance.

On their way out, Frieda stopped at the door. "Your plants need more light," she told Bohm.

* * *

On the drive back to Frankfurt, Inga tried to focus on Fred, on how he longed to take her to Malta to see the Dwejra Bay, but all she could think of was Rigmor lying in bed at night, awake and terrified, seeing shadows and having no one to comfort her, no one to bring her a hot chocolate, no one to brush her hair.

The first few days of Rigmor's absence, Inga shopped, read a book about Malta, organized her painting studio by subject matter, and met a friend for tea. But soon the novelty of freedom turned to a lack of purpose. Inga thought obsessively about Bohm's findings. Every day, fifteen minutes before the post arrived, she paced in the foyer, her heels clacking lightly on the tiled floor as she assured herself the news would be good. Or at least not terribly bad.

After two weeks, she took a trip to a spa in Baden-Baden. It wasn't a sanatorium, but it was a place of healing, of taking in the mineral waters, and though far from Rigmor, Inga felt the smallest of connections. She stayed at the finest hotel, soaked in the baths, and watched one couple in particular. The woman, fiftyish, had short dark hair and a round belly. The man, who looked younger, had broad shoulders and hair on his arms that reminded Inga of fur. But it was not what they looked like, it was the way he kissed the woman's neck, the way she shivered with delight. They existed only for the other, and Inga thought if she had that, that singular vision, perhaps she would cease to feel so restless and in need of distraction.

Fred visited. The afternoon he arrived, they ate lamb chops on the balcony, but the meal was cut short by his need to touch her, and for the rest of the day she felt as if she'd found her center again.

The following morning, they had breakfast in the main dining room. After he asked her to pass the orange marmalade, she looked into his brown eyes. "Would you ever leave your wife for me?"

He laughed. "Is that what you really want?"

"If it is, would you give it to me?"

He nibbled his toast. She brushed a crumb from the side of his mouth. "You already have more of me than anyone," he told her, which she knew to be true.

A good portion of his time was spent meeting clients to whom he could sell expensive luggage, purses, and briefcases. He also liked to meet politicians, more in England now than Germany. Yet still, he did not hide from the Nazis. He went to their clubs, talked diplomatically to them about their views, and tried to get a few of them to see how dangerous it might be to follow Hitler. He didn't have much success, but he was determined.

His life was like an overflowing cupboard. There was not enough space for everything he was interested in. Painting and fishing were his central passions, trumping even his passion for women. Inga knew that she was not his only lover. He had made it clear early on that he loved women, every aspect of them, and the one thing he couldn't tolerate was a jealous mistress. He already had a jealous wife to contend with, which was more than enough for him.

Fred picked up his coffee. "What do you imagine it would be like? To be married to me?"

She hadn't really thought much about the marriage itself, it was more the idea that it would ground her somehow, give her more of a purpose—*the wife of Fred*. She imagined it would stop the unease she always carried. "I would see you more often," she said, grinning.

"You would not worry that I would find another woman?" When he smiled, he had one small dimple under his right eye. She reached across the table and caressed his cheek.

"I know how to keep a man," she told him.

He nodded, his eyes catching the light reflected by the crystal chandelier. "I believe you do. But the same cannot be said of me. I'm afraid I would not be able to keep you."

"But you would have me," she said.

"Not for long," he replied. "You have a wandering spirit and excitement will always be right outside of your door. It will not, my dearest, be in your home."

She pouted playfully. "I have never been unfaithful to you."

"Because you are free to do what you like. If we lived together, we would disagree about what bread to buy, about if I should have two or three cups of coffee for breakfast. You would want paintings of landscape, and I would want still-life. We would become a pair of squabbling ducks."

She held her head high. "I prefer to be a swan."

"Yes," he said. "They have the more difficult disposition."

After breakfast, they returned to her bedroom. He left that evening, and although she was sad to see him go, she knew the building anticipation at seeing him again would be her reward.

Inga stayed another week at Baden-Baden. She took long walks in the Black Forest and thought about the freedom that marriage to Klaus provided her. If she divorced, she would be viewed as a societal inferior—or worse, a woman soliciting a man. Fred had understood her, perhaps better than she understood herself. A marriage to him would not make her miss her sister any less, or settle the apprehension about leaving Rigmor in a place that had not inspired quite enough confidence in Inga.

Chapter Thirteen

Tablecloths

Belmont, Massachusetts
1984

Sabine's knee bounced as she twisted off the cap of the saltshaker, while Helen painted her nails.

"I didn't want Omama here. She would have made me crazy." Sabine screwed the lid back on. "But I feel guilty for making her leave. I should have been nicer."

On top of the guilt there was the fear that her panic was worsening. The previous night had been rough. Only a couple of hours of sleep, and a nightmare in which she was tied to a bed as a tarantula crawled on her chin, one of its legs dipping into her mouth.

Helen blew on her fingertips. She had rounds the next morning, and no one went to rounds looking more perfect, more put together, more unlike a patient, than Helen. And no one came out with fewer privileges.

"You probably weren't as bad as you think," Helen said.

"I wasn't nice," Sabine insisted. "She gets under my skin. Telling me how to keep a man. It's ridiculous. What year does she think we're living in?" Her leg bounced and she wondered if a Xanax would help.

"It sounds as if it's better that she left." Helen polished the nails on her other hand.

Frank charged in. "You have a visitor," he said to Sabine. "They brought the artillery."

Sabine glanced down the hall, her eyes widening. It couldn't be. There were two people, her grandmother being one. The other woman wore a nursing uniform, pushed a stroller with one hand

and carried something that looked like a folded playpen in the other. Omama pulled a large suitcase on wheels. *What the fuck?* "Omama." Sabine walked toward them. "I thought..."

"I decided I still had a purpose here." She stopped. "Come, help me pull this case."

Sabine didn't move. She looked into the stroller, saw Mia, who was clutching a yellow plastic key ring, and reached in. But a hand pulled her arm away.

"She just finished eating," the nurse said. "She had a good burp. I think it's best if you leave her where she is." Her manner was firm.

"Please get the case for me," Omama instructed. Also firm.

But Sabine couldn't not hold her baby. She reached in again.

"You can pick her up as soon as we settle in the dining room," Omama said. "It won't be long."

Feeling as if she was in the middle of some alternate reality, Sabine did what her grandmother asked.

In the dining area, Omama pointed to the left corner. "I think that is where we should set up," she told the nurse, who kicked up the lock on the stroller and proceeded to open the playpen.

"Sabine," Omama said. "Please put the case here." With two fingers, she gave the desired table a few firm taps.

Sabine looked at Helen, who watched, amused and baffled.

Omama unzipped the suitcase, taking out diapers and wipes. "I hired Cathy. She will fetch Mia in the morning from her child-minding center, bring her to my hotel, and then we will all come here." She counted the diapers and stacked them on another table. "She is fully licensed and is excellent with babies."

"But..."

"There are no buts," Omama stated. "This is what must be done. Tanner is a busy man, and one day he will do well for you. But he must be given the time he needs."

There was no way this was going to be allowed. Out of the suitcase came baby clothes, a can of formula and a few burp cloths.

Sabine leaned over the stroller. Whatever was happening, as surreal and Mary Poppins as it felt, the ache that was lodged in her throat all morning was gone.

"I think you should keep Mia's clothing in your room," Omama said, handing Sabine a few dresses, tights and onesies.

Sabine put the clothes on another table and reached for Mia.

Cathy rested a burp cloth on Sabine's shoulder. "She's a beautiful baby."

"Thanks," Sabine said, not sure how to act with this new nurse, or was she a nanny? Was she going to tell Sabine how to be a mother?

"She might need to be changed soon," Cathy said.

Sabine backed away from the woman whose mouth slanted downward.

In an hour, or in ten minutes, this whole caravan would probably be asked to leave, and Sabine was going to make sure she made the most of the time she had.

"Cathy is a good nurse," Omama said.

"I don't need a nurse to help with Mia," Sabine whispered, not wanting to hurt Cathy's feelings.

"You wanted to see your child," Omama said. She broke the stack of diapers into two piles.

"I did. But tomorrow is rounds, and I was going to ask them if I could have Mia stay with me alone now. John said I might get that privilege."

"It should not be a privilege for you to have your baby here. It should be a right."

Sabine moved back a few more steps and nodded to Omama, so they could speak privately. "They probably won't let Cathy stay," she whispered.

Omama did not whisper. "I interviewed four people yesterday and she was the best."

The weight of Mia on Sabine's chest felt glorious. "I'm really grateful that you did this. But…"

"You needed the help," Omama said. "And it is here. I have spoken to a doctor who is very high up. He has agreed to this, so you needn't worry."

"Who?" Sabine asked.

"A man with the name of Holgart."

"But I don't need a nurse."

"Someone must fetch her in the mornings and bring her back in the evening. I cannot drive. And the nurse is paid for a month. You may use her as you see fit."

"I won't be here that long." A month felt unfathomable. If she was locked up for that long, she would definitely go crazy.

"Then you can use her to help around the house, if you like. Most women have nurses after they have a baby."

Sabine didn't argue that that was actually not the case. At least not in this country, not in nineteen eighty-four.

Cathy finished setting up and Mia began to fuss. Sabine walked back and forth with the baby, cajoling her, jiggling her—whispering to her. Cathy handed Sabine a bottle of formula.

"She might need a top up on her lunch."

"Thanks." Sabine took the bottle that she would have preferred to get herself and went to sit with Helen, leaving Omama and Cathy in the corner by the playpen, stroller, diapers, and various other baby necessities.

Mia ate with gusto. "This setup is insane," Sabine whispered to Helen.

Helen looked at the baby. "At least you have her."

"You think they're really going to allow this? To have a nurse and my grandmother on guard?"

"Technically they're visitors," Helen replied. "If they leave by eight, they aren't breaking any rules."

Sabine heard rustling in the background, but didn't turn around. "What's going on?" she asked Helen, who grinned.

"Your grandmother brought tablecloths. White ones. Linen I

think."

"She did not."

Helen leaned to the right, her face open and happy. "She most certainly did. And honestly, they look good."

A couple of minutes later, Omama gestured for them to move out of the way. She shook out the tablecloth like a picnic blanket and then covered the cheap veneer.

"They're never going to allow these," Sabine said to Omama.

"Why on earth not?" she asked.

Sabine couldn't think of a good answer. "Because this is a mental hospital, not a hotel."

"You might not believe I know much of anything," Omama said. "But sometimes it's the small things that help. When people have a nicer surrounding, they are more apt to feel better. You'll see. And they will agree because Holgart has made sure to allow it."

"How did you meet him?" Sabine asked.

"A friend of a friend." She walked to the next table.

Mia finished eating, and Sabine asked Helen if she wanted to hold the baby. "Really?" Helen asked.

"Why not? We'll just get Dr. Holgart to approve."

Helen looked content as she rocked Mia, and Sabine felt happy she could give something to her friend, who was so generous, always willing to listen to whatever was on Sabine's mind.

Sabine watched Omama put ivory lace overlays on top of the tablecloths.

"Thank you," she called across the room.

The arrangement, which Sabine discovered when Omama had finished with the tables, consisted of Cathy bringing Omama and Mia to the hospital at about one in the afternoon every day, and staying until six, at which time, Cathy would bring Mia home, and get her ready for bed so that Tanner could be free to do whatever he wanted to do. Probably drink a few beers and watch a hockey game.

Among the nurses there were shrugs mixed with smiles and a few frowns of disapproval, but John liked it. He claimed people were more polite to one another, and the overall mood of the hall improved.

Omama continued to bring in more items—a kettle, a small vase with fresh flowers for each table. There were new teacups, still plastic, but white with a golden rim. She brought fresh cookies that she insisted were biscuits, a fancy word that most of the patients went along with, except Brenda, who kept saying the whole situation was fucked. People weren't here to be served in a teahouse, she said, they were here because they were sick, and they didn't need some old hag rushing around, serving them, or some weird woman with the face of a weasel standing there in a starched white uniform.

Sabine thought Brenda made some good points.

* * *

The florist's assistant delivered daises, carnations and roses at two in the afternoon. The laundering service came for the linens at three. Inga checked daily on the supply of tea and biscuits, and considered adding cake and fresh fruit to the menu. Those were the simple tasks. More difficult, and much more important, was the question of what Sabine would do with herself when she got out.

She wouldn't have Helen as a constant companion. She wouldn't have Cece's entertaining stories, or Keith, who leaned on Sabine as if she was a surrogate mother.

Inga sat at a small table, next to the swinging door of the kitchen. When Sabine returned from therapy, she asked her granddaughter to join her.

"What will you do when you leave here?" she asked.

Sabine pulled back, as if the question was some sort of affront. "I'll be fine. I'll take care of Mia. I'll still go to therapy with Dr.

Lincoln."

"Yes—but what will you do for you, for Sabine. What is it that you want?"

"All I want is to be well enough to take care of Mia."

"But that is not enough," Inga said. "Having children is wonderful, but you must have something for you."

"What did you have?" Sabine asked, a ripple of anger under the question.

Inga took a breath. She was here to help, not to antagonize. "Well, for one, I had Fred."

Sabine gave a sideways glance.

"We travelled all over the world," Inga continued. "It was interesting and exciting. I learned about different cultures and spoke different languages."

Sabine half chuckled. "I'm not about to become a world traveler."

Inga smiled. "Agreed." She and Fred had climbed Machu Picchu, visited the pyramids in Egypt, and walked along the Great Wall of China. The more foreign the culture, the more at ease Inga felt. "But there are many other things that you can do that are fulfilling."

"Aside from Fred, what else did you do?" Sabine asked.

"I painted. As you know." Inga looked around at the blank walls. "I did watercolors. Then I began to paint porcelain. I was involved in classes. I play bridge now, which is good for the brain. I help my neighbor, Frau Chop. I do the floral arrangements for the nursing home in the village on occasion. I am still very active with my garden. I..."

"OK, I get it," Sabine said. "I should find a hobby."

Inga shook her head. "You should find a passion. Something you want to learn about. Something you are truly interested in. I never really got the idea, since you were just a child, that you had a lot of interests. I remember how Henri, even as a small boy, would go to the woods and sit for hours, waiting to see deer." She smiled. "And now your brother is almost finished getting his doctorate degree from Cambridge University. At this very moment he is in Africa tiptoeing in the jungle, trying to find some new species of rat."

Thinking of Henri always made Inga feel bubbly. Sadly, that feeling was often followed by one of dismay at how Gerald had treated Henri.

"That your father was so horrible to him. I cannot forgive that."

"He wasn't as bad as you think."

The muscles in Inga's face tightened. "I was visiting one summer. You might have only been four." Even just thinking about that man made her blood feel hot. "He actually kicked Henri, the way some people kick a dog. And poor Henri, he was so utterly shocked and hurt. He had done nothing wrong."

"My father was angry, but I always felt kind of bad for him. Like underneath everything he was just frightened."

"That is probably the case, but it's no excuse."

"Mutti told me he was beaten by the Nazis before he fled, but he won't talk about it."

"Yes, Fred said something similar. I have to admit that when I met your father, I found him reasonable, although he did have a habit of staring at the ceiling as if he was always contemplating some obscure particle." She chuckled. "I suppose that's what particle physicists do."

"He's a theoretical nuclear physicist," Sabine corrected.

Inga waved a dismissive hand. "He is what he is. But he is correct in not talking about Germany. There is no reason. And I will say this, your mother was very brave to put up with him."

"Maybe," Sabine replied. "But she kind of likes to be the winner at everything."

"What on earth do you mean?" Inga asked.

"She was the bravest. She's competitive. You have to be to win a national skating championship."

"I had never thought of it that way." Inga smiled. She liked this version of Lisbet, the competitor, not the weak woman who was so afraid to be alone, she put up with a brute. Inga's mind worked quickly at revising. Yes, Lisbet allowed Gerald to yell, but in no way did that give him the power. In fact, now that Inga thought of it, Lisbet did exactly what she wanted. She wanted to have the children, and so she made that happen. She wanted to teach skating, and so she made that happen as well. She was able to get people on her side, including Sabine.

"You know," Inga began. "I remember when you and your mother were at the chalet and she cried so about your father. You were such a comfort to her. The way you caressed her arm and told her she was wonderful. In that way you were very much like my sister."

"You had a sister?" Sabine asked.

"I did." Inga felt her heart skip a beat.

"I never knew that," Sabine said.

"Ancient history." Inga glanced across the room at Cathy.

"Where is she?" Sabine asked.

"She died many years ago. Long before you were born."

"Oh." Sabine paused. "In Germany?"

Inga twisted her watch.

Cece walked toward the table. "Hi Omama. Hi Sabine. Can I join you?"

"Yes," Inga said.

"Not right now," Sabine told Cece, who paused for a moment, worried she might have done something wrong.

"I just need to talk to Omama about a few things," Sabine said.

"Right." Cece moved on.

Sabine turned back to Inga. "How did your sister die?"

"Some," Inga began, "some sort of chest problem."

"Were you close to her?" Sabine asked.

"Yes." She took a breath. "But enough about that."

"How old were you when she died?" Sabine asked, keeping her voice soft and low.

"I said, enough," Inga protested. "It was a long time ago." She looked directly into Sabine's eyes. "Hashing over the past will not help your present situation."

"But it's interesting," Sabine said. "I'd like to know more about it. What it was like in Germany before the war. How did you decide on Switzerland? No one ever talks about it."

"What will you do with yourself?" Inga asked. "What interests do you have?"

"I'm—" Sabine hesitated. "I don't mean to sound pushy, but what interests me is what life was like for you in Germany. Before the war. How were you treated?"

"I try not to think too much about that time. I find it unhelpful to dwell on a past you can't change."

"What if the past can, you know, help us not make the same mistakes?"

"Yes, I understand that. God forbid we allow another man like Hitler to have power. But my life, that is rather insignificant."

"Maybe not to me," Sabine said, and smiled.

Inga sighed. "I will tell you that it was not always pleasant. I recall waking up one morning and seeing the words 'pig Jew' painted on the stone wall that surrounded our garden." The story was true, although it had not bothered Inga much at the time. There were graver concerns. But Sabine wanted something, and this was harmless enough.

"And your sister—was she there when that happened?"

"I believe she was away at the time." Inga reached for her tea, but her hand trembled so severely she could not pick up the cup.

"Are you all right?" Sabine asked.

Inga's heart fluttered. "Yes. Would you mind getting me a glass of water?"

Sabine stood immediately and Inga was glad for the reprieve. That she allowed the conversation to get so out of hand was either a sign of her old age or an indication of a strength that Inga had not previously seen in Sabine. Or perhaps it was neither. Perhaps it was a slow and painful excavation of a past that was getting more difficult to keep buried.

Chapter Fourteen

Diagnosis

Prina, Germany
1935

For the first month that Rigmor lived at Sonnenstein, she only left her room to meet with Bohm. Arnold tried to get her to tour the gardens, but every time Rigmor reached the threshold, her shoulders curled, and as she placed a hand on the doorframe, she claimed the room spun. They would turn around and Arnold would suggest the couch, but she insisted she felt too weak and needed to be in bed.

He visited her on his lunch break and at dinner time. He asked what sort of tests Bohm was using and she told him—nothing more than interviews and a few cards with words and splashes of ink. Arnold hoped that Bohm would discover something that he had missed.

In conversations with colleagues, Arnold became aware of his complete insignificance. No one had known he was coming. Rigmor, on the other hand, was well-known, as a "Jewess," "artist," "heiress," or "hysteric." Arnold even caught a snippet of a malicious rumor, that Rigmor and Bohm were lovers. Nothing could have been further from the truth.

Arnold enjoyed his work with the feebleminded patients. He liked making the rounds and asking people how they were feeling. He would often sit with patients and play chess or cards. No one rushed. Arnold did not adhere to any formal model of psychotherapy. For the most part, he simply listened. His favorite patient, Wilhelm, was a stout country lad, with the shoulders of an ox. Wilhelm talked of milking cows and planting potatoes. At Sonnenstein, he helped with the garden and impressed everyone with his knowledge of flowers. He knew every class, subclass, genus, species, order, and variety of plant. He knew the colors, the smells, and the lifespan. He also loved to listen to football games on Sunday and plan for his return to the family farm. Asked by Arnold why he resided in Sonnenstein, Wilhelm muttered something about a misunderstanding. The doctor in charge of the ward told Arnold that Wilhelm had fornicated with a sheep and that the likelihood he would return home was slim to none. Arnold did not believe the story about the sheep and decided that he would help Wilhelm in whatever way he could.

In the evening, as was dictated by the Third Reich, Hitler's speeches were broadcast, but few people at Sonnenstein listened. Wilhelm and Arnold often visited the gardens during those times. One particularly beautiful evening, as the clouds flared in shades of orange and pink, Wilhelm explained the life cycle of the bluebell, that they grew from bulbs buried deep underground where there was more moisture, that their journey began after the germination of the seed on the surface, and that the small bulb sprouted special roots that contracted and pulled the bulb downward. Wilhelm knelt next to the flowerbed and held the head of a blue flower.

"Dr. Richter," a voice called.

They both turned. An orderly raced toward them, arms flailing.

"What is it?" Arnold asked, fearing terrible news about Rigmor.

"You are late for a meeting with the Director. It is nearly six and the meeting was for half five."

"I don't recall having a meeting," Arnold said.

The orderly ran ahead. Arnold followed.

Bohm was tending to his plants when Arnold arrived.

"I didn't have an appointment on my calendar," Arnold said. "I'm sorry I am late."

Bohm waved a hand. "No matter now. Close the door. Let us

discuss my findings."

Arnold sat.

Bohm walked to his desk, picked up a folder, and began to pace. "It seems very clear. It is Dementia Parecox."

Arnold put a hand on his chest, feeling as if a metal bracket compressed his heart.

"But, you can hardly be surprised," Bohm said.

"It wasn't what I expected. It's not what I would have diagnosed her with."

"Under whose standards?" Bohm snapped.

Arnold needed a minute to consider and twisted the button on the cuff of his shirt. "I have read all of Blueler's work," he said. "And Kraepelin's, and I don't believe that Rigmor fits into their criteria."

"Well, they are certainly not the only two psychiatrists who have studied schizophrenia," Bohm said.

"No," Arnold answered, taking a deep breath. "If I remember their first-rank symptoms correctly, I would say Rigmor has none of those."

Bohm shook his head vigorously. "She most certainly does. In fact, you were the one who told me about the things she calls shadows. How can you not see that as a first-rank symptom?"

"I believe her shadows come from lack of sleep."

Bohm resumed his pacing. "And the lack of sleep? And the constant nervousness? Are those not symptoms? Both Blueler and Kraepelin have cited those." He looked at Arnold, as if he had won a point of debate.

Arnold needed time, not combat.

Bohm stopped at his desk and took out two cigars. He handed one to Arnold. "And negative traits? Have you taken note of those?" he asked, and gave Arnold a silver lighter.

Arnold placed the lighter and the cigar on Bohm's desk.

Bohm lit his cigar and sat. "She has a lack, emphasis on lack, of emotional expression. Her answers to my questions are often characterized by a flat, monotonous voice and avoidance of eye contact. She does not want to leave her room. She seems motivated to do nothing, even though we have many outlets for her here, including a painting studio and music rooms. In fact, we went to a room with a piano, and I asked her to play me something. Anything. Do you know what she played?"

Rather than answer, Arnold thought of Rigmor's favorite piece, Chopin's Nocturne in B minor.

"She played a nursery rhyme, and with one finger. It was if she was a child of five."

"Perhaps she was nervous," Arnold said. "She never liked to play for an audience. I can attest to having heard her play very complicated and difficult pieces."

"But is that not part of the disease? A decay of the mind?" Bohm smiled with an affected sadness. "Dear man, I have been crass. Of course this hurts on a personal level, and I have not been sensitive to that. You are a human being first, a doctor second. And as we all know, when we are close to someone it is hard to look realistically at the situation."

"I do not believe her visions, or whatever you may call them, are a sign of deterioration of her brain."

"I am not here to have a debate. I understand you might not agree with me, but I was extremely objective, and went above and beyond, so to speak, what another doctor might do." Bohm opened the folder. "I did a number of word associations, and I categorized many of hers to be loose."

Arnold sighed.

"Are you in love with her?" Bohm asked.

Arnold jerked backward. "Of course not."

"Diagnosing patients properly can only help them with treatment," Bohm said. "It is apparent that her symptoms put her squarely in the diagnosis of schizophrenia."

Arnold nodded, although he remained skeptical.

Bohm leaned back. "Let me tell you a story, if I can." He

inhaled and blew a mouthful of smoke upward. "I loved my father very much. When I was young, he would kick a ball to me in our garden. He was kind and often showed affection to my brother and me. But then, when I was seventeen, he would talk at dinner sometimes for hours. Most of what he said did not make sense, but I still believed him to be a brilliant man. He drank too much. One evening we had some friends over, and later, I overheard them telling my mother that my father was ill and needed to stop consuming alcohol. I barged into their conversation and told them they had no right to make that judgment." He leaned forward. "So, you understand," he said.

Arnold did not understand, nor did he care. He could only think of Rigmor, and how she suffered, and how he'd hoped that Bohm would find she was merely in an acute phase of depression and would recover. He had been naïve to think that. He had been naïve to promise Inga and Frieda that schizophrenia was not a possibility.

"Will you tell the family?" Arnold said.

"I have already written a letter."

Arnold imagined Frieda reading the letter and collapsing. "And treatment?"

"At the moment I am leaning toward a sleep treatment. Aside from the positive effects, I believe her body could use a good rest."

"Perhaps," Arnold said, as his thoughts raced. Would it be better to take Rigmor out of this place? To hire a good nurse and let her rest at home?

"I do understand this has been difficult to hear, but let me leave you with this thought," Bohm said. "We are on a new leg of this journey, and there will not be a constant need to try to fix things, as now you know that is impossible."

When Arnold left the office, he felt as if he was walking against a strong wind. His legs moved like trunks of lead.

Most nights, he brought his dinner to Rigmor's room. Tonight, he didn't bother with food. She smiled the moment he appeared, but her expression changed when she saw his distress.

"What is it?" She pushed a few peas around on her plate.

Not telling her would be wrong. And telling her would be heartbreaking. These moments were by far the worst part of a doctor's work. He began slowly, talking about the different criteria for mental illnesses, and how doctors didn't always agree on diagnoses. She held his hand and looked into his eyes as if he was the one hearing bad news. Finally, he said the word schizophrenia.

"Don't take it so hard," she told him. "Diseases affect people differently. Maybe I have a mild case."

"I disagree with Bohm's assessment," he said.

"Will there be a treatment?"

"There is a new cure that involves the patient sleeping quite a lot."

She smiled. "I could use some sleep."

He tried to return her smile, but his lips barely moved. "Before you are given any sort of medicine, I will make sure I fully research the effects."

"I am not frightened of the procedure. What frightens me is that nothing will be tried. Then the situation is hopeless."

"You are far from hopeless."

"Let's talk of something else."

They could talk about how little she was eating, or how she barely got out of bed, or how the nurses were treating her. But knowing Rigmor as he did, he knew that she needed to talk about something that didn't involve her.

"Would you like to learn about the life cycle of the bluebell?" he asked.

Her face opened with delight. "I would like nothing more."

* * *

Inga read the letter eight times, and each time she saw the words Dementia Parecox, her heart sank deeper

"I have just received the letter from Bohm," she told Arnold over the phone. "It is a mistake."

"I agree."

"Did Bohm get the wrong patient? Did he send the incorrect information? That they would make this sort of mix-up and devastate a family shows tremendous lack of responsibility."

"It is not a mistake. At least not in terms of the letter and Bohm's assessment. He believes that Rigmor has schizophrenia."

"But you told him that was incorrect?"

"I did."

"We will take Rigmor out."

There was silence.

"We will come and fetch Rigmor," she said more loudly.

"She is weak at the moment, and there are other factors."

"What other factors?"

"Patients diagnosed with schizophrenia are not allowed to leave unless they have been sterilized."

She shook her head. This was exactly what Frieda had predicted and feared. Exactly what Inga was sure would not happen. "We must find a way around those rules."

"I have spoken to Rigmor about Bohm's findings," Arnold said. "She was not as upset as you might think."

"Because she doesn't understand the full consequences. But if she knew."

"She would like to try the treatment Bohm has prescribed. It is a sleep therapy that was invented a few years ago by a well-known Swiss psychiatrist, Klasei."

"I have heard of him."

"It could help. The treatments are safe, and Rigmor will get the rest she needs."

"I will make enquires." Inga hung up the phone.

Later that morning Frieda asked to speak to Inga in the

drawing room.

Inga explained that Dementia Parecox was a condition of the brain that sometimes left the patient with disordered thinking. She used terms of science—auto-intoxication, endogenous, aetiology, metabolic—to purposefully confuse Frieda, to soften the blow. But Frieda was not easily fooled.

"Bring her home."

"There is a treatment. One that may be very helpful."

"You and Arnold have done nothing to improve Rigmor's situation. Living in a place where there are others who are sicker than she probably gives her ideas. You are feeding this illness, when I believe it should be starved."

Inga stiffened, steeling herself against her mother's instigations. "Let me find out about this new treatment, and then we can decide."

"The evidence must be compelling," Frieda said, and left the room.

Inga called Berne University, where Klasei worked and, by using Rudin's name, was able to get an appointment over the telephone. A number of his patients had gone into prolonged remission when treated with Somnifen, Klasei said. And although he was reluctant to use the word *cured*, he did believe that the possibility existed. He stressed the importance of speaking with patients even as they slept. He had witnessed the sickest of patients come out of sleep treatments with an uncanny ability to solve a difficult mathematics problem, or understand something about physics that they did not previously grasp. He told Inga about the dosage he used, and the varying length of time for treatments—a few weeks to a few months, even half a year.

Inga relayed the hopeful news to Frieda, who grudgingly agreed that it was worth a try.

Chapter Fifteen

Visions

Belmont, Massachusetts
1984

Moving from table to table, Inga picked out a wilted daisy here and there, and straightened the tablecloths. When she finished, she sat at the table next to the kitchen door—her spot.

The day after Inga met with Holgart, he came to the ward to check up on her. She treated him with a cool, polite graciousness. He also met with some of the nurses, smiling generously, if a bit condescendingly—patting them on the back, looking pleased with both himself and the staff. No one questioned Inga after Holgart's appearance and, although she would never like the man, she was grateful for his assistance.

Yesterday Inga sat with Helen. The conversation began in a guarded manner, both of them proceeding cautiously, as if they were positioning pawns at the beginning of a chess match. Inga's goal was to get a better sense of whether Helen could be trusted as an adviser for Sabine.

"May I ask you something?" Inga said, after they had talked about the weather and the food.

"Of course." Helen smiled. She was such an attractive woman, so composed.

"What do you hope for?" Inga asked.

"Hope for? In terms of the world? The people here? Sabine?"

"The question is an open one. Any hope you have."

"Well, I hope Reagan won't be president for long. I hope that the snow will melt. I hope they let me out of here."

Inga opened her notebook to a clean page and began to sketch Helen's face. Of late she had found herself drawing again, trying to get the essence of a character on the page. "If you did get out of here, what is the first thing you would do?"

"Get an ice cream sundae at Bubbling Brook."

"And after that?"

Helen gave a joyless chuckle. "Find a final exit strategy."

"So relatively speaking," Inga said. "You are safe in here."

Helen tucked her hair behind her ears. "That depends on how you define safe."

Inga paused in her drawing. "Yes, I suppose safety is a much more relative term than we generally think or want it to be."

"Where do you feel safest?" Helen said.

Inga had never given the question any thought. She felt safe in her chalet, but it was an ordered kind of safety, built on routine. "I suppose at the North Sea."

"Because?" Helen asked.

Inga imagined herself sitting on the beach, listening to the roar of the waves, smelling and tasting the ocean air, watching the seagulls, and digging her fingers into the sand.

"I suppose that I would be too occupied with the sounds and smells to contemplate my inner worries."

Helen smiled. "I love the ocean too."

Their conversation had floated gently on until Sabine returned from her session with Dr. Lincoln. She checked in on Mia, who was still napping, and then joined Helen and Inga. Sabine had said it was nice, *and sort of weird*, to see her grandmother and best friend chatting.

* * *

Today as Inga sat in her spot, Keith walked in, grinned at Inga, and then headed to the kitchen. When he returned, carrying a bowl of cornflakes, Inga asked him to sit. She took out her notebook, and Keith asked to see her drawings. She obliged and watched his hands, lean and strong. In a few years, he would be wanted by every woman who saw him, but he didn't know that yet. His gestures were still shy and hesitant. The only person he was really comfortable with was Sabine.

At first Inga thought it was because of the baby—the baby wouldn't judge him—but then she realized it was the way Sabine smiled, softly, and nodded to the chair next to her, welcoming him.

He flipped through a few pages. "When you first got here, I didn't like you," he said. "I thought you thought you were better than everyone else."

Inga chuckled. "Sometimes I do think that." She took back her sketchpad and began to form the outline of his face.

"What about now? Do you think you're better than us because you're not a patient?" For an instant, Keith's eyes changed, as if a shade had been drawn.

"I think when I do think that, it's a defense. I'm protecting myself against people who aren't nice, and I do that by telling myself that I'm better."

"Who isn't nice to you?"

"The list is quite long." She grinned.

"No, really, tell me about someone who isn't nice to you." His curiosity seemed genuine, and Inga was pleased that he felt comfortable enough to ask.

She put down the sketchpad and glanced out the window. The sky, a hazy blue, relaxed her. She described for Keith her Uncle August, how he had been cold to her, had told her that no man would ever like her because she was too headstrong.

"I think my mother thought the same thing," Inga said. "What about you?"

"I'd have to go with my brother," he said.

"Brothers can be hard on each other. Did he do anything in particular?"

Keith gave a sharp laugh. "He did a lot of things in particular, like leaving a dead rabbit under my blanket."

Inga had been drawing Keith's eyes. She stopped. "That is awful. It sounds as if your brother is the one who needs to be here."

"My parents were thinking of sending him away." There was a hard flash in Keith's eyes again.

Inga waited.

"We fought, in the kitchen. I grabbed a knife." Keith looked out the window. "It was an accident."

"He died?"

Keith nodded, and Inga reached across the table, giving his hand a gentle squeeze. She saw the sorrow in his eyes and understood, probably better than he, that its core, the dense nucleus of guilt, would remain forever.

* * *

The following day, as Inga sat at her table, she opened her book to the same page she'd left off on three days ago. A few minutes later Cece shuffled in.

"Hi Omama. I hear you're doing portraits." She sat and took off her baseball cap. "Can I see them?"

Inga pushed her notebook across the table.

Cece grinned. "The one of Frank is amazing. Will you do me?"

"I can try."

Cece turned. "Do you want to do a side view? Although I kind of have a double chin. I probably should just face you." She looked back at Inga.

Cece's teeth were crooked, her nose had a hook, and she had darkish circles under her eyes. Yet the whole of her was attractive. Inga had first guessed Cece to be in her twenties, but the more she had seen of her the more she realized; with the crow's feet fanning from her eyes, the scattered gray hairs, and the thin lines around her mouth, she might be in her late thirties.

"So when people come to this seat, what do they talk about?"

Cece asked.

Inga smiled. "Whatever they feel like." The pencil moved. "Sometimes the weather, sometimes their family."

"I want to talk about my dreams."

"I'm not any sort of analyst. You do have a doctor, don't you?"

"She doesn't get me. But I bet you would understand. I mean, look how nice you made this room."

"I don't see the connection."

"I remember how Sabine was on that first day with you. Even the second day. Like she didn't trust you, and she wanted you to go back to wherever."

"Switzerland," Inga replied.

"You figured out a way to make her want you to come. You hired that fancy nurse over there, who never smiles." Cece leaned forward. "What is wrong with her?"

"Nothing. I believe she is just a very serious person."

"I guess," Cece said. "Anyways, I get these dreams. Only they're not dreams, they're visions. They're people coming to visit me."

"I see," Inga replied as she kept sketching.

"The problem is my uncle. He was an asshole." Cece put her hat back on.

"Go on."

"When I was five." She tugged on the bill of her cap. "I had an accident. I peed my pants. It happens — right? But we were at his house, and he still had a kid in diapers. So he made me put on a diaper. I had to take off my clothes and I could only crawl and say wa-wa like I was a baby. When I tried to stand up, he kicked me. They laughed, his older kids, and my dad, too. So I told him he was going to get hurt really bad one day."

Inga stopped drawing. She hated this uncle, and Cece's father as well. "Did that happen?"

"Yep. Stabbed and killed at work five years later. But now he haunts me. The bastard! Comes at me with a switchblade like the one that got him. He says he's gonna get me back. As if it was my fault."

Inga glanced at her notebook. "It's your dream, correct?"

"Yes."

"Then you have the control. Take the knife from him and tell him you will stab him if he comes back." The advice felt preposterous, but so was the situation.

"I knew it. I knew you'd get it." Cece ran around the table to give Inga a hug.

A nearby staff member cleared his throat, reminding Cece, and Inga too, of the no-physical-contact rule.

"Yes, yes." Inga patted Cece's arm. "Now go and sit again so I can finish this."

Cece returned to her chair. "Remember when we first met? How I saw that woman with you?"

Inga nodded.

"She's there now."

Of course Inga didn't believe in the nonsense Cece spouted, but still it unnerved her. No one needs to hear that a dead woman is standing over her shoulder.

"So how did you come to be here?" Inga asked.

"That's not really very interesting. You don't want me to tell you about the woman?" Cece gazed at the space above Inga's head. She chuckled. "Strange. She's trying to hand me a hairbrush."

"Enough," Inga whispered.

"I know it can freak people out. I didn't mean to frighten you."

"What brought you to McLean?" Inga asked again, as she began shading the small portrait.

Cece kicked up her feet. "I knew there was going to be a fire at the halfway house I was living at. I tried to warn people, and then when it happened, guess who gets the blame?" She made an exaggerated gesture of pointing to herself.

"That doesn't seem fair."

"Yeah, well, whoever said things were gonna be fair—right?" She laughed. "So, I don't mean to be nosy and stuff, but the woman, she's like always there."

Inga put the pencil down. "I don't believe in seeing the dead."

"Yeah, I get that. Most people don't. It's just that I'm getting this feeling. I don't know. Like she's here for a reason. Like she wants to talk to you, or for you to . . . I don't know exactly."

"It feels rather warm in here."

"Yeah, your cheeks look kind of red. Maybe you're getting sick." Cece glanced down the hall. "Sabine's back," she shouted, and waved for Sabine to hurry.

Thank goodness, Inga thought and then felt surprised. She had never considered Sabine's presence particularly comforting.

"Omama doesn't feel so great," Cece said as Sabine approached.

Sabine pulled out a chair. "What's going on?"

"It's nothing. I am better now."

Sabine looked at the sketch of Cece. "This is really good. I didn't know you drew faces. I always thought you liked to paint flowers and stuff like that."

Inga took back the notebook. "Never mind."

She remembered a time in the studio in Frankfurt with the wall of south-facing windows. Rigmor was working on a watercolor of two field mice, and Inga had just finished a pencil sketch she'd made from copying a photograph. Frieda charged in, smiled at Rigmor, then looked in disgust at Inga's drawing, telling her she didn't have the talent for faces. Inga ripped up the sketch and threw it in the fireplace.

"Omama," Sabine said. "Are you sure you're all right?"

Inga glanced down at her notebook. She had torn out the page with Cece's portrait and crumpled it.

"It's no good." She stood, keeping her hand on the table for support.

"But it was good," Sabine said.

Inga shook her head. She hadn't meant the picture. She had meant to say, *it's no good remembering the past,* but she felt too weak at the moment to explain that. A splash of cool water would help, she thought, and told Sabine and Cece she needed to use the lavatory.

* * *

Sabine followed Omama into the bathroom where she tossed the picture of Cece in the trash, turned on the faucet, and then rinsed her face.

"What's wrong? Did something happen with Cece?" Sabine asked.

"Nothing at all. I only need a bit of cool water."

Omama didn't lie. In fact, she tended toward brutal honesty.

Sabine stood near the door, and glanced at her grandmother in the mirror. She was smaller than Sabine had remembered — more beautiful too.

Omama looked at Sabine's reflection.

"Sorry," Sabine mumbled, as if she'd been caught spying.

"It's quite all right my girl. But I do wonder what you were thinking."

That your hair is curly and frizzy like mine. Only I never noticed. That sometimes I hate you, and yet I feel drawn to you and I'm so grateful that you're here, yet I could never say it.

Sabine walked to Omama, reached out to touch her, but then stopped. Omama had always been the matriarch, the one in charge, and it felt awkward and confusing for things to be reversed.

"Do you want to go to my room and talk for a few minutes?"

Omama yanked out a paper towel and dried her face.

"Yes, but who will mind the baby?"

"We have a full-time nurse, remember?"

"Of course," she said with a light chuckle.

Omama sat on Sabine's bed, now covered with an eiderdown.

"So, what did you want to talk about?"

"Are you sure you feel all right?"

"I am quite fine. No need to worry. But I must say, very sweet of you."

Sabine wasn't convinced.

"Sometimes Cece can say strange things. I don't believe in seeing ghosts. But, you know, Cece does."

"It was all perfectly normal." Inga looked at the poster of the rainbow Cece had taped to the wall. "I am tired. Perhaps I will go back to the hotel and rest."

"You can rest on my bed if you want."

"It's a generous offer, but I'd prefer my own room."

Sabine called a cab and waited with Omama in the dining room, peeling an orange for her. When the cab arrived, Sabine walked her grandmother downstairs and told the driver not to leave the hotel until she was safely inside.

That evening, after Cathy left with Mia, Sabine returned to her room. Cece was lying on her bed with the boom-box blaring.

"Hey," Sabine shouted above Led Zeppelin. "Can you talk for a minute? Did something happen with Omama?"

Cece sat up and turned down the music. "She drew that picture of me, and I told her about a woman who was standing behind her."

"Oh?"

Cece looked down. "A dead woman."

"Who was she?"

"I dunno. I probably shouldn't have said anything." She ran her fingers through her hair. "Sometimes I wish I'd be able to keep my big mouth shut." Cece wiped her nose with her sleeve. "Who's to say it's wrong to see things?"

Cece smiled. "You ever seen a dead person?"

"Nope." Sabine moved to her dresser and took out a T-shirt.

"I'd be scared shitless."

"Not if you'd been seeing them your whole life."

"What did the woman behind Omama look like?"

"Sort of like you."

"You don't think that means I'm going to die or anything?" Sabine asked.

Cece laughed. "No. This person was already dead."

As Sabine drifted off to sleep that night, she wondered what Omama's sister looked like, and why no one ever mentioned her. Maybe she'd died in a concentration camp and it was just too painful for Omama to think about.

Sabine couldn't move. She couldn't scream. She couldn't talk. The sunlight streamed in her window and stung her eyes. Why didn't they close the shades? She tried to get out of bed, but her legs and arms wouldn't work. They were like concrete blocks. She smelled the smoke, felt it blanket her. Rats nibbled at her feet. But she couldn't wiggle her toes to get the vermin off her bed. She was paralyzed. Dying. Unable to cry for help.

Sabine gasped. She sat up, her head foggy, her heart beating too fast, her back damp with sweat. She'd been in that room before. She'd died in that room, even though she knew she couldn't die in her dreams.

Chapter Sixteen

The Letters

Prina, Germany
1935

In April and the beginning of May, Rigmor underwent a series of sleep treatments. In the morning, often after a lengthy time trying to wake, she ate a small amount of porridge and, in her flowing pink robe, was escorted to the lavatory. She then returned to bed and received another dose of Somnifen. During her short interludes of wakefulness, she slurred her words and could barely open her eyes. Sometimes she would ask where she was and whether Inga was near.

Arnold sat with her at least twice a day, talking about their walks in the Palmengarten. He held her hand, noting that her fingers looked like delicate twigs. She was so thin her cheekbones had become visible through her papery skin.

One morning he walked to the east wing to check on his patients. The warm May day invited those who could to come outside. Arnold expected to find Wilhelm in the garden. But only a few patients milled about.

On the ward, Arnold sensed an unnatural quiet. He approached a nurse and asked her if something out of the ordinary had happened.

"Many patients received their letters today," she told him.

His mood plummeted. He knew this day was coming, yet he still felt shocked.

"Wilhelm?" he asked.

"Yes."

Arnold didn't believe Wilhelm fit all of the criteria of feeblemindedness. He read at the level of an eight-year-old, but he had been able to learn so much about plants and flowers, and also had a vast knowledge of weather patterns. Had he come from a family with more means, they might have bought him some good clothes, and taken him to a barber. Outward appearance often played too much of a role in diagnoses.

Arnold found Wilhelm sitting on his perfectly made bed. He disliked any sort of wrinkles or creases. He washed the floor in his area at least twice a day, and did all of his own laundry. Pictures of his parents were taped on the wall next to the bed. His mother had the same easy, happy smile as Wilhelm. His father had weathered skin and was missing his two front teeth.

Wilhelm gripped the folded letter.

Arnold sat on a wooden visitor's chair. He was grateful the beds near Wilhelm's were unoccupied at the moment.

"I don't understand," Wilhelm said.

"Would you like me to read it to you?"

"I know what it says—I know it says they will take away my manhood—but I don't understand why."

"They will certainly not take away your manhood."

Wilhelm seemed on the brink of tears. "I am to be sterilized."

"That does not take away your manhood." Arnold hesitated, but then thought it best that Wilhelm have the correct information. "You will still ejaculate. You just won't have the sperm anymore. So you will be able to perform as a man. Sterilization stops people from having children."

"What if I want children one day?"

That was a much harder question. "The State has decided that many people should not have children, even if they might want them."

Wilhelm sat for a few moments, contemplating.

"Will it hurt?"

"Of course not," Arnold replied, a bit overenthusiastically, glad he was able to deliver a positive piece of news. "It's a very simple procedure. If you like, I will come with you."

Wilhelm smiled. "But why me?"

"Has anyone ever talked to you about your diagnosis?"

"A nurse once said I was feebleminded, but I am nothing like Eva or some of the others, who drool and walk like ducks."

"Can you tell me more about why you think you're here?" Arnold had heard bits, but he had no clear picture.

"I had too much to drink. Ten beers. Maybe more." He looked at his feet. "It felt good at first. It made me happy. I stole them from the Hubers. They live down the road. The beer was in boxes behind their house."

"Sometimes we have a bit too much to drink. Was it because you stole? Is that how you came to be here?"

He shook his head. "I don't remember it all. I was in the barn, and I think I fell asleep. I put my head on one of our sheep. She made a nice pillow. And then suddenly it was morning, and there was a man standing above me shouting. I saw that my pants were down. I must have gotten up to urinate in the middle of the night and not pulled them back up. My mother came running out of the house, and then my father, all while I lay on the dirt floor. Finally, my brother gave me a hand."

"Have you told all of this to the doctor in charge?"

"Yes. I didn't do anything," he cried.

Arnold sat next to Wilhelm, patted his back, and told him it would be all right.

Wilhelm shook the letter. "I don't want them to do this to me."

"You can appeal the recommendation. But you will have to take some tests, and answer many questions in front of a health court. The doctors may not be pleasant."

"What does appeal mean?"

"You explain why this shouldn't be done to you. Why you don't believe you are feebleminded."

Wilhelm wiped his face with the back of his hand and gave Arnold a strong hug. "I am going to appeal," he shouted. He lifted his hand in the air and charged down the corridor, yelling, "I am going to appeal."

There was little chance Wilhelm would succeed in his appeal. Perhaps it was wrong to give him hope, but in times when one often felt so powerless, at least he would have something to fight for.

* * *

Rigmor's windows were open and Arnold, sitting on the chair next to the bed, heard birds chirping and cowbells tinkering. A light breeze tickled his face.

He reached for Rigmor's hand. He talked about the constellations, about Hydra and its main star, Alphard. Well into his descriptions, he sensed another presence in the room. When he glanced up, he saw Bohm standing on the other side of the bed.

"She is a beauty—yes?"

"I didn't hear you come in," Arnold said.

"You were very engrossed in your vivid depictions. The sea serpent is a favorite of mine." Bohm smiled. "I have found Prina to be a spectacular place to gaze at the night sky. Don't you agree?"

"Yes." Arnold placed Rigmor's hand on the blanket. Only nurses of the same sex could touch a patient undergoing sleep treatments.

"I was told I would find you here," Bohm said.

"Are you here for me, or to check on Rigmor?" Arnold stood.

"Stay where you are. I am here for both you and Rigmor."

"Should Rigmor be hearing this?"

Bohm scratched his bald head. "She is asleep."

There was no point discussing what patients could or couldn't hear during sleep, Arnold decided.

"What is it then?"

"A small thing. But I thought you could help me out with it." Bohm rubbed his chin. "Rigmor is to be sterilized."

Arnold looked down as a wave of distress swept over him.

"The question," Bohm continued, "is how do we tell the family?"

"We?" Since the day Arnold arrived, he had not been involved in a single decision when it came to Rigmor.

"I would like to stay on good terms with Frieda Blumenthal," Bohm said.

In other words, he didn't want to lose the donations that came with having a patient such as Rigmor. The law would require sterilization, but to get the family's blessing for it would be a boon.

"I'm not sure how I can help," Arnold said.

"I have thought long and hard about this. I think it would be best to do it in stages. First, you can phone Inga and inform her. She did not seem so opposed to the procedure. Perhaps if you can soften the blow to her, she can in turn relay it to her mother. And most of all, make her understand that we are required by law to do this. The doctors who run the health courts are in control. Not us."

Bohm gave Arnold's shoulder a quick, forceful squeeze. "It is a difficult task I am asking of you. I realize that. But I believe you are the right man to do it."

"I will do my best."

"Good man. And please do tell Inga to come and visit us. She will appreciate the gardens, and a walk along the river. Perhaps you can find out what is playing in Dresden. A good symphony feeds the soul. Don't you think?"

What kind of a man talks about forced sterilization and the symphony in the same breath?

Arnold thought of his mother, how she considered him her greatest joy. To take away the hope of offspring, of raising a child, smacked of cruelty.

Bohm gazed down at Rigmor and laughed. "She does have magnificent hair. I am always envious of hair, as I'm sure you can understand." He walked to the other side of the bed. He hesitated a moment, as if he knew he shouldn't, and yet he did. He picked up a lock of Rigmor's hair and caressed it.

Arnold glared at Bohm. "She only likes her sister to touch her hair."

"Yes, of course," he said, letting go. "It is good you are here to protect her." Bohm walked to the door. "Let me know how it goes with Inga."

Two days later Arnold telephoned Inga, expecting her to be furious. Instead, she calmly explained that the best way forward was to proceed with the operation *without* informing Frieda. At first, Arnold thought he must have misheard her. So Inga explained again, speaking too loudly.

"Won't your mother be livid when she finds out? You don't plan on keeping this a secret, do you?"

"Of course not. But the truth is that my mother does not want grandchildren. She is terrified of the pain that love for children and grandchildren bring." Inga gave a harsh laugh. "Naturally, I am excluded in that regard." She paused. "My mother is also terrified of surgery. She can't tolerate the thought of a person lying on an operating table and being opened up and poked at. She just doesn't believe people can be closed back up and return to what they were prior to the surgery. She is old-fashioned in many ways. Once the surgery is complete, and Rigmor is well, my mother will not give it a second thought."

After saying goodbye, Arnold walked along the riverbank. The conversation should have left him with a sense of relief. There had been no disagreement, no yelling, no telling him he should have done things differently. Yet, something troubled him. A feeling of darkness, as if he and the Blumenthals were headed into a tunnel and there was no turning back. First sterilization, and then what? Binding and Hoche had written about such things years ago, how institutions for idiots lavished the best of care on life of negative worth, while the strength of humanity, the soldiers—able, healthy young men—were sacrificed on the battlefield.

Arnold tossed a small stick into the river and watched the current carry it away, with no regard for its destination.

Chapter Seventeen

Needs

Belmont, Massachusetts
1984

Omama had suggested Sabine spend time alone with Tanner, that she speak to him in a way that made him feel as if he was important to her, even if she had to exaggerate a bit. Omama made it sound easy, and Sabine wasn't sure she could do it, but she did want to find a way back to liking him, at least to being content with him. It would make the transition out of McLean easier.

Sabine and Tanner had been housemates the summer before her junior year in college, his senior year. He was coaching at a hockey camp, and she worked at a diner, a passable excuse not to have to go home. As far as she was concerned, he was way out of her league—leading scorer on the hockey team, big man on campus, full of charisma, and in possession of a Boston accent that sounded foreign and exotic. But he noticed her, called himself a leg-man, and insisted Sabine had the best legs he'd ever seen. He'd wait for her on the fake velvet couch with broken springs. When she came home, he'd pat the cushion next his and tell her that her uniform turned him on. He persisted, and she gave in. They had sex. His mouth tasted of beer and salt, and she was sure that after their hook-up, after he'd won his game, he'd lose interest. But he still waited for her, and if she held back, even a little, he came at her with more desire. She had never felt so visible, so wanted.

At parties together, she felt proud to be seen with him. She would giggle when he said random, ridiculous things, like that he invented paint, or that he was an emissary from Mars. She loved being around him, loved how he drew people to him, how he seemed genuinely interested in everyone's story. Sometimes he would give her piggy-back rides across campus, her long legs dangling at his sides.

When Sabine graduated from college, she moved to Boston, where she and Tanner rented a one bedroom apartment. She enrolled in a PhD program at Boston University medical school. But then one day, five weeks into the program, she stood at the bus stop in front of the Public Library where she handed out cigarettes to the homeless, and could not get on the bus. She didn't feel sick or even nervous, but her foot simply would not lift onto the stair of the bus. A woman behind nudged Sabine to *move already*. She turned and walked back to the one bedroom apartment and didn't leave for two weeks. Tanner brought home pasta and Parliament cigarettes. He tried to coax her out, but every time she got to the doorway she was sure she was going to pass out. He watched TV with her and told her that sex would help. But nothing helped, and Tanner suggested she move back with her parents for a while.

She lived in the basement of the yellow spilt level of her childhood. She didn't leave the house, and the curtains had to be drawn because light felt as if it drilled through her eyes. The voice came and went, sometimes telling her she was a failure and loser, and she should just kill herself, and sometimes telling her to run. Just run! Don't trust ANYONE!

Sabine's mother cried and rubbed her eyebrow and asked if it was her fault, if she'd failed as a mother. Sabine tried to reassure her mother that she was perfect. Sometimes that would make her mother fret more. *Then vhy*, she would ask. *Vhat is the matter vith you?*

Sabine's father was not as tolerant. He would trounce down the basement stairs after work, tremor with anger, and yell that it was high time Sabine moved on and pulled up her socks. Did she just think she could hide in a basement forever?

It took months before she could climb up the basement steps and walk outside, into the back yard. Eventually, she began to drive her mother's car around the neighborhood, then to the local convenience store for cigarettes, and finally one day she made it to the grocery store. But she had to abandon her half-filled cart because her heart was beating too hard and her hands shook violently.

Her mother continued to fret. Her father continued to yell.

After four months, she was able to take a plane to Boston. Tanner picked her up and they went to his new, cheaper apartment to have sex. She owed him that. Perhaps it was then that the tally board was started. They drove to Maine, rented a cottage on a lake, picked blueberries, drank, and had more sex. One night, after he'd had six beers, enough to relax him, he asked her to marry him. She knew her mother would be relieved, that this would make Sabine seem normal. And of course her father would be pleased to be rid of her.

So, she said yes, and was grateful to Tanner for saving her.

With financial help from Omama, Sabine and Tanner bought an old colonial in a suburb of Boston. For a time, Sabine felt as if she was managing. She even got a part-time job at an animal shelter, and adopted a mixed hound dog that shook whenever she heard the jingle of an ice cream truck.

But it (she had no better word to describe the fear and panic and guilt that breathed down her) never really went away. Having other people around helped, and so she and Tanner had friends for pizza and poker games. Somewhere in a hazy part of her consciousness, she realized that the need for others had to do with her lack of interest and enthusiasm for her husband. But she owed him and hoped that maybe she'd wake up one morning and feel the way she had felt for him in college. She'd call up memories, like the time a puck had smacked him and gashed his forehead. He'd refused to go to the hospital until the game was over. As he sat on the bench, wiping away the blood, banging his stick on the floor when his team scored, she thought he was a warrior. Her warrior.

Then the sleepless nights and the dread returned in full force and Sabine decided that having a baby would cure her. Tanner said they should have more in savings, but she promised that her mother and grandmother would help if there were bills they couldn't pay. He pressed her for a guarantee and was happy about the sex part of the arrangement.

Sabine had always felt defective and assumed that it would take at least a year to get pregnant. It took a month.

Her mood during pregnancy was surprisingly stable. But only a few days after Mia was born, all of the symptoms Sabine had managed to stave off, returned with a new and bold ferocity. By the three-month mark she could not cope.

Now here she was in her room at McLean with Tanner sitting on Cece's bed, as Omama held court in the dining room. How crazy was it, she thought, that she'd rather be with her grandmother, Helen, Keith, Cece and Frank. That'd she'd rather be laughing about Frank's paranoia of leprosy in the floors, Helen's thesis about humans having the right to kill themselves, and Cece's ghosts. Even talking to Cathy about the weather felt preferable to being alone with Tanner. Of course Sabine recognized how wrong her feelings were, and she wanted to adjust them, but they were stuck. She would have to pretend.

"So what's up?" Tanner asked.

"Not much," Sabine answered, wishing again she was in the dining room, but knowing she needed to attend to her marriage, and show Tanner that he was important to her.

"How's work?" she asked.

"Good. Getting a few clients." He rubbed the scar that ran through his eyebrow.

"Great," she replied.

He patted a spot on Cece's bed. "Come sit with me."

"You should probably sit on my bed."

He practically dove across the room, situated himself right next to her, pulled her close and kissed her neck. He smelled a little like a campfire.

She tried to be still, to tolerate his kisses, to tell herself she liked being close to him. But his lips made her squirm, and she pulled away.

"It's been a while," he said.

"I know. It's just not the right time. I mean, here in the hospital." She and Cece had been moved to the twenty minute check wing, the least restricted of the hallways. The checks person had just poked his head in, so no interruptions were imminent.

Tanner brushed a hand against her breast. "A guy has needs."

She glanced at the floor, at the scuff marks that made a path to the door. "I know. I'm sorry. I think it's the medicine I'm on. It makes me, you know. Not really want to do stuff like that." She paused. "It's not about you," she added quickly.

Tanner scratched his neck. "How long will you be on the medicine?"

For the rest of my life, she thought. "I don't know."

"I get that you need to be here. And I want you to get better and everything. But I have needs too. That's all I'm saying." He spoke casually—a light banter. The world had always seemed so easy for him to live in, that was one of the things she had been attracted to, one of the qualities she hoped would magically seep into her.

"What kind of needs?" she asked. "Aside from sex?" Maybe they could have a different, more mature conversation.

He had a full mouth and thick lips that she used to think were sexy, like Mick Jagger's.

"I guess I have to eat." He laughed.

She smiled mechanically, and then said, "I'm not talking about eating and sleeping and breathing. I'm talking about emotional needs. Needing someone to listen to you and understand you, help you figure out why you're the way you are." As she said it, she realized they weren't things she'd asked for before she had started therapy and her daily rundowns with Helen. Sabine was changing the rules, mid-marriage, and she wasn't sure that was allowed.

He sat pensive for a moment. "Yeah, I understand that's what *you* need. But not me. Just pretty much food and sex for this guy. Hungry and horny. H and H."

He laughed and went for her neck again. Under his happy-go-lucky shtick was a man who read Proust, a man much more sensitive than he appeared. But he didn't want to reveal that—not even to her—and she only knew because she had seen the books he kept on his nightstand, and the occasional glances of sadness for others. Lately his compassion was directed toward Frank, for whom he'd bought two new shirts.

In therapy, Sabine had come to the conclusion that Tanner's easy-going air was a protection against failure, against disappointing his father, who had claimed Tanner was a hockey prodigy at the age of seven. Better to swagger and act as if he never cared in the first place, than reveal the hurt of sitting in the penalty box, not getting a second interview at Fidelity, or driving an old Ford instead of a Mercedes.

He was a pretender. Like her mother. Pretend you never feel anxious. Pretend you are Jewish in front of Jews and Christian in front of Christians. There is no harm in playing both sides.

But now it occurred to Sabine that she didn't have her mother's gift of pretending. She never had. Sabine pushed Tanner away. Yes, this was what she'd wanted when they'd met. But the conditions had changed.

"Your Omama was telling me that this might happen," he said.

"What might happen?"

"That you might be frigid for a little while."

"She used that word—'frigid'? About me?"

"Not sure about the exact word, but hey, she was only trying to help. Don't be so hard on her. I mean look at everything she's done for you. She hired that Nazi nurse."

"Don't call someone a Nazi," Sabine snapped.

"Jeez. Relax. I was joking. It's just an expression."

"Don't use that word in front of Omama."

"You know, you have her all wrong. She's generous and nice, and she never criticizes like you always say she does. I think it's kind of up here for you." He tapped his head.

"She's always liked men better."

"She likes your friend Helen."

"Maybe it's just me then." Sabine scooted away from her husband.

"I think you shouldn't be so hard on her. She came all the way here. She's paying for daycare."

"You didn't tell me that."

That Omama was paying for daycare wasn't a surprise, but the way he slid it in felt off, as if he was considering keeping it a secret so he could take credit for paying all of the bills.

"You're not working," Tanner said. "Money is tight."

Shame prickled her skin. The thought of getting a job was overwhelming. She didn't even have privileges to leave McLean yet, nor did she really want them. She felt safe and protected here, and she knew that was wrong and weak.

"You're right," she mumbled. "I would just rather we didn't take anything from her. That's all."

He chuckled. "You don't think that nurse she hired costs anything? You think all of those fancy tablecloths and flowers are free?"

"I didn't ask for those."

"But you have accepted the nurse, because then you get what you want. So maybe you're being hypocritical."

She shrugged. Sometimes she hated the scoreboard of their marriage, the way he kept track of who did the chores—shoveling the driveway, mowing the lawn, washing the dishes, putting oil in the car—and who had a debt to pay. He always wanted to be paid back in sex, and she was always behind. Especially since this last episode, before being admitted to McLean. She needed rides, and needed him to go to the grocery store. She had become an incredible burden, and she hated herself for that.

Tanner slapped his hands on his thighs and smiled as if he knew he was in the lead, as if he'd been reading her emotions, which, after all, wasn't that difficult.

"I've been thinking," he said. "Since you're in here, and it's sort of like you're getting a break from everything. I could use a break too. I haven't been skiing in a while, and some of my friends are going to Sun Valley."

"Yeah," she said. "You should go."

She didn't point out that he'd just said money was tight. She didn't want to argue; she wanted him to go, and that made her feel guilty, because it wasn't that she wanted it for him—she wanted it for herself. Not only would he be away, she'd also gain points on the scoreboard.

Chapter Eighteen

Another Ward

Prina, Germany
1935

Bohm kept a regular routine with Rigmor's sleep treatments—
four days on Somnifen, three days off. The drug flowed through
her blood so that even on her off days, she barely woke.

Summer came with bright flowers and lush green leaves.
The spring rains had been good for the flora. Arnold walked in
the woods and along the river. He spent time on the east ward,
visited Rigmor, and sometimes even ate dinner with a colleague.

Wilhelm applied for an appeal and Rigmor's operation was
delayed due to her weakened condition. As far as Arnold was
concerned, she could always be in need of getting stronger, so
therefore the procedure could be indefinitely postponed.

One evening in the dining hall he made the acquaintance of a
young doctor named Guenther.

"I work on the east ward," Arnold said, trying to get a
conversation started.

"Do you like your work?"

"I do. And you, where do you work?"

"On a small ward."

"Which one?"

"Children's." Guenther looked at his watch. "I must get a
move on," he said, leaving his unfinished meal.

"I didn't know we had a children's ward," Arnold answered,
though by now Guenther was halfway across the dining room.

Over the next week, Arnold investigated, and finally received
his answer from a cleaning woman. She explained that the
children's ward, if you would even call it that, was very small

indeed, and that in order to get there, Arnold should walk all the way around the west wing of the building, then almost when he thought he had come to the end, he would see a few steps leading to a white door in disrepair.

As he debated about whether or not to visit, he did some brushing up on treatments for children, and came across an interesting paper by Hans Asperger, an Austrian physician, who seemed to have a special talent for understanding children who had trouble communicating emotions.

Arnold knew it would be heartbreaking to visit sick children, but he had free time in his schedule. He could play ball, or take a child for a walk in the garden. Wilhelm could teach the patients about flowers. The more Arnold thought about it, the more ideas sprang to mind.

On a warm evening, he found the rear of the building. Broken twigs and old branches littered the area. The uncut grass looked coarse, and the few blossoms that survived were more than likely weeds, although his knowledge of flowers, even with Wilhelm's instruction, was still limited.

He climbed the four steps and knocked on the door. No one answered. He was surprised to find it unlocked.

A nurse sat reading a book in the reception area. She kept her head lowered as Arnold carried on. He pushed a glass door that he guessed led to the ward. The smell of urine and mildew startled him. Sonnenstein prided itself on hygiene, and signs posted throughout the hospital read, *cleanliness is next to godliness.* Arnold covered his mouth and nose with his handkerchief. Although the evening light still shone outside, the ward looked like a maze of shadows, with a few dim bulbs plugged into the baseboards. Arnold guessed that the children, if there were any, had been moved elsewhere. Still he walked on, his eyes adjusting to the darkness. There were small cots on either side of the room. He heard nothing.

To his right Arnold noticed a lump under a blanket, probably a pillow. But when he approached the cot, a stick-like arm rose. Some sort of optical illusion, he thought—a trick of sight or a shadow on the wall. He moved closer to the bed and to his horror saw a child, too weak to call out. Arnold could not tell if the child was male or female.

"Good evening," he whispered.

The child's hair, short and fuzzy, reminded him of down on a baby bird. Arnold knelt next to the bed.

The child, he guessed female, because she had such fine, delicate features, reached out a hand. Her fingers were so light and frail, Arnold felt as if the bones of a small animal rested in his palm. He looked into her wide eyes.

"What is your name?"

She opened her mouth, but the only noise that came out was a whimper.

"My name is Arnold." He glanced around the ward, wondering why the girl had been left alone.

Her fingers curled around the side of his hand. He used his other hand to feel her forehead, which burned with fever. Then he felt her pulse, weak and slow.

"I will take you out of here." Arnold pulled down the blanket, ready to scoop her into his arms. Her legs, no more than sticks, appeared deformed from rickets. Her stomach protruded from starvation, and every rib was visible. Without the best of care, this child didn't have a day left in her life.

Just as he threaded an arm underneath her, he heard a sound coming from another bed. He covered the child and went to see if there was another forgotten patient.

As he tiptoed from one bed to the next, Arnold witnessed similar conditions. He counted eight children, some asleep, some with wide, desperate eyes—all starving.

It seemed unlikely that they were all forgotten.

At the far end of the ward Arnold found a sink and a few tin cups. He went from bed to bed giving the children water. He kissed their foreheads. He planned on getting help, but before he left, he once again knelt by the bed of the first patient he had discovered.

"Blau," she managed to whisper.

"Blau," he repeated, confused.

She turned her face toward him and closed her eyes. At least for the moment, she seemed comfortable. He caressed her hair and said a silent prayer.

"Good night, dear one."

The girl looked as if she wanted to smile, but then, suddenly, her body seized. A few seconds later, she released a long breath. Her skin was cool to the touch, even though her forehead burned. Arnold could not leave her. He sat on her bed, cradled her in his arms and sang Silent Night. Another child hummed along. Blau died fifteen minutes later.

Arnold hurried out of the ward and approached the nurse he had seen when he first arrived.

"Excuse me." His voice faltered. He pointed to the ward.

"Oh dear." She closed her book and slid it under the desk. "Why are you here?"

"A child... A child has expired."

She gasped. "You were in there?"

"A child has died!" He pointed again, frantically.

"We don't allow visitors. No one gets past this desk." Her dark hair was pulled back, her lips painted a bright red. "It is not allowed." She glanced over her shoulder and appeared relieved that it was only Arnold.

"It is my job to make sure no one goes in there. I have three children to care for at home and no husband to help. My God, I could lose this job—and then what?" When she covered her face with her hands, Arnold noted she wore a thin wedding band.

"A child has died," he said again.

"You won't tell anyone. Please sir." She grabbed onto the lapel of his jacket. "I could lose my position. I was wrong to be reading. But it's just that sometimes, sitting here, day in, day out, it gets dreary and lonely."

"I do not care about your job or your book." He slammed his hand on the desk. "I have been trying to tell you that a child has died. Can you please call the doctor who heads this ward?"

She shook her head. "No. They like to wait until the morning. It can be frightening to the others if we come in and turn on the lights and remove the body. It's much better in the daytime, when we can create a bit of commotion so the children who are still with us can look away."

"But the doctor needs to know." He shook his fist. "A doctor will need to write the death certificate, and time of death, and cause."

"Yes, yes. He will do all of those things. But sir, please do not tell anyone you were allowed in. I promise you that all will be looked after." She was like a train with no brakes barreling down a mountain. "We write kind letters to the parents. We tell them that their child did not die in pain, that he or she had pneumonia or some sort of heart trouble. We assure them." She stroked her hand along the counter as if she was patting a cat.

"But who runs this ward?"

"Well, the Director of course." She looked at the entrance. "Was the door open? How did you get in? It should be locked. I always check it. But maybe it was because the director brought that fellow here. Have you heard of Pfannmuller? From Elfging?"

Her hands clasped as if she was praying. "Dear God," she said. "If the director finds out someone just walked in here, I will lose my job."

"The door was unlocked." His voice rose. "I am a doctor here, so I would have been able to come in anyway."

"No, no, you can't come in. It doesn't matter. I have to have a phone call from the Director himself. They are doing some sort of secret experiment." She put a finger to her lips. "What is your name?"

"Dr. Richter," he said, exasperated. "I am very concerned about the child who died. Can you call the Director and ask him what should be done?"

"I know what should be done. We lose children here. We wait until the morning. That is how it's done. That is the order from the Director. I know the rules. It might be different than on some of the other wards."

He was done with the nurse. He would go now and speak to Bohm about this situation. Whether this woman, who could not shut up, lost her job or not, did not concern him.

Outside, as stars sprinkled the night sky, Arnold's body raged. How could a child be allowed to die and not one person come to her aide? The invisibility of the event shook him. That the other children were in the room with the dead child shook him further.

He could feel the purpose and anger in his stride as he walked toward Bohm's office. Appointment or not, he planned to see the Director.

Stefan sat at his high stool behind the long desk.

Arnold ignored him, and opened Bohm's door.

"You cannot," Stefan screeched.

A nurse was bent over Bohm's desk. Her arms were stretched forward, and her fingers gripped the opposite side from where Bohm stood. She looked back at him as he pushed himself inside of her, giving a moan of satisfaction, and Arnold remembered the sheep dogs from his youth, how watching them mate had been disturbing. But not nearly as disturbing as what he saw now.

Arnold cleared his throat.

"Why on earth are you here?" Bohm asked, stepping back from the nurse and pulling up his trousers.

"I have visited the children's ward," Arnold said. Having adjusted her uniform as best she could, the nurse scurried from the room.

"That is a private ward," Bohm whispered angrily. "You have no right. We are in charge of protecting innocent lives.'

"Protecting? They are starving."

"Out with you!" Bohm yelled at Stefan, who was standing behind Arnold.

Bohm buckled his belt. "You must get ahold of yourself," he said to Arnold. "You can't waltz around the hospital spouting such things. We will have a riot on our hands."

"They are starving."

Bohm paced behind his desk. "I have been asked to help in a study."

"Do the parents know?"

"They know their children are incurable, and have been sent to a place that can treat them."

"But that is a lie."

Bohm patted his potted plants.

"Why?"

Bohm turned. "You are naïve. We are certainly not the only ones conducting such treatments."

It couldn't be true. "I have never heard of it, and I'm sure when I tell other doctors here what is going on, they will be equally shocked."

"Be careful. It would not be a good idea if you began to spread this information."

"Why? Because you'd be put in jail?"

"Do you think I came up with this idea? Do you really think me that sort of monster? This is what we must do. This is what the authorities are telling us to do. Expenditure must be cut, and it was decided that the least cruel way was to let the children go in an easy manner."

"Starving is not an easy manner."

Bohm paused for longer than usual. "No, I suppose it is not." He sat and picked up a pen, began to tap it on his knee. "Pfannmuller believes that the use of injections can be traced, and that might provide a slanderous campaign for the foreign press." He set the pen on his desk. "I do what I am told."

"So you are against it?" Arnold asked.

Bohm pondered the question. "I am not against euthanasia for our sickest patients, and starvation has its benefits. It appears a more natural cause. But none of this is easy for me. This position comes with great responsibility." He looked at Arnold, his expression unusually subdued.

Arnold could do nothing but shake his head.

"I must tell you," Bohm said. "If you begin to spread the news of this, it is not I who will get into trouble, but you. You will be considered a political prisoner, and very quickly you will be sent to a concentration camp. I am not saying this to be difficult or threatening. I find you a kind man and a reasonable doctor. I would very much like you stay on here. But that will not happen, I guarantee it, one hundred percent, if you talk about this."

"A child died in my arms," Arnold said. Tears sprung to his eyes. "While I held her and sang to her. She might have had rickets, but otherwise she could have been perfectly fine. And now she is gone."

"She would not have been perfectly fine. Trust me. We do not make these decisions lightly. There are numerous forms to be filled out and those are then studied in Berlin by experts." Bohm stood and walked to Arnold. "Come and sit for a moment. You have had a very upsetting evening."

Arnold sat because he didn't know what else to do.

"When I first heard that this was something to be carried out," Bohm said, returning to the chair behind his desk, "I was mortified. I almost quit that instant. It seemed to me that I would be carrying out the devil's work. But as I slowly—very slowly—came to terms with it, I began to understand that there is mercy and relief for the children, and the parents."

"No." Arnold would never believe that losing a child, of any kind, at any age, under any circumstance, would bring relief.

Bohm opened a drawer and took out a few letters. He began to read. *We were terribly saddened to hear of the death of our dearest Ruddy. He will always occupy a large portion of our hearts. We are grateful for the care he was given, and also that he no longer has to suffer.*

"And did they know that Ruddy was starved? Or was another cause of death given?"

"We do everything we can to ease the pain on all sides. We write compassionate letters and give a cause of death that will not cause shame or guilt. It is easier to say your child died from pneumonia or encephalitis than from a mental illness." He returned the letters to the drawer.

Arnold could not sit in this vile man's office a second longer. No reasons, none, could ever justify what he witnessed tonight.

Staying at Sonnenstein, knowing what he knew, would make him complicit, and that was unacceptable. It was also unacceptable to leave Rigmor in the hands of this monster. He would phone Inga, and together they would make a plan to rescue Rigmor.

Chapter Nineteen

Links

Belmont, Massachusetts
1984

Inga sat at her table making notes on what needed to be done for Christmas. She had ordered little fir trees for the tables, picking out decorations for each. There would be baskets with fruit and nuts and chocolate. She didn't want to overdo it, but the residents deserved a decorated room and a few indulgences. And although it was awkward, she checked with Holgart to make sure her small touches and donations would be allowed. Perhaps out of guilt for overstepping his bounds when they first met, he was enthusiastic about Inga's generosity, and typed a letter telling the head doctor that Inga had full authorization to *spruce things up*.

She glanced across the room to where Cathy read and Mia slept. It was during this time, after lunch, when most patients were in groups or in therapy, and Mia napped, that Inga found she could focus on her tasks. But today she gave her mind a moment to wander. When she was young and visited the University library, new ideas flowed easily. Her mind was curious. Over the years, she'd lost that curiosity, but now, as she sat at McLean, she felt some of it come back, and it excited her. Her old self wasn't as much returning as it was peeking out from the years of fences and walls and balustrades she had erected.

When she saw Sabine walk down the hall, returning from Lincoln's, Inga noticed a change, a forcefulness in Sabine's gait. Sabine headed right to her grandmother's table without checking on Mia first.

"What is it?" Inga asked, closing her notebook, intrigued at

Sabine's newfound confidence.

Sabine pushed a piece of paper across the table. In front of Inga sat a picture of Rudin. His hair and creased brow were unmistakable. Inga picked up the page, some sort of mimeographed copy of a newspaper article.

"Was this the man you were friends with?" Sabine asked sharply.

As Inga drew her finger down the bridge of Rudin's nose, the excitement she'd felt a minute ago turned to dread.

"I'm not sure I would have called him a friend. But yes, I knew him quite well." She didn't like seeing him. Even so, she found it impossible to look away from the picture.

The date at the top of the page read *Tuesday, August 21, 1945. With a shock of white hair, china-blue eyes and tender pink cheeks....I am sure that Prof. Rudin never so much as killed a fly in his 74 years. I am also sure he is one of the most evil men in Germany.*

"Where did you get this?" Inga asked, unnerved to see Ernst after all of these years.

"Dr. Lincoln gave it to me."

Inga raised her eyebrows. "He had this? I recall him saying he had never heard of Rudin."

Sabine let out an impatient huff. "He hadn't. But he likes history and I guess he was interested in some of the things you mentioned. So he looked him up. But that's not the point. The point is that you were friends with this man."

Inga read a few lines. *Rudin will tell you, that as professor of race hygiene, he had to expound various racial laws passed by the Nazis... but that his point of view was always scientific and not political.*

"There is nothing in here that seems out of the ordinary," she said to Sabine. "Ernst was a scientist." She folded the page in half, not wanting to look at it anymore. The dread moved up her throat.

Sabine grabbed the paper from her. "You didn't say he was a Nazi."

"I was uninterested in his political views." Inga took her handkerchief from her pocket and wiped her forehead. "Tell me, should I get equal amounts of dark and light chocolate?"

Sabine opened the paper. "It says he was a commentator on the sterilization law. And that he would insist he knew nothing of the merciless killings of child and adult inmates at Elfging or Sonnen...something."

"Sonnenstein," Inga whispered.

The last time Inga spoke to Rudin was in 1940, when he telephoned her with a question about the Swiss bank she used. He had wanted to transfer his money out of Germany. She gave him the information he sought and then told him that she was no longer interested in psychiatry and had broken all of her ties with people in that field of study, which was the truth. Their views, which she once understood, had become repugnant as she realized that the human soul was forgotten in their quest for eliminating disease.

"Were those places concentration camps?" Sabine asked.

Inga was recalling the garden party Rudin had attended at their home in Frankfurt. She had thought him so distinguished and important.

"Pardon?" she asked Sabine, feeling bewildered by the way time leapt from there to here.

"Were those places—Elf and Sun-something—concentration camps?"

"No, of course not, why say such a thing? They were asylums, good ones. Not so different from McLean. Ernst was a doctor." She opened her notebook and looked at her lists. "I always think oranges and nuts are good on Christmas."

Sabine raised her voice. "Did they kill people in mental hospitals?"

"Shush," Inga said. "This is not something we should talk about in a public place. Especially here. It may be frightening to some."

"They sterilized people," Sabine said, shaking her head.

Inga took a deep breath and steadied her voice. If Sabine wanted to learn about this, then Inga would organize her thoughts and teach her granddaughter.

"My dear child, they did it in America first. I am not taking a side, but you must at least be aware of your own country's history before speaking with such scorn about another. It was everywhere. Germany did not invent eugenics. In fact, in some ways they were behind. There were societies studying these things all around the world."

"People weren't sterilized here," Sabine said.

"But of course they were. I believe, but am not certain, that California took the lead. Many other states had similar laws. I think some still do. Perhaps Lincoln should have explained that to you before giving you this article, which seems to have excited you in a negative way."

"So you think that this country believed in sterilizing and killing mental patients?"

"There were theories. Ideas. You have heard of natural selection?"

"Of course."

"Some doctors believed that extending lives that weren't meant to survive went against the natural law."

"So you did believe in killing the children in that home near your chalet?" Sabine sounded as if she'd already drawn a firm conclusion.

"I think I made myself clear on that. I hated to see how miserable some of them were."

"And who determines misery?"

"That is a question that I fear is unanswerable."

Misery as Inga had come to understand it was rarely objective. She thought of a girl in Arlesheim, a daughter of a friend, who had Down Syndrome. Inga had initially been wary of meeting the child, but in time Inga saw something that sparkled in the girl, a light of pure kindness.

"Did you know anyone who was sterilized?"

There was a hard glare in Sabine's eyes, and Inga felt too old and too tired to argue about what happened in Nazi Germany.

"I did not know anyone," she said sternly, closing her notebook.

She thought of the hospital in Hamburg where she had voluntarily chosen to get tubal ligation in 1935. After reading countless papers on heredity and genetics, Inga calculated she had a fifty percent chance of carrying a recessive gene for mental illness. Inga did not want to give birth knowing the child might inherit a life of pain and suffering.

"I just don't get how you believed some of these things," Sabine said. "That Rudin was your friend. I mean, they made you leave, and you seem to subscribe to the Nazi beliefs. How did it make you feel that they said you were an inferior race because you were Jewish?" Sabine glanced at the picture of Rudin.

"I did not think Jews inferior. Ever."

"But Rudin did." Sabine tapped her finger on the article. "He says, and I quote, 'they swindle. They're dishonest. They're not creative.'"

Inga pounded a fist on the table. "I am not Rudin. I did not say I believed everything he believed in."

"It just sounds like if you weren't Jewish, you might have joined the Nazis."

Inga had sacrificed her womb for the good of future generations, and here was this impertinent child trying to make her into some coldblooded monster.

"I hated the Nazis." She placed a hand on her chest and recalled the brown shirts and clicking heels of their boots. "They were greedy. They wanted their fat sausages and more land. They were stupid." Her eyes stung. "They did not understand culture or modern art. They called some of Klimt's paintings pornographic. Klimt. Can you believe it? His portrait of Trude

Steiner was priceless, and now it is gone. They destroyed the soul of Germany and fed the masses with propaganda of being the master race." She shook her head. "You have no idea."

"I'm sorry." Sabine's cheeks were red. "I shouldn't have said that. I know you weren't a Nazi."

"No, you shouldn't have. To even think that you would entertain such thoughts." But a creaking door had been opened.

"It's not about that. I guess I just don't know the history."

"No, you do not." Inga paused. "I have been thinking that since it is Christmastime, it might be nice for me to visit your mother. You have Cathy, and things seem to be going relatively well."

"Yes, you should go. But not because of what I said."

Inga pursed her lips. It wasn't because of what Sabine said. She had been thinking of Lisbet lately, how she missed her. Yet she couldn't deny, not entirely, that she felt an inkling of wanting to flee Sabine.

"I am in the States, and it's important that I also see your mother. But for future reference, I would prefer not to speak about the Nazis."

"I get it. I'm sorry."

Inga reached her hand across the table. Sabine gave Inga's fingers a gentle squeeze, a sign of goodwill.

"I will explain to Cathy what needs to be bought," Inga said. "I will call the florist and make sure everything is nice on Christmas Day."

"Omama, you don't have to do that. And if you want, you can take Cathy to help you. I'm getting driving privileges in a day, so I don't think we need her anymore. I'm going to pick up our second car. I'll be able to come and go any time I need to."

"I have paid her for certain tasks that she will continue to perform. If you don't need her on Christmas Eve or Christmas Day, I am sure she would be happy for the time off."

Inga booked a plane ticket for the following evening. Tanner volunteered to take her to the airport, which she welcomed. She liked riding in cars, especially with a competent male driver.

Before Inga left, she wrote lists for Cathy and reminded Sabine to sit straight, wear her hair in a bun, and thank people when they held the door. Most of all, she told her granddaughter, spend time holding the baby. Inga hadn't planned on giving that last piece of advice. It simply came out.

Chapter Twenty

A Mischling (Mixed Breed)

Germany
1935

The August heat refused to lift even after sundown and Inga decided to stay in the drawing room, where it was a few degrees cooler. At nine, the butler knocked on the door.

"Sorry to disturb. There is a phone call for you."

At this time of night, it could only be Fred.

When Arnold announced himself, Inga felt a faint panic. "What is it?" she asked.

"Not a dire emergency. Nothing to do with Rigmor."

"Thank God." But then why was he calling at this hour? She gripped the edge of her chair.

"It's time to take Rigmor home."

"The treatment isn't working?"

"The treatment is coming along."

"Then what is it?"

"There is not urgency for Rigmor. But..."

"Have you been let go?"

"It has nothing to do with me. Or Rigmor." He paused. "I am only thinking that because of the times we live in, I find some of the methods used at the hospital, to be blunt—barbaric."

"What methods?"

"I cannot say over the phone."

"The purpose of this call seems only to frighten the wits out of me. I will come and see for myself."

The following morning she hired a driver to take her to Sonnenstein. She did not tell Frieda, Klaus or Fred of her plans. Her intention was to see Rigmor, even if she was sleeping, to make sure she was all right, and then to have a talk with Arnold about his phone call.

She waited in the lobby of Sonnenstein as an orderly went to find Arnold.

"Inga," he greeted her, surprised. "I didn't expect to see you."

"I told you I was coming," she said, looking into his brown eyes, trying to assess if the problem was somehow with him. She stood and picked up her handbag. "First we will go and see Rigmor, and after that we will sit together in the garden and you will explain the reason for the call."

He led the way to Rigmor's tower room, where a nurse stood at the window. Rigmor lay on her back, her dark curls falling around her lovely face.

Inga ran to the bed, dropped her handbag on a chair, and kneeled on the floor. "I have missed you so," she whispered.

Arnold stood behind Inga. "The nurses will wake her soon for lunch. Sometimes she is alert enough to engage in a short conversation."

"I would like to be the one who wakes her," Inga said.

The nurse approached the bed, instructed Inga to stand next to Rigmor, and gently pull her to a sitting position. Arnold retrieved a cool washcloth that Inga dabbed on Rigmor's forehead.

"It's me, Inga."

Rigmor's eyelids quivered.

"I am here," Inga assured, rubbing her sister's hand.

Finally her eyes opened. She recognized Inga and smiled.

"It's so good to see you," Inga said, feeling a giddy relief.

Rigmor struggled to keep her eyes open. Arnold went to get a glass of water.

"You poor thing, having to sleep all of the time," Inga said. "But not for much longer. The treatments are almost finished, and I'm sure you will be better than ever."

Rigmor clenched her hands as she strained to take a breath.

"What is it?" Inga asked.

"Nothing," Rigmor answered.

Rigmor took a sip of water. "Mother?" she asked Inga.

"She is well."

Rigmor braced herself again, and Inga glanced at Arnold.

"Stomach pains?" Arnold said.

Rigmor nodded.

"Is it from having your period?" Inga asked.

Rigmor closed her eyes as she breathed through another cramp.

"I know how tired you are, but I think it might help if you sat up a little more," Inga said. "We could even try a walk. Just around the room. It is the best thing for cramps. To move a bit."

Rigmor nodded and pushed her hands on the mattress to gain leverage.

"It is too warm in here," Inga told Arnold. "She shouldn't have such a thick eiderdown. There must be a lighter one." When she pulled down the blanket, she noticed the blood. It was indeed a very bad period, Inga thought. Perhaps the sleep treatments caused irregular menstruation.

"Come," Inga said to the nurse. "Help me get Rigmor to the lavatory and get her cleaned." But Rigmor clutched herself again, and Inga noticed a large protrusion. This was more than just a strong period.

"Arnold!" Inga said. "What is this?" She pointed at her sister's stomach.

Arnold shook his head. "A tumor of some sort?"

Was he asking her? Wasn't he the doctor?

Rigmor folded in pain.

"Get some help," Inga shouted.

Arnold told the nurse to call for an ambulance.

"Rigmor," Inga said, caressing her sister's forehead. "Has the pain been going on for long?"

She shook her head.

Inga glanced up at Arnold. "Was this the reason for your

call last night?" she asked, baffled that he wouldn't have said something then.

"No," he replied, watching Rigmor. "I had no idea of this."

Inga looked at Rigmor's stomach again. "But how could you not notice something was wrong? A slender girl like Rigmor with such a large growth?"

"I have only seen her covered."

"I don't understand," Inga said. "Get some warm facecloths."

Inga reassured her sister that help was on the way. It seemed ages before the nurse came running back up to tell them the ambulance had arrived.

Arnold carried Rigmor down the stairs. He and Inga rode in the back of the ambulance.

Rigmor was rushed into surgery at the hospital in Dresden. Inga sat next to Arnold, a few meters outside of the operating room.

Inga's breaths were short and ragged, distressed. "How could you not have noticed?"

"I don't know." Arnold raised his hands to his face. "The nurses change her. The bleeding must have started after breakfast."

"But they didn't notice the protrusion?"

"They let her toilet herself. And in her long nightgown and robe." He shook his head. "I know it all sounds impossible. But I swear to you she has been getting excellent care."

Inga leaned her head back against the wall. "This would never have happened if she were at home."

Arnold paced in the waiting area, combing his hand through his hair.

The door to the operating room finally opened and a surgeon approached. His gown was covered in blood. He pulled off his mask and gloves and shook Arnold's hand.

"Dr. Schmitt," the surgeon said.

"Nice to meet you," Arnold replied.

Inga felt like screaming. This was no time for introductions.

Schmitt caressed his chin. "It was the placenta," he said. "It was torn completely from the uterine wall. We see this in about one percent of pregnancies. We have no real idea why this happens." He gave a compassionate shrug. "I think in the case of this young woman, she was undernourished and weak."

"The placenta?" Inga asked. "What are you talking about?"

Schmitt eyed Inga warily and continued talking to Arnold. "She is very weak. She has lost a lot of blood. If she can make it through the night, I think she will survive."

"What do you mean, think?" Inga shouted. "She must."

Schmitt spoke to Arnold. "We will try our best to keep her stable."

"Of course," Arnold mumbled.

Inga pushed in front of him. "She was pregnant?"

"You didn't know?" Schmitt asked.

"Is there a baby?"

The surgeon glanced upward. "Yes. She is very small. Two kilograms. Possibly only five months along."

"Oh dear God," Inga cried. "But how?"

The surgeon sidestepped her, trying to engage with Arnold. "We are doing all we can for the mother and the child." He took a long breath. "But I am not an obstetrician or pediatrician. This was an emergency surgery, a completely unexpected caesarian section. We had no idea the patient was even pregnant when she first came in. I can say this: The baby is grossly underweight. Taking into account the complications of the pregnancy, and the illness of the mother..." He sighed again. "The patient is schizophrenic? From Sonnenstein? That's what I was told."

"Correct," Arnold said.

"She is not schizophrenic," Inga interjected.

"I read the report that was given to me—that is all," said Schmitt. "If the child should survive—" He hesitated. "Let's not to worry about all of that now."

"Worry about what?" Inga asked. She wanted to grab this man and shake him.

"Children born in such circumstances, when the mother is mentally unfit. They are often... you know."

"I do not know," she said.

"Look, it really doesn't matter at the moment. Let us first make sure the patient survives."

"Tell me about the children," Inga insisted.

"Rigmor is unmarried and has schizophrenia. The child will be a ward of the state. There are homes for them." He looked at the floor.

"I have heard of such places." Inga covered her mouth.

Schmitt turned to Arnold. "We are doing our best," he said, and then walked back into the operating room.

Thirty minutes later, a nurse came out and told them that Rigmor would be asleep for the rest of the night, and it would help no one if they stayed sitting in this uncomfortable waiting area.

Arnold escorted Inga to the Bulow Palais Hotel in the middle of Dresden. He sat with her in the lobby, wearing his blood-stained blazer. He asked Inga if she'd like to call Frieda or Klaus.

"Only Fred," she said. Thankfully, he was home and told her he would drive to Dresden first thing in the morning.

"Can you bear the night alone?" Fred asked Inga.

"It is not I who has to bear anything. It is Rigmor," she cried.

Arnold brought Inga a glass of sherry.

"How?" she asked him.

"I can only think of one man who would have." His face turned a bright red.

"Bohm?" she asked.

Arnold nodded.

* * *

223

Arnold left Inga at the hotel and returned to Sonnenstein. At two in the morning, he changed into his pajamas and crawled into bed. He had never felt so weary, yet he couldn't sleep. Over and over, his mind returned to the same image—Bohm touching Rigmor's hair.

At seven in the morning Arnold walked to Bohm's office and stood outside the door. At twenty past seven, Bohm and his secretary, Stefan, strode down the corridor. Arnold grew tense. It would take all of his control not to punch this man.

"She could have died," Arnold barked. "Did you know that?" He took a step toward Bohm.

"Calm down, man." Bohm held a hand in front of his face. "Perhaps we need a drink."

"You have a busy morning, sir," Stefan told Bohm. "I think it would be wise if Dr. Richter came back a bit later. Perhaps after he's had some time for his nerves to settle."

"I am perfectly settled," Arnold shouted.

"Let us be," Bohm told Stefan. He unlocked his door and nodded for Arnold to go ahead.

Arnold walked in but didn't sit.

Bohm opened the curtains, careful not to knock over any of his plants. Then he walked to his desk, where he retrieved two cigars, and tried to hand one to Arnold, who once again refused.

Bohm struck a match. "Do you think this sudden illness of Rigmor's has anything to do with the sleeping treatment?"

"She was pregnant," said Arnold seething. "Five or six months along. Around the time when you began treating her."

Bohm laughed. "You can't be thinking that I had something to do with it."

"I saw you with her. I saw how you touched her."

"Get ahold of yourself, man." He puffed his cigar. "If it wasn't so amusing, I would have you taken off the premises."

Nothing about this was amusing. The fact that Bohm took it in so lightly, or at least pretended to, convinced Arnold that the director was guilty.

He marched around the desk and aimed his fist straight at Bohm's nose. The cigar flew into the air and landed on the desk. A piece of paper caught fire.

"Stefan," Bohm yelled.

Stefan ran into the room, took off his jacket and smothered the flame.

Arnold raced out. He had never hit a man before. He didn't have siblings to tussle with, and his father had never laid a finger on him. His mother wouldn't have tolerated it.

Once outside, he made straight for the road that led to Dresden. Of course he would be fired, but that seemed inconsequential in the scheme of things. All that mattered was Rigmor.

He walked a good half-hour before a car slowed alongside him. Arnold needed to be alone. He was ready to thank the driver for his generosity when he saw that it was Fred.

"You look as if you could use some company."

Arnold got in and focused on the road in front of him. If he turned, if he glanced at Fred, if he saw even the tiniest bit of compassion, Arnold was afraid he would start sobbing and not be able to stop.

* * *

Inga had been up most of the night. By eight in the morning, when Fred still hadn't arrived, she hired a car to take her to the hospital, where a tired-looking woman sat behind the reception desk.

"I need to see my sister," Inga told her. "Rigmor Blumenthal."

The woman looked through her leather binder. "Maternity ward. Second floor."

Inga let out a breath she hadn't realized she was holding. Rigmor wasn't in the morgue.

Inga pushed aside the swinging doors and walked straight to

the main desk on the maternity ward. "I must know the condition of my sister, Rigmor."

The nurse placed her hands on the wooden armrests and pushed herself up. "We ask that you keep your voice down. There are women trying to rest."

Inga replied by waving her hand for the nurse to hurry. Behind a blue curtain, Rigmor slept on her side.

"Shouldn't she be on her back?" Inga asked.

The nurse had a gentle manner. "She is asleep, and seems peaceful. My suggestion is to leave her for the moment. Rest is what she needs now."

Inga caressed Rigmor's forehead, and then followed the nurse back to her desk.

"And the baby?" Inga whispered, expecting to learn she had died in the night.

"She just fell asleep," the nurse answered. "She seems to have her night and day mixed up. That is often the case with new ones."

"Is she terribly weak?" Inga whispered.

The nurse inclined her head. "She is a small thing, but I would not say weak. She has the cry of a baby with strong lungs."

"But she is only five or six months—that does not make babies weak?"

The nurse smiled. "Yes, it would do that. But your sister's child was not preterm."

"I'm afraid there is some sort of mix up," Inga said.

"There was only one baby delivered last night."

"Yes, and Dr. Schmitt said the baby was very early and frail. He did not think she would survive."

"She is small, and there was some confusion about how far along the child was, but after she was examined, it was clear that she was full-term and is a healthy little bunny." The nurse smiled. "The mother is undernourished, and from the papers I received, suffers from a major mental illness. That is surely the cause of the low birth weight."

"The mental illness?" Inga asked, feeling off-balance. The baby was full-term. How could that be?

"The mental illness and the lack of good nutrition. A combination."

"But the baby." Inga stopped and calculated. The baby was not Bohm's. It was Arnold's. He did not have faulty machinery, as he had claimed. "The baby will live?"

"I believe so," the nurse said.

Inga thanked her and left the ward. Her legs felt weak. She walked to the end of a corridor, where she found a chair inside a small alcove. It couldn't be. For all of the precaution Inga had taken not to have a child, and then for Rigmor, who was so ill, to give birth? She took a deep breath, and tried to slow her thoughts. It was Arnold's, not Bohm's. That was a good thing. One good thing. She took another breath. Yes, better it be Arnold's. He did have a kind disposition. Although full-term would mean the baby might live, and the poor dear child...what a life would it have?

Inga covered her mouth when she recalled hearing about a child born with microcephaly, a small brain. The baby had been taken from its mother and brought to a home where it had undergone a horrible surgery and died. The baby was returned to the parents without its brain.

There was no tolerance for weak or sick babies, and though Rigmor's baby was not sick—the fact that she was small, that her mother was ill, and Jewish, and her father, German, that the Nuremberg laws prohibited sex or marriage between Jews and Aryans, that obsession of race gripped the country—all of those factors would dictate that the baby would be viewed as a Mischling, a mixed-breed. Defective. She would be taken in a matter of days. Perhaps even today. They would place her in a decrepit home for idiot children and leave her to cry alone in a metal crib.

Inga paced.

The circumstances could not have been worse. And there was Rigmor to consider. If she woke, if she saw the baby, fell in love with the tiny thing, and then had to separate from her, she would not survive the heartbreak. It was all too awful.

Inga walked to the main lobby, arriving just as Arnold and Fred strode in. She ran to Fred.

"How is she?" he asked.

"Rigmor has made it through the night."

"Thank God," Arnold replied.

"Go to her," Inga snapped. "Second floor. Maternity ward." Arnold obeyed.

Fred put an arm around Inga's waist and walked her to one of the sofas. "Why the icy treatment for Arnold?" he asked.

The words raced out as Inga explained that Arnold was the father and now the baby was about to be carted to some horrible institution where she would be shown no love.

"So then Arnold is not a homosexual." Fred took out a cigar.

"This is no time to smoke," Inga told him.

"It is the perfect time."

"What are we going to do?"

"This is certainly not the first nor the last time that an unwanted baby was born," Fred answered. "These things are manageable. I will make inquiries with the head of the hospital, and we will see to it that the baby gets placed in a good home."

"No one will take a baby from a mentally ill, unwed Jewish mother."

"Perhaps not in this country. But my sister is in Basel. She can keep the child for a time while we find a suitable home. You needn't say the mother was mentally ill. You could even say she died in childbirth and she wasn't married. It's common enough."

"But we cannot wait. Surely they will take the baby soon. And on top of that, I don't want Rigmor to see the baby and then have to say goodbye. It would finish her. As if she hasn't endured enough." Inga took a handkerchief from her handbag and blew her nose.

Fred rubbed her back. "We can leave today. We will hire a nurse, who we can pay handsomely. I will find the director and phone my sister."

"What if it won't be allowed?"

"There are ways. I do have some money. You needn't worry. It will be one less thing for the hospital to concern themselves with. They will be glad to have this situation so easily resolved for them."

"This is just too horrid," Inga cried.

Fred took a long pull on his cigar, blew the smoke upward, and reached for her hand. "You have been through a lot. I suggest you go to the dining hall, get a cup of tea, freshen your face, and by that time most of the details will be ironed out."

She rested her head on his shoulder for a moment. "You are a good man," she whispered.

He patted her knee. "And you are a good woman."

She went to get a cup of tea, but she did not wash her face, or put on another coat of lipstick. Instead she sought out Arnold, who sat on a chair next to Rigmor's bed.

"I must accompany Fred on a business trip," Inga told Arnold.

He didn't reply.

"Did you hear me?" she asked.

"Yes," he muttered. "I will watch over her."

"Do not leave her alone for one moment." She approached the bed and caressed Rigmor's hair.

"I will be here," he said.

Inga lowered her head. In a few seconds she would tell this man a lie that might very well keep him from knowing his only progeny, a lie that would likely ensure he would never have the chance to be a father. But there was little choice, and perhaps Inga was doing him a great favor, saving him from monumental worry and distress.

"The baby died," she finally whispered. "I will have her cremated."

Arnold gasped.

"It's probably best this way," Inga said. "Perhaps Rigmor was unaware she was pregnant. I would suggest not bringing up the matter." She kissed Rigmor's cheek. "Goodbye my darling," she said, and was about to hurry off, but then she stopped and rested a hand on Arnold's shoulder. "She must always be protected."

Arnold nodded.

Fred had been more efficient than Inga thought possible. He met with the director of the hospital, who agreed that taking the baby out of the country was best. Inga did not ask if money was exchanged. The director knew of a young nurse, Brigitta, who needed financial aid to help her sick mother. She would travel with them and stay with the baby as long as she was needed. As far as the other staff at the hospital, aside from the head maternity nurse, everyone would be told the baby died. Fred had offered money to the head nurse for her assistance, but she refused. The baby's wellbeing was all that mattered to her and if that meant peddling a few lies, that was perfectly acceptable.

Brigitta was to meet them at the back of the building where there was a door used by the deliverymen. Inga and Fred waited outside.

"What if she is stopped?" Inga asked.

"She is a nurse. She will not be stopped."

"Yes, but she is carrying a baby. It might look..."

Just then the door opened, and a nurse wearing a white hat and black cape hurried out with a basket that looked as if it might contain two loaves of bread.

Fred waved a hand. The nurse scurried over. Inga glanced down at the light gray blanket covering the basket. She noticed a ripple of movement—a gentle ocean wave.

"Come," Fred said, and led the way to the car.

Brigitta slid into the back and carefully extracted the baby, a tiny thing with a bright red face.

"What is her name?" Brigitta asked, after they began their journey to Switzerland.

"Lisbet," Inga answered, not sure why that name popped out. She wiped her forehead. The car was suffocating, the heat turned up because Brigitta insisted that was best for the baby.

Inga leaned her head against the window and watched the green hills blur. That her dear sister, already so weak and vulnerable, gave birth to a child, who more than likely would suffer from mental illness one day, and that Arnold was the cause—it all seemed so impossible. And of course it had not escaped Inga's thoughts that she was the root of this tragedy. It was almost too difficult to bear. She closed her eyes and felt a steely, cool hatred. Not for Arnold, or Frieda or the baby. But for herself.

Chapter Twenty-One

Lisbet

Glen Grove, Illinois
1984

At Lisbet's home, Inga took her case to the cellar, or basement, as it was called in the States. Although it was colder than the rest of the house, the light from the high-set windows was adequate, and Inga had the luxury of a private bathroom.

On Christmas Eve, Inga sat at the table next to Lisbet. Robert, her eldest grandson, sat next to his girlfriend, across from Inga. Gerald sat at the head of the table. Inga folded her hands on her lap and pressed her fingers together. She was here to see Lisbet and Robert, to wish them a happy Christmas, and to persuade Lisbet to visit Sabine. She would not argue with Gerald regardless of how he provoked her and she would remember what Sabine had said, about Lisbet liking to compete. That notion would help Inga not worry so much about her daughter.

Inga wore a silk blouse instead of a cotton one, and her pearl necklace. Lisbet laid out her best china, although only four plates remained of the twelve Inga had bought. The fifth, nonmatching plate, which Lisbet used for herself, was smaller, lighter and cheaper. Inga wondered what had happened to the others. Had they all been broken?

Lisbet cooked a roast beef, boiled the potatoes and ladled peas into filo pastries. All very well done.

During dinner, Robert and Gerald argued about Reagan economics, and although they sounded acrimonious they were both actually on the same side of things. Inga might not like Gerald, but she had to admit that at the moment, he seemed very interested in Robert's views, and Robert appeared quite pleased about that. She remembered how much Fred had always liked Gerald, how he tried to explain to Inga that Gerald just had an excitable nature—that he was an electron unable to find its ground state. Inga had tried to soften to Gerald, but that had been impossible after the way he kicked Henri.

Robert's girlfriend was nice enough, but Inga doubted she would be anything permanent. She had remarkably long brown hair, large hazel eyes, and added very little in the way of conversation, just that one day she hoped to visit Switzerland.

Lisbet, as was always the case, could not sit still. She jumped to get another spoon, or to refill Gerald's ginger-ale. Sometimes she went to the kitchen and came back empty-handed. She had always loved movement, and skating had been a good match for her. When she wasn't on the ice, she was practicing moves in the garden or the drawing room.

Inga turned to Lisbet now, and could not deny that her overriding feeling was one of pride.

Just as they finished their main course, Gerald patted Lisbet's hand, stood, and walked upstairs.

Mother and daughter would have peace, a gift Inga hadn't expected.

"I should check on him," Lisbet said, and glanced behind her as if she might have done something wrong.

"Leave him," Inga suggested. "He is a grown man, and you have done nothing."

But Lisbet's mouth quivered, and Inga found herself of two minds, feeling as if Lisbet was performing and, at the same time, feeling a bit heartbroken for her daughter, who had made such an effort, not only with the dinner but also in her appearance: her hair was in a well-shaped bun, and she wore red lipstick and a blouse with a silver sheen.

Gerald returned a minute later, took his place at the head of the table, and held up his glass of ginger-ale.

"I would like to wish everyone a very happy Christmas and

good health for the New Year. And to my beautiful wife, who works too hard and never sits down, I am very grateful to have you in my life."

Lisbet leaned over and kissed his cheek. "Oh darling."

Gerald handed her a small box wrapped in gold foil. Lisbet tore off the paper. "You shouldn't have." She picked up the miniature blue Faberge egg, another charm for her bracelet.

"It's beautiful." Lisbet kissed Gerald again. She was a tall, happy sunflower.

After tea and strudel, Jessica pawed Robert amorously, hardly shy about what she wanted. A few minutes later they said they had to leave to meet friends and Gerald announced he would retire to his study.

Inga helped Lisbet with the dishes and then suggested they sit in the living room, furnished in part with the few pieces the family had been able to save from Germany, including a very old dollhouse that had once belonged to Inga's grandmother.

"I remember playing with that doll's house when I was a child," Inga said. "I always wanted a canopy bed like the one in there. It's nice that you take such good care of it."

Lisbet had added some new pieces, each made by her own hands, something Inga found tender, a thread that linked the generations of women. One day it would go to Sabine, and then Mia.

Lisbet sat on the smallest chair in the room, her finger racing back and forth on her eyebrow.

"Dinner was excellent," Inga said. "And Robert seems well."

Lisbet's finger paused. "Yes, he likes his new job at the bank."

"I am a bit surprised to hear that. It all strikes me as too conventional for someone who has such a good mind. But he has time to change." She smiled, wanting to show Lisbet that she was not criticizing, but rather being open to the future.

"His girlfriend is nice," Lisbet said.

Inga decided not to remark that that might change soon as

well. Instead it was time to broach the reason for her visit. "It would be nice if you came to Boston to see Sabine. I think she needs her mother at the moment."

"I hate to think of her in that place." Lisbet's shoulders drew together.

"It's not so bad. The rooms are quite big, and her roommate has some charm. The baby can visit. But I do think it might give her a boost to see you."

"It is my fault that she is there."

Inga had little patience for martyrdom. "That is utter nonsense. It is no one's fault. These things happen."

"Grandmother warned me."

Inga and Frieda had agreed that they would not speak of mental illness in front of Lisbet, that there was no point in her knowing anything about Rigmor, or frightening her with stories of madness.

"What did your grandmother say?" Inga asked, not hiding her surprise.

"She just said that if I ever felt my mind betraying me, or if I felt my nerves get the better of me, then I should tell myself I was fine, and not give in to those inclinations."

"But you were always fine. So I don't understand how you could think you might be responsible for Sabine's condition?"

"I didn't tell anyone. When Sabine was a baby, I was desperate. I cried every night. I had terrible dreams. I had dizzy spells, and once I even..." She lowered her head.

"You even?"

"I saw a woman in my bedroom. I woke up Gerald, and pointed to the woman, but he said nothing was there. He was so kind to me during that period. He brought me tea, and asked me if I wanted to go on walks with him. I know you think he's awful, but he helped me then."

"I am glad to hear of it." Inga remembered visiting Lisbet shortly after Sabine was born. It had been a trying time with two young boys and a new baby. Inga had cleaned, played with the boys, organized the sitting room, made shopping lists, cooked dinners, but still there was always another mess, a crying baby, a diaper that needed changing, more washing.

"Do you remember when I came to see you in England after Sabine was born?" Inga asked.

"Yes."

"One night I had woken at two in the morning. I went to fetch a glass of water and you were in the kitchen tearing off the wainscoting, which I thought very peculiar. It was that night you told me you were moving to the States and I felt as if a strong wave from the North Sea had knocked into me. But now I understand. You weren't well, and you were frightened, and perhaps you thought fleeing would help. I was convinced you were running from me."

Lisbet shrugged. "I didn't know what to do."

"There was a time, when I was much younger, before you were born, that I believed it was good to get things out in the open. To talk. Somewhere along the way, I changed my mind about that. But now I think that was wrong. I think it might help you to speak of these things."

"I was so afraid of being put away. The way Sabine is now. Afraid that...I can't say it."

"But you must, my dear, or you will never be free of it."

Lisbet drew in a breath, as her eyes seemed to shiver. Inga had never seen a person's eyes do that, tremble back and forth in their sockets.

"Grandmother said that... I can't."

"You can," Inga told her.

"That I needed to be careful of you. That if you knew, you might want me to go to a sanatorium, but I must understand that sanatoriums were not what they seemed. People never came out. I thought living in the States would be safer."

Now, twenty-six years later, Inga once again felt the wind

knocked out of her. This time by Frieda.

"She had her own fears, and she should never have put those onto you." Inga shook her head. "Perhaps she wanted to protect you, but to do so at my expense, to make me into some horrible person that would get you locked up, that you had to run from — that was not fair. To me, or to you."

"Do you think I gave this to Sabine?"

"None of us knows exactly how much of who we are is genetic or cultural, but I am absolutely sure you were a kind and generous mother, and what you gave to Sabine had more to do with love than anything else."

Lisbet looked as if she might burst into tears. Inga was about to get her a tissue when she heard a door upstairs open and close. It was a sign that there might not be much time before Gerald came thundering down. He hated to share his wife, especially with Inga.

"You must not blame yourself, or me." Inga paused.

She remembered the afternoon Frieda had died in a hospital in Dornach. Lisbet had been beside herself and moments before Frieda took her last breath, she grasped Lisbet's hand and told her she would win the championship. Two days later that prediction became a reality. Whatever Frieda's faults were, she did adore Lisbet.

"You also must also not blame your grandmother," Inga said. "She had her beliefs for her own reasons. Sabine mentioned something to me the other day about learning from the past. I think that is wise. But we also must not get stuck in it." Inga touched Lisbet's hand. "I think it will help if Sabine sees you, if she learns that you once felt this way."

Lisbet lowered her voice. "When we came to this country, I even thought maybe I should go and see one of those doctors. A psychiatrist. That maybe they could help me. But then I knew I mustn't."

"I wish you would have. Perhaps they could have helped you

understand that you were always strong. Look how you have managed, with your husband, your career, this house? And three children."

Lisbet seemed encouraged—a little, at least—and Inga was glad to be making headway. But then the door upstairs opened again, and Gerald descended the stairs.

"It is time that Lisbet goes to bed," he said.

Inga stood. "Stop." She pointed to the stairs. "Go back to your room and let me speak with my daughter."

"I did not invite you," he shouted.

"Go."

"You interfere where you shouldn't."

"I do nothing of the sort," Inga replied, sounding sure of herself, but feeling less so.

Gerald marched back up and slammed the door.

Lisbet's shoulders rounded.

Inga sat. "I should not have come. I will leave in the morning."

"I don't think I can go to Boston tomorrow," Lisbet whined. "It's Christmas Day."

"Perhaps in a week's time," Inga said.

Lisbet nodded, and Inga decided she would push no further.

"I'll make an agreement with you," she said. "I will not ask you to visit Sabine. I will not beg you to come to Switzerland for an extra week in the summer or tell you to write me long letters. But you must promise that you will find a psychiatrist to talk to about what you're going through. Then I will leave you alone."

The beginnings of a smile curved at the side of Lisbet's mouth. "I have never wanted you to leave me alone."

Inga's throat tightened as she held back tears. It was the kindest thing her daughter had ever said to her.

Chapter Twenty-Two

New Directions

Dresden, Germany
1935

As he had during her sleep treatments, Arnold sat next to Rigmor and spoke softly. He told her he had punched Bohm, that he was sorry he hadn't kept a better eye on the man, and that as soon as she recovered they would leave Sonnenstein and return to civilization in Frankfurt. He told her that Inga and Fred had gone on a short business trip, and that he would find a gramophone and play her Bach. He caressed her hand and promised that she would soon be eating normal meals, and that he would make sure that she had as much potato leek soup as she wanted.

He took no notice of the time. He planned to sit by Rigmor's side all day. Babies cried, mothers talked, husbands brought flowers. Rigmor slept.

Arnold asked Dr. Eichner, the obstetrician, if perhaps it would be better for Rigmor to have a bed that wasn't on the maternity ward. The baby noise might be upsetting.

"Medically," he said, "this is by far the best place for her." He glanced around. "She is not the only mother who has lost a child." After a pause, he gave a kind smile. "And please, call me Rudiger. We are both doctors, no need for formalities." He had dark, heavy eyebrows that touched each other and made him appear angry, even though he wasn't.

At eight that evening, a nurse informed Arnold that visiting hours were over. But he refused to leave. The middle of the night was the most common time for patients to slip away.

"If we allow you to stay," the nurse said, "soon all of the husbands will be asking for the same favor."

"But I am not a husband. I am a doctor. Her doctor. I am a psychiatrist from Sonnenstein."

"What is she diagnosed with?" The nurse took a step back, as if she was afraid she might catch something.

"Schizophrenia."

Arnold was allowed to stay.

In the morning, a different nurse came to wash Rigmor. Arnold went to the dining hall for coffee and toast. When he returned, Rudiger was leaning over the bed listening to Rigmor's heart.

"She seems to be doing well," he said. "We will reduce the sedative, and in five or six hours she should open her eyes."

Arnold felt a rush of adrenalin. He would not lose her.

"When she is awake, do you want me to explain to her what happened?" Rudiger asked.

"It might be best if I talk to her."

"We realize she wouldn't have been able to care for the child, but had she hoped to see the baby?" His eyes looked sympathetic. He would have made a good psychiatrist.

"To be honest, I'm not sure what Rigmor is aware of," Arnold said. "She was under strict sleep treatments for the past five months." He sighed heavily. "The baby was early and so small, and Rigmor might not have even known she was pregnant."

Rudiger squinted, confused. "But the baby was not early. She was very small, but that is because the mother is completely malnourished."

"No." Arnold shook his head. "The baby was only five months. Perhaps you have confused her with another patient."

Rudiger moved closer to Arnold. "I have examined Rigmor's uterus," he whispered. "Full term."

Arnold sunk into the chair next to the bed.

"I am sorry to have shocked you." Rudiger said, patting Arnold on the shoulder. "I did learn from the nurses here that the baby died peacefully, although that is hardly consolation."

Rudiger was correct about one thing. It was no consolation.

Arnold was left alone with his foolish, dimwitted, irresponsible self. He had been doing everything, hovering and protecting, and trying to keep Rigmor safe, when it was he who had caused the most damage. It was his fault she was at Sonnenstein. It was his fault the sex had been so careless. It was his fault that they now had a child—a dead child.

At around six that evening, Rigmor's eyelids fluttered. Arnold whispered her name and she turned and smiled with parched lips, asking for water. He leapt up and practically attacked the first nurse he saw, telling her she must immediately bring something for Rigmor to drink.

Rigmor took a few sips of water and asked where she was.

"In a hospital in Dresden," Arnold answered.

When a baby cried, Rigmor smiled. "Is it a boy or a girl?"

"I don't know," Arnold told her, wishing she didn't have to listen to the healthy wails of infants.

"You have not seen the baby yet?"

Until this moment he hadn't realized how much he hoped she would be unaware of what had happened.

"I am sorry," he whispered. "It was a girl. She was too small. Her lungs were not developed enough." He stared into Rigmor's wide gray eyes. "She did not survive."

Rigmor blinked slowly, like a butterfly pressing its wings together for the last time. A tear rolled down her cheek.

"I'm sure she was beautiful," Rigmor said.

Perhaps she was calm because the sedatives still ran through her blood, or perhaps it was because she somehow expected this, as if she didn't deserve happiness or children—as if she knew better than to hope. There was resignation on her face that suggested she had understood, a long time ago, that in this lifetime she was meant to know only loss.

"I wish..." Arnold began and wiped a tear from his face. He didn't know what he wished for—to turn back time? A baby that survived?

"We mustn't. The best we can do is close this window."

His heart felt as if it was dissolving, breaking into thousands of little pieces that would swim through his blood and leave an empty hole in his chest.

* * *

Frankfurt, Germany
1935

For two nights, Inga and Fred stayed at Hannah's home in Basel. She was older than Fred by three years. What she lacked in beauty, she made up for in doting kindness and intelligence.

Inga called the maternity ward multiple times a day. Rigmor was recovering. But before Inga returned to Dresden, she needed to speak with Frieda, and it was not the type of conversation one could have by phone.

Fred drove Inga to Frankfurt and left her at the front of the house. As she watched his car pull away, she already missed him—his insights, his humor, the smell of the soap he used, the way his toes wriggled in his sleep.

The butler held the door. Inga planned to go upstairs, have a bath, put on a clean dress, and then face Frieda.

"Inga," Frieda called.

She hadn't even made it to the staircase. "I'm going to change," Inga said. "Then we can talk."

"No. Now," Frieda demanded.

They sat in the drawing room, a fair distance apart.

"That man from the institution called," Frieda said. "I feel as if I'm living in a horrible dream. He said that Rigmor was recovering well and he was sorry to hear that the baby died, but he wanted me to know, emphatically, he repeated, that it wasn't his."

Inga had hoped Frieda would never know there was a baby.

That Bohm had telephoned without first checking with Inga was stupid and insensitive, likely done in haste because he feared losing a benefactor.

"There was a baby. She did not die," Inga said. "Fred and I took her to Switzerland. She is safe, with Fred's sister, and a nurse. I am looking for a good home for her."

Frieda's eyes widened. "Alive," she whispered. "A girl." She sat a bit taller, and even smiled.

"Yes."

"You will not give her to anyone. Who is the father?" Frieda asked, as her fingers moved, likely counting the months.

"It's complicated," Inga answered.

Frieda shook her head. "They never went to the concert. Arnold and Rigmor."

Inga nodded.

"And what does he know?" Frieda asked.

"He was informed that the baby died." She hesitated. "I thought it best to keep him outside of matters at this point."

"Yes, we must keep it that way." Frieda stood and walked to the mantel. In that short distance, she seemed to redirect the course of her life. "I will move to Switzerland." She paused. "We will be forced out soon enough. You will find an institution in Switzerland where Rigmor can recuperate. Let us be rid of this hateful country."

But Inga was not ready to leave her country. "I will help you find a place for the baby, but I don't intend to leave Germany."

Frieda shook her head. "The baby will not be put in a *place*. She will have a home with us, and as far as the world will know, the baby belongs to you and Klaus."

"To me?" Inga said, shocked. "But I am not meant to be a mother."

"Perhaps that is true. But I think we both know that this happened because of your machinations, and now you must do the right thing. There is no other choice." Frieda walked to the door, reached for the handle, and then turned to look at Inga. "You were prudent in saving the baby. But you were very careless in getting Arnold and Rigmor together, and were unwise in sending her to Sonnenstein."

The moment the door closed, Inga's head drooped, her shoulders fell inward—her foundation faltered.

She was not ready to leave Germany, or her life. She was not ready to mother a child. But Frieda was correct. It was Inga's fault, and her belief that she knew best had not withstood her own actions. And now it was necessary that she fight—for the baby, for Rigmor, and for a new life in a country she didn't know. Like it or not, Inga had no choice but to submit to Frieda.

Later that day, she telephoned Rudin. He boasted that of course he had connections in Switzerland—after all, it was his native land. Then he sighed.

"But," he said. "Switzerland is not an easy country to get into, even in the best of situations. Their mental hospitals are overcrowded, and they will not look kindly on a schizophrenic German refugee."

Inga withered—*schizophrenic refugee*. Those words seemed so extreme and wrong.

"And," Rudin continued. "If you were able to find a bed for her, something I could help with, you must remember she will be placed on a general ward. She will be sleeping near people who not only have mental illnesses, but infectious diseases as well. She will not have a room of her own that overlooks some of Germany's finest countryside."

"But she will be safer in Switzerland."

"She is perfectly safe in Germany," he answered. "She is at an excellent institution with a first-rate director. I know Bohm well, and one of his best attributes is that he does not judge. At least not in the way of race, or color of skin. Rigmor will not be treated badly because she is Jewish. If that is what worries you."

"It's one of my worries," Inga said.

"One that can be erased. And then there is the question of paying for care in Switzerland. They will most certainly expect to be compensated, and as much as I disagree with some of the recent laws, I do know you will not be able to take your wealth out of this country."

He was correct about that. Fred had looked into it. Inga felt desperate. "I just don't think we can leave her here," she said. "If she can't be in an institution, then we will care for her at home."

"Has she undergone the sterilization procedure?" Rudin asked.

"Not yet," Inga answered, feeling as if he had dealt yet another blow.

"That will be an impediment."

"Surely we can have someone write a letter and say that she had the operation."

"I doubt a doctor would ever lie about such a thing, not to mention the danger it would put him in if he was caught." Rudin paused. "Personally, it is not something I would risk—after all, the surgery is quite simple. The best thing for your sister is that she have consistent care in an institution that is known for excellence. She will be safe and well looked-after, and you can visit her whenever you like. It is only a few hours' journey by car. And," he added, his voice more animated. "Didn't I meet a man at your home once? By the name of Richter? He was hired to care for her. Wasn't he? He might be the kind of chap who would be amenable to looking after her."

"Yes," Inga said, feeling the cold irony of it all.

"If you want to ensure she is well cared for, have people you trust look in on her. I assure you that is the best option."

Inga relayed the information from Rudin to Frieda. It would have been easier if her mother railed, yelled, and cursed. Instead she sat in silent condemnation.

* * *

Dresden, Germany
1935

By the time Inga and Fred returned to Dresden, Rigmor was sitting up in bed and eating small meals. The nurses expected that she would soon be able to walk with assistance.

Inga brought Swiss chocolates, yellow roses, and a silk robe. Arnold watched the sisters, the vibrant, worldly risk-taker, and the modest, humble introvert—each the harmony for the other.

That evening, she and Fred took Arnold out for dinner at a dimly lit tavern.

"We have news," Inga began, her tone brusque.

Arnold nodded as he chewed the first bite of meat until it nearly dissolved in his mouth. He found it difficult to swallow. The next bite was not much better, but after a few more pieces, his body seemed to wake to its hunger, and he finished his meal paying more attention to the laughing and talking in the background than to Inga or Fred.

After his second beer, Arnold said, "I think Rigmor should return to Frankfurt. Sonnenstein is not the place for her. She can get a nurse. I will return as well. She will be better there."

"My good man," Fred said. "Have you heard anything we have been telling you?"

Arnold set down his beer. "I was distracted."

"We are moving to Switzerland," Inga said.

"You and Fred?" he asked Inga.

"I have already moved my family to London," Fred answered. "Inga and her mother will be moving to Basel."

"And Rigmor?" he asked.

Inga's gaze dropped. "That is a concern."

"She cannot stay here," Arnold protested.

"It is not ideal," Fred said. "But at the moment, it is the safest and best option."

Arnold looked at Inga. He wanted the news from her, not Fred.

"I spoke to Rudin, and when we considered all of the factors, it seems Sonnenstein is the best place for the moment," Inga told him.

"There are things..." Arnold began—but then stopped. Talking about what he had seen in the children's ward could put them all in danger. If Fred went to a newspaper with this information, they would be carted off. "She should not live at Sonnenstein." Arnold placed his hand firmly on the table. "You must believe me."

Inga picked up a serviette and dabbed her eyes. "We are trying. I promise you. I wish I could take care of her myself, but that is not possible. She must get stronger before we can move her. You will stay with her, make sure she is well cared for. We will be extremely generous in our contributions to the asylum and you will be well compensated."

"I don't care about the money," Arnold said, feeling insulted. "I want only what is best for Rigmor."

"Then do what Inga says," Fred barked. "We will visit regularly and you will keep us abreast of any new developments."

A few patrons began to sing, *Deutschland, Deutschland, Uber alles, Above all else in the world!*

Fred stood. "I cannot listen to this rot." He found the waitress, shoved some money at her, and waited at the door for Arnold and Inga.

* * *

When Bohm requested a meeting, Arnold showed up unshaven and wearing a wrinkled shirt.

"We are in a precarious situation," Bohm said. He touched his nose, a sly reminder of where he had been hit. "Under normal circumstances, you would not be here. But these are not normal circumstances, are they?"

"No," Arnold said, keeping his head lowered.

"What the Blumenthals have asked for is rather simple. You will be Rigmor's doctor. You will have no other patients. Your quarters will be moved. A steward will show you to your new room. You will have no contact, at least no medical contact, with other patients. You can work on a volunteer basis and play cards or serve drinks, and clean night pots. At the moment, you will retain your medical license, but only for Rigmor's sake. If we happen to run into each other, we will be cordial. If you ever touch me again, I will tell the SS you have been secretly trying to have patients avoid the sterilization laws. I have already had papers made up to prove this. The SS will put you in a camp, and within a week, they will declare your case a suicide. Is this clear?"

"It is," Arnold said.

"Inga is not subtle." He rubbed his chin. "I actually find that an attractive quality. But that is not the point. She suggested that I change Rigmor's diagnosis. That is out of the question." He slammed a fist on his desk. "I could get sent away for that. Imagine that she had the nerve to ask, and after the lot of you practically accused me of doing unspeakable things to a sleeping patient." He shook his head. "Her diagnosis cannot be changed. And don't think other doctors haven't tried such things. Their fates have not been pleasant."

"I will ask nothing of you."

Bohm nodded to the door.

Arnold's new residence was a cell-like room on the second floor of Building Two. A cot, rickety wardrobe, and meager bookcase furnished the area. One small window overlooked the road, and on the wall, above the head of the bed, was a framed print of the Nazi insignia—the broken cross. He took it down.

As long as he could see Rigmor every day the size of his room was inconsequential, as were the mice behind the wall. At this point in his career, his dreams of contributing to the field of psychiatry had faded.

Arnold visited Wilhelm. The health court had declined his appeal, and Wilhelm had been sterilized. It wasn't so bad, he said, in a voice that closed the subject for good.

After the loss of the baby, Rigmor sunk into a deep depression. Some days Arnold would plead and cajole for hours just to get her to a sitting position in bed. But he never grew weary of trying, and soon she was dressing without help from the nurses, and going for daily strolls.

* * *

Her last night in Frankfurt, Inga kicked off her black pumps and slouched on the sofa, one of the few pieces of furniture left in the great room. In the past two weeks she had taken on the task of giving their artwork to museums, furniture and clothes to homes for the elderly, Oriental carpets to friends, silver and china to servants, and first editions to the library. In a few hours she and her mother would be leaving Germany, and Inga, who had filled her time with symphonies of Mahler, Schoenberg, and Bartok, lectures by Tillich and Jung, and all night dinner parties, would soon be living in a small Swiss village with no library or opera house.

Klaus had moved into a flat a few weeks earlier. Inga had legally separated from him so that he could continue on as a professor. Married to a Jewish woman, he would lose his position. Of course, emotionally and physically, they had been separated for some time. In fact, aside from having sex in their first few weeks of marriage, they had never really been together as man and wife.

Inga looked up at the painting of Rigmor. The family could not give the portrait away, and it was much too large for any home they would reside in.

She closed her eyes and the images flooded in. She and Rigmor playing in the garden, painting in the studio, sneaking their first glass of port. For just a little while, Inga would think only of happy occasions. About the parties, her couture dresses, the time she flirted with Dietrich and watched Fred from the corner of her eye. How Fred had looked jealous, hungry and excited all at the same time.

A knock on the door jarred her. She sat up and neatened her hair.

"Come in."

Erhard stood in the threshold. "I was wondering if you wouldn't mind if I went to bed now. It is two in the morning."

"I did not realize how late it was." She smiled at him. He had been their butler for eighteen years, and yet, she realized in that moment, she hardly knew him. Still, it felt nice to have a friendly presence in the room with her. "Please, join me for a few minutes." She thought of offering him a drink, but the buffet cabinet had been given to the Philanthropin School and she didn't want him rushing about searching for whiskey and glasses.

"If you wish," Erhard said. He sat in an armchair on the other side of the room and folded his hands carefully on his lap.

She glanced at the painting again. "Do you remember when this was done? The entire household had been in an uproar."

"I remember," he said.

"The painter made a miniature in order to ensure this was exactly what my mother wanted." She laughed lightly. "Did you know there was one of me made as well? A year or so earlier?"

"I did not."

"It was dreadful. The artist was second class, and my mother told him to burn it."

"A shame," he said.

She paused, giving them both a few moments. "It's mad, don't you think, the world we live in?"

"Some would say that."

"Dear, Erhard." She grinned. "There is no need to be formal.

Tomorrow I will be gone, and both of our lives will be irrevocably altered."

"I suppose that is true."

"But you will still have your home and your family."

She hadn't meant it quite as it came out, as if she was lamenting her own situation. Yes, it was difficult, but she was also lucky in many respects, and she would not allow herself to forget that.

"I am grateful," Erhard said. "And grateful for the service I have been able to provide your family."

"And we are grateful to you. But let us not get maudlin. Tell me how your children are. A boy and a girl, if I remember correctly?"

"Your memory is correct."

"How old are they now?"

"My daughter, Gerta, is fifteen. Bertie is nineteen."

"I have always loved the name Bertrand. My grandmother had a beagle named Bertie. He had one blue eye and one brown. Most unusual."

Erhard nodded like a well-mannered puppet.

"And are they in school?" she asked, determined to engage Erhard in a conversation.

"Gerta is." He turned his head away from her.

"And Bertie?" she asked.

Erhard squared his shoulders and faced Inga. "He has joined the SS."

"Oh." Her heart dropped a bit. She glanced away. "Yes, I see."

"It was his choice," Erhard said. "But we are proud of him for wanting to serve his country."

"It is important that parents are proud of their children," she muttered. It had been stupid to imagine that she could find some last-minute camaraderie.

An awkward silence followed.

"I need your help," Inga said finally. "The painting must come down."

Erhard stood on his chair, but his arm span was not sufficient. She dragged into place one of the wooden chairs that were usually kept in the kitchen. It had likely been used as a stool in the past few days as things were moved out. Together she and Erhard lifted the painting and placed it on the floor, carefully leaning it against the wall.

"Will that be all?" he asked.

Her plan was to lay the painting face down and sever the canvas from the frame.

"Please fetch me a knife."

As soon as he left the room, Inga tried to move the painting. But it was too heavy. She would need Erhard's help.

Erhard handed her a carving knife. Her arms tensed. Rage coursed through her. Damn them, the Nazis and Hitler. Damn Sonnenstein, and Arnold, and her mother, and the stupid young men blinded by extremism. Damn Bohm, and the officers who would live in this house. In a burst of fury, she plunged the knife into the canvas.

Erhard grabbed her arm. "The Fuhrer has made it illegal to destroy any art that may have value."

"As if I take my orders from that hideous man."

"Do not speak of him that way," Erhard scolded.

"Let go of me," Inga shouted. "Do you think I would leave this painting for those disgusting people to gaze at? I would never give them that pleasure."

Again, she stabbed the knife into the painting, this time dragging it downward.

* * *

On a brisk day in April of nineteen-thirty-six, nearly eight months after the baby was born, Inga and Fred drove to Sonnenstein for an unannounced visit. Inga had been listening to Fred's dire predictions about the Nazis for some time now and she believed it would be best to simply take Rigmor out of Germany. Only Fred knew of the plan. Inga had decided that although it would be a shock for Frieda, it would be easier to sort out the details in Switzerland rather than making elaborate schemes for months on end.

As soon as they arrived, Inga ran to Rigmor's room, but she wasn't there, nor was she in any of the studios. They looked in the gardens and in the dining hall.

Arnold and Rigmor returned from their morning walk an hour later. Rigmor's cheeks were rosy with health. Her hair was thick and luxurious. But most importantly, she was not too thin. Rigmor approached her sister and hugged her.

"What a wonderful surprise."

"We thought we could take you out for lunch. Perhaps in Dresden," Inga said.

Rigmor glanced at Arnold. "Without the proper paperwork," he explained, "it will be impossible for Rigmor to leave the grounds."

"But you were just on a long walk," Inga said. "Surely there are myriad ways to get out of this place."

Rigmor bit her bottom lip.

Arnold stood between the two sisters. "There are fences along the property line. The only way out is across the river, and the current here is extremely strong."

"Well then," Inga said, glancing at Fred. "We will just get into our car and drive. I'm sure if we explain that we are only leaving for an hour or two, the guards will not stop us."

"They will stop you," Arnold replied. "They are very thorough."

"Fred is rather a genius with these types of matters." Inga reached for Fred's hand. "Aren't you, darling?"

"I wouldn't use the word genius. But I do know how to ply a guard or two."

"I'd prefer to eat here," Rigmor said.

"But my dear," Inga said. "You need a change of scenery. It will be good for you."

Rigmor's face drained of color. "I don't want to be stopped at the gate."

"Arnold can help," Inga said. "He's a doctor here. Surely the guards will see that it's all right if he's in the car."

Arnold shook his head. "I'm afraid I have no special authority when it comes to allowing patients off grounds. Without the proper documents, it will likely be hopeless."

Inga took a few steps back and motioned for Arnold to follow. "You were the one who said we should get her out."

"Yes, but to come here and think you can just drive away." He tugged at his collar. "It is a bit naïve."

They lunched at the dining hall. Rigmor barely touched her food, and then claimed she needed to rest. Inga accompanied her sister and sat on the chair next to the bed.

"What is it?" Inga asked.

Rigmor covered her face with her hands. "You will hate me."

"I could never hate you."

"I don't want to leave this place. I have friends. I have Arnold. I paint. I even teach patients how to draw." Her voice trembled. "I don't want to live on the outside. And I don't want you and mother to race around trying to fix me. When I have an episode, it feels terrible, but I have the comfort of being surrounded by people who understand." She paused. "Here one doesn't have to try to pretend to be fine. I have everything I could want, and as long as you keep visiting me, what is the harm in my staying here?"

Inga held Rigmor's hand. "I understand. And maybe for the time being, these walls will protect you. But I do not trust the Nazi Party, and I do not know that you will always be safe here."

"When the time comes, you will know. Fred will know. And then I will do whatever it is you wish."

Inga kissed Rigmor's hand. "I do love you so."

* * *

Arnold discovered a small glen. The sun poked through the space in the trees where wildflowers grew. A brook trickled through and an old log, curved in the center, as if nature had carved a seat, rested next to the stream. He and Rigmor often brought books, a picnic basket and a blanket. In late September, as the leaves all but dripped with color, Rigmor appeared to be at peace with her life.

* * *

A year passed. Inga continued to visit, although she claimed that moving across the border was becoming more difficult. Her papers were checked thoroughly, and she was questioned as to why she wanted to come back into the country. She told the guards she had a husband in Frankfurt, which, legally speaking, was true.

Frieda wrote to Rigmor, claiming she missed her terribly, but could not return to German soil. Each letter ended the same way. *Soon, mein liebschon, we will be reunited.*

Arnold and Rigmor were not lovers in any conventional sense, but he had never felt love as deeply and as precisely as he felt it with her. He could read even the slightest change of expression on her face. Her eyes, which changed from the color of thunderclouds to that of a docile sea, expressed a thousand emotions, more than he even knew existed, more than he could put words to. He knew when she was thinking of her home in Frankfurt. He knew when she was daydreaming about dancing in a field of flowers. He knew when she worried about Frieda, when she wanted to feel the breeze on her face, when she needed to hold his hand.

He knew when she thought about their baby and how she privately mourned the loss.

Sometimes she asked him to brush her hair. Once she even tried to teach him how to make plaits, but his fingers were too clumsy and the result was two crooked lumpy twists. They laughed. He knew how her hair curled differently as the weather changed, but how she always had one small coil, a stubborn thing that fell right in the center of her forehead.

She had a wireless in her room. They listened to symphonies. Sometimes the broadcast would be interrupted by one of Hitler's rabid speeches. When his voice came on, Rigmor immediately shut it off.

Rigmor painted. At first, watercolors of fruit, flowers and landscapes, but soon she began to paint faces—first of nameless children, then of patients in the hospital. More people came to her for drawing lessons, and her pictures were hung in the wards. It was even rumored that Bohm had one of her paintings in his office.

Still she suffered. Two good weeks were often followed by days of crying spells, paranoia, a lack of appetite, bouts of dizziness, and sleepless nights. In time, the fits would pass, and interestingly, when Rigmor recovered from her disoriented states, her mental acuity seemed heightened, as did her artistic ability.

There were moments when Arnold felt as though he were living in some sort of fantasy world in which they were a wealthy English couple, overseeing their estate, making sure their tenants were happy and well cared for.

Chapter Twenty-Three

Day Pass

Framingham, Massachusetts
1984

On Christmas morning, Sabine sat with Helen, Keith and Frank in the festive dining area, with the little fir trees, and baskets of biscuits, fruit and chocolates that Omama had ordered.

Tanner would arrive in an hour; Keith's parents were taking him for the day; Helen and Frank would be left alone.

"I can stay here with you," Sabine told Helen as they drank coffee.

"Absolutely not," she said. "Mia needs to spend her first Christmas with her mother and her family."

It felt wrong to Sabine that Helen had no one. Her brother wasn't allowed to visit, and her mother refused to come.

Tanner had dressed Mia in a red velvet dress with white lace around the collar. They joined the group, and Keith picked up one of the fir trees and showed Mia the different colored bulbs.

After some chitchat, a middle-aged couple approached and Keith's arms clamped to his sides. Keith's parents, Barbara and Jim, introduced themselves, and then Barbara thanked Sabine for taking Keith under her wing. Her bob haircut hit at chin level and thin lines framed her eyes. She wore a camel coat and a pained smile. Jim gave Keith a quick pat on the back.

"We've decided we're going to Aunt Jane's today," Barbara told Keith.

He nodded, showing no emotion. Sabine guessed that wherever their destination, Keith would find it difficult.

A few minutes after Keith left, Sabine said goodbye to Helen, and walked out with Tanner and Mia. But a mile from the hospital, her heart began to race, and she felt dizzy and nauseated. She wished she could talk to Dr. Lincoln, but he was away for four days. When he first told her he would be out of town, she threw a tantrum, accusing him of abandoning her. She understood that the reaction was part of transference, but it still embarrassed her.

Tanner and Sabine barely spoke on the drive to his parents' house. Watching the snow hit the windshield, she told herself to get it together, to show some grit. She wanted this day to be uneventful. But she felt as if she was in one of those dreams where she wasn't prepared for the exam.

Holidays accentuated the voids in her life. Sabine had no presents to give anyone, even Mia. She didn't feel bubbly or joyful. She missed her own family, and her brothers, and especially her mother. She missed Omama too.

Tanner's parents had always treated Sabine well, if in a distant sort of way. She never quite fit into their clan. She wasn't from the east coast, she didn't vacation on the Cape or in Maine. She wasn't familiar with Filene's Basement. She didn't have a Boston accent or know anything about the Red Sox or the Patriots.

Tanner parked in the driveway of the light-blue Cape. A pine wreath decorated with cranberries hung on the white door. As soon as they walked in, Sabine smelled the ham. Tanner's older brother, Rick, whose plaid shirt blended in with the plaid couch, stood to greet them. The tinseled Christmas tree was set up in the corner.

Rick, who like his father had become a plumber, asked if anyone wanted a beer. Tanner raised his hand.

Tanner's mother, Martha, stood at the edge of the kitchen wearing a flowered apron. She was so different from Sabine's mother, who would have greeted them with her arms waving as she exclaimed exuberantly how beautiful the baby was. She would have scooped Mia up and praised her to the point of absurdity. Yes, she might be too frightened to visit McLean, but if she'd had the opportunity to have Mia at her house, she would have been ecstatic.

On the other hand, Martha waited. Finally, when her husband, Will, brought Mia to her, she smiled, and Sabine took a deep breath. Mia would be the center of attention today, and the pressure would be off of Sabine. Tanner's parents wouldn't think about the fact that their son had married someone who got locked up in a mental hospital—someone who had always been a bit of a stranger, with parents from Europe, and a father who was physicist.

Martha served dinner and Sabine sat squashed between Tanner and Rick, who were both unnervingly fast eaters. Her throat was tight. She couldn't shake the fear that her hands were about to start trembling.

But she made it through dinner, then changed Mia, and helped Martha with the dishes. She was finding her rhythm, and by the time she sat in the living room, she was sure she had made it through the hardest part of the holiday.

Tanner napped on the couch with Mia resting on his chest. A commercial for Denny's build-a-breakfast-for-$1.99 came on, and Tanner's father looked at Sabine. She expected him to say something pleasant, that it was nice to see her, or maybe that she was looking better.

"Places like the one you're in, they make people worse," he said in a low rumble. His eyes were round like Tanner's.

She tried to smile, but her lips barely moved. "I'm getting better," she said, even though at that moment, panic stirred in her chest.

Leave, she heard. She didn't move, didn't turn, didn't want anyone to have an inkling that she was hearing things.

"It would be better if you got out," Will said.

"Got out?" Sabine said, only half-paying attention, distracted by the voice.

"Of McLean. Pretend like it didn't happen, and do normal things. I knew this guy once who couldn't get a job after he was in there."

She thought of a teacher on her ward who suffered from severe migraines and depression. She stayed in her room most of the day with the lights off. The rumor was that she had been fired.

Will tapped his head. "It's mind over matter. Ignore the problem and it will go away. That's what I do. You stay in a place like you're in, you're just feeding your worst fears." He turned back to the TV.

The room was stuffy, the man announcing the football game shouted, and the smell from a beer on the coffee table sat in Sabine's stomach like curdled milk. She stood, woke up Tanner and told him she needed to go.

"But we haven't had dessert," he said, groggy. "And there are presents for Mia."

"I don't feel well," she said, looking forward to the Xanax waiting for her at the ward. She hurried Mia into her snowsuit and rushed out the front door.

"Why the quick exit?" Tanner asked, after they were all buckled in.

"Your father thinks McLean makes people worse."

"Sabine," Tanner said slowly. "You gotta relax. You take him way too seriously." They turned at the end of the street. The wipers squeaked.

"He said people can't get jobs if they've been in mental hospitals."

"He wasn't talking about people like you." Tanner rested a hand on her knee. She wanted to move it, but he was trying to be nice. "He means people like Frank. Besides, my dad does sort of have a point. You can't stay there forever."

She pushed Tanner's hand away. "I love Frank."

"You're getting way too worked up. My dad probably won't even remember saying any of that stuff to you. He doesn't mean it. Let it go."

Sabine thought of her own father, of how he yelled and how she would always defend him even when he was wrong. That was the nature of childhood. Parents love, parents try, and parents make mistakes, big and small, and children stand by them. Tanner was going to stand by Will, and Sabine could not fault him for that.

"You're right. It's no big deal." She leaned her head against the window, looking forward to returning to McLean, debriefing and analyzing the day with Helen.

"Hey," Tanner said. "I have an idea that will take your mind off of everything."

She knew what he was talking about, and it was the last thing she felt like doing. But she hated to be so ungenerous on Christmas. And to give him what he wanted might make going back home feel easier.

"We have Mia," she said.

"She's asleep."

"You're driving," she told him.

"I can pull over. Just a little blow job."

Her stomach knotted. She thought about swimming in the ocean. If you went in slowly, let your feet get numb, then your knees, then your thighs, you got used to it. Maybe if she began slowly with sex, she could handle it.

They parked at the end of a small street behind a corrugated steel barrier. A yellow street lamp blinked on and off. He pulled down his pants.

She told herself she could do this. It would be good for her. She leaned over and tried, but she gagged and her head went black.

She sat up, covered her mouth, and turned away from Tanner. "I feel sick," she said.

"Sick like as in you're getting a cold, or sick like as in doing this makes you sick?"

"Just sick."

"Want me to do you? Would that help?"

She did not want to be done, but she wanted to give it another try, to prove to herself she could do this. There were nights in college, and after, when she did want to have sex, and there were nights when she didn't, but she always managed to give Tanner what he wanted, and she was proud of that, proud that she wasn't a prude.

This time she counted, but she only made it to ten. "I can't." She held a hand over her stomach.

Tanner tousled her hair. "No worries," he said. "You don't mind if I step out for a minute. You know. And finish off?"

"Go."

Sabine stared off in the other direction. She focused on one green pine needle holding a perfect pearl of ice. Tanner wasn't going to take this well, even if he pretended otherwise. There would be marks against her on their scoreboard. But worse, soon they would be sharing the same bed, and his H and H self would be waking her up in the middle of the night wanting to do things she simply couldn't do anymore.

Chapter Twenty-Four

Mercy

Brandenburg, Germany
1939

In the summer of 1939, rumblings of war were impossible to ignore. Yet inside the boundaries of Sonnenstein, life remained, for the most part, placid.

One evening when Rigmor had fallen asleep rather early, Arnold decided to visit the library. He found a small alcove with a cushioned armchair. There he read *The Sorrows of Young Werther*, a novel he hadn't read since he was seventeen. Back then, he was convinced he was a facsimile of Werther—despondent, hopeless, and destined for a life of unrequited love. But now, he realized that he had overcome Werther's self-pity. Arnold, stronger than Werther, had learned that romantic love was the weakest of the loves, and that his relationship with Rigmor consisted of much more.

Arnold heard footsteps and was surprised to see Dieter approaching. For the most part, Arnold was left alone by the staff. His purpose was to attend to Rigmor, and remain obscure, although on occasion Dieter had expressed interest in Rigmor. He had published a paper on the benefits of art in treating the mentally ill.

"I have been asked to visit Brandenburg," Dieter said, taking a seat across from Arnold, who gave a slight nod.

"They have built some new sort of facility," he continued. "I am to give my opinion on it."

"Good," Arnold said.

"You must come with me," Dieter said with a burst of emotion.

Arnold smiled, feeling a bit like an old uncle who had resigned himself to a peaceful, unambitious life. "I think it's probably better to have someone who might be more interested."

"No, you must come. You will be objective and wise. I would appreciate your opinion above anyone's."

"That is kind of you to say." Also surprising, Arnold thought. "But I'm not terribly involved in new treatments."

"I was given two invitations. I think your opinion would be valuable."

"Do you know anything about the facility?" Arnold asked, perplexed by Dieter's insistence.

"It is modern and will change the course of psychiatry."

"When do you plan on taking this journey?"

"Three days from now. We will have a private car."

Very curious, Arnold thought. It was not often the hospital splurged on such things. "I suppose if you really think I can help."

Dieter gave one large clap. "Marvelous," he said, and bounced up.

The day they traveled to Brandenburg Hospital, a hypnotizing rain drummed on the roof of the car, and Arnold found himself dozing as Dieter rambled about another paper he was writing. Arnold nodded at what he hoped were appropriate points.

The car pulled up to the front of the hospital, an austere brick building with none of Sonnenstein's charm.

Dieter and Arnold were led to a large drawing room dimly lit by a chandelier. The room was chilly and thick with cigar smoke. Arnold wished he was back at Sonnenstein drinking a cup of hot tea with Rigmor.

About twenty-five men milled about. Ten or so were in uniform. Dieter grabbed Arnold's arm and pointed to Philipp Bouhler, a man with an aura of authority and confidence. His black hair was slicked back. His spectacles were round and his face perfectly proportioned.

"He is Chief of the Chancellery," said Dieter. "I wonder why he is here."

There were too many men in uniform for Arnold's taste. "I will sit for a moment."

He wanted to detach himself from Dieter and this setting. But just as he was about to take a seat, he noticed Bohm in the back corner of the room, waving his hands as he spoke.

Arnold pulled Dieter close. "Did you know Bohm was attending this event?" Arnold asked.

"Actually," Dieter answered, "he was the one who gave me the tickets and asked that I invite you." He lowered his gaze.

Arnold felt his stomach turn. "So this had nothing to do with you wanting my opinion on the matter?"

Dieter put his hands in his pockets, sheepish. "Your opinion and thoughts are of value. I apologize if I misled you."

"But why would Bohm care?"

"I haven't the faintest idea." Dieter kept his gaze lowered. "He made the terms clear. I would not be able to attend unless you escorted me."

"I have a good mind to leave," Arnold said.

"Please don't," Dieter replied. "I'm sure it won't be terribly long. And since you are already here, why not see what is going on?"

Arnold decided he would get through the day by keeping his mouth shut and staying out of everyone's way.

A waiter brought glasses of champagne. Arnold declined and sat quietly as Dieter found a more suitable companion.

As Arnold watched his peers, he noticed exaggerated hand movements, sentences that ended in exclamation and a general air of excitement.

Soon, the director, a thin man with crooked teeth, called the room to attention.

"Thank you for joining us today," he said. "We welcome you, and hope that in our small way, we can illuminate for you what we consider to be our future. I would ask that you keep in mind the research and work that has gone into this. Working with unfortunate souls is never easy, and we must face many difficult hurdles and choices."

A number of the men nodded solemnly. Arnold felt a sense of alarm.

"We must try to rid ourselves of diseases that only cause pain," the director continued. "It will take courage and conviction. I hope what you see here today will show you the way to cure ourselves."

Arnold shuddered at the thought that came to him, that they were here to learn some new way to kill patients. He remembered the stick floating down the Elbe, how its destiny was already determined, and how he'd had a premonition about the gruesome lengths the Nazis would go to eradicate disease and decrease expenditure.

The director launched into a history of Darwin, eugenics, and genetics. He mentioned scientist after scientist and how one influenced the next. His language was dense, his voice monotone. Arnold's mind wandered. He imagined living in New York and starting a practice of his own. He imagined Rigmor visiting. They would spend hours at the art museums and in cafes.

Finally, the director finished his introduction and the audience clapped. Arnold joined half-heartedly, realizing that not applauding at all might draw unwanted attention.

When the group moved to the dining room for lunch, Arnold sat at the end of a long wooden table, hoping to go unnoticed. But Dieter joined him, and not long after that, Bohm strode over.

"Nice to see you here," Bohm said to both men, and then turned his attention to Arnold. "I thought it would be nice for you to see how the Blumenthals will help lead the way to the future."

"I don't know what you mean," Arnold said, staring into Bohm's eyes.

"With the help of their donations we will soon have a facility that is even better than the one here."

"I have yet to see anything here," Arnold said, keeping his tone neutral and composed.

Bohm grinned, showing his yellow teeth, and then walked away.

After apple cake and a sweet port, they were led outside, to the back of the building, where they walked on wooden planks that couldn't have been laid more than a few hours before. The rain had turned to a fine mist. The boards wobbled under foot as Arnold marched along with the others, his sense of dread heightening.

They arrived at a barn-like structure and filed into a small anteroom.

The director explained that the men would see three patients today.

"Patient One is a fifty-four year old man who has never been able to care for himself. He was born prematurely and, after his first year of life, it was clear that he was highly feebleminded. He has not worked a day in his life. His parents died long ago. He has one sister who has not visited him in years. He recognizes his name, but little beyond that. He has the mental capacity of a one-year-old."

The audience let out a collective sigh.

"Patient Two, another male, is twenty-eight, and has dementia praecox. He began exhibiting symptoms when he was nineteen and tried to hang himself in his father's shed. Since then he has been in a state hospital."

The third patient had also been diagnosed with dementia praecox, although his symptoms weren't typical for schizophrenia. This patient was obese, barely moved, and rarely spoke. Arnold questioned the diagnosis, but in the past couple of years, the number of patients diagnosed with schizophrenia had dramatically increased. It seemed an easy and convenient label to slap onto people. It left the doctors in control and the families believing there was little hope.

The director pointed. "The patients are being held in exam rooms behind this wall. I ask that a few doctors go into each room for a minute or so, and then rotate. Please do not speak when in the exam rooms, as we don't want to startle or frighten the patients, who believe they are here for a routine medical exam, a shower, and new clothes. If you have any questions, hold them until we gather again in this room."

In the first room, Patient One sat on the exam table, swinging his legs. He looked older than fifty-four. He had no teeth, and a large hump on his back. Patient Two was handsome. He had dark hair, a narrow, angular face, and suspicious eyes. It was immediately clear that he was paranoid, and Arnold averted his eyes, as surely all of these people watching him must have made him even more uncomfortable. Arnold was the first in his group to leave the exam room.

Patient Three lay on the exam table and stared, wide-eyed, at the ceiling. He did not respond to any stimuli. His feet and ankles were swollen, most likely from gout.

When all of the visitors had seen the patients, they were brought back to the anteroom.

The director waited for silence.

"We will put a small adhesive bandage on the backs of the men, between their shoulder blades. On the bandage we will mark the men with a number. All of the records will be filed under the patient number. After the treatment, condolence letters will be sent to the family, or next of kin. The letters will have varying causes of death—pneumonia, heart condition, and the like. We do not want to further stigmatize the patient or family by stating the true cause of death."

He smiled as if this was a gift. The procedure was the exactly like the one Bohm described for the starving children. Arnold's gut clenched. He had hoped his suspicions about this gathering were wrong.

"The chamber, approximately three meters by five meters in area, is fully tiled. There is a small pipe on the floor. It is covered and has little holes through which the gas can escape. When we turn on the main, the carbon monoxide will blend with the air. You will see that the room is comfortably fitted with benches around the perimeter. After the men have situated themselves, we will turn the gas on slowly. If it is turned on too quickly, a hissing sound can be heard, and that might disturb the patients."

Arnold looked over his shoulder at the door. He was afraid that if he didn't get out, he'd vomit. But something kept him frozen in his place. A voice that told him to get a grip, to wake up. For the past three years, as he lived in a bubble with Rigmor at his side, the Nazis had been devising convenient methods of murder.

"The whole process will not take more than twenty minutes. What we would like you to see here today is how gently these men will succumb. Their eyes will close, and then slowly they will fall asleep and stop breathing. In this way, we feel we have found the kindest method."

"There is one small peep hole through which you can observe the chamber," the director continued. "I will ask that you form a line and that when it is your turn, you look for a few moments, and then get back into the line." He held up a hand. "Don't worry, you will each have a number of chances to see into the chamber. Please keep the line moving calmly. Are there any questions?"

"What will you do with the bodies?" one of the uniformed men asked.

"Excellent question." The director smiled. "We have built a crematory that is attached to this building. Carting the dead bodies could cause alarm, so we are careful in this regard. I'm sure you will consider doing something similar. All of the architectural drawings will be available to the directors of the hospitals."

There were no more questions.

"I think we should begin. Yes?"

Arnold was in the middle of the line. As he approached the hole in the door, his jaw clenched, and once again he was afraid he might vomit. The heavy patient lay on the floor, the feebleminded man banged on the wall, and the third patient looked at the nozzle, waiting for a shower.

The words of the men surrounding Arnold were unintelligible, but the general mood seemed to be of shock. He was not the only one with a conscience, at least. On Arnold's second round, the large man looked asleep and the feebleminded patient flopped forward, while the remaining patient clutched his throat as his face contorted. This was not gentle, Arnold wanted to shout, but the room had fallen completely silent, and he was too shaken to speak.

The director clapped and asked that everyone remain calm. "We are still working on some of the details, and it seems the gas was coming out a bit too slowly. We have now adjusted for it, so these patients will not have to suffer any longer."

Arnold did not look at the patients again. Instead, he pushed through to the door and stepped outside. He gulped in the March air as he steadied himself on a wooden beam.

* * *

Prina, Germany 1939

The moment Arnold returned to Sonnenstein, he went to the lobby and called Inga. He could not give her details of what he had just seen, but he could insist that it was time to take Rigmor to Switzerland.

"When war breaks out, which I think will be soon, the laws will change. It will not be safe here."

"I will come," Inga said.

"It will be almost impossible to get her out without sterilization." The surgery had been postponed a number of times—because she had the flu, because the doctor was on holiday, because Arnold didn't think she was strong enough, because Arnold believed there was time.

"There is a slim chance her papers won't be checked thoroughly," he told Inga. "But that would be a risk."

"Not one we should take. How soon can she have it done?"

"I can speak to Rudiger this afternoon. He is an excellent surgeon, and has performed many of these procedures."

"I will work on getting passports," Inga said. "Phone tomorrow."

That afternoon, as Arnold and Rigmor had tea in her room, he described to her some of what he had seen at Brandenburg. At first, he fumbled over words such as new procedure and gentle death. But as she asked for clarification, he eventually told her everything—about the patients, the director, the way the gas was pumped in.

Rigmor's eyes shimmered with tears. "But that is illegal."

"We live in a fascist state," Arnold said. "The government does what it wants." He sunk his head into his hands. "We should have gotten you out years ago."

Rigmor moved next to him and rubbed her hand in circles along his back. "We will find a way," she said.

He lifted his head. "I have spoken to Inga. She will get you the papers you need to go to Switzerland. You will live with your mother and sister. But in order to leave the institution, you will need to have a small operation."

"I understand," she told him. "I am not afraid of the surgery. I never have been, and you needn't be frightened for me. I have talked to women who have had it done, and they have all reported it was much easier than they thought."

Two days later, Rigmor had a tubal ligation. When she woke from the procedure, she claimed to feel no pain. She was ordered to stay in bed for a week. After the third day she seemed completely healed and Arnold couldn't help but think of the last time they were on the maternity ward. The child, his child, had she survived, would have been four. He imagined she would have been beautiful, and kind, like her mother. Then he remembered how thin and weak Rigmor had been, and now, after years of stability, a nutritious diet, regular walks, and painting, she looked like an entirely different woman—her cheeks fuller, her eyes wiser, her skin a smooth, porcelain white.

Rigmor returned to her tower room at Sonnenstein, saying that she looked forward to giving drawing lessons again.

But the next morning, she had a slight fever. Nothing, she insisted—just a mild cold. She always got them in the summertime. Still, Arnold wanted her to be seen by a doctor. Hans Weber, staff internist at Sonnenstein, was a small, nervous fellow with large hands and halting speech. He wasn't alarmed by Rigmor's symptoms. But he said he would like to take a peek at her incision. With his fingers he tapped and prodded around her abdomen.

"I find it healing well," Hans said. "A bit of swelling. I think nothing to be concerned about." At the door he turned and looked at Rigmor. "Bed rest for one week. Then you will be ready to gallop on a horse." He laughed.

Three days passed and the fever persisted. The skin around Rigmor's eyes became discolored, and she found it difficult to walk. Arnold called for Dr. Weber again.

"An infection. I fear." He shook his head. "Not terrible. Sulfanilamide should take care of it."

But the next day a rash broke out on Rigmor's arms and legs. Welts the size of coins covered her body. Dr. Weber returned. He patted Rigmor's hand and said sometimes patients had reactions, but not to worry. There were other types. He prescribed Protosil, a different sulfa drug.

The rash receded. The fever remained.

* * *

Although Inga had a room at the back of the chalet, she spent most nights at her flat in Basel. She had first rented the apartment in order to have a private place to meet Fred, but after only two months of living with Frieda, Inga needed to escape the frowns, turned shoulders, and icy glares.

Now, four years later, Rigmor would be moving to Switzerland, and Inga needed to pack up the few things she kept at the chalet. Frieda would reside in what had been Inga's room, and Rigmor would take the larger front room. Inga carried an empty suitcase up the hill and hoped she would get a chance to see Lisbet without having to spend more than a few moments with Frieda.

Inga loved watching the child. She had such marvelous long legs that seemed to kick in all directions when she ran. She was shy, like Rigmor, but when she tumbled on the grass or played with her jumping rope, her timidity receded. Even when she first toddled, it was clear that movement made her happy.

In the small bedroom, Inga took out the dresses in the wardrobe and packed her perfumes, soaps and brushes. When she heard a creaking sound on the landing, she opened the door and saw Lisbet peeking out from behind the staircase.

"Come in my girl," Inga said. "I have chocolate. Would you like a piece?"

Lisbet nodded, but remained where she was.

"I won't bite. You needn't be frightened of me."

Lisbet crept up the stairs and stood a few meters from Inga.

"What is it my dear?" Inga asked, crouching down. "What are you afraid of?"

Lisbet's feet pointed inward as her hands clasped behind her back.

"Did someone tell you not to speak to me?" Of course that someone would have been Frieda. It was then Inga saw Lisbet's eyes shiver for the first time. "I would never hurt you," Inga whispered.

Lisbet tucked her chin down and crossed her feet, looking a bit like an exotic bird.

"We won't talk about this anymore. All right?" Inga fetched a piece of milk chocolate and gave it to Lisbet, who smiled as she put the sweet in her mouth. Just as Inga was about to embrace Lisbet, Frieda called for her. As Lisbet barreled down the stairs, Inga felt her heart sink. She realized that it wouldn't be terribly long before she would be pushed further aside. In a year, possibly less time, she would be immaterial.

She and Frieda had agreed then when Rigmor first arrived, she would be told that Lisbet was an orphan of a German Jewish friend and that Inga was her temporary adoptive mother. Eventually they would tell Rigmor the truth, parceled out slowly and judiciously.

* * *

The train stopped at the German border. Inga handed the officer her papers, a false German passport and a blood purity form that showed no Jewish ancestry for four generations. The officer studied the documents, looking at the passport picture and then at Inga. He nodded, handed back the papers and moved on.

Her clothes were damp with sweat, but she remained still. As she glanced around the compartment, she wondered how many others were doing the same thing, desperately trying to get a family member out of the country. It was as if they were all wearing costumes, dressed in peasant clothes, so as to look unassuming and unremarkable. She wore a long floral skirt, a blue blouse and a cardigan with holes at the elbows, cut only a few hours ago. To get into Germany she had a German passport. To get out, she and Rigmor had Swiss passports. They would be the Gruen sisters.

If all went smoothly, which Inga expected it would, they would be leaving Sonnenstein tomorrow, and taking the first train out of Dresden.

As the train chugged forward, Inga stared out of the window and thought about the chalet in Arlesheim. Rigmor would find it enchanting, with its sloping roof, heavy eaves, and flowerboxes hanging beneath each window.

The gentle rumble of the engine soothed Inga. As she imagined having Rigmor stay in her Basel flat, walking the cobblestone streets, stopping at bakeries for coffee and wandering in and out of book shops, she began to drift off.

Inga woke with a start just as the trained pulled into Dresden. She took her small case from the rack above her, disembarked and stood on the pavement, relieved. Then a hand gripped her arm.

"Papers," the guard said.

"But I have already shown them," Inga told him.

She felt his hold tighten. "Do as I say or go to the police station."

She opened her handbag and showed him her German passport. "From Heidelberg?" he asked.

"Yes."

"Why Dresden?"

"My mother is there. She is ailing." Her headscarf began to slip.

"I have seen you before." He stared at the passport and then at her.

"I don't think so," she said.

"I would never forget a face like yours." He tapped a finger on her passport. "It was in Frankfurt. At a nightclub."

"No, I've never been there."

"I am sure of it. You were dancing with a short, bald Jewish man. We joked about it. I remember now. We guessed he had something special in his trousers to get a woman like you."

"You have me confused."

At the screech of the train whistle, Inga wanted to run, but of course that would have been disastrous.

The guard pulled down her scarf. "Yes, it is you. I happened to think your hair was quite magnificent."

"My hair is perfectly ordinary."

"Are you arguing with me?"

"No," she whispered.

"I like beautiful women." He slapped her on her bottom with her passport and smiled. "Now get a move on."

She turned and strode with cautious purposefulness, not wanting to betray either her fear or relief.

When Inga arrived at Sonnenstein, she raced up to Rigmor's room, and then stood in the doorway for a moment taking stock of what was in front of her. A sister who looked pale and weak, and a doctor sitting at her bedside in an attitude of grave worry.

"My dearest," Inga said, dropping her suitcase and running to the bed. "What is it?"

Arnold moved aside. "An infection from the operation."

Inga held Rigmor's hand. "Certainly nothing terrible, I hope. We will feed you and give you tea, and you will be better in no time."

She smiled, although she hardly felt happy. The operation had been performed nearly two weeks ago. That an infection lingered was not good news.

"I'm mending," Rigmor said, her voice faint.

Inga pulled off her scarf and let it drop to the floor. She felt Rigmor's face and forehead. "You have a fever." She looked at Arnold, who shook his head.

"These new medicines are a miracle," Inga told her sister. "You will be well by tomorrow. You must be."

"How is mother?" Rigmor asked.

Inga sighed. "The same. Missing you. I cannot wait for you to see how sweet the house is. It's at the top of a hill on a street called Ziegelacker Weg. So very Swiss."

Rigmor smiled before closing her eyes. "Tell me more."

"We have red geraniums in all of the window boxes, and across from us is a piece of land full of raspberry and blackberry bushes, and apple trees. It is like out of a picture book. The air is clean, and you can hear the cowbells from the neighboring hills. It is really like Beethoven's Pastoral. There is even a castle nearby that you can see from the chalet. And the village is just as you would expect. Small shops, everyone friendly. The bread freshly baked and—"

Rigmor grimaced.

"Does it hurt terribly?" Inga asked.

"It comes and goes."

"Rest for an hour or so. Then we can talk about our plans."

As her sister slept, Inga spoke quietly with Arnold on the other side of the room.

"When did this happen?" she asked.

"The operation went smoothly, but about a week later she complained of a fever. We tried have tried two sulfa drugs. She is very weak and in more pain than she is letting on. It's difficult for her to walk. I don't know that she can manage the journey."

"I only have papers for three days. We cannot wait."

"I understand." His voice broke. "I just don't know."

"You said on the phone it would not be safe for her to stay. Why?"

Arnold shook his head. "What the Germans and Hitler want it is beyond what I could have ever imagined."

"Tell me," Inga demanded.

"They will begin a euthanasia program. Hitler will start it at the beginning of the war, when people will be too distracted to care about what is going on in the asylums."

"My God. It has come to this?" She felt shocked, even though rationally she knew this was always where the Nazis were headed. They had begun years ago with their propaganda films, claiming the mentally ill were weakening the race.

"I'm afraid so." He rested a hand on her arm.

Inga didn't want him to touch her—this man who seemed to always make things worse, not better. She glared at Arnold. "Why did she even need the sterilization if she was soon to be murdered?"

"The euthanasia program is not common knowledge. Only the doctors know. Things, for the time being, are to proceed as if all is the same."

"Then she will get out. We will make her better. There is simply no other option."

"We can pray that the fever goes down."

"Pray," she said bitterly. "That is what a doctor advises?"

She returned to Rigmor's side, sat next to her and touched her face every few minutes. It remained much too warm.

* * *

Arnold placed a cool washcloth on Rigmor's forehead. If the fever would break, there was still a chance. Perhaps Inga didn't believe in prayer, but he did. Silently, he said one after another.

The human will was much stronger than people realized, and now, with Inga here, Rigmor might rally. It would not be the first miraculous recovery Arnold had witnessed.

When the first rays of morning light shone through the window, Inga rested a hand on Rigmor's cheek.

"She feels cooler," Inga said, fresh hope in her voice.

Rigmor's arm looked mottled, like blue and pinkish marble: a sign, Arnold knew, that her body was struggling to push blood to her limbs.

"We will see how she does today," he said.

"She should eat a good breakfast. Two soft boiled eggs, some toast and orange juice. She needs her vitamins."

Rigmor opened her eyes and rested a hand on her stomach. It was clear she had something to say, but she couldn't get the words out.

Inga put a finger to her lips. "Just rest. There is no need to talk. You can have a little breakfast, and then you will feel stronger."

Rigmor gave a nod and then cried out.

"What is it?" Inga asked.

"It's as if something is twisting inside of me."

"We will get medicine." She glared at Arnold. "Now."

Arnold rushed to the ward where he used to work. He walked behind the nursing station and took two vials of morphine and a needle. Yes, he might get reported, and yes, they could drag him off to a concentration camp, but at this point it hardly mattered.

When he returned to Rigmor, she was curled into a fetal position and pulling her hair. Arnold slipped a needle under her arm, and within ten minutes, she settled.

"Is it very bad?" Inga asked.

"I think it will help if she hears your voice," he said gently.

* * *

Inga told stories of how they played when they were young, how they stole biscuits from the kitchen, how they snuck out of the house and pranced down the street wearing some of Frieda's finest jewelry. She caressed Rigmor's forehead, and told her that she must get better, that she had been through much worse.

The evening sky darkened to a glorious red. Rigmor cried, saying she felt as if there were snakes in her belly, and Arnold gave her another shot of morphine.

Rigmor's skin turned a sickly gray as she writhed in her semi-conscious state.

"How long?" Inga whispered.

"Two days," said Arnold. "Maybe three. Her body is young. Her heart relatively strong."

"We cannot allow her to be in so much pain."

Arnold hurried off to get more medicine.

Inga sat with Rigmor and cried. This was not how it was

supposed to end. There was a garden of fruit trees waiting for Rigmor, and a four-year-old girl who would benefit from a mother with a soft spirit—not Inga, who Lisbet didn't seem to like, or Frieda, who managed every minute of Lisbet's day.

"You can't leave me," Inga whispered, as she climbed into the bed and stroked her sister's hair. "There is so much to tell you." Inga sighed. This was likely the last chance she would have to tell Rigmor everything. That she was sleeping, didn't matter at the moment. "The most important thing is that you have a daughter. A girl, called Lisbet. She is a sweet child with dimples and legs like a Daddy-long-leg. She cannot sit still, which sometimes irritates Mother to no end. Her legs swing under the table and one never knows when one might just get a swift kick. She's a strong girl. She was from the day she was born. And now the doctor has said she has weak ankles and must take up skating. I don't know anything about weak ankles, but I am very confident Lisbet has no such thing. I thought you would meet her soon. I hoped one day she would know you were her mother, that she would know your kindness. Her hair is like yours, a bit lighter perhaps. And of course, she has given Mother something to live for, which I know will make you happy."

Inga talked about Fred, how he was still married to Hilda, and how that didn't matter. She told Rigmor about the lavender they had in their garden, how it was the best lavender on earth. She talked about how she had started to make her own jam, about the farm in the village, about the castle ruins at the top of the hill in Dornach. She talked until her words slurred, until she imagined the two of them in a meadow making daisy chains, the sun warming them, and the breeze tickling their necks.

* * *

For a few moments, Arnold stood in the middle of the courtyard as the heavens opened and rain poured down. The summer storms often arrived in violent bursts, sending people scurrying for cover. Arnold didn't want shelter, he wanted the downpour to dissolve him, to make the cleaving of his heart subside.

When he was back in Rigmor's room, he gave her two more doses, and within fifteen minutes she appeared to sleep comfortably.

For twenty minutes, as Inga stayed on the bed and Arnold sunk into a chair, there was quiet. Even the rain paused.

But then Rigmor stirred sharply and vomited, most likely a side effect from the morphine. Arnold turned her on her side and told Inga to fetch some water and towels from the lavatory.

He had hoped that her death would be peaceful, but it was not. Rigmor's legs flailed and her head shot back, hitting the wooden bed post.

"Do something!" Inga shouted.

Outside it thundered. Inside, the room flashed with light from the storm as Rigmor convulsed.

"More morphine," Inga yelled.

For the third time he ran to his old ward, and stole morphine, as the nurse in charge turned away.

But when Arnold returned, Rigmor was completely still, and Inga sat on the bed, clutching a pillow.

"Dear God," he said.

"Get out," Inga yelled.

He walked to the bed, picked up Rigmor's hand and felt her wrist for a pulse. There was none.

"Get out," Inga shouted again.

This time he did what she asked. There would be no private goodbye for him. Inga, always the brave one, had done what was needed.

Arnold went outside, took the path behind the building, and kept going until he reached the river. He sat on the muddy bank as the rain pounded, and the strong current below invited him to jump.

Chapter Twenty-Five

Truths

Belmont, Massachusetts
1984

On the flight from Chicago to Boston, Inga sat next to the window and listened to the engine. The stewardesses were particularly friendly, perhaps because it was Christmas, or perhaps because they thought she was a lonely old woman. Yet for once she did not feel lonely. Lisbet had not pushed Inga away. In fact, quite the opposite.

A stewardess refilled Inga's coffee cup. She slipped off her pumps, wriggled her toes inside of her silk stockings, and felt at ease.

Back in Boston, she unpacked and then took a good look at herself in the hotel mirror. Yes, she was in her late-seventies. But her cheeks had a natural pinkness to them, and although her eyelids drooped a little, her eyes seemed a clearer, less muddied green. She would go to McLean. Sabine would likely still be with Tanner, but Inga would check on the baskets and fir trees, and perhaps Cece or Helen or Keith would be around. It would be nice to have a bit of company. Funny, she thought, how when one doesn't feel lonely, one is more open to companionship.

The front desk ordered her a taxi, and by the time she arrived at North Belknap, the sky seemed lit with diamonds. As a child, she had believed invisible strings dropped from the stars and tethered the earth in place.

Paul, with his bland expression, opened the door. "She's in the dining room," he mumbled.

"Who?" Inga asked.

"Sabine."

Inga glanced at her watch. It was only half past five. As she approached the dining room, she smiled when she saw the red tablecloths, but then she noticed Sabine. Her hair was coming out of its bun and, if she'd put on makeup for the holiday, it was now worn off. There was an old-world beauty about her. Perhaps it was the way the dark window framed her. But she did not look happy and Inga thought of the saying *you are only as happy as your unhappiest child*. It fit for grandchildren as well.

"Sabine," Inga said. Pieces of a chocolate bar sat on the table. The wrapper lay with its shiny insides exposed to the ceiling.

"Omama?" Sabine said, clearly pleased to see her grandmother. Quite a difference from the first time Inga had come to this ward.

Inga took off her scarf and coat and sat across from Sabine. She would wait a few moments before asking what was wrong. "A happy Christmas to you, my girl."

"Same to you. Did everything go OK?"

"Some things went better than expected," Inga said.

"You came back early. I didn't think you'd be here until after Christmas."

Inga smiled. "Your father was not one of the things that went well."

"Oh," Sabine said, appearing to sink a bit.

"He has always been a difficult man for me to understand." She picked out a walnut from the basket. "But your mother is happy with him, and that's what really matters."

Sabine glanced down. Inga had been insensitive to bring up Lisbet. "Your mother will come."

Sabine held back her tears. "She will?"

"Not immediately. But yes, she will." Inga brushed her fingers along Sabine's hand. "Let's talk about your day. Did something not go well?"

"The baskets are really nice," Sabine said.

Inga glanced around the room. There were two large ones and three smaller ones. Aside from the one at their table, most of them seemed untouched. "Yes, they are well done. I'm pleased. And where is everyone?"

Sabine sighed. "Helen is in the quiet room. Everyone else, aside from Frank, is out with families still."

"I see." It was inevitable that Helen would have trouble on a holiday, yet hearing the news left Inga feeling short of breath. "And you," she said. "Can we talk about you?"

Sabine shrugged. "I'm fine. Nothing bad happened. Not really. It was just something Tanner's father said." She ate a piece of chocolate.

"What did he say?"

"Just that places like this, like McLean, only make people worse."

"What an absurd thing to say. This is a good hospital." Inga sat taller. "Why would anyone tell a patient that they were in a hospital that wasn't helping? Did he think that would be useful?"

"I don't know. Maybe." She folded the wrapper for the chocolate into small squares as Inga took out a tangerine from the basket.

"It's probably best not to take him too seriously. After all, what does he know about psychiatry or medicine—right?"

Sabine nodded.

"Tell me how things were with Mia and Tanner."

Sabine smiled heartily for the first time. "Mia was happy."

Inga handed a tangerine slice to Sabine. "Tanner?" she asked.

Sabine shook her head.

"Why?"

Sabine frowned. "I'm not really sure."

Inga believed Sabine was beginning to recognize that she had fallen out of love with her husband, and might now need help accepting that fact.

"The last year and a half of Fred's life, he finally moved into the chalet, something I had wished for, for so many years," Inga said. "But when we did live together, we argued constantly.

About everything."

She thought about their last fight, how he had once again tried to defend Gerald, and she had once again insisted Gerald was a brute. They had been so angry at each other they didn't even say goodnight. And then in the morning he was gone. The man who had truly understood her, had held her hand for days on end after Rigmor's death, the man who had walked by her side even if he hadn't been her husband, the man who made living feel worthwhile had been stricken by a heart attack in his sleep.

Inga looked at Sabine, who seemed intrigued with the story, although Inga had forgotten what point she had wanted to make. Something about Sabine leaving Tanner—and yet here she was thinking about Fred's death.

"But you loved him?" Sabine asked, holding her head a bit higher.

"Of course I loved him. But so what? Is that what we really need? I think I needed more of a companion than a lover at that point in my life. But we really are going astray here. Do you want Tanner to be your lover?"

"No," the word almost spat out of Sabine. Her face reddened. "I mean not at the moment."

Inga tilted her head. "My girl, you do not have to be in love with him. That is not a requirement for marriage."

Paul moseyed into the dining room, inspected a few of the baskets, and took a bar of Lindt chocolate.

"Now there is a man no woman would want," Inga whispered.

Sabine smiled. "Brenda likes him."

"My point exactly." Inga laughed.

For a moment Sabine looked happy.

"You see, it's not all so bad," Inga comforted.

One of the lights above them flickered, and Sabine seemed to sink again. "Mutti didn't call me today."

The poor thing. Her marriage wasn't going well, and her

mother hadn't even telephoned. No wonder she felt bereft.

"Yes, you did seem rather lonely when I walked in. But your mother will call. She needs some time. Can you be patient with her?"

"I suppose there's no rush." Sabine rotated the basket. "Mutti used to be the one person who could make me feel better. But now the only time I really feel OK is when I'm here. In McLean. As soon as we drove off the grounds today, I could feel the panic and the fear come back."

"But that is to be expected. Your depression didn't just appear one day; it was likely building for many years. Perhaps you were able to hide it well, but eventually, these things come out, and then they must be treated. Naturally it will be frightening when you step outside of here. You don't have the comfort and support, and you have people like Tanner's father, who will never understand."

Inga tapped the table and glanced up at the light as it flickered again. She felt a flash of anger— at the world, at men who were unable to fix things or replace light bulbs.

Then she felt a push, not on her back, but on her heart. As if it was ready to burst.

"Are you all right?" Sabine asked.

Inga nodded. They sat together in silence for a moment.

"Water? Tea?" Sabine suggested.

Inga placed a hand on her chest. "No." She took a deep breath. Everything was calm here, she told herself. Very calm. In fact, there was no one else around. Nothing needed to be done. And yet something did need to be done. "I have had experience with places like this before."

"You were in a mental hospital?" Sabine asked.

"No. My sister." She paused. "Her name was Rigmor."

"That's a beautiful name," Sabine said.

Inga nodded. "She was a beautiful woman."

"Why was she there?"

"You weren't supposed to know. No one was." Inga held onto the edge of the table. "It was a secret, in order to help you. And your mother. We didn't want your mother to get ideas into her head. But it was stupid not to say anything. It didn't make it easier for her, or for you. I see that now."

Inga let go of the table. Her strength began to flow back. The years felt as if they tumbled outward, and a heaviness was lifted.

"So there was mental illness in our family?"

Inga took an apple from the basket and placed it in the middle of the table. "Above all, your mother was to be protected. And the way to protect her, my mother believed, was to never speak of any of this." Inga took out an orange and placed it next to the apple. "My mother was terrified that your mother might suffer. She believed I was in large part to blame for Rigmor's decline. I investigated new treatments. I proposed various ideas. I wanted so much to help. In the end, my mother thought all of my suggestions and research and talking only made things worse."

Sabine picked out a few walnuts and placed them around the fruit. "That wouldn't make her worse."

The light blinked one last time and then went out. They both looked up. "I suppose I will never know if I made her worse. For years I blamed myself. And then I tried to forget."

"What was she like, your sister?" Sabine asked.

Inga rested her hands on the table. "She was sweet. Very sweet. Shy as a child, quiet, not at all like me. I remember when she was only a baby, I felt in awe of her. I was only four at the time, but I remember telling our nanny that she was mine. My Rigmor, I used to say. Mine. I was a stubborn thing."

"Was she young when she got sick?"

"She wasn't a child. As a child she was so talented in art and music. She could sketch anyone, and so quickly. Her hands were nimble." Inga smiled. "She didn't have much fashion sense though. And she didn't care. I picked out all of her clothes.

Nothing too chic or modern. She never wanted attention drawn to herself. She had the most beautiful curls. Like yours," Inga said.

"Like mine?" Sabine asked, surprised. "But you have always hated my hair."

"Hate is a strong word. I think I wanted to help you with it. To tame it and plait it. I used to do that with Rigmor's. Wrap the braids around her head so that she looked as if she was wearing a lovely crown. But then things got worse. She couldn't sleep. Her moods were dark. She had stomach problems and became frightened to leave the house. At night shadows tormented her soul, and during the day if she heard Hitler's voice on the wireless, she would get so stiff and tense, she could barely move."

"She had psychosis?" Sabine whispered.

"Yes. But there were good times. She loved yellow roses and hated chamomile tea, which my mother was sure would help. A few times Rigmor and I emptied that tea into her night pot." The memory made Inga smile.

"Am I like her?" Sabine asked. "I mean not in art or music, but like her in the way I'm sick?"

"The kindness you show to Keith and Frank, the way you let Helen hold the baby. You are generous in those ways, like she was." Inga looked at Sabine. "But I don't believe you are as ill. You don't have delusions."

Sabine bit her bottom lip.

"So you have had a few?" Inga said.

Sabine nodded.

"Have you told Lincoln?"

"No."

"It is frightening, to be sure." Inga paused. "But not uncommon. When depression goes untreated for long periods, people are prone to psychosis. It's called depression with psychotic tendencies. I would advise that you share this with

Lincoln. Do you see things?"

"Sometimes. I have terrible dreams. And I hear a voice. I mean, not often. But…you know. Once in a while."

"Is the voice kind?"

Sabine shrugged. "It's not unkind."

"It doesn't tell you to hurt yourself or someone else?"

"No."

"People hear voices at different points in their lives. As long as they are not directing dangerous behavior, they can be lived with. Do you mind it terribly?"

"I mind that it happens. I'm afraid that I will get crazier."

"It is highly unlikely that it will get worse, especially since you are on medicine. It's tremendous the ways in which people can now get help. That was not the case in my sister's time."

"I'm sorry," Sabine said.

"No need to be sorry, my girl. We must be happy that things have progressed in such a positive way."

"I guess."

Inga reached for Sabine's hand, and this time she gave it willingly. They sat quietly for a few moments, Inga caressing her granddaughter's fingers and then her wrist.

"I noticed this small wound on the first day I saw you." Broken white threads ran through the red scars.

Sabine pulled her hand away.

"Did you hurt yourself?"

Sabine nodded. "Sometimes the physical pain…"

"Yes, it can be a relief. I have read that." Inga wanted Sabine to know that she understood. That she didn't judge. "It looks a bit like a four-leafed clover," Inga said.

Sabine chuckled. "I wasn't trying to give myself a tattoo, but I guess a four-leafed clover is as good as any."

"You and your mother were always good at finding them. Do you remember?"

Sabine nodded. "We were always looking down."

"True," Inga remarked. "Rigmor liked them as well. I did too, until a friend told me such a sad story about them. After that I could barely look at a clover, even a three-leafed one."

"What was the story?"

Inga was annoyed with herself. She shouldn't have mentioned it, but she could hardly not tell. She disliked when people started to say something and then refused—out of some moral obligation, or embarrassment—to finish what they had begun.

"My friend had been in a concentration camp. On a very wet and cold day, she was taken in the back of a lorry with another group of prisoners. Some were even children. They were left off in a field of mud. Nothing else, just cold hard mud. The Nazi soldier told them that the first one to find a four-leafed clover would be set free." Inga shook her head. "Can you imagine? And so they all got on their hands and knees and dug until their fingers bled." Inga opened her pocketbook and took out a handkerchief. The story always made her cry. "The hope that humans possess even in such situations is remarkable." She blew her nose.

Sabine looked at the clover on her wrist. "That's terrible," she said.

"Humans are the only animal that have the capacity for such abject cruelty." Inga sighed. "Will you let me braid your hair one day?"

"That would be nice," Sabine said.

There was a resemblance to Rigmor, Inga noted, not only in the hair, but in the shape of the eyes. They were long and narrow. And Sabine's nose was broad at the top, like Rigmor's.

"It's strange how I didn't see it. The similarities you have to my sister. And to think I believed I knew so much about psychology and I never understood why there were times I was so frustrated with you, and also so drawn to you. Perhaps I wanted you to be Rigmor. Perhaps I felt angry at times when you weren't." She took a breath. "How unfair for you."

"No, it's fine. And I'm grateful you are telling me now."

"You are forgiving in nature. As was she. But Rigmor was born at a time when mental illness was seen as a deformity." She looked at the darkened window behind Sabine. "In the end . . ." she said, but then her throat tightened. She shook her head as she coughed.

Sabine jumped up and poured a glass of water in the kitchen. Inga managed to take a sip. "Better," she said.

"Are you getting a cold?" Sabine asked.

"No, it's nothing." Her voice sounded old and raspy. "What was I saying?"

"Something about the end."

Inga gripped the table again. "The Nazis only wanted to exterminate." She pursed her lips.

"Did she die in a concentration camp?"

"No." Inga picked up one of the walnuts. She inched back her chair. "No," she said again, realizing they had reached a point she could not go beyond.

"How did she die?" Sabine asked.

Inga's eyes were playing tricks on her. It seemed as if there were two Sabines sitting at the table. "I think," she began slowly, trying to get her focus back. "It would be good to have a cup of tea." Her mind was murky. "I would prefer not to talk of death."

She glanced at her reflection in the dark window—a blurry composition, an ageless aggregate. She remembered the walks she and Rigmor would take in the Black Forest when they were girls, how they imagined fairies hiding behind the huge fir trees, and how the sunlight poked through in spots, like daylight stars.

Inga walked to the kitchen and waited as the kettle heated, giving herself and Sabine time to adjust to their shared knowledge—a new intimacy.

She brought out two cups of tea and opened a new bar of chocolate. "So I suppose you understand now, that you are not alone."

"Yes. Thank you."

They sat together for another twenty minutes, eating fruit and chocolate, talking about Mia and Helen and the weather. By the time Inga left, she felt tired and woozy—not sick, but light-headed. Perhaps a more unconstrained version of herself. On the ride back to the hotel, she put her hand in her coat pocket and felt the walnut she had taken. Its exterior was hard and bumpy, yet there was a smooth quality to it. She ran a fingernail along the seam and thought about breaches, how Fred had often talked about the point in a painting where light finds its way in.

* * *

The New Year started on the right foot for Sabine. She and Tanner had two cars, and she drove the older one to fetch Mia. Cathy, of late, seemed in the way. With nothing else to do, she began sweeping the hallway. When the head nurse asked her to stop, Inga did not intervene. Instead, she told Cathy to take a few days off. Soon Sabine would leave the hospital and it was time for Inga to begin making preparations for her return to Switzerland.

She sat at her desk at the hotel and began to write.

My Dearest Arnold,

It has been a very busy and interesting few weeks.

I suppose I must first tell you of my visit to your friend, Holgart. I did not like him, but he was helpful in the way I needed, and I thank you for that.

I have met some lovely people here. My favorite is a young man named Keith. He is highly intelligent and had the misfortune of having a deranged brother. In the end, there was a terrible accident, and Keith's life can never be normal.

But as I glance over the past weeks, I have a new appreciation for that word. I wonder if there is even a normal in terms of personality. Our lives are so intrinsically unique, don't you think?

There is a woman, Sabine's roommate, Cece, who believes she talks to ghosts. A year ago, I would have described her as completely mad and, although I find her fantasies farfetched, I wonder if there is something in them. I remember laughing when you told me that your mother read palms, but I was wrong to laugh. I read once that only a closed mind is certain. I believe my mind is creaking open, and I think that will make you smile.

Helen is Sabine's closest friend. I worry about her. She is much too sane. Which must sound odd, but I'm sure you understand. For her it is not biology at all. It is completely the fault of her upbringing. I am quite sure some unspeakable things were done to her as a young girl.

I have seen Sabine come to life. Every day she appears to be more capable and have more energy. Many of her symptoms are similar to Rigmor's, but I cannot say how similar, nor can I be sure if it's the medication that is making the difference. If medicine can cure such hopelessness, it would be a very great thing to have lived this long and to have witnessed such advances.

The baby is utterly and completely delightful. She has very full cheeks, as if she is a squirrel hoarding nuts. Her eyes are the shape of almonds and the color of dark chocolate.

I am tired of late, and sometimes I feel that time plays tricks, that I am in the past and then the present, and then nowhere at all. Perhaps time is not what we think it to be. Perhaps we are all of our ages at once, and our outer body is only an illusion, a reminder that we cannot stay here forever.

When you and I parted that final day in Germany, I wanted nothing to do with you, or anything that happened. I can't say that I fully regret my choice. I was strong-headed and grief-stricken. But I now wonder if I left you rather stranded and alone. For that I am sorry.

With fondness,

Inga

Inga put the letter in an envelope. She would post it in the morning. At the moment, she felt bone-weary. Although her bed was only next door, it seemed a long journey.

She did not have the energy to put on her nightdress or brush her teeth. The last time she felt this way, she was in the jungle, stricken with malaria. For three weeks she had sweated under a mosquito tent as Fred shouted at the nurses, insisting they do more.

Her forehead burned and she shivered.

She had no idea of the time when the phone woke her. She reached for the receiver, her lungs tight and congested, her throat raw.

It was Cathy, who said she had another opportunity to nurse a child with cerebral palsy. The family needed her to start immediately.

A godsend. "Yes, go. By all means," Inga said, and hung up the phone. She got herself a glass of water, and climbed back into bed. As soon as she had the energy, she would phone Sabine and tell her she wouldn't be visiting today.

Chapter Twenty-Six

After

Arlesheim, Switzerland
1939

When Inga returned to Switzerland after Rigmor died, she told the driver to drop her off at the bottom of the hill. She wanted to approach the chalet with stealth, move so quietly that no one would notice her. She would slip into her room, crawl under the eiderdown, and hide for the rest of her life.

She opened the gate. The pebbled path, freshly raked, made a soft crunching sound as she walked along it. The sun shone too brightly and everything around her felt too vivid, too close, too constraining. She turned the corner and walked to the back steps. There, standing at the top, was Frieda, her arms crossed in front of her, her face hard, her eyes searching.

Inga gripped the handle of her suitcase. She did not move. The five steps ahead of her seemed a mountain of stone.

When she opened her mouth to speak, only a small rasp came. Inga looked down at her worn boots and gave her head a tight shake, hoping that the gesture would convey everything, and that words wouldn't be necessary. But then she glanced up and saw the lines in Frieda's brow.

"The train journey?" her mother asked.

"Fine," Inga whispered. "Where is Lisbet?"

"Sleeping upstairs."

"That is good," Inga said, more to herself than Frieda.

"So then?" She was not a stupid woman. Surely she'd surmised that things with Rigmor had gone terribly wrong. "Was she not well enough to travel?"

The sun's heat bore down. Inga kicked a few pebbles.

Frieda turned and walked inside the house, giving Inga an opening to climb the steps. She stood at threshold and watched her mother take out an umbrella.

"It won't rain today." Inga set her suitcase carefully on the floor.

"One never knows about the rain." Frieda brushed her hand along the umbrella, a distracted movement.

"Mother," Inga began. "Where are you going?"

"To Germany." Frieda took a black overcoat from the closet. She wrapped a long silk scarf around her neck, and pulled on a pair of leather gloves. The warm day certainly did not call for such protection.

Frieda pointed the umbrella, gave it a small joggle, instructing Inga to step aside, which she did. Yet Frieda did not move forward. Instead she placed the metal tip of the umbrella on the burnt red ceramic tiles and shifted her weight. She was not walking out, and Inga understood then that her mother knew, at least somewhere in her brain, but the information had not yet seeped into her heart.

"I will be in the dining room." Inga walked the short distance from the foyer to the glass door. She sat at the round mahogany table with the white linen tablecloth. She folded her hands together and glanced at the miniature oil painting of Rigmor that sat on the desk.

Frieda finally joined, coat and gloves still on, umbrella in hand.

Inga picked at the skin around her thumbnail. "She got an infection from the operation," Inga mumbled and glanced up.

Frieda clutched her umbrella. "How many times did I tell you she shouldn't have the surgery? Why did it have to be done?"

Of course Frieda knew why. She was aware of the laws.

"Mother," Inga said, so softly she could barely hear herself.

Frieda shook her head, not ready yet for the news.

"She didn't respond well to the sulfa drugs." Inga could feel the thread growing thinner. "We tried."

Frieda looked away. She needed time.

Inga needed time. If only they could reverse the clock. Never have to face the moment that stood so cruelly in front of them.

"She died," Inga whispered.

The words hung in the air, as if they were too far away to be heard, and at the same time so loud that the result was a sort of deafness. Inga's throat constricted. Her head, her lungs, her mouth, everything felt completely dry, as if all of the water, the life had been drained out, and only dust remained.

The sound that came from Frieda was an inhuman wail. She fell to the floor dragging the tablecloth with her.

Inga gripped her knees, unable to move, unable to help her mother, unable to pick up the tablecloth that lay haphazardly across Frieda's legs.

"It cannot be." Frieda pounded her fist on the carpet.

"Mother," Inga said, wishing Frieda would get up, that they could find a way grieve together, that Frieda could understand how hard Inga had tried.

But Frieda stayed on the floor and turned her head just enough to look at Inga. "Out," she screamed, and pointed to the door.

In the foyer, Inga picked up her suitcase and left.

* * *

For weeks after Rigmor's death, Arnold's thoughts were incoherent. He lived in a haze and felt as if his blood had turned to tar.

Slowly, fragments of the night returned— morphine shots, Rigmor's marbled skin, the metal bowl next to the bed, Inga begging him to do more. As the memories began to coalesce, he was overcome by his total and complete inadequacy.

In October of 1939, Hitler signed a euthanasia decree.

The life of a person, who because of incurable mental illness requires permanent institutionalization and is not able to sustain an independent existence, may be prematurely terminated by medical measures in a painless and covert manner.

The autumn foliage burst into vibrant reds and oranges.

Bohm called Arnold to his office, almost certainly for the purpose of dismissing him.

When Arnold entered, Bohm stayed seated behind his desk. "I am sorry for your loss. I have been told you have suffered." A cloud of cigar smoke hovered above his head.

Arnold nodded and remained standing. "I will pack my things and be on my way."

Bohm picked up his cigar and took a long, languid pull. "That is not necessary, unless you already have another position."

"I do not."

"I might have something that interests you."

Arnold highly doubted that was the case, but he inclined his head showing that he was willing to listen.

Bohm pulled out a large piece of paper. "We have been chosen by the T4 committee to be one of the euthanasia centers." He nudged up his round spectacles and spread the paper on his desk. "The front buildings will be redesigned, as you can see in this drawing. We will still house patients and some refugees in the back buildings. In that way we are a little different than some of the other centers. Special, I like to think."

"I am not interested," Arnold said.

Bohm held up a hand. "Give me a moment. I understand you are sensitive. In some ways that is a very admirable quality for a psychiatrist." He looked as if he was having a debate with himself. "In other ways it might be a hindrance. But that is neither here nor there. I would not task you with anything traumatic. Your position would be mainly clerical. We need a doctor to provide the correct diagnosis of death."

"Will you have a similar gas chamber to the one at

Brandenburg?" Arnold asked.

"I think ours will be nicer." Bohm placed a finger on the diagram. "Building Two will hold the main facility. There will also be a crematorium there with two stationary ovens."

Arnold's room would be two floors above the chamber. His mouth went dry. "So why do you need a doctor to provide diagnoses if the patients are to be gassed?"

"I cannot tell how much sarcasm is in that question." Bohm folded the paper. "We are in the position to help families. They will receive compassionate letters with a realistic diagnosis of how their loved one died. For example, we do not want to make the mistake of saying a patient died from acute appendicitis when he or she had already in fact had an appendectomy."

"What you are offering me then is a job in which I would make up lies of how a patient died."

"If that is how you want to look at it, then yes, that is what I am offering. But I am also offering you a place in history. What we are doing in these centers has not been done before. It has been discussed among psychiatrists and eugenicists for years, but no one has been able to move forward with it. No one has had the courage." Bohm sat squarely in his brown leather chair.

Arnold listened as Bohm detailed Gekrat bus transport. Sonnenstein would receive patients from institutions in Saxony, Thuringia, and the Prussian province of Silesia. As soon as the patient arrived, a letter would be sent to the family notifying them of the patient's safe admittance and good health. In actuality, the patient would die within twenty-four hours—a fact that the family needn't know. Then, after about ten days, a death notice would be sent to the family home. Arnold would be given an alias. His name on the forms would be Dr. Bader.

Bohm handed Arnold a sample letter.

We are so sorry to inform you that your daughter NAME OF PATIENT, who was moved to our institution on SAMPLE DATE, died suddenly and unexpectedly of pneumonia on SAMPLE DATE.

Medical intervention was unfortunately not possible.

We offer heartfelt condolences for your loss and beg you to find comfort in the thought that your daughter was released from a severe and incurable illness. She died in peace, without pain.

On orders of the police we had to cremate the body immediately to prevent the spread of infectious diseases, which during the war pose a threat to the institution.

Arnold placed the letter face down on the desk. As he stared into Bohm's eyes, he wanted to spit at this wretched man. But instead of allowing his anger to consume him, he gathered the energy, wound it into a tight coil and decided to dedicate himself to a new purpose.

Arnold agreed to take the position in order to secretly gather information. Once he had what he needed, he would write to newspapers all over the world. He would be killed for treason, of course, an idea that he found strangely liberating.

Three weeks into the work, he had lost twenty-six pounds. His hair was thinning, and he found himself blinking constantly, as if his eyes wanted to close themselves to this madness.

One morning, he carried his clipboard into the exam room where a young girl sat on the table. She shivered. He took off his white coat and placed it over her shoulders.

"Danke." She wrapped the coat around her and felt inside the pockets, curious.

He glanced at his clipboard. Elsa Winkler. Diagnosis: Feeblemindedness.

"Your name is Elsa," he said. "That is very pretty."

She smiled, and he continued to read.

At age fourteen, Elsa performed at an age level of six on the Binet-Simon intelligence test, indicating a lag of eight years.

During the testing, her general knowledge was not commensurate with her age. She was unable to state her date of birth or the date of the testing. Her verbal expressive ability was primitive and frequently ungrammatical. In arithmetic, she could only perform operations in the first two basic forms of calculation with numbers from one to ten. Her performance in technical areas was equally poor. She had difficulty understanding the technique of braiding, and could work only with assistance.

We see no sign of any vocational interest or any degree of improvement.

"Would you like a sweet?" he asked.

"Yes."

He opened the tin he kept in the cabinet and handed Elsa a chocolate.

She grinned and hid it behind her back.

"But you must eat it," he said.

"I am saving it for after dinner."

"There will be many more after dinner," Arnold said. "Enjoy this one now."

She placed it in her mouth. Her light hair fell over her shoulders as her feet swung, banging the exam table.

Arnold did not think he could bear this work any longer. His hands trembled as he checked Elsa's breathing and heart.

When it was time for her to get down, he held her hand and told her to keep the white coat.

A nurse took Elsa into the hallway where she waited with a group of female patients. In less than an hour they would all be dead.

After Arnold filled out the form stating the cause of Elsa's death to be encephalitis, he went to his room, and slid under the covers, fully dressed. He didn't even take off his shoes.

For two days, he hid. Only when Nurse Adalet came to inform him that the Reich was looking for doctors to tend to German soldiers in Nazi-occupied France, did Arnold stir. At first he was sure the news from Adalet was a dream, but she led him to an office off of the main lobby where he signed papers and volunteered to leave Sonnenstein. Once in France, he knew he would never set foot on German soil again.

Arnold stayed in France for a month, tending wounds, and sitting with young men who would not make it home to see their families again.

One afternoon, a small crew of soldiers talked about heading to Norway. Arnold found the commandant and told him he had a sister in Oslo who was ill. He was allowed to join the cadre.

In Oslo, he took a ferry to London. He brushed up on his English, and a few weeks later took a boat to New York.

He found a small apartment at the edge of the city, and sent letters to the New York Times, The Washington Post, Chicago Daily News, and the San Francisco Chronicle. He made sure all of his contact information and his credentials were available. He guessed that in a few days, he would be receiving phone calls from reporters.

No calls came.

He sent the information to the Los Angeles Times, New York Herald, Baltimore Sun, Denver Post, and Dallas Morning News. Again, he received no response. But he did not stop. Finally, he received letters from The Des Moines Tribune and the Courier in Louisville. The editors thanked him for sending along his disturbing, but rather unbelievable, report. Without corroborating documentation, they wrote, they could not print his accounts.

He saw no alternative other than to march into the newsroom of the New York Times and speak directly to an editor. A secretary pointed him to a room with crowded young journalists clacking at typewriters.

A young reporter named Thomas shook Arnold's hand. "How may I help?" he asked.

Arnold explained that he had recently arrived from Germany, where he witnessed ghastly horrors. Thomas nodded, asking Arnold to sit.

"It is hard to know where to begin," Arnold said.

"Wherever you feel comfortable."

Arnold told Thomas that he was a doctor who had watched the Nazis act on their theories of a superior race.

"They are murdering mental patients," Arnold said, as Thomas took notes.

"Patients are weighed, photographed and given a number before disinfection." Arnold pulled out a handkerchief and wiped his brow.

"Disinfection?" Thomas asked.

"That is what the Nazis have termed euthanasia."

"Go on," Thomas said.

"About twenty patients at a time entered the gas chamber. The staff made sure the door and ventilation shafts were properly sealed. Then the gas valve was left open for about ten minutes. Usually most patients were unconscious after five minutes."

"And people do not know of this?" He sounded incredulous.

"People have some ideas perhaps. The residents in the town complain of the stench from the castle. They see the billows of smoke. The children run behind the buses that deliver the patients. They call them the murder boxes."

"But there has been nothing written of this?" Thomas stopped jotting.

"The Nazis are doing everything they can to hide what is happening."

"You seem like a good man," Thomas said, and sighed. "But I must tell you, this sounds a bit...well, rather implausible."

Arnold stood. "I am not fabricating this." His back was damp with sweat. "They often had to disentangle the corpses before putting them on a clay grill—a baking pan." He shook a fist in the air. "A baking pan," he shouted.

Two other reporters stood and moved toward Arnold and Thomas. Arnold turned to the older of the two men. "They call it mercy killing, but it is anything but. They are killing any people who are unfit for work, people they claim are unworthy of life."

The elder man approached and firmly gripped Arnold's arm.

"You are making people nervous," he whispered.

Arnold tried to shake off the man's hold. "Don't you see," he began. "This is just the beginning. They will soon expand their gas chambers to the concentration camps. They will kill in large numbers. You must believe me."

"Calm down, man."

"I cannot be calm. No one should be calm. Not when innocent people are being killed." He was out of breath. Sweat trickled into his eyes, but he could not stop. "The Germans are profiting from these murders. The stokers extract gold teeth which are collected in a paper carton. I have seen those cartons. That's just a small part. All of the people and agencies who pay for the patient's upkeep, they pay until the day of death, which is postdated. They are raking in millions."

"Come," the man said, and led Arnold to a private office. "My name is Richard. Let me take your name and address. I will make calls to some friends of mine who are psychiatrists and then get in touch with you."

Arnold slumped onto a chair. He hadn't realized how exhausted he was, how frustrating it had been to get someone to listen. Finally though, here was a man willing to take action. "Thank you," he said, feeling as if he might cry, out of gratitude and relief. Carrying this burden alone had been too much.

"How long have you been in the States?" Richard asked.

"Only a few weeks. I was a doctor in Germany. A psychiatrist. I worked for one of the most evil men in Germany. I tell you, they have no feeling left. It was not long ago that I sent a young girl to her death. And for what? Because she couldn't do her math as quickly as she should?" He shook his head. "All I could do was give her a chocolate."

Richard pulled up a chair and sat across from Arnold. "It will be good for you to talk to someone in your profession."

Arnold wasn't quite sure what Richard meant. "Yes, I will talk to other doctors, if that's what you think I should do. But I also think it needs to be written about in the papers."

"I think it will help for you to talk about these things with a doctor who will be there just for you."

"Me?" Arnold felt confused.

"Yes, you seem very nervous and upset. Your pants are swimming on you. And it looks as if you might not have slept or eaten in weeks."

"Of course I haven't slept," Arnold barked. "I am exhausted beyond belief. But I have no intention to stop until people hear what I have to say."

"A good psychiatrist will certainly listen."

Richard wasn't going to call people to corroborate Arnold's story. He wanted to find Arnold a psychiatrist. In another situation the irony might have been laughable.

Arnold stood. "One day you will understand what a disservice you did by not listening."

He visited smaller papers. Some journalists would hear him out, but no one believed him. A month later, when he was nearly out of money, he accepted a job as a waiter at an Italian restaurant. Sill he didn't give up. He couldn't. What had he lived for—what had Rigmor died for—if not to expose these devils?

The staff at the restaurant where he worked liked him, and he became friends with one of the cooks. Night after night, Lester listened as Arnold spilled one story after the next. He began with the most recent, and moved backward, from Sonnenstein, to Rigmor to the Blumenthals. Eventually he got to his work at the University, and his attraction to men.

When all of the words had been released, Lester pulled Arnold toward him and kissed him. It was that night that Arnold began to come out of his trance. Slowly he cobbled together a life for himself. He stopped going to the papers. It would be left up to others to tell their stories and reveal their nightmares.

Arnold had a chance to start again, to establish himself as a physician in a country that believed in human dignity. He passed the required medical exams to become a resident doctor at Columbia University, and a year after the war ended, he opened a private practice.

The past slowly disappeared beneath the present tides. Inga, and Sonnenstein, and Frankfurt—so much good and so much bad—rested in the sediment beneath the waves. Once in a while a few grains of sand, or a small rock—a memory—was dragged out from under the water, and Arnold would hold it, study it, but ultimately return it.

Rigmor, on the other hand, lived in the light, becoming ever more present, ever more vivid—an energy he would never, not even for a moment, relinquish.

* * *

Every morning after Inga woke, she did her exercises, had her one cup of coffee with one sugar, and got dressed as if she had somewhere important to go.

She lived in her small flat in Basel near the train station. In nineteen-forty, the rumbling often woke her, and her first thought was always that of a bomb.

The world had lost its mind. Switzerland shuddered daily from fear and blitz attacks too close to its borders.

It was difficult to travel, difficult to see Fred, difficult to continue. But she did. Every day she walked the city until her legs were so tired she knew she would sleep.

She visited cafes and shops, and it was the treatment she received from store owners, from waitresses, from book sellers, that helped fortify her. Her hair was always nicely done. She wore pearl earrings and a pearl necklace, and people spoke to her as if she was someone. They curtseyed and bowed and made sure her table was wiped clean. She didn't speak their Swiss dialect yet, and was initially worried they would judge her for being German, but it was rare that she received a dismissive glance. It was the working class people who saved her, who greeted her kindly when she had only scattered dust inside of her.

The pain didn't lessen as much as it changed form. Once a scorching fire, it was now a hollow reed.

She was not a mother.

Or a wife.

Or a sister.

Or a German.

Or a Jew.

Or a Swiss.

She had no country. No home. No friends.

She was a well-coiffed, properly-mannered, beautifully-adorned, nicely-scented, pretty shell with dull, defeated green eyes.

In time, she trained herself to stop. Stop thinking. Thoughts of Frankfurt, Arnold, Sonnenstein, or Rigmor still crept in. But each time, she imagined a red stoplight, and forbade herself to continue. Some days the stoplight came up a hundred or more times. Still she maintained the practice, and on good days she barely saw the red light at all.

Eleven months after Rigmor's death, she felt strong enough to visit Arlesheim. She took a tram and walked to the chalet for Lisbet's fifth birthday.

There were two young mothers with their children sitting at the round dining room table with cups of tea. Frieda greeted Inga in front of the guests as if she was a cherished family member, telling the other women that Inga was the mother of Lisbet and a highly educated world traveler. The truth was somewhere in between.

The other children were young skaters whom Lisbet had met during her lessons.

"They are not nearly as gifted as Lisbet," Frieda said to Inga, not quietly enough. One of the mothers turned. Frieda gave a polite smile. "Her instructor has told me he has never seen a child take to the ice the way Lisbet has."

As soon as the guests left, Frieda refused to look at or speak to Inga. At dinner, when Frieda wanted the salt, she faced Lisbet and said, "Could you tell your mother to pass the salt?"

Inga laughed. "I can hear you," she told Frieda, who ignored her.

"Tell your mother if she chooses to stay away for almost a year, I will not speak to her for twice that time."

Lisbet, her small face quivering, looked at Inga. "My grandmother," she began, and burst into tears.

Frieda opened her arms, and Lisbet jumped into them. "There, there, my dear girl. It's nothing but a small disagreement. Isn't that correct, Inga?"

"Yes, nothing to be upset over," Inga said.

Frieda put Lisbet to bed, and Inga washed the dishes. It was nearly eight, time to get back to her flat, but she didn't want to leave. Being in a home that had visitors, that had a child, that had life, even if it also had Frieda, connected Inga to a world she had severed herself from.

"You are still here," Frieda said, as she walked to the buffet cabinet to get her whiskey.

"Lisbet seems well," Inga said.

"Yes," Frieda replied.

Inga ran a finger along the tablecloth. "I was thinking," she began, and stopped. "I know I stayed away, and I am sorry for that. But now that I am back..."

Frieda finished her drink. "And?"

"I thought it might be good if I moved back in."

Frieda let out a heavy sigh. "Why did you stay away so long?"

Inga couldn't find the words. She managed to say, "I shouldn't have."

"The child thinks she has no mother," Frieda said.

"I am sorry."

"It would be good for Lisbet to see her mother more than

once a year, but there are rules in this household."

"Of course," Inga replied. "I will follow them."

Frieda nodded. "But know one thing," she said.

Inga waited.

"I cannot forgive you."

Inga moved back in the following week. Some days were passable, even pleasant, especially when she could play hide-and-seek with Lisbet, who never seemed to tire of the game. But much too often, Lisbet clung to Frieda, who made no secret about her dislike of Inga.

When it felt intolerable, Inga retreated to her flat in the city, for a week, sometimes a month, sometimes longer. She took up painting lessons at the art museum, learned how to play bridge, and began to see other men, not seriously, but to help fill the void. Four was the maximum number of times she would sleep with someone. After that, it might slide into more serious territory, and she wasn't looking for serious. She had Fred for that.

The war went from bad to worse to devastating, and Inga had to stop reading newspapers or listening to the wireless.

But it was impossible to shut the world out completely. Fred always had his stories, and there was talk in art class, and on the streets. All around her, even in neutral Switzerland, people staggered and sagged under the weight of loss.

Through it all—through the defeat of humanity, through Lisbet's growth spurts, through Frieda's callousness, through Fred's coming and going, Inga got up every morning, did her exercises—had her one cup of coffee with one sugar, and got dressed as if she had somewhere important to go.

Chapter Twenty-Seven

Home

Framingham, Massachusetts
1985

Sabine would be moving out of McLean soon, and she felt prepared. Almost. She just needed to feel ready to live with Tanner again. Dr. Lincoln asked her what made her anxious about going home. She skirted around the topic, saying that what frightened her most was not being able to sleep. Sleeplessness was usually the first sign of depression, she pointed out, and then sometimes hallucinations followed. When she had finally told him about the psychosis, he was concerned but not alarmed. His thoughts mirrored Omama's, which felt strange and good. Sabine really did have an ally.

One weekday afternoon, after lunch and a lengthy conversation with Helen, Sabine decided it was time to talk honestly with Tanner. She planned on telling him that she wanted things to work, but that she needed time. She would thank him for his support and explain that she had never really had a good sense of herself because she'd always lived in fear and guilt. She would apologize for being weak and needy at times, and tell him that so many of her decisions had been made in a desperate attempt to be normal. Nothing was his fault, nor was it hers, but for the time being it might be good to sleep in separate bedrooms.

She signed out of the ward, climbed into the dilapidated station wagon with the fake wood paneling on the outside, went grocery shopping and then picked Mia up from daycare.

At home, she played with Mia, and felt as if she was on solid footing. She was going to be able to do this. As Mia napped, Sabine called Omama, who was staying at the hotel for a day or two because she had a sore throat.

"Do you feel better?" Sabine asked.

"Much," Omama said. "And what about you, my girl? What will you do this evening?" Her voice sounded fainter than usual.

"I'm making dinner for Tanner."

"Oh," she said, with a bit more life. "Very good." She stopped for a breath. "I remember something Fred told me, near the end of his life." She paused. "He said that if a relationship went wrong, I always blamed the woman." She chuckled.

Sabine felt herself smile. It was such an Omama-ism. "Do you think he was right?"

"Yes. I did blame the woman. I tended to be extreme in my beliefs. But I was not always correct." There was both laughter and fatigue in that sentence. "At times a little more flexibility would have been in order. And you mustn't be too hard on yourself if it's not so perfect with your husband." The last few words were barely audible.

"You should rest," Sabine said. "I can stop by later."

"No, I do not want you or the baby catching this. I will be mended in the morning."

"But if you do need something…"

"I'm fine. Quite fine."

"Keith and Helen and Cece were asking about you."

"Very sweet," Omama said. "Phone tomorrow."

"They all—" Sabine hesitated. "You know. Everyone likes you." Now was the time for Sabine to tell her grandmother that she loved her. "I mean, I've never told you…"

But Omama had already hung up.

When Tanner came home at six, Sabine and Mia greeted him at the door. She felt a little like a housewife out of the nineteen fifties, but Tanner seemed pleasantly surprised.

Sabine got him a beer, and they sat together on the green couch she'd found at a yard sale. Tanner made faces and noises that threw Mia into riotous giggles, and Sabine began to feel as if this really was her home.

An hour later, when Sabine came back downstairs after putting Mia to bed, Tanner raised his eyebrows, tilted his head a little, and gave her something close to a wink. It was clear what he wanted. She did not want the same thing. She scurried through the living room and into the kitchen.

"I'll start dinner," she called, as if she hadn't noticed he had a different agenda.

Tanner joined her, placed his beer on the counter and his arms around her waist as she turned on the tap to fill the pan.

"You look good," he said, nibbling at her neck.

She nudged him gently with her elbow. "I have to boil the water."

"The water can wait."

"I'm supposed to be back at McLean at nine." She moved the pot to the stove and lit the gas. Tanner stayed behind her.

"You know what they say about watching pots," he said.

Sabine smiled and swooshed his hand away as she moved toward the fridge. "I have to make the salad."

He pretended to mope, but backed off and retreated to the living room, where he watched the news. She felt relieved he'd taken her rejection so well. Maybe he would be more understanding than she'd anticipated. Maybe she hadn't been giving him enough credit.

The spaghetti sauce was thick with hamburger meat the way Tanner liked it. When dinner was ready, she poured him a glass of beer and sat across from him at their small butcher-block table drinking a Diet Coke.

Tanner held up his glass. "Cheers." And then: "Where's Omama tonight? Hot date?"

Sabine smiled, although she didn't find it particularly funny. "Omama's at the hotel. She isn't feeling great. She has a sore throat."

"Tell her I'm sorry, and if she needs anything, I'd be more

than happy to bring it to her."

"I will."

As Tanner had a few bites of spaghetti, Sabine contemplated how to start the conversation about sleeping in separate bedrooms.

"It's weird," she said. "Don't you think, that Omama had a sister who was mentally ill, and that no one ever talked about it?" It seemed a good place to begin. The topic was serious but not personally threatening to Tanner.

He shrugged. "People were sicker back then. Lots of them didn't make it."

"It wasn't that long ago," Sabine said. "Plus, Omama seemed to be really close to her."

"I think you're giving all of this stuff too much attention."

She felt chastised for talking about herself—her problems, her illness, her family. "Maybe. How's planning for the ski trip?" she asked.

"What I meant was that sometimes you have to get outside of your own head. Don't just surround yourself with yourself."

"Yeah, I understand. I guess having therapy five days a week can lead to some self-absorption." She smiled and twirled a forkful of spaghetti. "So you are still going skiing, right?"

"It's not like I haven't noticed," he said.

She set down her fork and backed up her chair a little, feeling confused. "Noticed?"

"That you are not interested in me." His round eyes looked straight at her. There was nothing laid back or easygoing about them.

She took a deep breath. "I am interested in you. I keep trying to ask about skiing."

"You really want to talk about that?" He chuckled disdainfully.

"OK, I get it. I mean I know I'm in the middle of psychotherapy and I'm trying to figure out myself. But that doesn't mean I'm not aware of you and your needs."

"You pushed me away a few minutes ago." He pointed his fork toward the kitchen counter.

"That's what I'm trying to say. It's not about you. It's that I have this work to do, and I'm just not ready yet. To, you know, to be with you that way."

"So what am I supposed to do?" he asked.

"I was thinking that maybe I should sleep in the guest room when I first come home. I'm afraid I won't be able to sleep, and I think if I was in there I wouldn't feel so anxious."

He gave a hard grin. "And you think this is not about me?"

"It's not."

"How long am I supposed to wait?"

"I'm not sure," she whispered.

"A week?"

A week seemed way too soon. "Maybe a month."

He shook his head, coiled some spaghetti around his fork, then held it midair with the noodles swinging. His eyes looked like stones.

"Just so you know, if you ever try to divorce me, I will tell the judge that you were locked in a mental hospital, and I will get full custody of Mia."

"What?" She must have misheard.

"If you ever..."

She held up a hand. "No, I know what you said."

She inched her chair further back. She needed space and time, and someone to tell her who this man sitting across from her really was. Why was he being so mean?

One side of his mouth curled a little. "You think it's not obvious that you'd rather be with your friends in the nuthouse than me? You think I don't feel anything when you keep pushing me away? You think it's easy for me to take care of this house and Mia and get nothing from you?"

She'd felt inklings of his anger, little warning bells, but she'd ignored the signs, hoping that his core was truly laidback.

"I know it's been hard," she said, wanting to get to level ground. "But things will change."

"Sabine, they've already changed. You just don't want to look at it yet."

"I'm talking about in therapy."

"Listen," he said. "All I'm saying is that if you try, I will get custody."

Tears welled in her eyes. "I'll fight," she whispered. "I'll get Dr. Lincoln to write a letter. I'll get all the proof I need to show that I'm totally healthy."

"Ha," he chortled. "You can't just erase what happened."

"It's no different than being in the hospital to get your tonsils out. No judge is going to hold that against a mother."

"Seriously—tonsils?" Tanner laughed.

"I just don't get why you'd be so cruel."

"Because I've worked for all of this." He swooped a hand through the air. "I pay our mortgage. I've invested in stocks. I've started something, and I'm not just going to let you tear it down." She'd threatened his manhood and his wallet.

"I'm not going to tear anything down."

"The law says fifty-fifty. We'd have to sell the house, split the bank accounts."

"You can have the house and the money," she told him. Her face felt hot, and her legs weak. She was trapped in a negotiation for which she'd not prepared in the least.

Tanner's fork scraped the bottom of the plate. "You'll put that in writing?" he asked.

Sabine remembered a party she and Tanner had gone to in college. They sat around a campfire on the beach. Buddy, a short, popular preppy, was holding court. He wore a pink Lacoste shirt with the collar turned up and played a version of Lord of the Flies, passing around a conch shell, asking people about their first sexual experience. Thankfully he skipped over Sabine. Tanner, who was drinking too much, kept sprawling, kept taking up more space, expecting Buddy to choose him. But Buddy purposefully avoided Tanner, and later that night, when Tanner and Sabine were in bed in her dorm room, he said he would show that asshole one day. Buddy was right forward on the hockey team, and Tanner, who played center, never passed the puck to Buddy again.

Tanner was more than capable of following through on a threat.

"If you get the house and the money, will you put in writing that you won't tell some judge about me being in McLean?" Sabine asked.

"And how are you going to take care of yourself?" His words were tight.

"I'll figure it out." She just needed to know she wouldn't lose the baby.

"So it's done then? Us?" His voice cracked. "Did you ever love me?"

"Of course," she said, glancing at the clock above the sink.

"You can't even look at me."

"I was just checking the time," she said, forcing herself to look at him, realizing that she didn't find him sexy or charming, that she hadn't for quite a while. He was right, they were done, and of course he'd seen it, and she'd been the one in denial.

"What about when your grandmother dies?" he asked.

She sat back. "What about it?"

"If we get divorced, I don't think it's fair that I get nothing. If you add up all of the hours I've worked so you didn't have to."

Sabine felt something snap. "For fuck's sake," she yelled. "I haven't been at some spa. I've been in a hospital. And I'm sorry it's been hard on you. I'm sorry you've had to do so much. Believe it or not, I do feel guilty. But Omama isn't about to die, and I have no idea how much money she has. And whatever she does have will go to my mother, not me." She stared at him. "You greedy bastard."

"How dare you," he said.

She stood. "You're right. We are done. You take what's yours and I'll take what's mine."

She turned, walked upstairs, lifted Mia out of her crib, and dressed her. Mia would sleep at McLean tonight. Fuck the rules.

Chapter Twenty-Eight

Inga

Belmont, Massachusetts
1985

When Inga woke, it was still dark outside. She carefully moved her feet to the floor. Then even more carefully, she stood, keeping one hand on the night table. After counting to ten, she felt strong enough to walk. She took solid steps, and knew she was improving. She pulled aside the curtains and sat on one of the ugly hotel armchairs, covered with a material that felt plastic to the touch.

Sunrises anywhere were glorious, although nothing compared to the Rigi—to watching a small dot of light grow larger and eventually spread like a palette of melting colors across the sky. But even here, overlooking a parking lot, there was beauty, and as the sky transformed from gray to pinks and reds and oranges, Inga cried. She had no reason to stop herself. No one could see what a silly, sentimental old woman she really was.

When the sky announced its brilliant winter blue, Inga returned to bed. She needed one more day to recover fully. In an hour or so, she would phone Sabine, find out how things went with Tanner, and get an update of the ward.

Sometime later, she woke gasping, unsure of where she was. She needed a minute to orient herself, to recognize the mediocre hotel room with the unregulated heating system. She picked up the phone and called the front desk.

"The heat in my room," she began and stopped for a breath. "It is much too hot."

"I will send someone up."

A few moments later, there was thunderous banging on her

door. She thought of the morning the Nazis came to inspect their home in Frankfurt, looking to confiscate artwork.

"Come in."

"Hello," a man's voice called. "I'm here to check the heat."

She glanced down at her chest and saw that her dressing gown was open. She tugged it closed. "It is too warm."

"I'll take a look."

They were never far, those stupid brutes. She spoke with as much strength as she could muster. "You are in the wrong house."

"We're in a hotel," he told her.

Of course he was lying. The wise course of action was to play their game. "Yes, yes." She smiled, wishing her head did not feel as if it were two meters under water. "And you are here, why?" She reached for a tissue on the bedside table and wiped her forehead.

"The heat."

"The heat. Yes. The heat is too high."

He stood next to a small box on the wall. "Ma'am, it's at sixty. We can't make it lower than that in the winter. We don't want the pipes to freeze."

"Sixty," she repeated.

"Yes, Ma'am."

She saw two of him. Two men with uniforms, telling lies. A room at a temperature of sixty Celsius was practically an oven.

She pointed to the door. She was not going to be tricked into being gassed. "Get out," she told him.

"You don't look so good. Want me to have them call a doctor or something?"

If it wasn't so frightfully warm, she might have laughed. A doctor. They were the most dangerous of all. She remembered when she learned Bohm had been executed by guillotine for his crimes against humanity. It was a moment of vindication.

"Out," she said now. She meant to sound forceful, but instead the word seemed suffocated in a thousand feathers.

She could breathe a bit better after he was gone. She wrapped her fingers around the glass of water on the night table, but lost her grip as she tried to bring it to her lips, spilling water over the front of her robe.

She reached for the phone, touched the smooth plastic of the receiver, and thought about calling Arnold. Not because she needed him, or wanted his advice, but because it would be nice to talk to a friend. But she was too weak to pick up the phone again, let alone get a call through to Switzerland. She imagined sitting in the green room with him. She would explain how she had only recently understood that what she felt most of her life was emptiness. She had confused that with loneliness.

She remembered a time, many years ago, when Lisbet visited the chalet with the children. One afternoon when Fred had taken the boys to hunt for fossils, Inga planned to take Lisbet and Sabine to town for lunch. It was a sunny day, with a few white clouds that looked as if they'd been painted on the sky. Lisbet and Sabine held hands, swinging their arms as they walked down the hill, and Inga, without thinking, reached for Sabine's free hand. Maybe they could play, *one, two, three—up*. The boys loved that. But Sabine pulled her hand away and tried to hide it, and Lisbet pretended she didn't notice. It was such a small moment, and silly as well, yet the thought that came to Inga was Lebensunwertes Leben—*life unworthy of life*. The doctors had used that term, and then the Nazis took it for their own, declaring the mentally ill, the Jews, the Gypsies, the homosexuals, and the deformed children unworthy of life. Inga had never thought herself unworthy until she watched Lisbet and Sabine happily skip on without her. Her mother, her daughter and even her granddaughter pushed her aside.

Now she lay on the hotel bed with her eyes closed. She had tried. She had always tried, and finally the winds of her life had shifted. She was no longer unwanted and unworthy, and with that thought she drifted to sleep.

Then suddenly, she was being shaken. A hand held her arm. This time she was absolutely sure the Nazis had come to take her away.

"Omama, you have a fever," a woman's voice said.

The voice sounded distant. Inga turned toward it, and there in front of her was Rigmor. At last.

"I'm going to call 911," Rigmor said.

It made no sense. But that didn't matter. They were together.

"I think you have to go to the hospital."

"No," Inga told her. "Out." She took a shallow breath. "Out of the hospital."

"You're burning up."

Poor, dear Rigmor, so confused. "Time to dress." Inga felt around for her glasses. "We will get a train in Dresden."

"We're in Boston, Omama."

Inga blinked and in front of her stood Sabine holding a glass of water. The wall seemed to ripple and blur. And then there were two. Two women, both young, both with dark curls, one more of a shadow.

* * *

Before driving to the hotel, Sabine had dropped Mia off at daycare. Now Sabine followed the ambulance that took Omama to Brigham and Women's Hospital—to the medical intensive care unit.

"Is there someone you need to call?" a nurse asked Sabine, and pointed to a beige phone in a beige-looking hallway. "That phone is for family of patients in the ICU."

She knew she had to call her mother, but she hesitated. They hadn't spoken since the day before Sabine went into McLean.

It was ten in the morning, a time her mother should be home. Her students came to the ice rink before and after school.

Sabine dialed.

"Hallo," her mother said.

Sabine stared at the plant standing in a wicker pot and thought it was odd that the green leaves, plastic and fake, also seemed beige.

"Who is there?" her mother asked.

"It's Sabine." She wrapped the cord around her wrist. "I wanted to let you know that Omama is in the hospital."

Her mother gulped and said, "Oh."

"It's probably just the flu," Sabine said.

"When did it start?"

"I'm not sure exactly. Two days ago, she said she had a sore throat."

"Do you think she could have caught something from the plane?" Panic pierced the words.

"It could be from anywhere," Sabine answered.

"But, you know what they say about planes. How colds and flus live in the air ducts. She should have stayed here for longer. I should have—"

"Stop," Sabine said, sounding angrier than she had intended. "It is not your fault."

"She had a nasty fight with Gerald when she was here."

"I'm sure it has nothing to do with the flight." Sabine had imagined a number of ways a conversation with her mother might go. This was not one of them.

"Should I come there?"

Sabine couldn't answer. She had wanted her mother more than anyone when she first was admitted to McLean, but now the thought of having her mother around—of having to assuage the guilt and assure her that she hadn't done anything wrong— felt like a burden.

Dr. Lincoln had asked Sabine if she fought with her mother. The answer was no. Never. Not even a little. There was no reason to. *But you must have felt angry at times?* Again, no, not that she could remember. And now here she stood feeling her hand tense around the receiver.

"Come if you want," Sabine said coolly. "I'll call if things change."

She called Tanner next, to ask if he could pick up Mia while she stayed with Omama in the hospital. Tanner sounded concerned and asked if he could stop by, bring some flowers. Had he forgotten their conversation last night? Sabine thanked him and said it would be best if he took care of Mia and didn't come to the hospital.

Next, she called the ward and told them she would most likely be staying with her grandmother. Nurse Nancy told Sabine that she was required to come back, that she had to take her medication, that they had a group meeting. It was unheard of, she said, that a patient would just walk out in the morning and not return.

"I'm not leaving my grandmother." As soon as those words came out, Sabine remembered something Omama had said when she first came to McLean, about how people shouldn't be left alone in a hospital without family.

Omama lay on a bed with a mask over her mouth, an IV in her arm, machines beeping, and screens with red and green lines bumping along. A blue curtain separated her from someone on the other side.

Sabine pulled her chair closer to the bed. "Omama," she whispered. There was no response, not even a flutter of the eyelids.

A nurse came in and asked Sabine to fill out some forms. There was almost nothing Sabine knew, except name, address and age. She handed back the forms, and asked the nurse what the prognosis was.

"Has she suffered from pneumonia before?" the nurse asked.

Sabine shrugged. "Not that I know of. Will she get better?"

"We're doing everything we can." The nurse glanced at the

partially filled out forms and walked away.

Sabine stayed next to Omama for three hours, as nurses came in and out to listen to her heart and lungs, check the IV bag, and make sure the oxygen was working.

At around five, Sabine closed her eyes and dozed. She woke when she felt something skim her wrist.

"Omama," Sabine said, looking down at the bowed fingers gently raking her hand. "Do you feel better?"

Omama tugged off her oxygen mask.

"I think you're supposed to keep that on," Sabine said.

She shook her head. "Listen," she wheezed.

"Don't strain yourself." Sabine stood, ready to help put the mask back on.

"The baby."

"Mia is fine," Sabine assured.

"No." She held up a finger. "The other one."

A nurse hurried in. "She needs to keep on the mask." She lifted Omama's head off the pillow and moved the elastic, but in a sudden show of force, Omama pushed the nurse's hand away.

"The baby did not die," she gasped. "Tell Arnold."

"That's enough." The nurse adjusted the mask, and Omama's head sunk into the pillow. She slept.

Sabine went to the gift shop and found some lavender lotion. One of her favorite things about Switzerland was the smells. Omama made sachets from lavender that she grew in her garden and put them under the pillows. The linens were always crisp and air-dried. Everything smelled fresh—the shrubs, the raspberry jam, and the milk that came from the farm down the road.

When Sabine returned to the ICU, she took out the lotion and began to rub it on Omama's hands, one finger at a time. Her grandmother's bones felt light and fragile, and her skin was cool. Sabine talked about the chalet, about each room, about the golden hedgehog that stood on the mantel, and the locked glass cabinet in the dining room. She talked about the gardens and the fruit, and the cherry trees. She talked about the open windows, about the purple hue of the foehn from the mountains. Then she stopped for a moment and glanced around. She felt something. A slight draft, but there were no windows, and the door was closed. She glanced back at Omama and imagined her at the chalet, standing on the balcony, waving as a light breeze glided by. As quickly as the image came, it was gone.

Omama died that evening at seven fifty-eight.

Chapter Twenty-Nine

Arnold

Arlesheim, Switzerland
1985

At six in the morning, Arnold's door at the nursing home flew open, and there stood his favorite nurse, Erika. Her large shoulders blocked a good amount of light. He had asked her once if she was a swimmer. It was, he thought, a delicate way of learning why she had such an unusually muscular body.

Erika clapped. "Are we ready to greet the day, Dr. Richter?"

She entered the room like a large gust of wind, and then moved him swiftly and yet with great care to the bathroom, where she had the loathsome job of cleaning him and changing his diaper. She talked about her brother, the trouble he'd gotten into for staying out drinking and vomiting on the front lawn, where god forbid the neighbors could see. Her mother had attacked him with a frying pan. Wearing her yellow bed jacket, with her black hair, she looked like a large bumble bee, chasing him down the street. All of this Erika told Arnold as she sat him in the shower stall and ran a soft stream of warm water over him. She kept up her storytelling until he was dressed. She made the whole morning humiliation (as he called it) invisible.

"I am having a visitor today," he said, before she could begin a story of how she told off one of her boyfriends. "Do my eyebrows look too bushy?"

She seized his chin and studied his face. "They could use some neatening. I think a little trim of the hair as well."

After draping him with a black cape, she began her work. They talked about Inga, about how everyone in the home missed her, and then he told Erika that his visitor was Sabine, Inga's granddaughter, a woman he had never met.

Fifteen minutes before Sabine was due, Arnold asked to be taken to the green room. There he sat by himself, looking at the painting of the Matterhorn that Inga so often complained about. The perspective was wrong, she insisted. It looked as if the mountain was sitting on air. And the colors were too bright. The grays should have been more shaded and the purple more bruised.

The clock in the room chimed eleven, and Arnold felt the pulse of his heart in his neck. Aside from Inga, he never had visitors.

At ten minutes past the hour, Sabine arrived, carrying her baby.

"Hi," she said, her cheeks glowing with color. "I'm sorry I'm late. I turned left when I should have turned right."

"You are hardly late." Arnold grinned as he looked at the woman in the peach-colored dress and flat sandals. "Would you like something to eat or drink? Something for the baby?"

"We're good, thank you." She sat with Mia in the same chair Inga always chose, fishing a baby bottle from her large carpetbag that resembled something his mother used to carry.

"It was such a great surprise to get your call yesterday," Arnold said. "I must tell you that I had a stroke a few years ago. Hence my compromised position." He gestured to his wheelchair.

"I'm sorry," Sabine said, as Mia drank from her bottle.

"I was deeply saddened to learn of your grandmother's death," he said. "I was very fond of her."

Dark ringlets cascaded over Sabine's shoulders, and he noticed that she wore no wedding ring.

"Were you good friends with my grandmother?"

"Yes." Arnold hesitated, unsure of how much he should reveal.

"For a long time?"

"Well," he began, and sighed. "It would seem an easy question, yes?" He smiled at her. "But in this case, it is not so simple."

Mia finished her bottle and sat up. She was as glorious as Inga had described. Sabine pulled a few toys from her bag.

"Can she sit on the floor?" Sabine asked.

"Of course, if she likes."

Mia sat sturdily as Sabine surrounded her with a doll, some blocks, and a wooden cow.

With the baby settled, Sabine sat again. "The day after Omama died, I found a letter addressed to you in her hotel room. I sent it right away."

"Thank you," Arnold said. "I received it, and she wrote about you and the baby. How well you recovered, which I can see for myself."

"Yes, I'm good. I think." She dipped her head, and Arnold felt his heart flutter. There was something in her movement, something he couldn't place.

"Did you know my grandmother before the war, in Germany?" she asked.

"I did." He smiled again, wanting to show her that she could ask whatever she liked. "We knew each other quite well during that time."

Sabine looked out of the window, then turned back to him. "Did you know her sister?"

He nodded slowly. "I did know her, yes," he said carefully. "I am surprised that you have heard of her."

"My grandmother told me. She thought it would help me."

"And did it?" he asked softly.

Sabine hesitated. "Yes. I guess it made sense. My life that is. Everything seemed to fit. To sort of click into place." She glanced at the baby. "Did you know Rigmor when she was sick?"

It felt strange and perhaps a bit wrong to speak of this when Inga had always asked that they not speak of it, yet it was in a sense Inga who was now providing the direction. She had opened the door.

"I did know her." Arnold paused. "In fact, I was a doctor, a psychiatrist, and although Rigmor was not a patient, I did in some ways oversee her treatment."

"What was wrong with her?" Sabine asked, her voice a whisper.

He closed his eyes for a moment. When he opened them, the room dimmed as clouds obscured some of the light. "If I were to look with a modern-day lens, I would say she suffered from depression with some psychosis."

"That's what I was diagnosed with," Sabine said.

"If I may ask, did they put you on a suitable medication?"

"Yes, you can ask. And yes, they did. I didn't even know it was possible to feel as good as I feel now. If I look back, I probably had depression for most of my life."

"It is often the case. But thankfully, you seem well now and very capable. The way you manage the baby. Are you here on your own?"

"I'm actually living in Arlesheim. In Omama's chalet. She left it to my mother, who is coming soon to decide what to do with it. But I'm sure I'll be here for at least six months. I took a job working at the home for disabled children."

"Arlesheim is lucky to have you," Arnold said. "For however long you decide to stay."

"Thanks," she replied. "Can I," she began and paused. "I mean, can I ask more about Rigmor?"

"I think that's what your grandmother would want," he told her, surprised by how sure he was of this.

"Did she die in Germany?"

"Yes. She had an operation, and from that she got an infection that didn't respond well to the medicine they gave her."

"Was it an operation from being sterilized?" Sabine asked, lowering her gaze.

"It was." He rested his good hand over his lame one.

"I think Omama felt guilty, like she should have done something differently."

He glanced out the window. It had begun to rain. "Your grandmother had nothing to feel guilty about. I can assure you of that."

Arnold remembered Rigmor lying on her bed, begging for the pain to stop. "In the end, Rigmor suffered greatly. No one should have to be in that sort of agony. Your grandmother was there in those final hours. She was a great comfort."

The rain passed. Sabine glanced out at the roses. The yellow ones seemed to be looking directly into the window.

"Omama was a comfort to me too." She dipped her head again. This time Arnold recognized the gesture. It was exactly like Rigmor's. "I wasn't very nice to her at first."

He smiled. "Your grandmother wasn't always easy. But she cared deeply about the people she loved. She was so happy to see that baby of yours."

Sabine looked up, startled, as if she'd just thought of something.

"What is it?" Arnold asked.

"Was Rigmor married?"

"No," he answered.

"Did she have a baby?"

He hesitated. "She did. But the child died."

"No," Sabine whispered. "Omama asked me to tell you. It was the last thing she said. 'The baby didn't die. Tell Arnold.'"

Arnold was speechless. He massaged his bad hand and looked at Sabine. He coughed and tried to remember. Inga had said the baby was cremated, but he had never actually seen the baby or the ashes. And it had always seemed so odd, almost incomprehensible, that Inga rushed away from Rigmor when she was in such a critical condition.

"I see," Arnold finally answered, not knowing what else to

say.

"I mean—I should probably not even say this—but is there any way that baby was my mother?" asked Sabine. "Because, well, it would make some sort of sense. You know, or maybe you don't, how my grandmother wasn't in the picture much when my mother was young, and how my great grandmother, Frieda, raised my mother. I know I'm babbling, and Omama would think my form is terrible." She gave a half-hearted smile.

Arnold grinned. He liked her. Very much. "It's nice to hear your thoughts."

"Do you think—" she started. "I mean, is it even a possibility?"

He closed his eyes for a moment and felt the sun's warmth on his shoulders. "Yes," he said, trying to grasp the enormity of what Sabine was suggesting.

Sabine walked to the window as Mia crawled behind. She lifted the baby, and for a few moments they stayed there, their bodies a natural fit.

When Sabine turned to face Arnold, he had no doubt. "You would have liked Rigmor."

"Can I come and visit you again? To hear more about her?"

"Of course."

"My mother too?"

"It would be a tremendous joy to meet her."

And then Sabine did something completely unexpected. She walked toward Arnold and put the baby on his lap. He wasn't ready. He had only one good arm. But what choice did he have? He held Mia, looked into her deep brown eyes that Inga had said were the color of dark chocolate, and felt very glad indeed that he had lived to see this day.

House in Frankfurt am Main

Inga and baby Rigmor

Frieda

Inga and Rigmor as young girls

Rigmor age ten

Rigmor age thirteen

Rigmor in rose garden at Sonnenstein

Inga

Lisbet

Top Hat Books

Historical fiction that lives

We publish fiction that captures the contrasts, the achievements, the optimism and the radicalism of ordinary and extraordinary times across the world.

We're open to all time periods and we strive to go beyond the narrow, foggy slums of Victorian London. Where are the tales of the people of fifteenth century Australasia? The stories of eighth century India? The voices from Africa, Arabia, cities and forests, deserts and towns? Our books thrill, excite, delight and inspire. The genres will be broad but clear. Whether we're publishing romance, thrillers, crime, or something else entirely, the unifying themes are timescale and enthusiasm. These books will be a celebration of the chaotic power of the human spirit in difficult times. The reader, when they finish, will snap the book closed with a satisfied smile.

If you have enjoyed this book, why not tell other readers by posting a review on your preferred book site.

Recent bestsellers from Tops Hat Books are:

Grendel's Mother
The Saga of the Wyrd-Wife
Susan Signe Morrison
Grendel's mother, a queen from Beowulf, threatens the fragile political stability on this windswept land.
Paperback: 978-1-78535-009-2 ebook: 978-1-78535-010-8

Queen of Sparta
A Novel of Ancient Greece
T.S. Chaudhry
History has relegated her to the role of bystander, what if Gorgo, Queen of Sparta, had played a central role in the Greek resistance to the Persian invasion?
Paperback: 978-1-78279-750-0 ebook: 978-1-78279-749-4

Mercenary
R.J. Connor
Richard Longsword is a mercenary, but this time it's not for money, this time it's for revenge...
Paperback: 978-1-78279-236-9 ebook: 978-1-78279-198-0

Black Tom
Terror on the Hudson
Ron Semple
A tale of sabotage, subterfuge and political shenanigans in Jersey City in 1916; America is on the cusp of war and the fate of the nation hinges on the decision of one young policeman.
Paperback: 978-1-78535-110-5 ebook: 978-1-78535-111-2

Destiny Between Two Worlds
A Novel about Okinawa
Jacques L. Fuqua, Jr.
A fateful October 1944 morning offered no inkling that the lives of thousands of Okinawans would be profoundly changed—forever.
Paperback: 978-1-78279-892-7 ebook: 978-1-78279-893-4

Cowards
Trent Portigal
A family's life falls into turmoil when the parents' timid political dissidence is discovered by their far more enterprising children.
Paperback: 978-1-78535-070-2 ebook: 978-1-78535-071-9

Godwine Kingmaker
Part One of The Last Great Saxon Earls
Mercedes Rochelle
The life of Earl Godwine is one of the enduring enigmas of English history. Who was this Godwine, first Earl of Wessex; unscrupulous schemer or protector of the English? The answer depends on whom you ask…
Paperback: 978-1-78279-801-9 ebook: 978-1-78279-800-2

Messiah Love
Music and Malice at a Time of Handel
Sheena Vernon
The tale of Harry Walsh's faltering steps on his journey to success and happiness, performing in the playhouses of Georgian London.
Paperback: 978-1-78279-768-5 ebook: 978-1-78279-761-6

A Terrible Unrest
Philip Duke

A young immigrant family must confront the horrors of the Colorado Coalfield War to live the American Dream.
Paperback: 978-1-78279-437-0 ebook: 978-1-78279-436-3

Readers of ebooks can buy or view any of these bestsellers by clicking on the live link in the title. Most titles are published in paperback and as an ebook. Paperbacks are available in traditional bookshops. Both print and ebook formats are available online.
Find more titles and sign up to our readers' newsletter at
http://www.johnhuntpublishing.com/fiction

Follow us on Facebook at https://www.facebook.com/JHPfiction
and Twitter at https://twitter.com/JHPFiction